Swallowed
by the Cracks

Lee Thomas

Gary McMahon

S.G. Browne

Michael Marshall Smith

All stories are printed or reprinted here with permission of the authors.

Cover art and book design copyright © 2011 by John Everson.

"Typically Atypical" copyright © 2011 by Bill Breedlove and John Everson.

"Appetite of the Cyber Tribes" copyright © 2009 by Lee Thomas.
First published in *In the Closet, Under the Bed* (Dark Scribe Press).
"I'm Your Violence" copyright © 2008 by Lee Thomas.
First published in *Unspeakable Horror* (Dark Scribe Press).
"Before You Go" copyright © 2004 by Lee Thomas.
First published in *Chizine*.
"The Dodd Contrivance" copyright © 2011 by Lee Thomas.

"My Name Is Natasha Putkin" copyright © 2011 by Gary McMahon.
Originally published in a different form as "What Must be Done" in *Three Crows Press*, the Morrigan Books ezine, May 2009.
"Creep" copyright © 2011 by Gary McMahon.
"A Night Unburdened" copyright © 2011 by Gary McMahon.
"The Ghost In You" copyright © 2011 by Gary McMahon.

"Lower Slaughter" copyright © 2000 by S.G. Browne.
First published on *Horrorfind.com*, 2001, and in *Outer Darkness*, 2005.
"Dream Girls" copyright © 2011 by S. G. Browne.
"The Lord of Words" copyright © 2011 by S.G. Browne.
"Dr. Lullaby" copyright © 2011 by S.G. Browne.

"REMTemps" copyright © 1996 by Michael Marshall Smith.
First published in *Postscripts 10*.
"Dave 2 Beta 2" copyright © 2009 by Michael Marshall Smith.
First published in Michael Marshall Smith's blog.
"Death Light" copyright © 2011 by Michael Marshall Smith.
"The Stuff That Goes On In Their Heads copyright © 2011 by Michael Marshall Smith."

Printed in the United States of America.
First Dark Arts Books Printing, April 2011
ISBN-0-9779686-6-9
ISBN-978-0-9779686-6-4
10 9 8 7 6 5 4 3 2 1

DARKAR†8
B O O K S

Table of Contents

Typically Atypical

What if thinking about something really bad happening to you drew something REALLY BAD to you?

What if that interesting stranger in the Internet chat room was lying about much more than you'd ever expect – like about even being human?

What if the human brain was just a big tape recorder? How long until it was just another commodity? And how would you use it?

What if seemingly innocent medical trials for experimental drugs led to spontaneous evolution and a superhero known as...Diarrhea Boy?

Yes, these typically atypical questions (and so much more) will be answered in the latest Dark Arts Books anthology that you now hold in your hands!

Welcome, then, to the seventh volume of stories where – pretty literally – anything goes. Just like the six previous volumes in this odd little subset of literary adventures, *Swallowed By The Cracks* mixes and bends genres without apology, because boundaries are exactly the thing that fiction should break.

Dark Arts Books strives to present the best in dark fiction – but dark fiction can be uproariously funny or socially relevant as easily as it can be soul-searing and bone-chilling.

In many anthologies, the focus is often on a unifying topic – vampires, mummies, vampire mummies, etc. And twenty or so talented authors offer their take on that particular theme. Which is all well and good. But haven't you, in reading such anthologies, sometimes come across someone whose story was so different, whose perspective was so interesting, whose writing was... so right, that it left you wanting to read more? But instead of getting more from that author, there were sixteen more tales of those darn mummies. Sometimes you might jot that author's name down, and vow to look for more work by him or her – but just as often, life intervenes, and that moment of discovery is sadly, forgotten.

Eventually, it occurred to us: instead of having a set theme for an anthology, what if the authors themselves were the theme? The only way that would work would be to feature several tales, not just one, from each author. It didn't matter if they were new stories or reprints... it should simply be the authors' best, and – perhaps – most diverse work.

The key, as with any successful anthology, is to find the right authors for the right project at the right time. Once that is done, the smart move is to get out of their way and let them do what they do best – tell stories.

Until it's all said and done, we never know what we're going to get when we start out to compile a new Dark Arts collection – which is part of the fun. We're readers and lovers of stories and fans, too. Perhaps the best part of this gig is discovering these tales when reading them for the first time.

Swallowed By The Cracks has worked out to become Dark Arts' longest title, featuring more novelettes than we've ever published in a single volume. But it also includes several examples of taut, tight short works as well.

Maybe you are already familiar with all of these authors, but we're guessing that one or more will be somewhat new to you. One of our goals has always been to present fans with work from their favorite authors while cross-pollinating the work of other interesting writers.

Notice that we did not say "similar." Our unofficial motto has always been "typically atypical" and nowhere is that as apparent as in the tremendous range our authors showcase – both within their own work and as an aggregate. They all have their own wildly sly, stylistic ways of insinuating their visions into your head.

What these four authors all excel at is in creating a mood – weaving a whole world completely formed into the tightly-compacted mechanism of the short story.

This is a book of sensuous, lush tales.

Lee Thomas writes with sensuous lushness in almost all of his fiction. The characters ache so strongly the reader can almost feel their pain. And, that's usually before the real shit hits the fan. Lee puts the entire gamut of human emotions on display, and he mixes them all as expertly as an artist blending colors on a palette.

Lee opens these pages with "Appetite of the Cyber Tribes," a meditation on loneliness and the insularity that computers allow us to hide within... yet, ironically, it is that same technology that exposes us like never before. With "I'm Your Violence," he treads in *7even* territory, but with a deeply personal twist.

Then he switches gears to the Lovecraft-by-way-of-Jules-Verne stylishness of "The Dodd Contrivance" and then changes it up again with the chilling epitaph of "Before You Go." You'll think twice about doing things behind your spouse's back after that one.

Gary McMahon excels at building dread. Like an infinitely patient model-maker, carefully planning each and every detail, he draws the reader into his stories with the small things – a comfortable pub for a setting, a Radiohead song on the radio – and when the reader is invested fully in the characters (who, after all, inhabit a world just like he/she does), that's when he kicks the supports out from underneath and reveals the chaos ready – always ready – to attack our precious reality.

Whether it's the clarion call issued (knowingly or unknowingly) for the narrator in "Creep" or the disillusioned and lonely people in both "A Night Unburdened" and "The Ghost in You" who start out thinking they have it bad, and then soon enough find out how subjective "bad" can really be, Gary fills in those spaces with haunting perfection. His epistolary "My Name Is Natasha Putkin" offers the flip side of all those tired torture-porn tropes with a series of heart-wrenching missives.

The narrators in S.G. Browne's stories seem so... nice. So... pleasant. They are articulate, clever and bright. They're good company. What they say makes perfect sense, and it's fun to go along with them.

Until.

Until it's too late to turn back. Wait for the oh-so-gradual shift in "Dream Girls" where he takes a seemingly comical (and comically gauche) premise – insatiable female sex slave robots created to please every stereotypical male fantasy – and in a heartbeat turns it into something much, much darker.

"Lower Slaughter" and "Lord of Words" follow with a more traditional creep factor before he brings back a twist of the light in "Dr. Lullaby," a story of human guinea pigs who find some very interesting side-effects to their experiments.

Michael Marshall Smith is kind of like a one-man band, a whirling dervish of ideas and notions that, no matter in what direction he turns his keen intellect and amazing storytelling prowess, he delivers something unique and memorable. The four selections found in this volume are a testament to his prodigious gifts.

With "Death Light," he presents a British screenwriter on a depressingly pointless trip to Hollywood. But things go from bad to worse when he suddenly finds himself face-down on the hotel lobby floor accused of multiple homicides.

"The Stuff That Goes On In Their Heads" is a quieter and yet profoundly powerful look at the relationship between man and his son, while "REMTemps" toys with the conceit of the brain as a big tape recorder. What if you could store other people's dreams and memories for them? What if they'd pay you for it? What sort of things would they pay you to take from their minds for a bit?

Finally, we close Smith's section (and the book itself) with "Dave 2 Beta 2" which perhaps is the funniest and saddest commentary on Middle-Aged Man ever penned.

Funny, frightening, furious... sarcastic, sardonic, sensitive... the stories you're about to read send light into spaces you may never have looked in before. There are forgotten things to be found there.

Truths and abominations.

Fear and solace.

These are stories of things that slip between the cracks in our vision. Sit back, and let them swallow you for a little while.

Enjoy.

– Bill & John
Chicago, IL
March 2011

Lee Thomas

Lee Thomas is the Lambda Literary Award and Bram Stoker Award-winning author of *Stained, Parish Damned, The Dust of Wonderland,* and *In the Closet, Under the Bed.*

His novel, *The German,* was released by Lethe Press in March 2011.

You can find him on the web at www.leethomasauthor.com

Appetite of
the Cyber Tribes

When it came to the Internet, Walter knew that people weren't always what they seemed. The online world was, quite simply, a fantasy kingdom where any number of beings, some wonderful and some hideous, roamed about their realm wearing magical disguises. Cloaked in the woven spells of personal profiles and fabricated histories, the creatures of the web had the power to mask the truth of their being only to be exposed when they were conjured and drawn from that enchanted, digital land into the concrete domain of real life.

Walter knew this because he was one of those beings. Behind the guise of his screen handle, he was confident, funny and charming. But now on a chilly autumn afternoon as he approached the row of glass-faced buildings harboring shops and restaurants, he felt the weave of his magical persona unravel, and he wished he had stayed at home. He didn't like being exposed. He was an average guy in a world that demanded more.

All of the perfect young bodies – images that had once been relegated to porn sites – spilled onto the dating pages he frequented. He couldn't compete with the well-hung twenty-somethings who'd spent their adolescent-year allowances buying steroids. They were a VIP generation, and Walter couldn't get past the doorman.

He walked with slow, precise steps along the sidewalk toward Downing Street, his gut twisting in electric knots. His friend, Gary, would have called him a wuss for being so anxious about his date, but Walter wasn't like Gary. His friend hooked up with guys as easily as he ordered pizzas, but Walter's experience was far more limited. The chat rooms and dating sites allowed him to observe and sometimes participate in the rituals of the beautiful. He could be charming, even somewhat aggressive, online, but when it came time to swap pics, his confidence withered. On those rare occasions when sending his photo didn't end the conversation, and he actually hooked up, he sensed from the moment he met his date, that he'd been summoned for his convenience and little else.

In no hurry to endure the awkward first moments with another disappointed date, he paused, looked up to check his location and saw a throng of pedestrians meandering along the shopping district. A mother gave her son an ice cream cone and brushed a lock of hair from his brow; two men with perfect smiles and matching white fleece jackets entered the video store; a straw-haired woman stood in front of a new age card and candle boutique, chewing gum and examining her fingernails; and a man in a forest green trench coat stood on the far corner. The guy seemed to be watching him, but Walter figured that was his imagination – another bit of anxiety to add to his afternoon.

Above, the sky threatened rain, and on the near corner just beyond the new age boutique and the chewing woman, who now returned to the card shop's interior, stood the coffee shop where his date was waiting.

He didn't know why he was so worried; Barry was great. At least he seemed great. He liked Chinese food, Grisham novels and court shows like *Judge Judy;* Barry didn't much like crowds or bars, and he preferred DVDs to going to movie theaters, just like Walter did. But for all Walter knew, Barry was just another cloaked denizen of the fantasy kingdom, willing to lie to assuage his loneliness. A lot of people did that these days.

And what if... (and this was an even more uncomfortable prospect)... What if he hadn't lied? What if Barry was as great as he thought, and what if he didn't feel the same way about Walter? The questions made the anxiety in his belly roil and spit lightning through his gut.

He walked to the door of the coffee shop and rested his hand on the metal handle, letting the cold seep into his palm. Through the glass he saw Barry sitting at a table across the room.

He looked exactly like the picture he had sent: blonde hair, the color of wheat, short and spiky and only slightly receding. Large blue eyes gazed at the counter with a sparkle of anticipation dancing over the irises. His slender body rested in an overstuffed chair. He hadn't lied.

Walter stepped back on the sidewalk, away from the glass door.

Unfortunately, Walter could not make the same claim to veracity as his date. The picture he'd sent to Barry was nearly five years old, and though Walter looked almost identical to the image he had sent, he felt like a cheat and a liar for having passed the image off as recent. He looked at his reflection in the pane of the boutique window and saw round, chipmunk cheeks framed by a thinning hairline. His brown eyes were flat and uninteresting, and his lower lip looked too full. His sturdy build, when viewed in the reflective glass, appeared simply, fat.

Barry would give him a quick frisk with his eyes, find him plain in all of the least comforting ways; he'd finish his coffee; he'd explain he had another appointment; he'd leave and Walter would be sent home to entertain his disappointment.

The door of the coffee shop opened, and Walter's heart skipped into his throat.

A man with a shaven head, chambray shirt and black quilted vest stepped into the gloomy afternoon. Despite the day's gray cast, he wore thick, dark shades over his eyes. Casually, he regarded Walter, then turned his back and entered the crowd of wandering pedestrians.

Simultaneously relieved and disappointed, Walter felt any confidence he might have retained escaping him as if someone had punctured a balloon to release his courage into the atmosphere. If instead of the bald man, Barry had been the one to come outside, if he had seen him standing there, then he would have been forced to speak with him; they might have shared a cup of coffee; they might have had a really good time.

But Barry had not come outside, and Walter knew he wasn't brave enough to join him inside.

In submitting to his cowardice, he turned to leave and nearly collided with a woman.

She was a blur of dark brown hair, and her hand went quickly to Walter's shoulder to stave off a collision. In the wake of her touch, he felt a piercing sting in the meat of his shoulder. A fingernail or perhaps a sharp ring gem had cut him. Walter tried to get a look at the woman, but she was already beyond the card and candle boutique, walking with a purposeful haste along the glass front of the coffee shop, the tail of her green trench coat, whipping in the breeze.

Walter rubbed his injured shoulder and as soon as he touched the epicenter of his pain, the anguish soothed, faded and died away completely.

Walter cast a last, hopeful look at the door of the coffee shop. He turned away and walked back to his car.

~φ~

GDTLP: *He was probably a total Teek.*

Walter laughed, reading Gary's assessment of his failed date. His friend's use of cyber-slang was a wonder, constant and always changing. A few weeks ago, Gary had hooked into the term "Teek," (apparently "Troll" was passé) and now used it whenever he got the chance. Walter thought to ask Gary what the word meant, but he didn't want to suffer through his friend's jeering, so he decided to look it up when he had a minute.

Situated comfortably in his home and sitting before the glow of his computer screen, Walter was feeling secure again. Of course, Walter had mentioned nothing to Gary about his earlier anxiety or the evaporation of his courage as he looked at Barry through the glass door of the coffee shop. Instead, he lied to save his ego.

WH61: *He looked like a whale in a Wal-Mart tank top* ... he wrote.

GDTLP: LOL! *Teek bitch.*

Walter winced. He didn't like Gary calling Barry a Teek. Even though he wasn't sure exactly what the word meant, he'd seen it in enough chat rooms to know that it wasn't good. And he certainly didn't think the guy deserved to be called a bitch, but Gary was just being supportive of his friend. So...

WH61: *Teek is right.*

He rubbed his shoulder, feeling the memory of pain there and looked at the screen, waiting for Gary's reply.

After returning from his failed date, Walter had gone to the bathroom and stripped off his shirt to examine his wounded shoulder, but he'd found no cut or abrasion. A small disc of skin, maybe the size of a nickel seemed to be discolored, grayish, but that could have been the light. He hadn't been bleeding, and his clothing wasn't torn. The woman in the long coat had just clipped him on a nerve in passing.

GDTLP: *TTFN. Hooking up. C U ltr.*

Walter smiled, typed in C U, and pushed away from his desk. The phone rang, and anxiety writhed in his belly. That would be Barry; he'd want to know why Walter had missed their date.

He let the phone ring and walked into the hallway.

Walter's house was a big ranch-style job with everything he could possibly want. His furniture was sleek, efficient and well matched. The office, perfectly appointed with everything he needed for his job as a technical copywriter, had actually been the master suite of the house with a big bathroom and enough space for a sofa on the far wall. Since Walter spent most of his time in the room, he wanted it to be the most comfortable. He'd installed his bed and clothing in one of the smaller spaces across the hall. The living room was spare but nice with a flat panel LCD television he'd bought with money saved for a vacation he never took, and the leather sectional – forming an L at the room's center – could accommodate ten people, though Walter couldn't remember the last time he'd asked friends to his house.

In the kitchen, he retrieved a beer from the fridge, ran the cold bottle over his brow and closed his eyes in guilty frustration when the phone started a second round of intrusive ringing.

Not yet ready to be confronted or condemned by Barry, Walter ignored the phone's trill and returned, beer in hand, to his office. In the black manager's chair, he stared at the screen.

Walter sipped his beer and opened up Google to run a search on the word, "Teek." He couldn't visit any chat rooms for a while because Barry might catch him, and he certainly didn't feel up to getting any real work done, so instead he decided to satisfy his curiosity about the odd term.

He clicked on a couple of suggested pages from the menu, but they were all about some science fiction book by an author he'd never heard of, and he found no connection between the book's synopsis and the cyber slang his friend Gary tossed around. He scrolled down the listings, clicked on the second page, scrolled down.

Walter continued this casual scan until he came to a page listing with the title "The cyber legend Teek in today's interactive community." This sounded about right to him so Walter opened the page.

Derived from the word, Mortique and abbreviated as seems mandatory for the syllabically challenged denizens of the World Wide Web, Teek are to the Internet what the Bogeyman and Bloody Mary are to children: a myth for a wired society.

Well that's interesting, he thought. The page covering his screen was simple, with block type and few aesthetic touches; it looked like some college kid had posted a term paper on the web.

He sipped from his beer, scrolled down the page and continued to read.

~φ~

The term *Mortique* can be traced back to 1867 and the works of Jean Claude Van Maele (1830-1878). A Belgian novelist, Van Maele's early works, mostly short poems and prose fragments were collected in a volume entitled, *L'ombre de l'Esprit.* The title translates to *The Shadow of the Spirit,* though in researching Van Maele's history, it is suggested that his use of the word L'Esprit was intended to mean the less obvious definition (i.e. mind). The *Shadow of the Mind* as a title better suits this odd aggregation of experimental literature, particularly if one notes Van Maele's lifelong struggle with emotional instability.

Though Van Maele went on to become one of Belgium's most respected nineteenth-century novelists, his early works were written off by critics of the day as infantile "ghost stories" designed for the amusement of the lower classes. In *L'ombre de l'Esprit*, one such tale involved a young Marquis who stumbles into the courtyard of a crumbling castle and encounters a grizzled old man whom he finds squatting on a boulder. The old man puts a spell on the Marquis, causing the royal to wither and die. As his victim succumbs to the spell, the old man explains that he can only survive by ingesting the flesh of the dead. But plague and fear have driven the peasants from the neighboring countryside, and he has been left to starve in the broken keep. Once the Marquis is dead, the Mortique finds his personal papers and drafts a letter to the Marquis' beautiful young fiancée. The ghoulish man, writing as the Marquis, insists that the young woman join him in the countryside. When she appears, she too is placed under the creature's spell. Then, he writes to her loved ones – father, brothers and friends – and all come to the isolated fortress to become food for the aged monster.

The story itself might have gone completely unnoticed by historians were it not for the questionable success of Ian Harrison (1895-1948). A contemporary of Lovecraft and devoted reader of Poe, Harrison plagiarized Van Maele's tale of the Mortique. His story, *Hungry are the Lost*, was so unforgivably derivative that Harrison went so far as to call his hero Markus. Though the setting was changed to a dilapidated estate in New Hampshire, Harrison made no other efforts to hide his theft of Van Maele's work. The only concession to originality in Harrison's tale was a short passage that suggests the origin of the Mortique.

In Harrison's version, the old man tells the dying hero that he is descended from a band of religious pilgrims, who upon finding themselves lost and starving in a desolate wilderness, are forced to feed upon one another. But being devout to their god, they refuse to partake in the flesh of their brothers and sisters until natural decomposition signals the end of the fallen as spiritual beings. Once certain that the souls of the deceased have fled, the Mortique of Harrison's tale consumed their dead. Despite their caution they were cursed for their unwholesome behavior – damned forever to exist on a diet of putrescence and decay.

(Walter found this last line unduly grim, and he winced in disgust. He sipped his beer and an electronic voice announced that he had mail. He opened his mailbox and saw Barry's name in the sender field. Quickly, he clicked back to the description of the Teek, an action of avoidance more than curiosity at this point, though admittedly he was interested to discover how these anti-quated creatures had made their way from a nineteenth-century fairy tale to the present day.)

Van Maele's *Mortique* make their appearance in modern culture through the dreadful film adaptation of his tale. The 1982 film *The Voice on the Phone* is an updated version of Van Maele's story, in which a group of teens are drawn by a series of phone calls to meet their fate in an abandoned butcher's shop. The film's first victim (named Mark this time) is carrying his "little black book" and the killer (a rather embarrassed look-ing Cameron Mitchell in the title role) works his way through the phone listings to draw unsuspecting young women to his lair. Unlike Van Maele's villain, Mitchell uses a drug compound, administered with a filthy hypodermic needle, to expedite the death and decay of his victims (in one of the worst stop-motion animation sequences this writer has ever seen).

Certainly it is this last example of the *Mortique* that has spawned the cyber slang definition of Teek. The film rose to cult status in the late 80's and was a favorite of the midnight movie crowds including university students, many of whom went on to prosper during the Internet boom.

With the advent and proliferation of the Internet, new fears arose in the form of child molesters, serial killers and other con-temporary villains who used technology to lure their victims. Early on, the term Teek was relegated to these digital preda-tors, but has since evolved to include anyone who misrepresents themselves in chat room settings with fabricated profiles.

This takes us back to the wondrous element of anonymity the web provides for...

~φ~

Walter spent twenty minutes reading and musing over the origin of the Teek, and he thought they were a perfect addition to the web's fantasy kingdom. They could pretend to be anybody, court and lure their prey, and if they were skilled enough, even maintain the identity of their victims for a time so as to throw off suspicion and avoid discovery – a perverse kind of identity fraud.

He thought that was kind of cool, but it also disturbed him. After all, he worked from home. With Netflix and GroceryNow, he could go days without ever stepping outside. No, he corrected, he could go weeks. Add to that the fact that most of his friendships were web-based, and he actually got a chill. He really could disappear and almost no one would be the wiser. Of course, work was a different matter. He was in contact with his bosses and clients almost every day. Certainly they'd notice if he just vanished.

Walter's stomach rolled and a wave of exhaustion fell over him. The day's events, the beer and the reading had made him tired. He dropped his beer bottle in the wastebasket, stood and walked across the hall to his bedroom for a quick nap.

~φ~

When the dream started, Walter was standing in the middle of a city; it could have been any city. Tall buildings of concrete, glass and steel towered above paved avenues and streets that teamed with vehicles and pedestrians. People brushed past him and the touch of their shoulders, their hands and their clothing on him felt almost erotic in its intensity. But he was frightened. In addition to the libidinous sensations the caress of fabric and flesh brought to him, there was also a feeling of dread.

Because within the throng of executives and tourists, someone waited to grab him and hold him, though for what purpose he could not imagine. Eyes that probed with unwanted attention ran like a dry wind over his neck, his back and his cheek. His exposed skin chapped and flaked under the assessment of those arid stares.

Terrified that he should be turned to dust, Walter held out his arms as if to take flight and wished the city and its crowding populace away...

And his will seared the color and depth from all around him until Walter stood not on a city street but beneath towering, yet sheer panes of glass. The limpid sheets rose to a sky that had darkened from sunlit blue to a grim, brain-gray. The street below him shifted and crumbled until the city avenue was reduced to a desert of grainy sand, from which the towering panes rose. On the surface of the clear sheets, two-dimensional representations of the city's buildings and populace were etched. In the nearest pane of glass, he saw Barry's face concerned and pleading, staring out at him.

Through this panel, Walter also saw three people, still whole and with full dimension. All three wore trench coats of a deep forest green. Their faces were swollen, lumpy and covered in a sickly yellow skin. Their eyes were small, black and hungry.

Frantic to escape this flat, horrible world, Walter spun on his heels to run.

A woman in green touched his shoulder, and Walter cried out.

~φ~

His eyes snapped open as the echo of his cry faded. The room was filled with night's shade, the only light coming from the numbers on his alarm clock.

He had napped for over three hours and now woke with a parched throat and a bad belly that rolled and kicked painfully. Feeling achy and still tired, Walter climbed out of bed, went to the kitchen for a glass of water and ended up drinking three. But the liquid seemed to be exactly what his troublesome gut required for its revolt.

He barely made it to the bathroom in his office before his clenching stomach let loose. After struggling with the button and zipper on his chinos, he frantically lowered the toilet seat and perched on the porcelain just as a jet of hot fluid burned through his bowels and evacuated. Sweat popped up on his brow and Walter gasped for air as the molten stream left his body. Behind his eyes, a needle-sharp pain insinuated itself and blurred his vision.

Once he was certain that his body had nothing left to expel, Walter splashed water on the hot skin of his face and then leaned on the counter to support his weak legs. A moment later, his strength returned; his face and neck cooled and the pain behind his eyes receded, leaving only a vague ache.

Maybe the beer he'd had that afternoon had gone bad, or perhaps it was something else he'd eaten. Running through a brief list of his meals and snacks but identifying nothing that might have made him ill, Walter returned to his office and clicked off the screen saver.

His e-mail box had ten new messages; Barry's was the first, the rest were junk ads. Walter erased the spam, and with great hesitation he moved the arrow over the bold, subject line of the remaining message. He squinted in readiness as if Barry's accusatory words might cause the monitor to explode in his face and then clicked on the subject line.

Walter,

I'm so sorry to hear that you aren't feeling well, but it was very sweet of you to try to call the coffee shop and let me know (they really should have paged me). OF COURSE, we can reschedule when you're feeling better.

If you feel up to chatting later, I should be home after six. If not, get plenty of rest and know that I'm thinking about you.

Warm hugs and a kiss on the forehead (you are sick after all, LOL).
Barry

Walter read the message three times, feeling certain that he had missed something important, and yet experiencing a great sense of relief that Barry was not at home cursing him. Still, he had not written him an e-mail.

Had he?

Walter opened his "sent mail" folder and right at the top was a subject line that read – *Sorry, sorry, sorry!*

It was addressed to Barry.

He opened the note, which quite simply stated that he'd managed to get food poisoning, and it had hit just as he was leaving to meet Barry for their date. The note was brief, to the point and made it very clear that Walter was not a flake, just unforeseeably stricken. He'd even added to the deceit by noting that he tried to call Barry at the coffee shop but the clerk had refused to page him. In closing, he had begged, in a humorous yet sincere manner, that they reschedule.

Distressed and confused, Walter shook his head in wonderment and instantly regretted the action because it brought the needle sharp pain back to the cavern behind his eyes. His stomach flipped and a fresh dew of sweat broke out on his face. Despite his discomfort, he drafted a quick thank you, mentioning that he felt worse than he had, which was true enough, and assured Barry that he'd be in touch once the illness subsided.

The mysterious correspondence nagged at him, though. He began to think in earnest that someone might have hacked into his mail account.

Only last month, three guys had been arrested in Cleveland and the news reports said that they'd stolen data on over thirty thousand people. They'd used the stolen identities to rob bank accounts, max out credit cards and set up phony Internet businesses.

Maybe someone had pirated his account.

But his logic was not only faulty; it was just plain silly. Even if someone had been able to access his account and had read his correspondences to discover the details of Walter's date, who could have guessed that he'd back out of the meeting at the last minute? How could they have been so accurate in identifying a sickness Walter hadn't even experienced yet? Furthermore, why would they?

The whole scenario made for a rather impractical practical joke.

Still, the paranoia was in his head, and for the next hour he checked his credit card and bank account statements online. He studied each transaction and played it against his memory but his financial records indicated no action beyond the authorized deductions for automatic bill payments and the few charges for CDs and DVDs he'd purchased online. He returned to his "sent mail" file and read the note to Barry again.

Sorry, sorry, sorry!

Throughout his exploration, a dull ache rose in his joints and the pain in his head persisted. By the time he closed the note of apology this last time, still confused by its content and origin, his face was shiny with sweat, and his back hurt.

His thirst returned. He left the office and made it halfway across the living room before his knees turned to liquid. Walter saved himself from a damaging fall only by clutching the arm of his sectional. He considered calling an ambulance as he navigated himself onto the sofa cushions, but reconsidered. He'd had food poisoning before and in the previous instance it had been much worse than this.

Walter lay down to let the cool grain of his leather sectional soothe his warm cheek and neck.

But as he grew drowsy, Walter thought about a grizzled old ghoul, killing a Marquis and penning notes to the dead man's relations. He thought about *The Voice on the Phone*, and a dark shape inviting a young girl out for "some fun" while chewing on the decomposing flesh of her boyfriend.

The soothing coolness of the leather hardened, dried and became like ashes on his skin. Walter spun in a tight arc until he again stood on an avenue of dust in a city of glass.

This time, Barry stood at his side, holding Walter's hand in a painful grip. He stepped forward and yanked, trying to get Walter to follow. Walter resisted. The Teek, wearing forest green trench coats, wandered beyond the panels of glass. There were so many of them; they were everywhere. He tried to resist Barry's insistence.

But the man was strong and his efforts were supported by a gusting wind at their backs, and Walter's feet slid in the dust, kicking up filthy ephemeral wings from his heels. He struggled harder. He didn't want to get near the glass tapestries or the creatures that roamed between the panes.

Barry turned an angry face on him.

"You can't shut it all out, Walter," he called, his voice still barely audible over the desert wind. "You can't live behind the glass, because that is where they hunt. Do you understand that, Walter? Do you?"

Desperate to be free of Barry's demanding grasp, Walter yanked his arm so forcefully that the bones and cartilage in his hand snapped. Walter fell back in the dust and gazed up in wonder.

Barry was still in front of him, but a paper-thin sheet of glass the size of a common household door stood between them. Through the glass, Barry gave him a final, mournful gaze and then turned away, leaving him alone in a settling cloud of dust.

~φ~

The next morning, Walter woke on the sofa with a foul taste in his mouth and a horrible scent in his nose. He wiped his eyes and sat up on the sectional. A dull ache thudded in his belly and chest and the act of lifting himself from the cushions seemed to take all of his energy. He balanced on his feet for several moments until he felt that he could move without toppling over, and then Walter walked to the bathroom in his office.

Slowly, he brushed his teeth and covered the horrible taste in his mouth with minty paste. In the mirror, his face and eyes seemed to rest beneath a veil of dust.

...a drug compound, administered with a filthy hypodermic needle, to expedite the death and decay of his victims...

The fragment of text flashed into his head and was followed by the image of a woman in green, racing over a crowded sidewalk as Walter's shoulder flared in pain.

He shook as if a stream of ice water cascaded down his spine. He spit in the sink; the foamy white paste was veined with brown and burnt yellow streaks. Gray flecks floated on the unwholesome foam. Disgusted, he ran the faucet to clean away the ugly wad, rinsed his mouth, and felt another wave of freezing cold crash down on his neck.

...damned forever to exist on a diet of putrescence and decay...

The terrible definition of the Teek continued to play in his head and the images of his dreams – the arid plain, the towers of glass and the things behind the glass illustrated the tale. He stumbled from the bathroom and clutched at the wall to keep from falling.

Already his efforts to erase the miserable, filthy taste with brush and paste began to fade as the dull flavor of rot rode over his mouth on a tide of mint. Walter closed his eyes, which were already filling with tears. Panic surged and then faded, muffled by the pain that had begun to radiate from his shoulder.

He must call help; he needed an ambulance.

He fell into his desk chair and reached for the telephone.

It rang, and with an excruciating effort he lifted the headset from the cradle.

"Help me," he said, his voice raw and breathy. His lungs hung behind his ribs like dry bags of flour, heavy and rigid. "Help."

"Walter, what's wrong?"

The man's familiar voice was at first welcome, but the comfort of his tone soon rose to a siren-pitched alarm in Walter's head. He remembered snippets of his dreams, remembered the man with the wheat-colored hair trying to drag him toward the towering panels of glass and the creatures prowling the dust between them. As Barry continued to speak anxiously on the distant connection, Walter felt hope slip away.

Only briefly did he consider that his convictions were irrational, but that voice was a whisper among screams.

"Walter? Are you there?"

Their date had been a trap; he saw that now. Barry had drawn him out into the dangerous world and one of his kind, the woman in the green trench coat, had injected Walter with sickness. He had to get Barry off the phone, had to call for...

The weight of the phone doubled with every second he held it. Already it felt like he held an iron to the side of his head – then, a bowling ball. He couldn't keep his grip much longer as the ache in his shoulder had become unbearable.

"Walter, what's your address? Give me your address so I can help you. Walter?"

No, he thought, struggling to keep his grip on the headset. He didn't want him (didn't want *them*) to know where he lived. They'd come for him; they'd find him; they'd...

He dropped the phone and leaned back in the chair, his eyes locked on the glowing screen of his computer monitor.

An instant message box blipped open.

GDTLP: *Where ya been?*

Walter fell forward. He caught himself before crashing face first on the keyboard, his head swirling with hungry faces and transparent buildings. He gasped for air and the effort shot bolts of pain throughout his body.

After a tremendous effort, he got his fingers positioned on the keyboard and wrote.

WH61: *Hel...*

From the front of his house, he heard glass breaking. His head lolled on his shoulders and a cry of panic sounded in his torso. The front door opened with a dry whoosh and a foot clicked quietly on the tile in the entryway. But he might have been imagining these sounds; he couldn't be certain. His pulse was too loud in his ears; his head hurt so badly that he couldn't be sure.

GDTLP: *Hel? LOL! Can't even write hello?*

A board groaned in the living room. This time, he heard the sound clearly, like a sheep bleating from a great distance. He struggled to look away from the screen. More footsteps joined the first.

He panted frantically trying to fill his flour-sack lungs with air and again put his fingers on the keyboard. With great effort, he managed to write a simple note:

WH61: *911 intruders here*

Walter fell back against his chair, exhausted by his exertion as the sound of footsteps whispered in the hall.

GDTLP: *I know.*

Barely able to keep his eyes open, Walter squinted to make out the message. When the words became clear their meaning connected in his mind like the terminals of a battery. Panic shot in painful waves through his failing system.

GDTLP: *Our path led us from a woman named Tess to a man named Gary. From Gary we found a man named Walter and from Walter we will find the next.*

The lines of blurry script wormed into his head, and Walter spun in the chair, attempting a final act of flight. He made it to his feet and took one lumbering step forward, but his leg maintained its integrity for only a moment. The corrupted bone and muscle crumpled under his weight, popping and snapping as he toppled forward. He cried out as gravity took hold. A spray of filth jetted from his throat and over his lips, spattering the carpet moments before he crashed to the floor, pinning and crushing an arm beneath him.

Numb and broken, Walter scratched at the carpet with the arm that had not shattered. The nails pulled back and the tips eroded, coating the fibers in a foul porridge. Shadows fell over him, blocking out the glow of his computer monitor. The Teek entered the room and gathered around him; he saw their black shoes and the hems of their green trench coats, and he felt their eyes on him.

Something was spread out next to him. Walter tried to see

what it was, but couldn't turn his head. A moment later, he was being rolled onto a clear plastic tarp. They lifted him and carried him across the hall to the bathroom, set him gently in the tub. He tried to obey the panic in his mind and struggle, but his arms and legs were useless. One of the creatures carrying him leaned in to look at his eyes.

The woman's face was almost human. Thick brown hair swept back from a normal looking brow, but her eyes lacked irises, just a black dot of pupil amid a glistening lens of white. Pronounced and narrow ridges at the cheekbones gave the woman a gaunt appearance. Walter noticed her mouth was filled with short blunt teeth like those of a baby. Distantly, he wondered if she was the monster that had grabbed his shoulder.

Another Teek pushed into his view. He came at Walter with a pair of shears. Walter's heartbeat raced, bringing sharp pains to his chest.

Carefully, the Teek cut away his clothing. A layer of skin and hair peeled away with the fabric.

Don't, he thought. *Please don't.*

More Teek pushed into the bathroom. Now there were five of them. Walter lay naked, looking up at them, unable to bear the sight of his rotting body. They all had the same iris-less eyes and the sharp facial bones. One male lightly licked his upper lip as he stared down at Walter.

Tears spilled over Walter's cheeks. His struggle apparent only in the twitching of his left index finger.

His clothing, now nothing more than swatches of material, made filthy by his decaying flesh, was distributed among the tribe. The Teek lunged for their share of the fabric. They licked and chewed on the torn clothing, slurping at the foul meat clinging to the fibers.

Walter's body convulsed, but his weak muscles responded with little more than a shudder. *Please help me*, his panicked mind begged. *Please. Please. Please.*

His index finger stopped twitching. The tears stopped flowing. His body could no longer manage these simple tasks.

Then the numbness spread to his mind and the faces above

him blurred; they faded. And a flare of panic, like the popping of a flash bulb, ignited as he endured a final, desperate wonder: Would anyone, anyone at all, notice he was gone?

I'm Your Violence

The victim's name was Charles Clarke. He was fifty-eight years old and apparently in good health – prior to death. Clarke had plans with friends to try a new trendy restaurant downtown before catching the premiere of *Hole*, a somber little play at the Wilkes Repertory Theatre on Jackson Street. He never showed for dinner, and he didn't answer calls. These behaviors were unlike Clarke, or so his friends claimed when they called the police station just after 9:00 p.m. A patrol car was dispatched and finding the back door ajar the officers entered and announced themselves before investigating the scene. Clarke was found in his bedroom.

The officers who found the body reported the victim looked as if he'd been run through a food processor.

Detective Dean Kaiser rolled this information around in his head as he ground his cigarette into the car's ashtray and exhaled a cloud of blue-gray smoke over the dashboard. He stepped from the car. Icy wind sliced along the collar of his overcoat and caressed his cheeks like frigid palms. He pulled the coat tight over his chest and hurried toward the house.

Two patrol cars had joined the first in the street outside of the house for a total of three. Four officers wrangled the dozen or so neighbors who'd been drawn into the cold night by flashing lights and the prospect of a glimpse at some intriguing misfortune. A waist-high wrought iron fence ran across the front of the property, beyond it a low rise of lawn, beyond this a circular drive, beyond this a three-story Edwardian home, which in any other part of the city might have been considered a mansion, but amid the opulent domiciles in the Country Club neighborhood seemed simply typical.

An unattractive officer with skin like a bleached pumpkin rind met Dean at the door. The officer nodded. Despite the cold, sweat clung to the young man's brow. Dean pegged him as a rookie who'd just seen too much, trying desperately to keep from losing his dinner to the bushes.

That bad? he wondered. *Food processor,* he remembered.

Inside he found another young officer, this one built heavier with a soft pudgy face and cool blue eyes. He approached the kid.

"Where's he at?" Dean asked.

"Upstairs. Third door on the left."

"Has Detective Harper arrived?"

A nod of the round head sent Dean up the stairs. He followed a red Persian runner along the corridor. A shape broke the light coming from an open doorway ahead, casting a shadow in the dimly lighted hall.

Dean stepped into the room and saw Reg Harper on the far side of the bed. The man was looking down at the remains of Charles Clarke, which covered the bed in a crimson paste. His skin had been ripped away. Fluids still leaked from the body. The skull and sternum appeared to float in a puddle of blood and viscera. Bits of bone, yellow fat and pale skin showed like vegetables in a shiny stew. Blood pasted similar tissues to the headboard and wall in a ragged fan pattern.

"Watch your step," Harper said, his voice low and gritty. He pointed his index finger, which was gloved in latex. "He's all over the place."

"Jesus," Dean whispered, casting his eyes downward. His stomach rolled. He pulled a pair of protective gloves from the pocket of his jacket and snapped them on, before picking his way across the bedroom to join Harper. This vantage was worse.

The victim's right hand had avoided the kind of damage the rest of his body had endured. Slathered in blood, it hung over the side of the bed, dripping. Dean made out the shape of a ring with a large stone on the pinkie.

"You ever seen anything like this before?" Harper asked.

"No," Dean replied. "Any idea what did it?"

"I'm guessing it wasn't a butterfly."

"I meant the weapon."

Harper stepped toward the bed and reached out with a latex-covered hand to grab the dangling arm. Coagulating blood acted like a poor adhesive; the sheet lifted with the arm then peeled away.

"Look at the wrist," he said.

Dean leaned forward and immediately saw what Harper meant. The marks punched through the skin. Darker blood filled them.

They were made with human teeth.

~φ~

Dean stood on the porch smoking while the forensic teams worked over the house. The medical examiner had already confirmed Harper's supposition regarding the cause of death.

You're telling us he was eaten alive?

Not eaten. There's too much tissue here. Yes, his attacker removed the flesh with his teeth, possibly even masticated the tissue to some degree, but he spit much of it out. You can see it all around the body and on the floor. Clarke wasn't cannibalized, at least not completely. On the up side, your boys can make some good dental casts, and saliva samples are a given. You catch this guy and you'll have no trouble confirming the ID.

How long would it take to do that to a body?

As long as the killer wanted, the ME said. *On the short end it wouldn't take long. Fifteen minutes. Twenty. I'd only be guessing. I've never run into anything like this before.*

Neither had Dean, and he didn't know what to make of it. He took another drag off his smoke and surveyed the sidewalk and the crowd milling there. Concerned faces hovered above the low wrought iron fence. Many of the aggregated gawkers hadn't dressed for the cold. A woman in a terry cloth robe trembled. Next to her a man built like a linebacker, wearing nothing but cargo shorts and an olive green T-shirt at least one size too small for his stocky build hugged himself against the cold. The guy laid a hard stare on Dean, an expression of unapologetic lust.

Maybe some other time, Dean thought. The guy was attractive, no question, but his timing sucked.

Harper appeared in the doorway, his face screwed into an uncomfortable grimace. "You need to see this."

"There's more?"

"Yeah," Harper said. He sighed. "We just hit a whole new level of fucked up."

Dean dropped his cigarette on the porch and ground it out, then he bent down to retrieve the butt. He dropped it in the front pocket of his chinos and followed Harper into the house.

Harper led him back up the stairs but instead of returning to the bedroom and its grisly content they continued down the hall and entered a home office, where he found sleek furniture and multiple flat screen monitors on a broad glass and iron desk. Harper crossed the room to a laser printer. With a pair of tweezers he lifted a sheet from the tray and held it by the corner, dangling it in Dean's face.

A photograph had been printed on the paper. Though the image was clear his mind took several moments to process it:

A middle-aged man in ecstasy…
An adolescent boy in pain…
Both unclothed…

"Shit," Dean hissed. His blood grew thin and hot, racing through his veins like acid. His heartbeat turned to thunder in his ears. He jerked his head toward the photograph and asked, "The older guy our victim?"

"Looks that way."

Good, he thought.

"I'll bet his computer is choking on these things. The men with candy like their glossies."

"Could be," Dean replied. "It certainly gives us a hell of a motive if that kid's not a pro."

His pulse continued to race and his face burned. Dean's head grew light for a moment, and he drew in a deep breath to quiet his ragged nerves. He gave the disgusting picture a final glance then turned away.

The monitor on the glass desk before him swirled with colors. He reached out and jabbed the space bar on the keyboard with his index finger. The screen saver disappeared to reveal the computer's desktop.

Amid the folders and application icons displayed on the screen, a window was open in the center of the screen. Dean found himself looking at the crimson fluid pooling on Charles Clarke's bed. Men and women wearing masks and gloves – the forensic team – worked over the surfaces of the room.

"What the hell?" Harper asked.

"Video cam," Dean replied. "The sick fuck has one hidden in the bedroom."

"Remember, 'the sick fuck' happens to be the victim in this case."

Dean disregarded the statement. He stared at the monitor, the bed, the room, the people moving there unaware of his watching.

"If this thing was recording, our job just got a hell of a lot easier," Harper said.

"Yeah," Dean said. "Maybe."

~φ~

Lifeless stifling air poured into the office. Already uncomfortable, the stale atmosphere felt suffocating. Through the window on his door, Dean looked over the expanse of the station. Half of the desk lights were off, and the floor was deserted. His colleague's on the Clarke case were off in different departments, checking on forensics, running phone numbers, grabbing cups of coffee for the long night ahead. The scene gave him the creeps, and he turned away. Dean opened the window and stuck his head into the wintry night.

For now, Dean waited. Charles Clarke's computer was in the hands of the techs downstairs. Departmental procedures were in place to assure data wasn't corrupted. Plus, if the family of the victim came forward to claim defamation of character once Clarke's crimes hit the press, the department could cover its ass with reams of detailed paperwork.

Currently, this last point was likely far more important to the Barnard Police Department than the investigation.

After word of Clarke's twisted pastime had made its way through the crime scene, the attitudes of the on-scene investigators had immediately changed. The eagerness to find the murderer seemed to drain from his colleagues' eyes, making room for disgust. Dean understood the reaction; he'd felt it himself. Did Clarke deserve to die for molesting children? The law said no, but Dean certainly wouldn't lose any sleep over his passing. No, his slumber would be sacrificed to anger. In the aftermath of this crime, Clarke wouldn't be seen as a hebephile or pederast, he'd be seen as a homo deviant, emphasis on the homo.

Likely Dean's colleagues were already growling about it in the locker room, volleying misguided opinions through the sweat-thick air, liberally peppering their dialogue with words like "queer," "cocksucker," and "fag." Fortunately, they knew better than to get in his face with that shit.

It was infuriating; being painted with a brush frayed by the behaviors of a monster like Charles Clarke. Were all straight men rapists? Were all straight men responsible for JonBenet or Megan Kanka? No. But some fuck like Clarke gets exposed and the idiot faction processes it as another example of the predatory queer.

Harper entered the office carrying a cup of coffee and a thick folder. "We got the most recent pictures," he said, crossing to the desk and setting his mug down. "They cover the last two years. The techies are transferring the video clips to DVD now. They're starting with tonight and working their way back. Should have the disk in a few minutes."

"Why didn't they start with the vids? That's our best chance of catching this guy."

"You just answered your own question. My guess is they'd erase the things if they could. Hell, they'd probably buy the guy dinner and put him on a plane to Rio if they had the chance." Harper chuckled and placed the folder on the desk.

"Glad you're so amused," Dean said, still fuming.

"Don't play that shit with me," Harper said. "I know what's going through your head, and I get it. I do. We can discuss it all over breakfast or a beer, but right now we have the job. So save the rage; sit your ass down; and let's get to work."

Dean accepted Harper's direction and sat; his partner was right. He pulled the folder toward him and lifted the manila flap. "Sorry," he muttered, gazing at a photograph similar to the one he'd seen in Clarke's home office.

Dean shook his head, flipping through the two-dozen photographs. He identified seven different boys. At least one of them was from the streets; Dean could tell by the shabby jeans and tattered tennis shoes he wore, but this was the only kid that was dressed in the pictures. Others might have been runaways, hustlers or kids from Clarke's neighborhood. It was hard to tell. The very rich and the very poor had the same hairstyles these days.

As for Clarke, he was a bland looking man with a dark suntan. His white hair lay back against his scalp in a perfect wave, looking as properly coiffed as a banker, a real estate agent or a political candidate.

"I don't get it," Dean said.

"What do you mean?"

"The attraction to youth." That wasn't exactly what he meant. Dean knew the psychology. Clarke's crimes weren't about sexual attraction so much as they were about control and loathing, but every goddamn television commercial and magazine ad pushed this youth shit down his throat. Ten year olds dolled up to look like whores. Nineteen-year-old pop star has-beens. According to those advertising fucks, people were supposed to desire children. But if one of their neighbors actually acted on it and went all bad touch on one of their kids, they'd be the first ones to form an action group. The first ones to ask 'why my child?' It's a wonder the whole fucking country hadn't gone pedophile. "I just don't get it."

"What's to get? You have youth on the left and old age and death on the right. You keep looking to the left because what's on the right scares the hell out of you."

"I've never dated a guy under thirty." Truth was, he rarely dated men under forty. Younger men all looked somehow unfinished to Dean. He found a few of them pretty, but found none of them attractive. Only when youth was shed for a more distinct masculinity did men appeal to Dean. He knew it was uncommon. Some of his friends even considered his preference a pathology, but he didn't care if his friends got hard for his dates or not; they didn't have to fuck the guys.

"You're not afraid of death," Harper said.

"Come again?"

"Never mind. Look, we need to run these pics through juvy and social services and see if we can get a match."

"Did any names appear in Clarke's files?" Dean asked.

"Nope. He numbered them. Kept them all in a folder labeled 'Puppies.'"

"Charming," Dean said.

~φ~

Dean rewound the digital movie until the moment before the man entered Charles Clarke's bedroom. Clarke lay naked on his bed. Freshly showered, he looked relaxed and comfortable. No shades of remorse or shame colored the man's face in the aftermath of his abuse. The prick even waved at the camera and grinned. His unrepentant satisfaction infuriated Dean, disturbing him deeply and far too personally.

At fifteen, Dean had experienced his first sexual encounter, with a man three times his age. For Dean, it had been consensual. The man, Rick, had done nothing but present the opportunity, he hadn't gotten Dean drunk, hadn't drugged him or enticed him with porn. Rick asked if Dean wanted to get sucked off and Dean had said, "Yes." All of his friends at school talked about having sex, and Dean was determined to have it, though not precisely as his friends would have; his peers' tastes ran towards actresses, cheerleaders, and swimsuit models.

A month later, Rick was arrested for forcing sex on a nine-year-old boy. He committed suicide in a jail cell three floors down from where Dean currently sat.

The man's arrest, highly publicized in the local paper because of his position as a teacher, had terrified Dean. He listened, ashamed, as kids at school talked about the "fag teacher," emphasizing that suicide was too good for the pervert. For weeks Dean had lived in fear, convinced his friends already knew what he'd done or would soon know. The fear had filled Dean's chest like shards of glass. It would be ten years before he was again intimate with a man.

As an adult, looking back on that time in his life, the shame of that encounter rekindled, but not for the reasons some might imagine. His fear had changed over the years to guilt. He understood the teacher's aberrant behavior. Dean knew that he wasn't to blame for Rick's sickness, but he couldn't help but think his acquiescence had encouraged the teacher's crimes. Ridiculous, he knew. Rick had been a molester long before Dean had ever entered the man's life, but if Dean had known enough to deny the man, to stop him, a nine-year-old boy – an innocent who couldn't fathom let alone consent to the teacher's demands – wouldn't carry the lifelong scars of Rick's touch.

On the screen, Charles Clarke rolled from his bed startled and clutching at the duvet to cover himself as he scurried across the mattress. He shouted for someone to get out of his house.

Then another man entered the shot, standing in partial profile, head turned as if aware of the camera. He wore loose-fitting blue jeans and a black T-shirt. Dean noted the bulk of muscle beneath the garments. He estimated the man stood six-feet tall and weighed 240-250 pounds. He appeared to be younger than Clarke, but not young. His hair was thick, with salty strands lightening the near black hue.

"I have an alarm. The police are coming," Clarke claimed.

"The alarm isn't set," his killer said evenly. "You didn't set it. You never do after your crimes. You never lock your doors. When you're done with them and send them on their way, your deepest wish is for their return, their subservience, their adoration. You want them to misinterpret what you did to them as love."

"I'll pay you," Clarke cried. "I'll…"

Before he could finish the next sentence, the killer crossed the room in four quick strides, revealing nothing of his face. He landed a ferocious punch to Clarke's jaw. Even with poor sound, Dean heard Clarke's bones crack beneath the blow. The abuser dropped to the carpet unconscious. His killer bent low and lifted the man and tossed him onto the bed as easily as discarding a robe before dressing. Then the killer pulled his shirt over his head, revealing a powerful back and thick shoulders. He folded the shirt and removed his pants and shoes. He stacked the clothing tidily and carried it off camera, perhaps into the hall. Then he returned.

Clarke's murderer walked to the edge of the bed, head canted away from the observing lens. He leaned over Clarke and bit into the man's thigh. Skin ripped and gouts of blood poured over the leg. It happened quickly. No hesitation or clumsiness.

Then it happened again. The killer didn't chew the flesh, but rather spat it out in the rapidly forming pool of blood. Clarke came to then. Frantic eyes as wide and white as golf balls dominated his features. He opened his mouth to scream but all that emerged from his throat was a shrill hiss.

The killer changed his position, moving closer to the headboard. His palm went to Clarke's brow. He shoved the abuser's head back into the pillow, and then he leaned forward and ripped Clarke's throat out with his teeth.

Dean stopped the clip and rewound to the point just before the killer dipped his head to take out Clarke's throat. In this action he revealed more of his face – a full cheek, a strong jaw smeared with Clarke's blood, the crescent pool of an eye socket. The blood acted as a mask, making clear identification impossible, but Dean would know this man if he met him.

The killer reminded Dean of a teacher named Rick.

~φ~

Interviews with Charles Clarke's neighbors yielded nothing of value. Like all good neighbors, they minded their own business. The time counter on Clarke's computer put the time of death at 5:33 p.m., which meant there was still some light in the sky when the murderer let himself into Clarke's house, but of the neighbors who were home at that time of the evening none could "recall" seeing anything of interest.

The techs went through Clarke's computer several times, looking for the names or addresses of victims. They scanned his Internet browser history, trying to ascertain if he'd met his victims (perhaps his killer) in a chat room. They combed his emails, seeking evidence of pornography trafficking, possibly the names of other men who shared his disease. After twenty-four hours, they'd found nothing. Apparently, Clarke was a rarity: insular in his perversion.

The video itself was of little help. Though the murderer was distinct in appearance – muscular, middle-aged – there wasn't enough of the man's face to capture a functional image. They couldn't put the back of his head on the departmental website or the six o'clock news and hope to field accurate leads.

No, despite having captured their killer on tape, the break in the case required a little more effort. Clarke's cell phone records showed a call to Capital Taxi at 4:48 on the afternoon of his death. Based on the video clock, this would have been shortly after his abuse of the boy Clarke had labeled "Puppy Number 16a."

The boy was featured in several of Clarke's photographs and at least one video. He was the frightened boy with the grimace of pain in the photo Harper had lifted from Clarke's printer.

Following up with the cab company, Dean got an address for a home on Arnold Street in a rundown residential district called Four Points – about as far from Clarke's Country Club address as was possible while remaining within the city limits. The home was owned by a property management group and leased to Mr. Jesse Bolton and his wife Janis. The couple had been under lease on the property for just over nine months. They were currently two months behind on the rent. Both had records with the Barnard Police Department – drunk and disorderlies and a DUI for Mr. Bolton – and both were on file with social services, stemming from an incident involving their son, Matthew.

With the address plugged into the GPS system, Dean drove across town. Harper occupied the passenger seat.

"So how are we going to handle this?" Harper asked. "I mean if this is the Puppy's address."

"Could you not call him that?" It had been bad enough seeing the demeaning term listed among Clarke's documentation; he saw no point in encouraging its use from his partner.

"Fine. Regardless. We check the place out, meet Jesse Bolton and realize he isn't our guy, cross everyone off the suspect list, then what?"

"Then we inform the parents their son has been abused and suggest they get him therapy so he doesn't end up as fucked up as Clarke."

"You think a family in Four Points can afford to send their kid to a shrink?"

"There are services available."

"If they'll use them."

"That's their decision to make."

"I hate this shit."

"We all hate this shit," Dean replied.

He drove out of downtown and over a viaduct, spanning a broad ditch filled with litter, scrub grass and the cardboard homes of those who found even Four Points out of their price range. The houses on the far side of the bridge were single and double story wrecks with peeling paint and sagging porches. Shingles draped loose on rooftops like scabs displaced by eczema. Most of the vehicles – pickup trucks, cheap sedans, bloated mini-vans – offered transportation if not style. Grass browned by early frost and grown wild from indifference ran from property to property, the yards differentiated only by the junk littering them. Four Points was the colon of the city; a dismal and diseased organ processing a constant flow of waste and toxicity.

An exception to the decaying appearance of the district caught Dean's eye as he turned down Arnold Street. One house wore a fresh coat of white paint; it's roof looked healthy and the yard was, if not lush, well maintained and free of trash. It looked like a single healthy tooth amid a rotted mouth. At the corner of this house, Dean saw a man, wearing a red ski parka and blue jeans. His dark hair was brushed back neatly. White threads lightened the field of near-black strands.

A frisson of recognition ran through his chest.

Is that him? Dean wondered. He played back Clarke's video in his mind. The man beside the house on his left was certainly the right size, and the hair was similar if not identical. *Jesus, that could be him.*

"You missed it," Harper said.

"Missed what?"

"The house," his partner said. "The GPS chick said we arrived at our destination. Don't you listen?"

"Yeah, right," Dean said. He pulled to the curb, turning his head to keep the man in his field of vision. The front tire rolled up on the sidewalk, jolting the car to a stop.

"Watch the rubber," Harper said.

But Dean was watching the man across the street and two doors back. He stared in the mirror, refocusing his eyes as if the act might magnify the man's image or produce a clear identification.

"You see that guy?" Dean asked.

"Where?"

"Two houses back. Other side of the road?"

"No. Why? He and old boyfriend of yours?"

"Fuck off, Harper," Dean said. "He could be our guy."

The man stepped back into the alley beside the house. Dean kept his eyes on the mirror, hoping he would reappear.

"Are you serious?" Harper asked, turning to look over the seat and through the back window.

"I don't know," Dean said. "Probably not. There have to be a hundred guys in Four Points that fit the description. I'm probably just overreacting. On edge or something."

"Should we check him out?" Harper asked.

"I'll do it," Dean replied. He opened the car door and stepped out. Speaking to Harper over the roof of the vehicle, he said, "You check on the Boltons. More than likely this isn't our guy, but if it is and he thinks we're close he might bolt."

"Or he might blow your head off. I'm going with you."

"And what if the perp *is* Jesse Bolton? He sees us out here and tears out the backdoor because we went chasing geese? You handle the family, I'll go talk to this guy."

Harper wasn't satisfied with the arrangement – it wasn't procedure – but he nodded his head.

Dean turned to face the house across the street. The man in the red parka was there again, crossing to the front door. His head turned slightly as he attempted to unsnag a key ring from one of the jacket's pockets. Seeing the man in partial profile set off a web of chill at the back of Dean's head.

Shit, that's him.

~φ~

He stopped at the mailbox on the curb and read the name *Baker* on its side. Dean jogged over the man's lawn and paused on the front doorstep. He breathed deeply and released the strap that secured his sidearm in its holster. Then he knocked on the door.

When the man opened the door, Dean saw he had shed his parka. The bulk of frequently worked muscles pressed at Baker's white button down shirt. Thickly veined forearms grew from rolled up sleeves. The face was chiseled and striking; the eyes as clear and blue as the winter sky. The man's appearance unnerved Dean, caused a thick and inappropriate lust to settle low in his belly.

Watching the killer on the video, Dean had been reminded of a teacher named Rick, but Baker looked nothing like that man. There wasn't even a passing resemblance to the soft-faced teacher who abused boys and finally killed himself. Dean couldn't be certain what random connection he'd made equating the two.

"Hello," the man said.

"Hello, Mr. *Baker* is it?"

"I'm Paul Baker."

"Mr. Baker, I'm Detective Dean Kaiser with the Barnard Police Department."

"Yes detective," Baker said. "Do you want to come in? It's colder than shit out here."

"Yes, thank you." Dean stepped inside, his hand close to the gun on his hip.

The inside of the house was as impeccable as the exterior. The furniture, while not expensive, was clean and modern and fit the space well. White high-gloss paint covered the moldings at the ceiling and floor, framing walls painted a soft fawn color. Anywhere else in the city, the house would have struck Dean as pleasant, but it didn't fit the Four Points model. He found the neatness of the home wholly wrong.

"Mr. Baker, I'd like to ask you a couple of questions," Dean said, watching as Baker crossed the room.

"I assume this is in connection with the deviant?"

The statement was close enough to a confession for Dean's taste. He took a step back and removed his sidearm, which he aimed at Baker's torso.

"I'm going to ask you to lie down on the floor with your hands behind your head."

"That isn't necessary."

"My gun disagrees with you."

"So shoot," Baker said. "This body has already lived its time. Your bullets won't change the shape of things."

The serenity in the man's tone disturbed him. No one should sound that calm with a gun pointing at him.

"I said get on the floor."

Baker ignored the request and walked along the far wall, brushing his hands across the vertical blinds, making them clack and whisper. He paused and licked a thumb, which he pressed to one of the white plastic panels. He rubbed lightly as if to remove a stain.

"The boy would have damned himself without me," said Baker, seemingly lost in his massage of the blind.

"You're quite the guardian angel, now lie the fuck down!"

"That won't happen," Baker noted with amusement. "You'll find that Clarke wrote a check to Matthew Bolton's father; it wasn't a very large check. People pay more for a mediocre television set."

"Excuse me?"

"That's why Matthew couldn't go to his parents. Surely, you must have been wondering that. Clarke bought the boy's services and his parents' silence. Matthew really had no choice."

"But *you* did."

"Not so."

"Down on the floor!"

"You'll find Clarke wrote a lot of checks to a lot of people."

"I'm only going to tell you one more time."

"That's true," Baker agreed.

A blur of motion startled Dean. He nearly fired his weapon, but the target was gone; Baker no longer stood at the window. A thick arm slid around Dean's neck, clamping across his throat like a boa constrictor. Baker's other arm shot out and grasped the gun. With a painful twist, he freed the weapon from Dean's hand.

"You don't need this," Baker whispered, rocking the gun in Dean's field of vision. "I'm not going to hurt you, and you can't hurt me." Baker inhaled loudly, air rasping through his nose and throat. He let the breath out cold and dry on Dean's neck. "Now, I could snap your neck, or if I was feeling particularly cruel, I could suffocate you slowly. You know that, don't you?"

"Yes."

With the uttering of the word, Baker released Dean's throat and stepped away.

"Sorry, but guns have a way of making people deaf to the important things. Now, as I was saying, Clarke wrote a number of checks, to procure company and to keep things quiet. You'll find ample evidence of these transactions."

"If you know so much about this, you should have turned him in."

"That's not the shape of things."

"Because you'd rather kill."

"I have no choice."

"Bullshit."

"I was created with a purpose. I'm a fabric, a weave of needs, created from man's effluent."

"You're a fucking psychopath."

"No," Baker said, evenly. "I'm your violence."

Baker walked in front of him and pressed his face close to Dean's. He cocked his head slightly to the left, peering into Dean's eyes.

What is he looking for? Understanding? Fear? Fuck that.

Dean drove a fist toward Baker's throat. The man didn't flinch. His eyes remained locked on Dean's as he caught Dean's wrist in his hand.

"How frustrating," Baker said. "You so badly want to hurt me, but you can't. Not because you don't possess the determination but because you're helpless against me. Imagine a small boy with no place to turn, backed into a corner, betrayed by the only people in the world he thought he could trust. Imagine that. Imagine what that must be like for the boy. Just think what he might do."

"But the boy didn't do anything. *You* did."

"If I hadn't destroyed Clarke, Matthew would have. His thoughts were already leading him to it; he might have even succeeded, but then his soul would carry that soil, and I couldn't let that happen. So I intervened on his behalf. That is the shape of things."

"He told you to kill Clarke?"

"Of course not. If he had asked, he would have been complicit in the act."

"But he told you Clarke was abusing him?"

"His desperation summoned me."

"Let go of my hand, Paul. Come with me. I can get you help."

"This is a carousel," Baker said in frustration. "Perhaps another approach?"

Baker tossed the gun to the floor, and his hands shot to either side of Dean's head. He pulled their faces close. Remembering Charles Clarke's death at the teeth of this madman, Dean struggled against the grip, fearing his skin would soon be pinched and torn away, but his efforts against the sturdy hold were futile. Baker's lips crushed against his in a violent kiss. The skin of Dean's upper lip split with the impact. His head grew light, his struggles intensified.

A flash of blue light blinded him, and Dean fell back and down, his body shaking in spasm as if he'd just been struck by a taser. He hit the floor hard, and pain flared at his elbow, his hip, and his leg. Baker also collapsed on the floor, but unlike Dean the suspect was motionless.

Once the seizure-like tremors released him Dean crawled away from Baker's body. "Shit," he hissed. "Shit. Shit."

He stood and looked about the room frantically as if expecting another attacker to emerge from one of the archways. Dean's eyes fell on his sidearm laying on the floor less than a foot from Baker's clawed fingers. He scrambled across the room and retrieved his gun. From this angle Baker appeared dead. Glazed eyes stared blankly at the ceiling. His mouth, stained with Dean's blood, was open and slack. Dean thought to check the man's pulse, but feared his host was playing possum, waiting for a clean opportunity to strike.

Instead of touching the suspect, Dean fished his cell phone from his pocket and flipped it open, intending to call for back up.

His finger refused his command to dial. Dean tried again, thinking he must be in shock. He took several deep breaths, steadied himself and tried again. Still he could not force his finger to press the buttons.

Don't, a voice shouted.

Dean looked around, seeking the direction of the voice, but he shared the room with no one but Baker, and the man hadn't moved.

The walls about him began to melt, blurs and smears replacing hard edges and angles. This odd shifting forced Dean off balance. A moment later, he stood in a different room – a bedroom – and Charles Clarke was alive and offering him money in exchange for his life; he tore the man's throat out. The room spun, and Dean dropped to his knees. Strange faces appeared like memories behind his eyes. A slender, cruel-faced woman knelt before him as he brought a hammer down on her skull. A handsome young man in an expensive business suit flopped on the floor – a length of bailing wire tightly wrapped around his throat. A blubbery man with few teeth, dirt-splotched cheeks and watery eyes howled. He lay crucified on a floor of raw wooden planks. Dean gouged at the man's genitals with a broken whiskey bottle.

The ghastly show played behind Dean's eyes. He couldn't push it away, couldn't hide behind his own thoughts. His head swam with the grotesque images.

Then Dean was walking away from Baker's body. His mind cleared momentarily, but foreign thoughts surged over the moment of relief. Paul Baker's life and death surfaced in the wake of the blood-soaked montage.

Baker had pumped his body full of muscle enhancing drugs, had spent hours at the gym to reshape a body that had earned him the nickname "Porkster" in high school. Baker had been so obsessed with his personal beautification he'd drawn away from people. He'd slaved and struggled and sacrificed for a body considered perfect, but in the process had totally removed himself from the society he'd meant to impress with his newfound physique. The information came to Dean like a memory, like a fragment of his own life clearly remembered.

Recently. Late one night, Baker answered his front door. On the stoop stood a young boy with blond hair and an innocent but sorrowful face. (Matthew Bolton? Dean wondered) The boy showed Baker his palm, where a long cut ran from index finger to wrist. Baker took the boy's hand amid a flare of blue light.

And then this other – this Violence – moved into Baker's skin, the way it now resided in Dean.

Yes, a gentle voice whispered in his head. *The dead and dying… the weak. They give me shelter. Baker died only minutes after I joined him. The drugs he used to manufacture his physique destroyed his heart.*

Am I dying? Dean thought. *Am I dead?*

No, the other voice replied. *Your arrival interrupted my final duty to Matthew. You are simply being borrowed.*

Dean felt his body move, but he'd made no command for it to do so. He walked across the room to the front door and pulled it open. Dean tried to exert his will, struggled to make even a single finger move of his own volition, but his attempt failed. Inside his head, his own body, he was an impotent prisoner.

His thoughts twisted and tangled, knotted by an extreme and manic claustrophobia, but his body produced none of the phobia's physical manifestations. The sick gut. The sweaty palms. The clenched muscles. His mind struggled but his body was untouched by the fear.

Dean's body walked across Baker's lawn, his sidearm gripped in the hand at his side. A new collage of grisly images erupted in his thoughts. Blood. Bands of shredded flesh. Organs, glistening and twinkling wetly, but no longer serving the human machine.

Christ, Dean screamed within his head. *What are you?*

You already know, the voice replied.

My violence.

Man's violence. Emotional energy, like all energy, unbreakable and eternal. I'm woven of it. I'm the sum of it. But for you, violence comes with guilt and fear. I lack these obstacles, and I absolve you of them.

You're a creature of revenge, Dean asserted.

I'm a being of justice, unhampered by the viscous fluid of shifting moralities. This is my purpose. Others of my kind were woven of different emotions, with dissimilar purposes. Some are pure hate and others pure joy. Some have gone mad because they were woven of so many disparate threads.

And you're not mad? Dean asked. *You ripped Clarke apart with your teeth.*

With Baker's teeth, the voice corrected. *And the method is prescribed by the one I serve. Lacking a viable weapon, Matthew was led by tortured thoughts to a resolution not wholly common.*

Dean's foot stepped up on the far sidewalk. A gunshot echoed. It rang in his ears, but his body was otherwise unmoved by the sound.

Matthew's house, Dean thought, suddenly panicked. *Harper?*

He willed his legs to move faster, to run. Concern for his partner flared like static charges all around him, but his body was not his own, and it continued to stroll along the sidewalk at an aggravatingly measured pace.

Maybe that will make what follows easier for you.

Make it easier? What happened?

You'll see.

Harper? Dean asked.

Yes, the Violence replied, *Harper.*

They reached the house far too slowly. Dean's imagination played cruel games up to the second his hand wrapped around the front door's knob. He imagined Harper lying dead on the Bolton's floor. He clearly saw a hole punched between his partner's eyes. Then the door opened, and his body moved inside to find his teasing imagination hadn't been completely inaccurate.

Harper lay against a cheap and tattered brown sofa. A shimmering crimson stain blossomed across the left lapel of his coat. He struggled for breath, chest rising and falling in ragged gasps.

Across the room, in the archway separating the dismal room from another stood an emaciated couple. Their faces were tight and pale like latex masks pulled too tightly. Through these masks wild eyes scurried in their sockets like insects fleeing sudden light. Janis Bolton bit a fingernail furiously. She wore only a bra and a pair of blue sweat pants frayed at the cuffs. Her ribs showed through the thin membrane of sickly skin on her chest. Pale blue shadows accentuated the protruding bones.

Jesse Bolton wore blue jeans and a gray T-shirt with a beer company's logo printed on the chest. He held a narrow, cheap rifle at his side.

"We found him that way!" Janis Bolton shrieked, suddenly, pointing a bony finger at Harper. "He was like that when we got here."

The grossly ridiculous claim would have been humorous if its subject hadn't been Dean's partner. He felt the urge to shoot the woman on the spot. Perhaps fortunately, his body was not his to control.

"Yeah," Jesse blurted. "Yeah, this isn't mine. It was here."

He threw the rifle on the floor, where it clacked on the rotted wooden planks.

"You lying sacks of shit," Harper said weakly from his place against the sofa.

Dean's arm lifted. He took a moment to aim down the barrel. Then, he pulled the trigger. The bullet hit Jesse Bolton in the chest and threw him back to the floor amid a spray of blood.

Janis Bolton screamed. She started a silly jig, stomping back and forth in frantic steps, bent low as if trying to hide behind currents of air until her gaze fell on the rifle. Dean watched as she lowered herself to snatch up the weapon. Once her hands were on it, his finger tightened. A bullet entered through Janis Bolton's left temple. Her head was cocked toward him so the bullet traveled through her jaw, sending a spray of teeth flying from her mouth. She crumpled to the side, arms splayed, landing on the corpse of her husband. Again, the rifle clattered on the floor.

Dean lowered his weapon and holstered it. He crossed to Harper and put a hand behind his partner's head.

"You okay?" he asked. "Hey, Reg, can you hear me?"

"I'm not deaf," Harper muttered. "Shoulder wound. Broken collarbone. Blood loss. Get something to apply pressure. Thank god the asshole only had a twenty-two."

Dean stood from his partner's side. Only then did he realize he was again controlling his actions.

The Violence had released him.

He took no time to entertain his relief. Instead he spun away, searching for a suitable bandage for his partner's wounds.

A boy stood in the home's entryway. His eyes were soft, filled with tears, but Dean could see the boy's struggle, and it sickened him.

Matthew Bolton fought to keep a smile from pushing up the corners of his mouth. His lips trembled with the effort. Soon enough, the boy gave up the fight, and Matthew grinned happily as tears streamed down his cheeks.

~φ~

Dean walked into Harper's hospital room and presented him with a bag of barbecue flavored Ruffles potato chips. He sat in the gray chair beside the bed and looked at the floor. Two sleepless nights and days had passed. Moments of recent brutality mingled with incidents of long ago bloodshed to make a disconcerting loop in his mind, playing endlessly, showing him faces – familiar and strange – all in some pose drawn from the spectrum of anguish. The Violence had left him, but the visions it had brought remained, hardly discernible from Dean's own memories.

More disconcerting was the idea that this thing existed at all. It had violated him, used him. It called itself Violence, but what was it? This mystery haunted him. Naturally phases of disbelief punctuated his thoughts about the entity; it couldn't have been real. But Dean wiped away the skepticism whenever it arose; he wanted the thing to exist. He needed to believe in it.

"You're golden," Harper said, obviously trying to ease Dean's mind, though he was miles away from understanding the source of that unease. "As far as I'm concerned it was a clean shooting. I've already made my statement."

"Thanks," Dean replied.

Dean knew Harper was right. He didn't feel guilty for what had happened to those people. Though his finger had squeezed the trigger it was the Violence that had killed the Boltons. Dean had merely been a witness as the creature used his body to fulfill a duty, to complete the shape of things.

"Weird about that Baker guy, though," Harper commented.

"You heard about that?"

"Dumb ass M.E. Sometimes I think he makes all this shit up as he goes."

Initially, Paul Baker's time of death was placed at sometime on the evening *before* Charles Clarke's murder. Naturally, when forensics confirmed Baker's ID as Clarke's killer, the medical examiner adjusted his original report, adding twenty-four hours to his estimate. But even with this modification Dean's accounting of events was fucked; it seemed he had left his partner alone with the Boltons to go question a dead man.

Still, his superiors weren't making an issue of it. Harper had backed up Dean's statement every step of the way, going so far as to positively ID Baker as the man standing beside the house across the street from the Boltons, when Dean knew damn well his partner hadn't even seen the guy. Grudgingly, the medical examiner was forced to change his report a second time.

"You need to snap out it," Harper said. "In a couple days you'll have your hearing. I was there. Matthew was there. Neither of us are going to change our stories. You'll be back at your desk by Friday."

Matthew, Dean thought. *Jesus, that kid was going to be a wreck.*

Maybe the Violence had intervened on behalf of the kid's soul, but the boy still had to live with what had happened to him, would always live with the fact his meth-head parents had rented him out to a diseased freak like Clarke for a few blasts of crystal. Matthew's smile returned to Dean, and he tried to push it out of his head. It too had haunted him these last two days.

The kid was now in the custody of social services. Dean didn't know if that was a good thing or not.

"I saw some weird shit that afternoon," Harper said, "but I also saw both Boltons holding that rifle."

But Bolton dropped the gun before he was shot. Panic drove his wife to it. They didn't have to die.

"I will, of course, leave out all mention of hallucinations."

"Hallucinations?" Dean asked.

Harper smiled and shook his head. "Weirdest thing. Probably a result of trauma, but I could swear that someone was standing next to you when you fired on Bolton. I mean I couldn't see the guy's face or anything. It was like this blue-white smear. This shape. I thought I was seeing ghosts."

Dean's pulse quickened as the blood drained from his face. "You said you saw this thing *when* I shot Bolton?"

"Sure, I guess."

"Not *after*?"

"I don't know, Dean. Jesus, I wasn't exactly in the most focused of mental states at the time, what with the pain and the
bleeding. I'm not even going to mention it at the hearing, so
just relax."

"Was it before or after?" Dean insisted.

"What fucking difference does it make?"

All the difference in the world, Dean thought. The only thing
that had made the last two days bearable was the idea that he
hadn't been responsible for the Boltons' deaths. He hadn't followed procedure in the shooting, not even close. He'd walked
into the house and gunned the couple down. Clean. Cold. *Unhampered by the viscous fluid of shifting moralities*. He'd believed
the Violence was responsible, but now he couldn't be sure.

Had he used the entity as an excuse to execute that family
because they disgusted him? Was he capable of that?

Harper wanted to know what difference it made. It was the
difference between harboring a mystery and being one.

"Please," Dean said. "I have to know. Was it before or after?"

~φ~

The Dodd Contrivance

Imagine looking into a raindrop and seeing an entire world at work – the labor and the joy and the pain of its populace; the celebrations and the battles; the shifting currents of climate traversing miniscule continents and infinitesimal oceans – all encased in a liquid pellet with a volume no greater than that of an inconsequential breadcrumb forgotten between stove and larder. With this as your supposition, it is then necessary to discard the premise or become overwhelmed, because surely if such a world can exist in one drop, others must exist as well, and following this hypothesis it stands to reason that the real world, the one occupied by man and beast, king and servant, is likewise sheathed and similarly fragile.

And what should happen when those drops collide? Could gutter streams and filthy puddles be universes unto themselves, where the many worlds come together to struggle anew with fresh species from neighboring worlds, or merely confluences of destroyed planets with uncounted casualties that had briefly thought themselves immortal as they plummeted from cloud to dirt?

Samuel Beaufort smiled at this whimsical notion, sitting in his favorite chair at the window and listening to the rapping rain. It was a familiar fancy, one he revisited often, though only in his thoughts. In the one instance he'd actually voiced the idea to a small group of colleagues at the club, he'd been summarily excoriated with disdainful glares, so he'd learned to consider the theory a personal entertainment rather than a topic of conversation.

Coffee cooled in a china cup resting on the mahogany table beside him, forgotten as he gazed at the precipitation beading on the pane. Rainfall speckled the glass, smearing the light cast by the few lamps still burning in the city beyond. At his feet, the honey-colored hound whimpered and nuzzled his ankle. He looked down into the warm dark eyes and nodded solemnly.

"Of course, it's impossible. It's likely quite insane, but isn't that what makes it such an interesting study?"

The hound responded with a second whimper and a more forceful push at his leg. Then the animal stood, stretched out its front paws and began circling the Persian carpet.

The bitch was still quite young, though her exact age Samuel did not know. One afternoon just over a month ago she had joined him on his stroll through the central park and proved fine company, and since he lived alone – his long-passed wife having died in her twenty-second year – he thought to bring a second heartbeat into the too-quiet home. He'd named the animal Ruby after a particularly scandalous aunt, and though she often still bounded with the unrestrained energy of youth, he found her a pleasant companion in an otherwise empty home.

"You're quite right," Samuel told the dog while pushing himself from the chair. "We should take the next step and examine this phenomenon in greater detail. What kind of scientists would we be if we left all things in the realm of theory and speculation?"

After retrieving Ruby's tether, his own topcoat, hat and gloves, Samuel withdrew his umbrella from the stand at the front door and allowed Ruby to lead him into the storm. Samuel had always loved the smell of the rain, reveled in the clatter of a particularly forceful storm. When viewed through the pelting drops the buildings around him took on the texture of raw wool – gray, nebulous, and frayed. A climax of thunder cowered the dog, who pulled back on the lead, now uncertain about taking her constitutional in such dreary weather.

"Ruby," he said, "discovery is a terrifying thing, which is why so few have the heart to accomplish it. Now, let's explore."

Though apparently not convinced of her master's supposition, Ruby took a hesitant step toward him. Soon enough, she fell in at his heel, beneath the cover of the umbrella as Samuel guided her to the south.

The gray static of rain against the black backdrop of night soothed him. Streetlamp flames spluttered, flashing yellow auroras in the gloom. Carriages crossed the boulevard ahead, but the streets were otherwise unoccupied, and Samuel's fascination with worlds within the rain transformed into a new fancy. Turning away to allow Ruby some privacy while she relieved herself beside a stoop, Samuel began to consider what being truly alone might be like. What if the entire city, the entire world, were to be emptied of humanity, leaving only himself and his fine companion to wander smooth roads and grassy dales, seeing the important locations of the earth without the hindrance of a populace? Would such desolation prove soothing or maddening?

Ever since Leslie's death some ten years past, Samuel had been alone. Parents long dead and no siblings, his only remaining family consisted of an Uncle who lived in Charleston and another in Albany, along with a number of cousins with whom he'd socialized extensively in his youth but had seen rarely in recent years. His social circle was quite large, but his friendships few. The men at the club were such rigid creatures, never questioning their status or the social structure that allowed them it, but rather blustering on without a hint of inquisitiveness, reaffirming their position and denigrating those who fell beneath it. Samuel knew they considered him an odd-duck, perhaps even crazy for all of his chatter about what might be rather than extolling the virtues and vices of day-to-day existence. The only member of the club who truly intrigued him, though he could not claim friendship with the man, was one Hubert Dodd, a bearish braggart with a penchant for inappropriate often scandalous humor and the ability to weave gilded lies that engaged with their sheer brazenness. Though not close to the man, Samuel admired Dodd's imagination and listened intently whenever the man regaled the salon with one of his outlandish tales.

Often, Samuel had thought to invite Hubert Dodd to his home for a meal. He found the man at turns overbearing and standoffish, yet always fascinating. He'd thought to question the man in some detail about the adventures he'd recounted, perhaps even catch Dodd in a lie, though not to embarrass the man, but rather to show that Samuel thought the stories remarkable, regardless of their veracity. He felt a kinship with

Dodd. They both had suffered the hushed derision of their conservative peers, yet both were established enough in the society to remain on the guest lists for all of the right gatherings. But he'd never managed a proper introduction, let alone extended a social invitation.

Ruby's pleading whine and her wet haunches against his trousers alerted Samuel to her desire to leave his fanciful experiment behind and return to the warmth of the fire. He was about to acquiesce when a great bolt of lightning ripped the sky above them and a cannon-shot of thunder peeled.

His terrified hound backed away, ducking low to the ground, and before Samuel could calm her skittish nerves, Ruby had escaped her tether. The honey-colored hound barked furiously at the sky. Whimpered. Then she set off in a blinding tear, leaving Samuel with a damp leather strap and a look of surprise on his face. A gust of wind pulled hard against the bowl of his umbrella, sending him back a step, but this concession to motion proved to be a necessary goading. He ran after his dog, into the storm, through dim, empty streets, lit only by flickering lamps and flashes of lightning.

In the distance he heard the muffled yaps of his companion, and they guided him, but the clatter of the weather muddled his sense of direction. He turned right, certain Ruby's voice had risen from that direction, only to have the familiar bark rise at a great distance to his back. The poor creature was obviously traumatized by the storm, running aimlessly for someplace warm and dry, a place she would perceive as safe. If she were a rational animal she'd return home, flee to the north where an old soup bone and the roar on Samuel's hearth would assure her comfort, but for all of her fine companionship, Ruby was not a great thinker and instead had to rely on inaccurate instinct for guidance.

Samuel followed her on a winding path beneath tall brick homes. Caught sight of her twice, dashing like she had a fox in her nose, ignoring his calls and vanishing around a distant corner.

Finally he came upon his dear hound in an alley between two grand structures – a large, fashionable house and another building which, save for its intricate architectural detail, including a cornice of brass about the eaves, he might have taken to be a carriage house or stable. The corridor between them ended in a high stone wall, and rain coursed over the barrier, giving it the appearance of a great perspiring beast. The door to the house stood open, as did the one to the detached building. A dull glow oozed from the opening on his right, providing a trifling illumination to the scene before him.

Ruby crouched facing the corner between the outbuilding and the wall. Her growls were all but eaten by the torrential clatter, but she seemed to have cornered something, perhaps a cat or one of the raccoons that scavenged the city's waste. He hoped it wasn't a rat. Samuel loathed the creatures and a chill ran over his neck and spine as he considered having to face one.

But as he moved closer to the scene, a flash of lightning bathed the alley and Samuel gasped. The bleaching light revealed Ruby's prey in brief, vivid detail. It was no rat. But exactly what this creature *was* he could not say.

Though the size of an average cat, and possessing some feline traits about the head, this beast was hairless and the color of muddy water. Its legs jointed awkwardly, reminding him of sketches he'd seen of the crocodiles said to roam the Nile Valley. The unnaturalness of the animal lodged in Samuel's throat and knitted a web of uncertainty in his mind. His curiosity insisted he carefully observe and catalog this beast; understand something of its composition, but a potent dread kept him at a distance.

He called for Ruby, wanting to keep his precious pet from the mouth and claws of this sinister oddity, but she disregarded his appeals, focusing her full attention on the thing she'd cornered. Seeing no option, Samuel stepped forward, affixing a sliding loop in the tether so that it would secure tightly to the dog's neck unlike the manufactured collar attached at its end, which had proven something less than reliable.

Just as he reached Ruby, her head whipped up as if finally hearing her name being called. Samuel lunged forward, repulsed at the idea of getting too close to the unnamable creature, but instead of managing to slip the lead around the dog's head, the loop passed through wet air. Ruby eluded his attempt at capture and raced to the side disappearing through an open door in the building on his left.

Samuel backed away from the corner, uncertain if its occupant might find him less threatening than his hound had been. He shuffled several steps until he stood inside the threshold. Lantern light glowed at the far end of the hallway, and he saw Ruby at its center. He searched for the panel of the door but found nothing save splintered planks, barely clutching twisted hinges. The state of the door disappointed him as he should have liked a means to lock out the creature in the alley, but since this option had been denied him, he decided to collect Ruby quickly and get her home.

Setting off toward the dog, who sat at the edge of the dim light, Samuel fell under the distinct impression that he walked on a balcony, rather than an expanse of floor. To his left the wall seemed to end at his waist, forming a banister, and though he had no clear sight of the space beyond – merely shapes of gray atop sheets of black – he felt certain it stretched out and down from him. At his club, they had wired one of the studies with electric light in a rare concession to progress, and though this man-made incandescence was neither as soothing nor as dependable as the gas-lit fixtures, he thought it would be nice to bring illumination to this peculiar and unfamiliar space with the simple turning of a knob, but having no such modern novelty, Samuel bolstered himself and made his way toward the muted light ahead.

Yet he was forced to pause, because another shape had joined that of his hound. This form was decidedly human, though quite small.

"There's the pretty Milly," a girl's excited voice cried. "There's my ever-so good girl."

Samuel detected a lilt of brogue in the words, likely one of the Irish working as a servant for the owner of the adjacent home. But why was she claiming familiarity with Samuel's pet? Was it simply the exuberance many youths showed toward domestic animals, or had Ruby once belonged to this girl and gone stray only to find her way back after a month in Samuel's care?

"Excuse me?" he said forcefully, so as to be heard over the marching rain. "Miss?"

He now stood close enough to see the girl, but was surprised to find it wasn't a girl at all, but rather a fully-grown woman, though quite certainly petite. Her hair was the color of carrot soup and her skin as white as bone.

"The dog's mine," the woman snapped, clutching tightly to Ruby's neck. "You piss off home. He don't need you no more."

The vulgarity startled Samuel, and he puffed up with outrage as he was not accustomed to being addressed so harshly from the likes of a servant, but the woman's claim gave him ammunition. "You have no rights to that dog," he charged. "Clearly, you don't even know its gender. You said '*he*' doesn't need me, and it's quite apparent the animal is a female."

"Not the dog you nancy," the girl spat, "Him, the one that sent her to you... *He* don't need you no more. The dog is mine. He had no right giving her away."

"No one gave me that dog," Samuel replied, infuriated with the diminutive woman's impertinence. "The dog was left to stray, and I cared for her."

"You got all the brains of a shite stew," she replied. "That bugger, Mr. Dodd, sent her to you, made it all a game 'cause he thought it would be a fine story to tell." The woman pulled something from her pocket. She held it up and back so that it caught the light. "This here calls my Milly home," the woman said. She put the instrument to her lips and made a great show of blowing, but no sound emerged from the pipe. Still, Ruby's ears pricked, and she shot to her feet, searching the landing as if her name had been called. "You see that there? I don't know how it works, but it does. He trained her to come when this was blowed on. Proves she's mine. Now piss-off home."

"Miss, I will only warn you once about your language."

"Good," she said, swiftly returning the pipe to her pocket. "'Cause I don't give a piss if you like the way I talk or not, and I don't want to hear nothing more about it. I just want my dog."

"And what would your master, Mr. Dodd, have to say about the way you treat his guests?"

"Don't think he'd give a donkey's cock one way or another. He's right out of his fucking skull. Now get out of the way and let me and my Milly go."

Lightning flashed above, and the space to Samuel's left lit up as if it had no ceiling at all. Something large and confounding occupied the center of the space, but he'd only managed to see it from the corner of his eye. Before he could turn to take it all in, the atmosphere was again as black as velvet.

The lightning had a different affect on the woman. She yelped as if it had burned her, and as the thunder rolled through the rafters, rumbling the very walls of the structure, she quickly struggled to lift the dog.

Samuel's heart sank when he thought he might lose Ruby forever. In their brief time together, he'd grown fond of the bitch, liked having her at his feet and lying next to him at night kicking her legs as she scampered over dream landscapes. He loathed the idea of her being kept by this crass and horrible woman.

"I'll pay you for the dog," he said.

"Don't need it. Got my pogue from the bugger when he lost his mind, and after what he done to me, I deserve every penny. You know what it's like to serve a monster? You see what he did to that door? Him's got the luck I come back to board up the other down there," she said throwing her index finger toward the staircase at her back.

"I'll be quite generous. I have grown fond of the animal."

"He said he'd be generous, too. The only thing he ever gave me was this here dog, and then he took her away. The rest I'm taking myself, because he don't need it anymore and the dirty bugger don't deserve none of it no how. He's against God that one. He's the Devil himself. That there," she said, pointing into the vast space on Samuel's left, "that there is Hell, and you can go on down and wait for him in it."

Obviously, the small woman had lost her mind, and it occurred to Samuel that she may have become delusional and murdered the master of the house in her derangement. It happened all the time with the immigrant classes. Samuel bore them no ill will generally, and he certainly didn't believe they were the beasts his friends at the club often claimed, but they were raised harshly by rough hands and their morality – their value of life – differed from that of men like Samuel and Hubert Dodd. Her fixation on Ruby seemed to contest this cold-blooded perception, but Samuel felt an instant chill and wondered if his colleague from the club lay bleeding somewhere in the main house, struck down by a servant who'd succumbed to religious mania.

"Where is Mr. Dodd?" Samuel asked.

"He's in another Hell," the girl replied. Ruby wriggled in her grasp. "He made a Hell here and found one in his own damned head."

Seeing no use in arguing with a lunatic, Samuel decided to change his tack. He gripped the handle of his umbrella quite tightly, should he need to use it in defense, and then he squared his shoulders.

"I can run much faster than you," he announced.

"Who said we was gonna race?"

Ruby whimpered and looked at him with the same pleading expression she used when she needed her constitutional.

"My point being that with the dog in your arms, I can reach a constable and bring him back before you make it to the end of the road. Now, I have offered to pay you generously for the animal. I suggest you allow me to do so. Otherwise, I shall be forced to involve the authorities."

Apparently, Samuel's logic worked on the woman, because the tension left her shoulders and face. "Bugger," she muttered, surrendering to the futility of her situation.

She dropped Ruby, who had only a short distance to fall. Immediately the dog raced to Samuel, taking a seated position next to his leg. Samuel presented the servant with an ample number of bills, enough to make her eyes light.

"Take care of Milly," she said, tucking the bills into her boot. "She's a good dog. The only good thing to come out of this place."

A moment later, the dreadful little woman was gone, tromping through the mud in the alley toward whatever destination summoned such people. Samuel bent low to scratch Ruby behind an ear.

"I hope I wasn't being presumptuous," he told her. "If you'd rather accompany that foul woman, I should quite understand, though I think remaining with me will provide you a more comfortable future."

In response, Ruby opened her mouth as if to yawn, but instead gave a weak yap, which Samuel took as acceptance of his decision. Ruby pressed close to his woolen trousers, and Samuel was finally able to slip the tether around her neck without incident.

An explosion sounded at his back, startling both man and dog as a cloud of brilliant white erupted around them. Unlike the previous flash of lightning, this one did not come and go. Rather the light, shocking after so much gloom, remained. Samuel spun, his heart lodged in his throat. Surely, lightning had struck the building and the persistent illumination suggested fire, but what Samuel saw upon completing his turn was no natural element.

The ceiling of the building was made of glass. Hundreds of small panes captured in an intricate steel web partitioned the dark sky beyond into a grimly colored grid. A great metal pole descended from this ceiling, ending at an immense platform, which while no taller than a steamer trunk spanned a good thirty feet. From this suspended panel a series of tubes and wires and rods dropped to a great apparatus of gears the smallest being no larger than Samuel's head, while the largest being the size of a respectable carriage. Burnished wood, perhaps mahogany, and tarnished metal were used to fashion the complex series of cogs, all of which now groaned and cranked. The distance from Samuel's location on the walkway to the floor was no less than forty feet. There he saw the base of this grand mechanism: a thick glass column, wide enough for Samuel to stand within and stretch his arms. The tube rose into the heart of the complex works, which creaked and turned like the heart of a great watch. Within the clear tower, dozens of coils glowed, throbbing energy as if they had captured the lightning itself.

Samuel gazed on astounded by the intricacies of the contrivance before him. It was impossible and amazing. His gaze ran from ceiling to floor and then back skyward to the mesh of metal above. As he drew his attention downward again, he noticed a series of flat metal plates beneath the wooden platform, a detail eclipsed by the magnificence of the whole.

The plates, two dozen in all, pushed forward and back along narrow tracks like finely fitted drawers. A great ratcheting suddenly filled the hall. Only when it happened again did Samuel notice that the plates were locking into positions along the base of the platform. This seemed to cause the complexity of gears to become sluggish. One by one, the metal sheets came to a snapping rest, and though this technical marvel thoroughly intrigued Samuel, his gaze was soon drawn away.

A dark form moved across the far wall. Perhaps it had only been a shadow cast by one of the revolving gears, but the sudden motion caught Samuel's eye. He followed it over the wall with his gaze, and reared back from the banister when it came to a stop.

The floor and back wall of the chamber below the walkway were alive with motion. Hundreds of unidentifiable forms in a spectrum of unsavory colors – cheese mould green, rotten beef gray, the filthy yellow of infection's discharge – swarmed the lower room to create a foul bestiary in the heart of the city.

Among these insectile and reptilian specimens, another species stalked. This trio of creatures bore a resemblance to man, in that they traveled on two legs and swung two arms, but there was nothing human about them. Their skin seemed to be the color of porridge and it stretched tightly over twig-thin appendages punctuated by knotty, grotesque joints. Tufts of beet-red hair jutted from their scalps. Exhibitions of their savagery proved many, even in the momentary viewing. They beat and tore the others creatures. They stomped them beneath clawed feet. And from all of their adversaries, they took a taste.

Samuel rushed away from the banister, yanking Ruby along as he made his way to the door. So horrible had been the vision, he instantly wiped it from his mind, which proved to be a transient comfort at best, because he forced himself to turn back to see what his mind wanted him to never see again.

In the room below, the coils within the glass tube faded. Two more plates clicked into place, sounding like pistol reports in the vast chamber. And in the dying light, Samuel saw the writhing bodies of the unholy menagerie scrabbling for their places along the floor and the walls.

He ran back into the rain, following his eager hound, without opening his umbrella. Cold water drenched him and brought a little of his sense back, and he stopped in the muddy road, though Ruby struggled with the tether, attempting to drag him away from the perverse scene behind them. Hubert Dodd had risen in his thoughts to cancel his retreat.

No, they were not friends. Perhaps civil acquaintances, but certainly not friends. Surely the device and the monstrous creatures that guarded it were in some manner of Dodd's manufacture, but if this were the case, Hubert Dodd would certainly be the most brilliant man alive. And hadn't the terrible woman told Samuel that Dodd had arranged for them to meet through his discovery of Ruby? Something about a joke? A story?

Drenched to the bone, Samuel turned, taking great care to pull Ruby to his side so as not to add to the dog's ill ease. He took a step toward Hubert Dodd's home. Ruby complained, digging her paws into the mud and barking a frightened tune.

"Of course, you're right," he told her. "It's a foolish thing to do, but think of what we might learn should Dodd be alive to tell us it?"

~φ~

Indeed Hubert Dodd was alive, but just barely. They found him in the front parlor of his home, lying amid a clutter of discarded papers and strewn books, and Samuel believed the man had been attacked by the foul-mouthed servant girl with whom he'd bargained for Ruby's ownership. Dodd sprawled naked as a jay. His once hearty face now appeared gaunt and his intimidating bulk seemed deflated, with sallow skin creped at his joints and creased below the navel. On closer inspection however, Samuel found no cuts from a guttersnipe's blade, nor any indication Dodd had been accosted about the head. Rather, he seemed to be under the influence of a powerful opiate. The man moaned solemnly, then burst forth with a startling round of giggles.

The condition of the man and his surroundings appalled Samuel. Bodily waste had settled into the carpet and clotted on Dodd's skin in long stinking scabs. Further whatever intoxicant the man had consumed seemed to be acting as aphrodisiac as the sickly gentleman's penis remained in a state of erection.

Still not convinced that the servant girl was free of liability, Samuel considered the very real possibility that Dodd had been poisoned, perhaps with some exotic toxin he'd procured on one of his great adventures. Or Dodd may have been feverish from an illness given him by one of the strange specimens he kept in the adjacent building. Thoughts of disease caused Samuel to pause and wonder on his own well-being. Still, if he were going to be infected it would have already happened, and he couldn't leave Dodd to thrash and die in his own filth.

Only upon closer inspection of the man did Samuel believe he found the cause of Dodd's hysteria. Inside the man's thigh, very near his scrotal sack, a pale wormlike creature, long and thin like the lace of a boot, clutched the wrinkled skin. Samuel instantly thought of leeches. He had seen a jar of the black, slime-coated creatures at his physician's office, and though this parasite bore little resemblance to those horrible slugs, he imagined it was of the same genus. Without hesitation he reached down and tugged at the worm, which was dry and scaly, and not slick with vile excretion as he'd imagined, and while the central thread of it easily peeled away from the skin, it held firm on either end.

"Leave it be," Dodd bellowed.

But Samuel ignored the delusional command and grabbed firmly to the worm and yanked with all of his force, separating the worm from Dodd's thigh and discarding the dreadful thing to the carpet where he ground it into the filth and fibre with the heel of his boot.

Dodd appeared infuriated for a moment, then he closed his eyes and sank unconscious.

~φ~

With no chance of carrying Dodd up to his rooms – even withered, the man bore a tremendous heft well beyond Samuel's physical abilities – he located a large library on the first floor with a broad leather sofa and dragged the unconscious man along the hall atop a carpet. He hoisted Dodd onto the sofa and then set about matters of practicality. Certainly he would need to call a physician, but no servants remained to send about this task, and Samuel feared leaving the stricken man alone. He stoked the hearth in the library and did the same with the stove in the kitchen, on which he placed an ample stockpot that he set about filling with water from a ceramic pitcher. Ruby followed at his heels from library to kitchen and then up the stairs where Samuel came upon a guest suite. He removed pillows and blankets from the mattress and carried them back to the library. They remained piled on the floor while Samuel used warm water to clean Dodd's reeking skin. Then he wrapped the man in blankets and pushed a pillow beneath his broad head.

He thought to leave then. In part, his concern was for Dodd, thinking to hurry back into the storm to fetch a physician who might competently treat the man; but he also felt a profound disquiet as he considered the creatures occupying the building next door. Surely, he'd seen some of them scrabbling about the walls. Even if the door were locked as the servant girl had suggested, some might climb from the room and spill over the banister. He thought about the cat-like species he'd encountered in the alley, and his resolve to leave this place heightened. Upon making the decision to depart, the sickly man stirred and came awake. Confusion and exhaustion worked on Dodd's face. He looked like a drunk who'd woken to find himself in strange rooms.

"Samuel," he muttered, using the familiar name as if they were dear old friends. The name caught in his throat though, and he coughed violently.

"What have you done to yourself?" Samuel asked.

"The parasite?" Dodd asked, suddenly concerned. A great scramble beneath the blankets indicated he sought the thing out on his thigh.

"I've done away with it."

"Good man," Dodd said. "I was unable to do it myself. Its gifts were beyond my refusal."

"Gifts?" Samuel asked, confounded.

"Some manner of opiate," Dodd said before another racking flurry of coughs convulsed him. When the fit passed he continued, "Even when I first discovered it latched to me, I knew it was trading the blood it drew with an euphoric substance. I thought to document the effects of the creature before removing it, a clear indication that the opiate worked with an initial subtlety on my reason, and as the hours passed, I drew deeper into its thrall, until I was its prisoner."

"Where did you find such an odious specimen?" Samuel wanted to know.

"Dear Samuel," Dodd whispered as if to a dense child, "I did not find it. It found me."

"Because of that contraption?"

"You've seen it?" Dodd asked, seeming pleased with the information. "I dare say, it's a wonder."

"But what is it?"

"The contrivance is an accumulation of knowledge," Dodd said. "*Some* of that knowledge emerged from my own tinkering and experimentation, and some of it I quite simply stole, at the time not being aware of the comprehensive design. That came when I discovered the particular property of lightning."

"And what property is that?" Samuel asked.

"Do you remember regaling the men at the club with your theories about raindrop worlds? How you believed that each drop contained the possibility of realms and what might happen when those varied worlds puddled together?"

"Yes, but…"

"You were not incorrect, at least not in the broadest sense. That was one of the reasons I thought to bring you to me. Many worlds run adjacent to our own. They bump and caress and gather. Like the raindrops, these other realms are innumerable, shifting and fluid all part of the collecting puddle you imagined, but they are segregated by sheer membranes, which is to say the drops heap without dilution. But the lightning… the lightning creates a momentary tear between realms. It is a double-edged sword that slices the veils, and my device holds those lips of fabric open, making it possible to cross realms as easily as stepping over a threshold into a new and astounding room."

"You've made these journeys?" Samuel asked, dumbfounded.

Dodd snuffled a laugh and leaned his head back, letting it sink into the pillow. "I am not that brave," he said. "Were it not for the specimen you so kindly removed from my leg and that odd bird-thing I keep in the laboratory cage, I wouldn't have even known of the experiment's success, but it is apparent that if these creatures can slink into our world, then we could just as easily cross into theirs."

"And what of the others?"

"What others?" Dodd asked.

"The other specimens in the laboratory. It brims with them."

Dodd smirked as if having been made the butt of a joke, but then his eyes cleared and he pushed himself upward. "What day is this?"

"Day?"

"What is the date?"

"It is the Sixteenth of November."

Dodd's face slackened as if the muscles there could no longer sustain the weight of his skin. "November?" he asked.

"Yes."

"For the love of God, I've been in thrall for a fortnight? Maureen must have cared for me until she lost all hope for my recovery."

Samuel thought about the coarse Irish woman and couldn't imagine her caring for anyone, let alone the man she'd described in such callous terms, but perhaps she'd endured so much in the last two weeks that her harsher instincts had surfaced. Still, if her master had been so ill, why had she not summoned a physician for his care?

"What of the weather?" Dodd asked, attempting to drag himself from the bed.

"Is that really relevant?" Samuel replied.

"Has it stormed frequently?" Dodd demanded.

And then Samuel took his meaning. If Dodd's contrivance operated on lightning, nothing could be more important than the weather. The news on that front was quite bad. "Storm most days."

"And lightning?" Dodd asked.

"And lightning," Samuel confirmed.

"God help us. My contrivance lacks only the convenience of predictability. The rifts in fabric shift away from its hold and mend themselves, which is to say that the device may hold back the curtain for a moment or an hour or a day at a time, but cannot do so indefinitely. Had the weather been calm, my worries would be few, but with each fresh bolt that strikes my conductor a new tear occurs."

Dodd struggled to his feet, but his legs were not sufficiently recuperated for the task of sustaining his weight and the bearish man collapsed on the floor amid a great *Whush!* of air. Samuel and Ruby rushed to the fallen man. The dog hoped to soothe the tumble with licks to the man's face, while Samuel took the more practical approach of grabbing him under the arms and assisting Dodd back onto the sofa.

"What can we do?" Samuel asked.

"The device's controls are in the laboratory. If you could get there it is simply a matter of withdrawing the coupling rod from the lightning rod on the roof, or disengaging the coils from the base. Either would take no more than moments, but if the laboratory is as infested as you claim…"

Samuel considered wading into the writhing mass of exotic monstrosities and knew his courage fell well short of the task. The very notion of approaching that building raised gooseflesh on his neck.

"It must be burned," Dodd said. "There's no alternative."

The pronouncement startled Samuel. Much of Dodd's life and a considerable portion of his estate must have gone into the creation of the contrivance, and the sheer miracle of its existence contended a casual approach to its destruction. What might be discovered should the wonder of the device be controlled and utilized in the pursuit of knowledge? What existed beyond these folds? Surely they all didn't contain unsavory beasts. It seemed wrong to do away with such opportunity, and yet, Samuel knew such a dangerous machine could not continue to function unchecked.

A roar of thunder shook the house and Samuel looked to Ruby, who cowered at the edge of the sofa. Then he looked at the weak and sickly man.

"It must be burned," Dodd told him earnestly. "You'll find tins of kerosene in the cellar."

~φ~

But simply setting fire to Dodd's laboratory proved no easy

task. There was the possibility of the fire spreading to the house or to other homes on the block. Considering Dodd's incapacitation, the man would never be able to flee in time, so his evacuation of the property would have to precede Samuel's arson. A carriage had to be summoned, and the debilitated man packed into it. And so he was. Though Dodd continued to refuse the attentions of a physician, Samuel told the carriage driver to help Mr. Dodd into his house on Walnut Street and once having done so, fetch Doctor Meriwether with due haste.

He placed Ruby in the carriage next to a blanket-wrapped Dodd. She whimpered and tried on more than one occasion to leap from the coach, but Samuel was forceful, and though the dog never settled, she ceased her attempts at flight.

"As for you, young miss," Samuel said to his pet, "you keep an eye on our guest until I return. You're the lady of the house, and it's your duty to make visitors feel welcome."

She whined and leaned out to lick his face, tongue swiping and darting with affection. He chuckled, tickled by the wet tongue, and gave her a good scratch behind the ear before closing the carriage door and rapping the back, sending it on its way.

Then Samuel returned to the house. The first order of business was to locate Dodd's stock of kerosene.

He followed the man's directions, found the door to the basement, and after a deep breath, again reminding himself that the wonderful device could not survive, he pulled open the door and was immediately accosted with a stench not unlike sulfur. The foulness of odor clotted in his throat and Samuel removed a handkerchief from his pocket to cover his nose and mouth. With a lantern firmly clutched in the other hand he began down the stairs.

The atmosphere here was cold and damp and worked quickly through the wool and cotton of his garb to latch onto his bones. The meager light of the lantern only revealed four steps at a time, while the rest of the chamber swirled, shadows upon shadows.

A clicking sound deep within the basement startled him. Too fast to be a clock mechanism and too sharp to be dripping water, Samuel felt tremendous unease as he attempted to identify the sound. A number of possibilities occurred to him: a draft sending a bit of wood against a beam or window jamb; a rat gnawing its way into a wooden storage crate; but again he felt the noise was too rapid, too precise to fit into any scenario of which he could conceive. Another sound, like the throaty belch of a toad rose from beneath the stairs.

Samuel froze in place, waiting for the noise to come again, but only the tick-ticking in the corner sounded. Could some of the creatures from Dodd's laboratory have slipped into the house? Made their way to his basement? It struck Samuel as wholly unlikely, as the door above had been secured upon his entry, so he continued his descent until he stood on the hard packed dirt of Dodd's basement. The smell here was dreadful, working through the cloth of his kerchief like maggots digging in flesh.

Dodd had told him the canisters were lined against the wall directly ahead of the staircase. Samuel walked forward and lifted the lantern high. A wall of crates, tattooed with stencils rose to the left, but the light could not reach deeply enough into the room to reveal the casks he sought.

Another great belching filled the chamber. Samuel turned to it, and something skittered across the floor just ahead of his light. His heart leapt into his throat and panic cascaded down his spine like water from a melting glacier. The clicking multiplied until it sounded as if the entire basement were chock-a-block with racing metronomes. Motion displaced the air at his back, and Samuel spun around, swinging the lantern like a club, but it passed through the air harmlessly.

Upon completing this pirouette, Samuel found himself facing a hole in the wall of Dodd's basement. Its diameter spanned a good meter, more than enough room for a small man to have squirmed through, certainly large enough to accommodate any of a number of creatures. The dawning realization brought a fresh stream of icy tingles to his back.

Some faction of the hellish bestiary had managed to escape. A burrowing species had taken the initiative, and now shared the same dismal void in which Samuel found himself. The panic became too much for him to bear. The lantern clacked in his trembling hand. He begged his feet to move, wanting nothing more than to vanish from the hideous gloom and to reappear on the street or even in front of the mantle at his home, and though his mind screamed for his legs to take action, they resoundingly denied his pleas.

Only when the air again felt displaced very near his left ear did Samuel manage to turn away from the gap in the wall of Dodd's cellar. Samuel whipped around in a reflexive jerk. The lantern flew from his fingers, sailing into the darkness like a comet. It glanced off the side of a rapidly fleeing specimen, which was clearly of the same clan as the savage stick-men he'd viewed in the laboratory. Amid a crash of brass and the cracking of glass, a window of flame opened on the far wall, and in this sudden illumination Samuel noticed two things simultaneously: his lantern had made impact above a row of cans he recognized as kerosene containers; the other revelation came in the form of dozens of tiny specs hanging like fireflies about the back wall and ceiling. Moist eyes from innumerable heads reflected the spreading flames, and faces bathed in the orange light cast by the conflagration pushed tightly together like blossoms in an unholy garden.

A scream escaped his lips, and Samuel fled for the stairs. An unknowable appendage reached through the gap between the steps in an attempt to trip him up, but Samuel sprang past the terrible limb with a yelp of terror and continued to scrabble toward the dull light above.

He attained the landing and the room beyond and slammed the door. He searched for a lock but finding none, he backed away and quickly surveyed his immediate surrounding for something with which to secure the panel. Finding nothing, he chose flight, but instead of racing through the house, he made his way to the kitchen and the door to the alley, which remained open.

Another of the cat-like creatures had joined the first in the dim corridor. They groomed one another, only pausing long enough to eye Samuel curiously before setting their foul tongues back to task.

He thought to flee this block entirely, to run and keep running until he was again secure in his own rooms where the unspeakable creations of some alien god did not prowl with malicious intent. But his rational mind – sorely tested to be sure

– screamed at him to finish the task, to destroy Dodd's device and bring an end to this grotesque invasion. All he need do was cripple the contrivance so that it could no longer brace open the panels of veil separating his world from the others. A single lantern, well-thrown, could fulfill his duty. Perhaps the bulk of the mechanism would go unharmed but it could be disassembled at some future time, just so long as Samuel sabotaged it sufficiently to make it ineffective.

Lightning flashed directly above his head, thunder immediately accompanying the bath of light. He heard its crackle and pop. A brilliant glow of light rose from behind the banister beyond the door, and he knew that Dodd's contraption was again in use.

A small body with skittering claws struck his leg, and Samuel recoiled to the jamb of the laboratory door. He searched for the source of the attack and was shocked to find it came from a familiar face.

Ruby, his fine pet, raced in for another pounce, her tail whipping the air and her eyes glittering with happiness, unaware of the horrible spectacle surrounding her. She must have escaped the carriage and sprinted back to him – her unconditional affection drawing her like moth to killing flame.

"Beautiful dog," Samuel said. "Foolish beast."

Scooping her into his arms, he hurried onto the walkway above Dodd's laboratory. He followed it to the place where he'd spoken with the awful Maureen and continued to the stairs where he found the lantern she'd left behind. Balancing Ruby, Samuel lifted the lamp free of its hook, and dashed back to the walkway near the door.

Dodd's contrivance continued to fill the space below with light. The floor positively swarmed with unclean creatures, fleeing from and feeding on one another with abandon. A soft dove-gray animal appeared near the glass column, encasing the glowing coils. Much like a deer but very short and very plump, the animal gazed on in paralytic horror until a creature like a massive limbless scorpion dropped onto its back and buried its stinger in the unfortunate animal's haunches. Then both predator and prey fell beneath the swatting claws of one of the porridge colored stick-men.

Great washes of blood sprayed from the monster's claws, dappling the glass column and misting the surrounding beasts. The stick-man cast aside the stinging creature and fell on the soft body of the plump deer. Its teeth tore away at the pink belly, releasing a cascade of glistening organs and a wash of dark fluids that spread across the floor.

Ruby wriggled and whimpered in his arms, and Samuel attempted comforting words but what might be said to alleviate the terror of the abattoir below?

He considered where to attack the device, and felt certain the glass and gears would prove impervious to the minor threat of his lantern. Instead, he decided his greatest luck would come if he could set alight the wooden platform with its numerous locking plates. If the oil sufficiently set blaze to the structure it would cease function.

With no further thought on the matter, Samuel launched the lantern and waited, breath held, until it cracked open upon the upper deck of the device. Flames dripped down like brilliant wax, showering the menagerie below and causing a chorus of fearful screeches and chirps.

"Have that," he said triumphantly, observing the slowly spreading sheet of fire atop the platform. Pride welled in him as he heard wood pop with the burning, knowing it signified the likelihood that once the fire had fed in earnest the planks would collapse and with fortune, completely destroy the mechanisms below.

Confident in his success, Samuel nuzzled Ruby's neck and turned from the laboratory to face the alley…

And the abominations that looked back at him.

Two of the stick-men stood beyond the door, rain pasting their crimson hair to the gleaming skin of their brows. This was Samuel's first unobstructed view of the things' faces, and he wished to have never seen it. Eyes like shattered emeralds, faceted with ridges and fissures, glared hungrily at him, and beneath these horrible ocular configurations three narrow slits rippled like the gills of a fish. But the mouths were worst of all. The stick-man on the left yanked something forcefully from its jaws and tossed the hindquarter of one of the odd cat-like animals to the mud. Then its face opened. Oh that terrible gaping chasm, with hundreds of pin sharp teeth lining the roof and jaw, bits of prey still snagged on the barbs.

Behind Samuel, the laboratory glowed ominously with flame and the device's still-radiant coils. Something about the light had changed, but he daren't look back to observe the anomaly. The stick-men came forward cautiously, assessing the strength of their quarry.

A great explosion sounded in Dodd's house. The fire had made its way into the kerosene stock to create a firebomb that blew through the flooring and sent shards of glass flying across the alley amid enormous gouts of flame. Samuel thought he and Ruby's luck had shifted for the better, as the tumult distracted the stick-men, bent them low to cower from the tremendous force behind them. For a moment, as the hot wash of air blew over his face, he even allowed himself to hope the blast would send fragments of ruins at his assailants like shot from a rifle, cutting them down in the mud, but the hope lasted only a moment. Though distracted, the stick-men had not fled from the conflagration; it had simply pushed them over the threshold, blocking any chance for Samuel's escape.

Refusing to serve as repast for these terrible creatures, and horrified that Ruby might meet the same fate, Samuel clutched his dog tightly and backed to the railing. The stick-men recovered and righted themselves at the doorway, and Ruby greeted them with a fierce growl, but Samuel knew she would prove no match for the barbaric and perverse species.

Instead, he closed his eyes, holding the dog so tightly to his chest it made her whine painfully, and Samuel launched them backward over the railing. It was better to break apart on the floor below than to suffer the bloody intentions of the stick-men. Ruby would forgive him this cowardly end.

As they dropped, Ruby turned in his arms, scraping his cheeks and waistcoat with her paws. She yelped in terror and the sound cut clean to Samuel's heart, but this was better for them. Better than teeth. Better than claws. Better than…

~φ~

Grass bends in the wind along a great plain, pointing at a hillock upon which leafless trees stand as straight as columns, jutting toward the gathering clouds. Amid the trunks is a small shack with refined lines and a tower of stones through which smoke pours, like a daughter of the accumulation above, racing skyward to rejoin her parents. As the storm rolls in, announced by the first rumbles of thunder, a panel opens at the front of the shack and two creatures – no longer strangers to this place – emerge onto the hilltop. One of these odd beasts walks on two legs and the other on four.

Their names are Samuel and Ruby, and today as with all inclement days, they run down the hillside and into the field. They dash through the countryside, calling out to one another excitedly as if playing a game. Both seem to enjoy the rain and the wind, and when the sky splits with jagged light, they race toward the bolt, chasing the lightning as if they could catch it and keep it as a precious souvenir.

~φ~

Before You Go

You never listened to me.

I warned you about the cigarettes, begged you to stop a hundred times. You insisted it didn't matter – just like the steaks and the cakes and the flood of whiskey served neat in your favorite glass. You said these things made life worth living, these simple pleasures.

You were cold when I woke this morning. With your back to me, I saw the thread-thin scars on your neck, just below your freshly trimmed hair; I saw them every morning before I rose to make your breakfast, and I found them comforting. They were so particular to you. Today, I trace them lightly with my fingernails, knowing my touch won't tickle or disturb.

While sliding out of bed, the odor of you follows me. Judgment wouldn't accept you full of waste and water, so you expelled it on our sheets. I know you'd be embarrassed to have anyone find you soiled, so I pull on my robe and walk to the bathroom. I clean you like a child, roll you so I can collect the sheets and then ease you onto your back.

Even now, so many years from youth, you are beautiful to me. Strong.

Your death confused you; I see that. It's carved on your face. You must have woken knowing what was happening because you stare at the ceiling in wonderment. And I'm staring at you, your white hair, your brown skin, the soft wisps of down covering your chest. The hairs smooth under my palm as I comb them in neat waves, arcing their pattern over your nipples.

I notice that your nose hair has grown too long, so I search the nightstand drawer for the manicure kit. I find the leather pouch and the tiny gleaming scissors within. With them, I cut the stray hairs. They collect above your lip and seem to float in the black field of your nostril. Gently, I blow them away and a hollow tone sounds in your nose. I smile.

Your ears need trimming, too. I snip them, careful not to cut you especially when I trim the awkward bulb. A damp towel collects the threads, and finally, I close your eyes so that the lashes weave in two neat lines.

Peaceful now? Are you?

I run my hand over your belly, and the skin is rigid but oddly comforting in its chill. Your sex does not respond to my touch, so I hold it. After so many years between us, I'm surprised to find that it has never felt quite this way before. I try to explain this to you, try to make you understand that I've felt you hard and soft and at every stage between, but never have you felt like this.

You move.

Startled, I release you and step away. Your shoulder raises and then falls; the other does the same. I expect your eyes to flash open but they do not. I expect you to speak or grunt your continued participation in life, but you make no sound.

Again you try to move, but rigid arms and legs are useless so you roll back and forth on the mattress. Your struggle is that of a man trapped in cloth, wrapped in bandages.

Bound.

And I remember the scars on your neck; the scars I put there.

You were in Miami with one of your women. Not your first infidelity; not your last. But this was somehow different. You made so little effort to hide it that I felt you wanted me to know; you wanted me to admire the weapon you drove through my chest. So, I walked alone, wandering through the streets looking for something, escaping the beautiful cage you'd bought and told me to furnish, to paint, to clean.

My legs carried me in random directions – first south and then east and then back to the north. Anger was my engine; sorrow the navigator. I stopped in a bar on the other side of the city, a dark place that held the kind of wisdom we considered beneath us. The elegant crone in the tattered mink coat waited for me, or so I believed. She knew me and my need. Her lips parted in a terrible smile of black gums and violet tongue, more like the slit belly of a rat than the mouth of a woman. Speaking with a twinkling whisper, she pushed a small book toward me across the damp, pocked tabletop.

She called it *The Book of Wives*, and in its pages, I found the design that would bind your soul. I traced the arcs and the cross-hatched lines to memorize the pattern while you were at your office or your club or out entertaining clients and mistresses. Two months later I was drawn to the park, book in hand. A sobbing girl, barely out of her teens, sat on a bench, face in hands. Without a word, I placed the book on the bench beside her, walked away and returned to my opulent cage, where I began the work of wives.

Late at night, when you were exhausted from your infidelity or simply too drunk to wake, I drew on you. A scratch here, a gouge there. I worried the lines, made them bleed but slowly and over the course of many years. You never once noticed, or if you did, you never said.

Late in life, I let the fancy go, another souvenir of aspiration to be stored in a crate and never opened. My emotions healed, numbed and callused. I barely felt you any longer. So, I left the design incomplete.

You always said that I never finished anything.

Your body bucks on the mattress and the bed collides with the nightstand. The shiny chrome scissors rock on the edge and then fall to the carpet. Frantically, you try to sit up, but your muscles are petrified.

I know your struggle will loosen them and break death from sinew.

And you frighten me. Your unnaturalness makes me tremble and cry out.

I crouch low and come to your side. Reaching down with fingers made clumsy by haste and fearful palsy, I slap at the scissors on the carpet. Their tip jabs my finger and makes me bleed. The bed groans under your weight, and I grip the silver handle. On my feet, I shove with every ounce of me to get you turned over but age and gender have weakened me. When you were still, turning you was a simple task, but your struggles defy my strength. I'm nothing but an old woman now. Three times I try, and each time you convulse and land on your back.

On the fourth attempt you roll onto your stomach, face deep in my pillow, and you writhe like a landed fish, your arms and legs still immobile, but the rest of you frantic. My mind struggles to remember the final lines of the symbol from the book's page, and I drive the scissors into your neck, just below your neatly trimmed hair. I drag the point toward your shoulder then back up in a jagged check.

Your body lies quietly on the bed. There is no blood to stain the pillowcase.

With the scissors back on the nightstand, I roll you onto your back. Your hair is disheveled; it sticks out in wisps like torn cotton gauze. In the bathroom, I grab a brush. I fix your pillow, adjust your head at its center and brush your hair down so that it's smooth and you are handsome again.

Somewhere behind your eyes, you know I'm doing this. You feel the soothing stroke of the brush and appreciate the care and love of my efforts.

Conscious inside your failed body, you can feel every touch to your skin and hear every word I say. That was the promise of *The Book of Wives*, and now, the design is done, and you are bound. Your soul fills the skin of you, the meat of you, and the bones of you. Silently, without help or hope, you fight, but to me and all of the world, you look peaceful and beautiful.

I couldn't bear to watch you suffer.

Perhaps you're afraid now. I'll stroke your brow and calm you a bit.

But when they take you away...

They will take the blood out of you with a cold metal wand. They will shove it into your body, and you will lie there and accept it because that is what is expected of you, because you are capable of nothing else. They will do an autopsy because it is my right to demand one. Your sternum will be cut and split and their hands will tear into you, fondling your organs indelicately before shoving them aside. And when they bury you in the ground and the worms get through the box, and the beetles get in, you will feel them nesting and feeding, taking little bits of you with their mouths. In the end, having served and submitted, you will rot.

And you will feel every moment of it until the meat of you has fallen away and dissolved completely.

I run the brush over your chest to neaten the fan of hair. Licking my thumb, I smooth down your eyebrows before I kiss your lips this last time.

Now, you're presentable, and I can call the ambulance.

But I have some things to say first, and you will listen; you will hear me, and you won't interrupt. I have a lot to tell you before you go.

~φ~

Gary McMahon

Gary McMahon's fiction has appeared in magazines and anthologies in the U.K. and U.S and has been reprinted in both *The Mammoth Book of Best New Horror* and *The Year's Best Fantasy & Horror.*

He is the British-Fantasy-Award-nominated author of *Rough Cut, All Your Gods Are Dead, Dirty Prayers, How to Make Monsters, Rain Dogs, Different Skins, Pieces of Midnight, The Harm, Hungry Hearts,* and has edited an anthology of original novelettes titled *We Fade to Grey.*

Current and forthcoming are several reprints in "Best of" anthologies, a story in the mass market anthology *The End of the Line,* the novels *Pretty Little Dead Things* and *Dead Bad Things* from Angry Robot/Osprey and *The Concrete Grove* trilogy from Solaris.

Website: www.garymcmahon.com

Creep

You receive the first call when you are sixteen years old.

It is Saturday night; you are in the house alone. Your parents are out at some golf club dinner and your friends are spending time with their boyfriends. You don't have a boyfriend. You are small and dumpy and don't know how to make yourself stand out in a crowd. You aren't unattractive – you are bright enough to realise this fact – but you simply do not "pop" when so many of your friends do. The clothes you wear are all wrong. The words you use never sound as cool as everyone else's. Nothing you do seems to put you in a good light.

You are sitting in front of the television, a glass of coke and a half-eaten sandwich on the coffee table. Freddie the cat is sitting at your side, eyeing the popcorn in the bowl balanced precariously between your bare knees. You are stroking the cat's head, barely even watching the programme – some crappy game show – and wondering if the rest of your life will be made up of similar lonely Saturday nights, similar crappy TV shows, and similar scruffy cats.

When the phone rings you glance across the room, blinking your tired eyes. Pushing a slowly advancing Freddie away from the popcorn bowl, you rise slowly to your feet. The front of your dressing gown is gaping, exposing your oversized Zombie T-Shirt. Black cotton. Green face. Grasping hands. Red blood.

You cross the room and pick up the receiver. "Hello."

At first there is no voice on the line, just the weird rushing sound of empty air. Then, gradually, a faint, murmuring voice fills the space and creeps into your ear.

"Sorry, I can't hear you. This is a bad line."

The low voice keeps mumbling. You can't make out any words.

"Hello? I can't hear what you're saying. You'll have to speak up."

Then, as if someone has flicked a switch to stop the whisper of static and reveal the words hiding beneath, you begin to understand what the voice is saying. It is male; a man's voice. The voice is low and husky, with little trace of a recognisable accent.

"I know what you want."

Then whoever is on the other end of the line hangs up the phone to end the call.

You have seen all the films – those silly American chillers where the babysitter is stalked though the house by a crazed killer. It always starts with a spooky phone call; it always ends with the babysitter being stabbed or beaten or strangled to death.

You run out of the room and check the front door.

Locked.

You go into the kitchen and tug on the latch.

Secure.

Then you climb the stairs, turning on all the lights and making sure the windows are shut tight and the curtains are closed.

You are safe inside. There is no way in. Whatever is outside should stay there.

Feeling slightly more at ease yet still afraid, you go back downstairs and turn down the volume on the television. The game show is over. The popcorn no longer appeals. Freddie the cat eyes you with suspicion from the floor. You wait up until your parents arrive home, tired and drunk and acting just a little bit silly, like they always do after a boozy night out. Then, when everyone else retires to bed and the house is filled with darkness, you hear that voice from the phone call inside your head, repeating those words. For reasons that you cannot understand, you want the mystery caller to phone again. That moment – filled with an exquisite terror – made you feel alive in a way that nothing else ever has.

You stare at the phone but it does not ring.

Your fear recedes to a manageable level; the energy it leaves behind is almost pleasant. Now you are intrigued. How could anyone possibly know what you want when you have no clue yourself? You realise that you want *something* (because surely everyone does) and you know without a doubt that your life is so much emptier than those of the people around you – but you have no idea what that something might be, or where you are supposed to find it.

The thought that someone else might possess this information, especially a person – a man – you don't even know, fills you with a sense of dread that is almost erotic in its intensity. You have always lived with the certainty that sooner or later something would happen to you – an event over which you would have no control, possibly some kind of disaster. For years you pushed the thought right to the back of your head, where it couldn't hurt you. But now that thought is out in the open, and it has been given a voice.

~φ~

The next time you are twenty-one.

The partitioned Victorian house you share with your University friends is large, spacious: you have an attic room to yourself. It is a Monday evening, late autumn. The streets outside are littered with crisp brown leaves. The sky is dark, a vast charcoal sketch that seems to strain at the edges, as if it is about to rip open and reveal whatever lies beyond.

You are working on your essay – something about a feminist reading of 19th Century literature – and wishing that you could call it a day and open that bottle of wine in the fridge, the one your parents left behind the last time they came for a visit. They always try to buy you off with expensive gifts. It's the only way they know to show their love.

You chew the end of your ballpoint pen. Your eyes are closed as you listen to an old Hank Williams song on the radio. Bored now, distracted and looking for an excuse to forget about the essay, you maximise the browser window on your laptop screen and check your emails. The result makes you feel even lonelier than before. There is a single new message in your inbox. The address line is blank. The message line contains a series of dots: ....

Spam email: the curse of the internet age. Your cursor hovers over the little digital envelope, and then you double-click the left button on the mouse, opening the message. It contains five words. You know what they are before you even see them – a trigger has been pulled inside your head. Feeling nothing, thinking nothing, you read the words on the screen.

I know what you want.

You had almost forgotten the first time – almost but not quite. It comes to you in dreams, a trace memory; a vague echo of something you might only ever have imagined, or secretly hoped for.

But you did not imagine the long ago phone call. That voice was real. Here is the proof. Not that any proof were needed, because deep down inside, locked within the folds of your heart, there is a special emotion that fits neatly around this moment, completing it.

You turn around, glancing at the door. It is closed, just as you left it. There is no one else in the room, yet you feel watched. You sense eyes upon you; a hidden observer is eating you up with his gaze. You close down the browser and leave the room, needing the company of your housemates.

The stairwell is much darker than usual. The walls were never that close before. Your world is growing smaller, the minutes and seconds clenching around you like a fist.

"Sally," you say as you enter the living room. A single lamp sheds meagre light. A figure stirs in the gloom.

The girl – slim, tall, with a black spider tattoo on the right side of her throat – looks up at you, smiling around a beer can. "Hey, you finished?" She pulls out her earphones, turns off her iPod, and adjusts her position on the sofa, propping herself up against the worn, faded cushions.

You shake your head. "Nah. Couldn't settle. Something… something weird happened."

Sally sits up, her long, bare legs sliding across the battered leather seat. "Weird? I like weird." Her wide eyes urge you to continue.

"Years ago, when I was sixteen, I got this phone call. It was a man."

"Oh, yeah?" Sally giggles.

"No, not like that. A man's voice on the line. Soft, toneless. He said that he knew what I wanted and then he hung up." You realise that the tale sounds trite in the telling. What was frightening once now seems slightly absurd, a child's bad dream.

"That *is* weird." Sally smiles encouragement.

"It's happened again. I got an email a few minutes ago. He still knows what I want."

The room grows cold. Sally's humour vanishes and her face goes ashen. "Fuck. That's creepy." She gulps from her can, and then licks her lips. "Like, really creepy." Her eyes are glazed; she is at least half drunk. "Have you ever told anyone else?"

You lower your gaze, feeling guilty for reasons you are unable to express. "No. It only happened that once – twice now, I guess. And there's nothing to tell, not really. A voice on the phone. An email. A feeling that something bad is going to happen. That's all.

You could say so much more, but you are afraid that it might jinx you, drawing out the shape of your fears until a grinning figure is formed on the upstairs landing, the downstairs bathroom, or in the cramped hallway cupboard. The twitching movement at the corner of your eye is simply the shadows near the door, but you don't want to look too closely in case you see something else crouching there, waiting to stand and greet you as your scrutiny gives it substance, adding flesh to its bones.

"But still…it's creepy." Sally pulls a face, curling her bottom lip.

You nod, hug yourself against the chill. "Got any more of that lager?"

"It's in the fridge. Help yourself."

But you don't want to go out there, into the dark kitchen. Somehow this room feels like the only safe place in the house, and you are glad that you are not alone. You remember sitting up to wait for your parents that first time, and how relieved you were when they finally got home. You move closer to Sally on the sofa and stand by her side. She reaches up and takes your hand. You smile, but it freezes on your face.

"It's okay, honey," says Sally. "It's fine. I'm here."

But she isn't the only one in the house, because I'm there too. Peeking over your shoulder, or standing outside the door, with one foot resting against the skirting board and the palm of my hand pressed flat against the wall. I am not yet whole, but we have all the time in the world... one day I will be able to reach out and touch you.

Your unspoken desire summoned me, created me from dust and darkness, inviting me inside. The constant feeling you have that something bad will happen – that's me. I am the jinx, the genie from the bottle that should never have been opened. I am the cancer in the marrow of your bones, the toxins in your bloodstream. I know it all – I know what you want.

~φ~

The last time you are twenty-nine.

It is eight years later and that night in your student digs is just a memory, an echo of an episode that you've tried to forget. Nothing has happened since: no calls, no emails. Your life has developed a rhythm; the days fall into place, one after the other, slotting into the greater pattern of your existence.

Your life is normal in every way.

You have a good job with an insurance company and a fiancé who says he loves you but can't quite get you to believe it. Deep down inside you are still the lonely little girl with the cuter, more popular friends, and no amount of flowers and attention can lay that particular ghost to rest. Her image walks always alongside you, not allowing you leave her behind.

You are working late. It isn't quite dark yet, but neither is it light. The sky is flat and grey outside the office windows and the traffic moves sluggishly along the dismal streets. It has rained for a week now, and the downpour only let up a few hours ago.

You pick up the phone and dial your fiancés number, and then wait until his voice mail kicks in. It is too early for him to be home – he will be at the gym, flirting with fitter and prettier girls than you and arranging a night of drinks with the boys. The thought makes you feel like that dumpy teenager all over again; the one who never had any boyfriends and often stayed home with the cat on a Saturday night, wishing that someone would call.

Until somebody *did* call – and that somebody was me.

"Kev, it's me. I won't be back at the flat till late this evening, so if you want to call me make it after nine. I'm tired. I'm going to get a curry and go straight to bed. If I don't speak to you before, I'll see you tomorrow. Have a nice time." You make a move to replace the handset, and then raise it again to your ear. The mouthpiece hangs like an unspoken invitation before your lips; a wordless open mouth, perhaps waiting to be kissed. "Love you." It is an afterthought; you don't even believe it yourself, so why should he?

An hour or so later you are ready to leave. All the paperwork is beginning to look the same: page upon page of identical text, row after row of increasingly meaningless figures. You close the folder, shut down the machine, and put on your coat. The office lights flicker. You pause, shake your head, smile, and walk across the room to the door.

A shadow passes outside the door. You catch sight of it through the glass, and are afraid to go out into the hall. The cleaners have all gone home. It is dim out there, along the hall and on the short landing. Memories stir like snakes inside your head: a voice on the phone, a brief email you should never have opened. The same old words, spoken over and over again...

Gritting your teeth, you push open the door and step out onto the landing. Your pace is quicker than usual as you make your way to the stairs. You are too afraid to wait for the lift, and the realisation makes you feel embarrassed, even though there is no one else around to see you.

Nobody, that is, but me.

Your mobile phone buzzes just as you reach the ground floor. You pull the phone out of your handbag and fumble with the buttons. There is no caller ID: the message on the screen does not show a name. You try not to press the button, but it is too late. Your thumb jerks involuntarily, an instinctive reaction, and the message flashes before your eyes.

You are not surprised. You have been waiting for this. You have waited your entire life for this. You know exactly what's going to happen, like a movie you've seen countless times before.

The words on the tiny screen are like a a greeting from an old friend: *I know what you want.*

Even after all these years, you are filled with an emotional charge. In the past, you have spent sleepless nights and harrowing mornings trying to figure out what it is the mystery messenger knows. An answer to a question you dare not even ask yourself?

You type out a reply, quickly, before you can change your mind.

You don't even have to read it over before pressing Send: "What do I want?"

That one response is all I need; the final piece of the puzzle.

Traffic sounds outside the walls. A helicopter hovering overhead. Distant music, perhaps from a loud car stereo. They're playing our song.

I step out from the shadows at the bottom of the stairs, dragging my crippled left leg behind me. It is always a struggle to walk at first, to make those first few newborn steps in the real world. The transformation from fearful thought to feared flesh is not an easy one. Sometimes my legs bend the wrong way, my feet point backwards.

I try to smile but it is difficult with a face so deformed, so twisted and incomplete. You step back, alarmed, and I reach out to touch you. Disgust mars your features – it always does, though you are expecting this. Even with the ones who have asked for it, or have begged for me to appear. The truth, when they see it, is often too much to bear. But I didn't choose you; you chose me. You are the mother of my invention, the author of my fiction. I belong to you.

Your eyes are big, so very, very big, and my hands are small.

"No," you say, or try to say. But it is immaterial. You no longer have a choice. The only choice you ever had was long ago, and you made it.

I nod once. Up close, I can actually taste your fear.

You begin to scream, but by the time I reach you it will be too late for anyone to come. And then I will be gone, like always; I will blend back into the dusty shadows and wait for someone else to summon me, another willing victim. Someone who wants what I have.

Somebody who needs what I know.

Because I do, I really do know what you want.

And the reason I know this is because I know exactly what you do *not* want.

You do not want me.

You don't want this.

Not ever.

~φ~

A Night Unburdened

t was almost a week after Bonfire Night but still the air smelled of smoke. Jack closed the car window, wary of the stench infiltrating the vehicle, and watched late-flowering fireworks light up the sky over the council sink estates.

The radio was tuned to a local station. A traffic report interrupted the music: a husky female voice speaking about a bad accident on the A19, near Testo's roundabout. Several vehicles had been involved in a pile-up; three people were reported dead.

Jack reached out and pressed the button to switch the stereo to CD mode. The Arctic Monkeys filled the car with their chirpy brand of antagonism.

He pulled of the main road and into a new estate. The old houses had all been demolished by the borough council, and each of these replacement dwellings was built from the same kind of inexpensive red bricks, lending a slightly toy-like appearance to the rain-slicked rows of near-identical semi-detached properties.

He pulled up at the end of the drive, checked the address chitty that was taped to the pizza box on the seat next to him, and opened the door. The warning alarm chimed, but he left the headlights on. He would only be gone a few moments.

Carrying the cooling pizza, Jack jogged up the drive, past a tiny silver Nissan with a football pennant pasted on the rear window, and rang the doorbell. A lower corner of the living room curtain twitched, revealing a small pale face; seconds later a light went on in the hallway.

When the front door opened he recognised her immediately.

"A large thin-crust Pepperoni, extra cheese, for Crossly." He held out the grease-damp box. A single firework detonated overhead, momentarily flooding the area outside the door with sultry light.

"Thank you." She handed him a ten pound note, her long fingers brushing against his open hand. When he passed her the limp box a quizzical expression crossed her narrow face. Multi-coloured lights died in her eyes. "Don't I... Do I know you?"

She had not changed much. Her long blonde hair, flecked now with grey, was pulled back from her face, displaying fine, broad cheekbones, thin but naturally red lips and a flawless complexion.

"Yes. Yes, you do. Well sort of." He was stumbling over the words; even now, years later, she made him feel like a clumsy teenager.

"Yes. Your face. I know it... did you go to my school?"

"Yes, Mrs Crossly. My name's Jack Bentley. You took me for English."

She flashed a smile; Jack pretended it was flirtatious, enticing, when in reality it was simply the result of recognition. "Oh, yes. Jack. How are you?"

"I'm good, Mrs Crossly. I... well, this isn't my real job. I'm studying journalism at Uni, and do this in the evenings to pay my bills." Why did he feel the need to explain himself, to justify the dead-end night job?

She shook her head. Strands of hair came loose from the ponytail, tracing the line of her jaw. "No need to explain your choices to me, Jack. This is honest work – a lot more honest than some of the things far too many of my ex students get up to." She had taken an unconscious step backwards, away from the door. Her hand clutched the pizza box delicately, as if she were itching to put it down.

"I'll let you get on," he said.

"I was just about to invite you in. Unless you have another delivery to make?"

He stared at the front of the tight white T-shirt encasing her large breasts; at her thin waist and those long, slender legs whose image he'd masturbated over in his cramped single bedroom with the door wedged shut during so many lonely teenage nights. "You were my last one. My shift ended ten minutes ago."

He noticed that her feet were bare. She wore a decorative silver ring on the right big toe.

"Well? There's an open bottle of wine on the table, and I'm bored of drinking alone." She moved back, into the hallway, expecting him to follow.

Jack did just that, trailing her through into the kitchen like a little lost dog.

"I'll have this later. I prefer my pizza cold, anyway." Her smile was now playful; its edges twitched, perhaps a slight nervous tic. "Go on in." She cocked her head in the direction of a dimly lit lounge. "I'll close the door."

He watched her firm, trim jeans-clad backside as she stepped lightly to the front door, closed it, and turned off the hallway light. Her face hung in the darkness, an after-image of untouchable beauty, a trace memory he'd once lusted after with such desperate longing that it still shocked him to recall.

"I'll be with you in a second." She moved slowly to the stairs – gliding, really – and disappeared into the darkness at the top of the house.

Jack walked into the lounge, leaving the door to the kitchen ajar. The room was lit by a low lamp in one corner. Open on the sofa was a paperback book, the cover of which he could not identify. There was an illustration of a naked man with grubby feathered wings on the front of the book, but the title evaded him because the font was so faded.

On the walls were a handful of original landscapes. They looked like the work of a local artist, well below the level of what he would call professional: poorly sketched representations of faded skies, rotting jetties and a sombre, unoccupied rowing boat. No people were present in these pictures. They were all scenes and objects, and held a coldness he didn't much like.

He heard a toilet flushing upstairs, footsteps moving over his head.

The furniture in the room looked expensive. A large-screen TV formed the centrepiece, whatever DVD she'd been watching when he arrived was paused at a scene showing a close-up of a woman's sweaty screaming face. The lamp flickered. From somewhere outside came the disassociated hissing of a sparkler: the sound seemed to be drawing closer, was almost inside the room.

"I hope you like it red."

Jack spun around, his fists clenched.

"Whoa, child!" She was laughing, a long-stemmed wine glass held out before her. "I was talking about the wine." She passed so close by him that he felt her heat. One of her breasts brushed against his upper arm, and he was frozen to the spot by the sudden shock of contact.

"It's merlot. My favourite." She poured him a drink and sat down on the sofa, next to the open book. Her free hand fell across it, obscuring the cover: bloodless fingers splayed out like bleached spider legs.

"Thanks. That sounds lovely." Jack crossed the room and sat in the armchair beside the cabinet on which she'd placed the glass. He picked it up, raised it. "Cheers, Mrs Crossly."

"Please, you're not my student now. Call me Judy."

The wine was lukewarm, but tasted good. He closed his eyes and savoured it, feeling the alcohol hit him immediately.

Mrs Crossly – Judy – crossed one leg over the other. Her bare sole flashed white; there was a sticking plaster across the ball of her foot. "I hope my invitation didn't make you feel uncomfortable. I'm afraid this is my second bottle, and the sight of a familiar face made me act on impulse." Again, there was that coy little smile. "I'm not in the habit of inviting young men into my home."

"Don't worry about it. I was at a loose end, anyway. I have a report to work on, but I can't seem to muster the enthusiasm. "It's good to see you after all this time. I feel daft saying this, but you were always... my favourite teacher." He looked down at his glass, cheeks burning. Had he really just said that?

"You're sweet. As an educator, you always try to make an impression."

Glancing up, he smiled. Judy's face was frozen for a moment, as if caught in the act of something unnatural, but the smile slid quickly back into place. "So," she said. "Tell me what you've been up to since school. I seem to recall that you did well in your exams."

Voices passed by outside, becoming almost loud enough to hear their conversation, and then fading away just as he thought he might recognise a word or a phrase. "Well, I got into Newcastle Uni – which is what I wanted. I've just started the second year of a journalism degree. I always loved to write."

"Yes, I remember. Your fiction was always particularly striking. Vivid." She sipped her wine, not taking her eyes off him. "It's good to know all that natural talent hasn't gone to waste."

Flustered at the compliment, Jack glanced around the room. The wallpaper was a dusty cream colour, delicately patterned; a narrow wooden picture rail ran around the wall several inches below the white-painted ceiling.

That was when he noticed the photographs. There were quite a few of them, standing on the mantelpiece, the window sills, the occasional table. Each photograph was of a different person, and the one nearest to him – on the cabinet where she'd put his drink – showed the portrait of a stern young man dressed in army uniform.

He reached out and picked up the photograph. The young man's eyes were intense, as if he were staring at something he didn't like. "Is this your boyfriend?"

Judy laughed lightly, leaned back on the sofa. "No, but I'm flattered. That's my son." The joviality left her voice as she continued. "He died last year, in Afghanistan." Her face took on a strange expression, not of pain or regret, but of lazy contentment.

"Oh." He put down the photo, straightening it. The young man looked nothing like her: different coloured eyes, dissimilar features, the suggestion of a mixed race background in the dark skin tone.

Jack's hands were shaking. "I'm sorry. I didn't know." How old was she, anyway? She looked young, but must be at least in her late forties, possible her early fifties. Firm body. Smooth skin, Clear eyes. How did she remain so flawless? "I didn't know you had a son. Or a husband."

Her face darkened; just a shade, but it was there. "My husband's dead too, I'm afraid. Cancer. Five years ago." Again that well-fed look; like a cat after a bowlful of milk.

Shit. Could this be going any worse? All thoughts of fulfilling his youthful fantasies left him; she was just a lonely, messed-up woman who wanted someone to talk to.

"Don't look so worried. I'm not going to cry on your shoulder, or break down in front of you. I've done all my grieving." She uncrossed her legs. The sound of denim on denim was like a whisper in the quiet room.

Jack was running out of things to say. He felt embarrassed that he'd been imagining some kind of tacky porn-mag scenario: fucking an old teacher he'd been in lust with years before. He wasn't a bad person; he really wasn't. Just a weak one.

"Do you like music?" She stood and moved towards a silver boom box that stood on a book shelf at the front of the room. She made no sound as she stepped lightly across the floor, her feet barely making in impact on the soft pile of the carpet. She was like a ghost, a beautiful and untouchable phantom.

"Yeah. I like most kinds." His voice was strained; he coughed gently, just to clear his throat.

"How about some jazz? But not the weird kind. This is nice. Sexy."

Did she really say that, or was he merely imagining it? Suddenly, the mournful sound of a horn cut through the air, snaring his attention. Judy turned around, her glass almost empty, and swished her hips. Once again she was smiling. Her teeth were very white – clearly she had a good (or expensive) dentist. She moved fluidly to the music, her body a visual form of poetry. Her full hips beckoned, her tight runner's thighs moved fractionally apart.

"More wine?" He grabbed the bottle and refilled his glass. She was suddenly beside him, holding out her own empty vessel. The neck of the bottle clinked loudly on the rim of the glass. He filled it to the brim, almost making it overflow.

Judy returned to the sofa. She sat down, stretching her legs, moving her head from side to side as if ironing out the kinks in her neck muscles. "Tell me more about you. Your family."

The pain was still there – it would never fade – but these days it was less of a burden. "I don't know if you remember, but my mother was murdered just before I finished school. It happened the day after I got my exam results." He blinked, expecting the threat of tears, but none came.

"Yes. Yes, I do remember that. I was so sorry. It was such a tragedy. Did they ever... you know, find the killer?"

Bitter memories: of a courtroom, a man in a cheap suit with a faded sparrow tattoo on the side of his neck, yelling barristers, a sour-faced judge and a solemn jury. Tears. Fury. Rage.

"Yes, they got him. Banged him up for life." He swallowed the entire contents of his glass, and groped for more.

"At this rate I'll have to open another bottle."

He glared at the empty bottle in his hand; clutched the half-filled glass. "Sorry. I'm being rude."

"No," she said. "But I am. I shouldn't have asked about your mother." Her eyes looked bigger, wider, yet strangely empty. The alcohol was already working on his brain.

"It's fine. I can talk about it now. I couldn't back then, just after it happened, but now at least I can tell people about it without bursting into tears." The wine tasted even better the more of it he drank; it was like a soothing balm in his mouth, loosening his tongue.

Judy shuffled forward on the sofa, her cleavage exposed as the wide-cut neck of the T-shirt sagged beneath her throat.

"I went through a bad time just after it happened. Then, with the court case and all that, I almost lost the plot. Drink, drugs... casual sex. The lot. I was a walking cliché."

Her eyes. So big, so empty, as if waiting to be filled... filled up with his pain.

Her chest rose and fell as her breathing became more urgent, as if she were aroused. And he felt it too; his cock stiffened, his back began to sweat.

"I wanted to kill him myself. Just five minutes in a room, alone, with my mother's killer. I would've given anything for that."

Judy let out a tiny moan, so quiet that he suspected he might even have imagined it.

"But I'm fine now. I've sorted out my life."

Her shoulders sagged, her eyes receded, becoming smaller; she was spent.

Slowly, she placed her glass on the floor. When she stood, she knocked the glass with the side of her foot, upending it, and red wine spilled on the carpet, forming a dark stain that would never come out. That stain would be there forever. It was a thought that seemed somehow relevant, but the sight of her looming in his vision sent it scuttling away.

"You poor boy." She held him, her arms wrapping around his head and pulling him towards her. Jack breathed in her scent – it was dull, flat, and a little disagreeable. But he held his breath and enjoyed the moment: the soft press of her cool breasts against his cheek, the sound of her heart beating in his ears, its rhythm speeding to match that of his own racing pulse. His mother appeared in his mind, a stark image of loss, but parts of her began to break away. Large jigsaw segments vanished incrementally from his mother's silent image to reduce her presence to a mental echo, something he now struggled to connect to his past life. Rather than causing him more pain, the process was a relief from all the pain he'd suffered since her meaningless death.

Then, all too soon, Judy pulled away. He felt like he had lost something; or, more specifically, that something had been snatched cruelly away from him.

"I'm sorry. I shouldn't do that. I should exercise more self-control. But then again, you're a man now, not a boy." She paused. "I always knew you had a crush on me, you know." Her eyes sparkled, but it was the false allure of fake gemstones.

For no reason that he could pin down, Jack was afraid. Her presence was threatening in a way that was both obscure and oddly direct. "Can I use your toilet?" He stood, almost knocking her down, and moved to the door, confusion robbing him of grace.

"Upstairs," she said. "The little room at the top of the stairs." Her smile was wide and white.

He climbed the stairs in darkness, and found the door open. Closing it, he opened his trousers and attempted to urinate through his throbbing erection in the dark. It was like trying to force water through a short length of steel tube attached to floating balloons: a strange airy heaviness that made his head spin and his crotch ache.

He left the room without flushing and just as he began to ascend, heading for the front door, he caught sight of another open door across the landing. He stepped backwards, and then headed for the door. There was a lock on the outside, but she had failed to use it. He pushed open the door, unsure of what he was expecting. This whole situation was so weird, so like a dream, that he was ready for anything, however unusual.

The room was empty. There was no bed, and no furniture; not even a computer or a desk and chair were present to identify the room as an office. But the walls were covered with countless framed photographs, each one showing a different face. People of all ages, all races, and both sexes, adorned those blank white walls, with no spaces between them. Like a cobbled-together family, a montage of orphans, they stared at him, pleading for something he didn't even think he could give, searching for a connection he did not feel.

The only thing he knew for certain was that Judy Crossly had no son; and her husband, if he had ever existed at all, had not died of cancer. Normal human relationships were beyond her reach. She clung instead to something different, something extraordinary. She craved whatever was represented in these pictures.

His head spun. He raised his hands to rub his eyes, but saw that his fingers were so pale that they were almost white. He moved his fingers, bending them, and realised that they looked thinner than they should. His ring – the one belonging to his mother – that he always wore on his wedding finger rolled loose below the knuckle. Before, it had always been too tight to remove.

He returned to the bathroom and turned on the light. Standing before the mirror that hung above the shining sink unit, he barely recognised himself. His face was sallow, the bones prominent. His eyes had sunk into their sockets, the white parts bearing a slight yellow tinge. He looked... *withered*. Reduced. Less than he'd been when he entered the house.

He turned off the light and went downstairs.

"Are you okay?" She stood framed in the kitchen doorway, a freshly opened wine bottle in one hand and an old-fashioned cork-screw in the other. He could only describe the look on her face as *knowing*. She *knew* something that he did not; it was apparent in every gesture, each studied rearrangement of her features.

"I... I have to go. Sorry. Thanks for the drink." Back-pedalling, he came up against the door. Groping behind him, he was unaccountably relieved to find that the keys were still in the lock.

"Come back," she whispered, advancing towards him, dropping the corkscrew and much of the pretence. Her face was avid. "Come back any time."

The worst thing – the very worst thing – was that he knew, eventually, he would do exactly that. He would return because, despite the fear, and the threat of the unknown, she had somehow, in some small but definite way, made him feel better.

He ran out into the wet, hazy night; saw the yellow splash of the car headlights he'd foolishly left on. He unlocked the car and climbed behind the wheel, praying that the battery wasn't flat.

She floated up the drizzly path, drifted to the low metal gate. Her hand rested on the concrete gatepost. She was smiling.

The car started on the third try, the engine sputtering reluctantly to life. He pulled away from the kerb, wincing as the tyres screeched on the road surface, and watched her retreat in the greasy rearview mirror, her form diminishing but her power – whatever that meant – remaining just as intense, perhaps even growing stronger.

A cluster of fireworks detonated above her head, bathing her in sickly colour, making her look like a vision from hell: a smiling, sexually-charged demon, the depth of whose hungers would always remain unfathomable.

~φ~

Three days later he went back. Of course he went back: there was never any doubt that he would go, it had simply been a question of when.

He had regained the weight so abruptly lost that aching night; his ring was once again tight enough to cause the finger to swell and the top layer of skin beneath to flake away. His face was his own again, and he had almost convinced himself that he'd simply been drunk and emotional that evening, that Judy Crossly was nothing more than a desperate widow looking for company on a bad November night she could not face on her own.

He told himself all of this many times – so many in fact that he began to believe it. And always, behind the scenes, deep in his back brain, he thought of her still-lovely face, her wondrous breasts; imagined what she would look like naked. She had promised him nothing but suggested everything, planted the seeds in his mind and in his libido. And he could do little to fight what was growing deep within him.

He found himself parked outside her house, a pizza destined for another street on the same estate cooling on the seat beside him. He could smell cheese and overcooked sausage. His belly churned while his mind raced.

He left the car, this time turning off the headlights, and headed towards the house, his feet silent on the road, his hand clutching a photograph in an expensive gilt frame. He didn't want her to think he was cheap so he had bought the frame the day before, using the last of the previous week's wages.

He didn't even have to knock. She saw him coming; he was expected. He wondered, idly, if they always were: those just like him, the ones who wanted to further unburden themselves and offer this woman the dread weight they carried and were sick of carrying. The people who had grown sick of the taste of their own pain.

The door opened and he stepped inside. No words were necessary; she knew why he'd returned. This time when she smiled it did not look at all human. It was a rip in the mask, a gaping imperfection through which there peeked the very essence of what she really was and where she came from: a cold, dead hungry void.

He followed her across the threshold and up the carpeted stairs. She stood outside the spare room, the sad gallery he had stumbled across last time, with her hand held out to accept his gift.

Jack handed her the photo of his mother, relinquishing it, when the time came, with a surprising ease. It saddened him to discover that he was not even able to put up the pretence of a fight.

She went into the room and hung the photograph on the wall, among so many others just like it. His mother's face seemed somehow diminished, as if those around her had absorbed something vital that could never be replaced.

"Come," said Judy – or whatever she was really called. Did names even matter now? Where they in any way valid or meaningful?

No, all that mattered was whatever came next; and not even what came after that.

He followed her into yet another upstairs room, this one without a window. The only furniture inside was a dirty double bed without any sheets, its mattress stained and faded. The damp walls crawled with a thin black liquid that did not pool upon the floor but simply flowed across the plaster walls and along their rotted skirting, forming a series of dark mirrors which reflected nothing but nothing but nothing...

She unfolded onto the bed, throwing off her clothes and her perfect, perfect skin; shedding her ordinary disguise to reveal the dark wonder beneath. Without the bland costume, she was all about desire: a hungry creature made up of all the second-hand grief that had ever been sent her way, every ounce of human agony that had been spilled in her presence.

Beyond the shiny black liquid walls, a million sucking mouths opened; a billion blind eyes blinked across a vast and empty darkness without end.

Jack felt nothing but nothing but nothing.

Presently, he followed her down onto the spongy mattress, and opened himself up to her scrutiny. Weeping with a fearful kind of joy, he poured out his woes in a long, thrilling cascade, so that at last she might begin to feast. And those above and beyond her – the cold, sightless ones she served – fed vicariously, supping from the vessel she had become.

~φ~

The Ghost In You

"An idea, like a ghost, must be spoken to a little
before it will explain itself."
-Charles Dickens

"Ghosts only exist for those who wish to see them."
-Holtei

1

It was raining again when I looked out of the office window and into the car park below. The tall sparse trees overlooking the tiny asphalt parking area gently lowered their moulting heads in the wind, the sky above was dour and unreadable, and light spatters of rain kissed the window pane.

In the distance, beyond the constant murmur of traffic noise from the nearby road, I could hear the high arrhythmic dirge of a muted car alarm. A bus growled past unseen. Someone shouted a name I couldn't quite make out, and then shouted it again.

Then there was a lull during which all sound compressed into a small conceptual space. My ears rang; my head began to throb gently, as if someone were pressing against the skull with large, hot hands. It felt like I was about to see or experience something beyond the realm of the senses, but the moment soon passed, leaving me empty and distraught.

I looked at the photograph of my son on my desk. He was smiling, his hands thrust deep into his pockets. Danny. Five years old. Happy. Unknowing. His T-shirt had the words LITTLE MAN printed across the chest, and he was wearing a badge that featured a smiling cartoon sun.

The tree branches rustled outside the window, whispering in a secret language. The traffic had gone quiet. The empty building opposite – an abandoned church – had wire mesh across its broken windows. The yellow stone walls were stained with grime and parts of the roof were missing – small gaps where the slates had either been blown off or stolen.

I gazed across the outside of the structure, picking out the finer details: faded graffiti, the airbrushed, anatomically incorrect outline of a monstrous penis, a stone windowsill scraped bare of its dark paint, the scraps left behind resembling old scabs on ancient flesh. As I watched, a lone figure walked past an upstairs window, as if crossing the room. I heard music – something sombre and bluesy – but it soon faded: ghost-music, something felt in the blood rather than genuinely heard.

The sky darkened by degrees, as if a thin veil were being drawn across it. The rain intensified.

For some reason I thought of my mother. Her thin, frail arms, the way she moved across a dusky room when she thought nobody was looking, the plaintive sound of her voice when she sang late at night. My eyes were wet with tears. I brushed them away, disgusted. My mother was fine; I'd spoken to her a few days before. But eventually, just like everyone else, she would die.

"Idiot," I murmured. "Maudlin twat."

"Sorry?" Mick: the guy who sat opposite me. We shared a huge cluttered desk in the open office space.

I smiled. "Nothing, mate. Just talking to myself."

Mick nodded, went back to his work. His eyes narrowed as he examined his computer screen.

I returned my attention to the window, the fluorescent office lights flickering at my back. I watched a plane as it rose into the dark ocean of sky above Leeds-Bradford airport, located just a mile or two away. It flew at an acute angle, nose pushing through the clouds, and eventually it vanished from view into the whirling grey haze.

I blinked, trying to clear a slight prickling sensation from my eyes. For a moment there, lost in my own inchoate thoughts, I'd imagined that I'd seen tiny figures standing on the wings of the plane.

When the telephone rang I stared at it before answering. Short double rings: an external line, which meant that it might be a personal call. I picked up the receiver, pressed it against my ear.

"Hello."

There was a pause during which I could hear music playing in the background – something crappy from the eighties. "Hi, Simon. It's me."

"Polly. This is a surprise." Understatement had always been my forte.

"How are you?"

I considered lying, and then opted instead for the truth: "Not good. Shitty, actually. Why, what do you care?"

"Still wallowing in self-pity, I see. Congratulations on that."

I tried not to smile, I really did. "How about you. Everything okay? I mean, I'm assuming this isn't a social call."

The line hummed; someone had turned off the background music. I wondered where Polly was calling from – was she at work, or did she have a day off?

"Well?"

"There's something I need to talk to you about." She paused again. I could almost hear her licking her lips. She did that whenever she was nervous: a quick flick of the tongue like a lizard on a rock. "Any chance we could meet for a drink one evening this week?"

For some reason I glanced at my watch but didn't register the time. "I'm free tonight, actually. Unless that's too soon?"

"Tonight will be fine. How does seven-thirty grab you?"

"Yes. That's good for me. Where do you want to meet?"

"How about The Porcupine?" Somewhere neutral, then; clearly she wanted a *serious* chat.

"Okay. See you then. Do I need to bring a weapon? Ammo?"

"Just bring yourself, Simon. Or, better still, leave one of yourselves at home and come alone." She didn't wait for an answer before hanging up the phone. She had always been good at exit lines.

I got up and walked across the office, ignoring the rest of my co-workers who were staring at their screens as if hypnotised. Leaving Mick at his computer, tapping at the keys like an inquisitive monkey, I went out onto the landing and headed for the disabled toilet – I never used the able-bodied one; when I shit I like to shit alone, without anyone else hovering around to sniff my arse.

I kicked open the door and went inside, locking the door behind me. I took a piss instead, closing my eyes and listening to the sound. Then, after a short pause, I reached out and flushed the toilet.

Turning to wash my hands in the undersized basin, I looked at my reflection in the small, square mirror attached to the wall. I didn't recognise the face that stared back at me; it was blotchy, bloated, loaded with too many full nights and empty promises. I opened my mouth and stuck out my tongue. It was an odd yellow colour, like the leaf of some kind of exotic plant.

"Blah!" I said. Then I said it again.

The room was tiny, the walls pressing in, closing me down. I shut my mouth and tried not to scream, the sound of my teeth snapping together far too loud in the enclosed space.

Outside, on the landing, I ran into my boss coming up the stairs. He was returning from a meeting in Bradford, and was adjusting his tie as he gained the landing. "Hi, Simon," he said, frowning. He was a big chap in cheap shoes but with an expensive haircut

"Hello, Brendan. Good meeting?"

"Listen, I was going to come and see you later, before lunch. Do you have a few minutes? There's something we need to go over in my office." It was not an invitation; I was expected to say yes and follow him.

"No problem, Brendan."

We walked silently through the door and into Brendan's inner office. He closed the door behind me, smiling.

I sat down without being asked and stared at the pictures on the walls. Photographs of his bland wife and their ugly kids; a bad watercolour landscape depicting some seaside scene I didn't recognise; a framed University degree in something I could never quite maintain the interest to read.

Brendan squeezed his large frame behind his long desk. The wheels on his chair squeaked as he shuffled forward. He clasped his hands on the desktop, his fingers wrestling on an ink blotter covered in doodles of little men and women and what looked like big dogs.

"I've been meaning to have a word with you for some time."

"Yes?" I stared him right in the eye; I knew he respected the direct approach – or at least he pretended to after reading it in some shallow management pamphlet.

"It's about... well, it's about your recent work."

Something over his shoulder caught my eye and I shifted my gaze to look out through the window.

"Your focus isn't what it should be."

From where I was sitting, I could see the *Farm Foods* car park on the opposite side of the road. At that time of day there were not many vehicles parked there, but the shop was open for business.

"I mean, you don't seem to be concentrating. Your work is suffering. Tell me, are you still interested in what you do?"

A man stood at the centre of a parking bay near the side entrance – a spot where nobody ever parked, even when the store was busy. I'd always found it odd that a perfectly good parking space was never filled, but the one time I had tried to park there I was unable to use it. The spot had an atmosphere, a raw and shifting sense of... what, dread? Horror? It was difficult to tell, but the small rectangular patch of cracked concrete felt *unwelcoming* in a way that it was impossible to deny. I'm sure it's the same when the interiors of certain buildings are said to be intimidating, or accident-heavy stretches of modern motorways hold a cold, anxious atmosphere which makes drivers put their foot down on the accelerator...

The man was not moving. The rain fell upon his head and shoulders like shredded strips of polythene thrown from above. His arms hung loose at his sides and his hands were closed into fists, the fingers curled tightly into his palms. His mouth gaped, as if he were silently singing; a single long note held way beyond its breaking point. I imagined that I could almost hear it.

"Simon? Are you even listening, Simon?"

For as long as I stared, the man remained motionless. His long black overcoat didn't even flap in the wind.

"Simon!"

I turned my head sharply towards Brendan, blinking, feeling like I'd woken from a short nap. He was glaring at me, red stains blooming at the centre of his cheeks. "Sorry. Sorry, Brendan. What were you saying?"

"For God's sake, Simon." He stood up too quickly and knocked a mug filled with pencils onto the floor. Neither of us bothered to pick them up. "This is exactly what I'm talking about. Your lack of focus, the way your mind is never on what you're doing."

I tried to care but couldn't summon the energy. Glancing back towards the big office window, I noted that the man had moved on. There was now a small white van parked in the space next to the one he'd vacated.

"Do you like your job, Simon? I mean, times are hard, we're in a recession, and redundancies might be on the horizon. You aren't doing yourself any favours here." He sat back down, mellowing. "I know things have been rough for you lately – God knows, we all liked Polly. You had a good thing going there..." He trailed off, unable to complete the thought.

"Can I go now?" I blinked at him, seeing through his shabby pretence. He was a sad man playing at being a manager. People like him didn't care; they simply acted like they did while they sharpened the knives they'd use to stab you in the back.

"Yes, Simon." He sighed, rather theatrically I thought. "Yes, you can leave." Then he picked up some random papers and shuffled them, as if punctuating the end of our meeting.

I got up and left the room, not bothering to close the door behind me. I heard Brendan sigh again as he crossed the room to slam it.

I messed about until home time, killing the final few hours of the working day by answering emails, browsing the internet for cheap flights, reading badly written film and book reviews on badly designed websites. At 5:15 p.m. I tugged on my coat and headed for the stairs.

"G'night," said Mick, speaking to my back. I ignored him and went straight to my car, which was parked across two spaces in the private car park reserved for company directors. The dark surface was stained even darker in patches by the rain. My hair was wet and my scalp began to itch.

The short drive home was miserable and rather taxing. It seemed that all the bad drivers in Yorkshire where on the road at the same time. Which meant, of course, that everyone who owned a car was out there: Yorkshire people drive like old people fuck.

I parked outside my rented flat and entered the building, shaking off the rain. The stairwell echoed hollowly as I ran up the building's core to the top floor. My door stuck when I tried to open it, so I fixed it by repeatedly kicking the thin steel strip along the bottom and swearing at it.

The flat smelled musty, as if no one actually lived there. The floor was littered with days-old newspapers, takeaway cartons and empty beer bottles. I went straight to the fridge, shrugging off my coat and slipping off my shoes. Grabbing a bottle of Molsten, I continued through into my bedroom to change out of my work clothes.

I put on a pair of faded jeans and a black shirt that hid my beer belly. On my feet I wore some running shoes that were so old the right one had a hole worn into the area above my big toe. I examined myself in the mirror and turned quickly away. I looked worn-out, wasted; my lifestyle was draining me of any good looks I might once have possessed.

I took a second beer from the fridge, half-drained it in one swallow, and then poured myself a vodka from the bottle I kept in the freezer. I knew I was drinking too much, but I didn't really care enough to stop. It was something to get me through, a crutch to lean on now that my human support had gone away. God, that sounded like the lyric to some antiquated blues song.

I rang a taxi and drank another glass of vodka while I waited for it to arrive. I would be in town early, so decided to stop in at the North Bar – a cosy little place where they sold a good selection of foreign beers.

If Polly was going to tell me something I didn't want to hear, alcohol would anesthetise whatever part of me was cut away.

2

It was still early so the bar was almost empty. There was a new jukebox in one corner and someone had pumped in enough money to play a Nirvana album all the way through. I liked the band, so felt immediately at home.

I ordered a draft Budvar from a bored-looking barmaid. She had green strips dyed into her shoulder-length blonde hair and a gold stud was stuck to one snotty nostril like a pimple. She sniffed as she served me the drink, sneezed into her fist.

"I hope you wash your hands before you offer me any nuts."

She gazed at me, more bored than ever. "Fuck off, old man."

That put me firmly in my place. I smiled, raised my glass, and fled towards the back of the room.

"Well done, Valentino." A female voice rose from a table pushed against the wall. I glanced over and saw the red tip of a cigarette poised above a wide, easy grin. She had short dark hair, green eyes and a snake tattoo running down the left side of her throat. Her black leather jacket was torn at one elbow and her hands were unnaturally large, the fingers bony and big-knuckled.

"I always did have a way with the ladies." I sipped my drink. She got up and walked across to my table. Her bare legs were short for her body; they hung chunkily beneath a short pleated skirt. If she bent over, I bet myself that I would get a flash of her knickers.

"Mind if I join you?" She sat down without even waiting for an answer.

"Only if you're in the mood for my scintillating banter and witty comebacks."

She smiled; this time it was slightly guarded. Using the nail of her right index finger, she flicked cigarette ash onto the damp tabletop. I stared at it and watched as it dissolved into the spilled beer.

"My name's Diane," she said, holding out one of those work-men's hands. I stared hard at it before giving it a shake.

"I'm Simon. Come here often?" I took another swallow of cold beer.

Laughing, Diane scratched her ear and blinked those wonderful gemstone eyes. The more I looked at this woman the more attractive she became. Despite her weird hands and short, stumpy legs, she possessed a lazy sexuality that I found oddly appealing.

"I was supposed to be meeting a friend – he comes here quite a bit. The bastard hasn't turned up, though, and his mobile seems to be turned off." Her smile didn't waver as she told me this, so I guessed that she wasn't too hurt by the snub.

"It's rough when a date stands you up. Maybe you should've promised him something at the end of the evening…"

She shook her head. A nose ring winked in the light from a ceiling-mounted fixture; it was like a tiny eye, keeping watch to make sure I made no sudden moves. "Oh, I never put out on a first date. Unless it's for money."

I laughed, almost spilling my beer. "You're a one, aren't you?"

"Depends what one is." She narrowed her eyes and, and in that moment I knew that we'd made a connection, however tenuous; then I mentally kicked myself for such bad timing. I looked at the clock on the wall above the bar. 6:30. In an hour, I had to meet Polly.

"Listen," I said, shuffling the bar stool along the wooden floor so that our thighs were touching under the low table. "I'm meeting my ex-girlfriend. I don't know how you're fixed, but I'm not expecting it to take long – she's going to give me some sort of bad news, so I'll need a good drink afterwards. How about meeting me back here at, say, eight o'clock?"

She stared into my eyes, those strange green emeralds widening to draw me in deeper than I was prepared to go. "I don't usually arrange to meet up with strange men."

"I'm not strange, just a little odd and needy."

She laughed again. "Okay. I have a few calls to make, and I'm picking up some weed from another friend at eight, but I can be back here for eight-thirty. But if you stand me up, I'll find you and I'll kill you." The smile disappeared and I felt like I'd suddenly missed the joke. Then it was back, slow and sly. The snake undulated across the skin of her throat as she swallowed her drink.

Thirty minutes later I was walking towards The Porcupine, the taste of Diane still in my mouth. She'd leaned over and kissed me as I got up to leave, a teaser for later that evening. I'd enjoyed the way her tongue had pushed into my mouth even before our lips made contact; it was dirty, expressive, and just a little bit scary. She tasted of smoke and white wine, and underneath those was another more unusual flavour that I couldn't nail down.

It was dark and the traffic was busy. Someone ran in front of a bus on the Headrow, prompting what sounded like a hundred car horns to blare in unison. A woman carrying too many shopping bags pushed past me on the footpath and I stumbled into the gutter. I twisted my ankle, but it didn't hurt a bit; the alcohol in my system acted as protection against such everyday injuries.

I stood and waited to cross the road. Cars and buses streamed past me, a continuous line of blurred, washed-out colour. I looked for a gap to dodge through but none appeared. The traffic lights refused to turn green and I was starting to get jumpy.

A single-decker bus trundled towards the junction just down from where I was standing at the kerb. Its lights were out, signalling that the vehicle was off duty, but a single figure sat curled on the back seat, its right upper arm pressed against the window. The figure was dark, hunched, and seemed to be staring right at me. I couldn't be sure because the interior of the bus was so dim, but it looked like the figure had its mouth open wide in a dark and silent scream.

More horns blared; a mournful siren approached rapidly from the top end of the Headrow, causing the traffic to pull in towards the central reservation. When I looked back at the bus it was empty; the back seat was unoccupied. A police car sped past, the siren still going.

Polly was sitting at a table in the window as I approached The Porcupine. I stood there under a set of defective traffic lights, watching her as she examined a drinks menu. Her nimble hands held the menu delicately, as if it were a precious volume. She was biting her upper lip, as she always did when she was engrossed in a task. Her long ash-blonde hair was swept back from her face, held in a loose ponytail by a thick red elastic band. She looked lovely there in the window: a glowing display in the tidy shop-front of a perfect life.

I was unable to move, so I waited until the sense of awe and grief passed. Polly glanced up when a waitress approached her table, pointed to an item on the menu, and then said something through a smile. The waitress, tired-looking but with a nice smile of her own, nodded her head and laughed.

I waited until Polly had her drink, then I moved towards the door, rain on my shoulders and pain in my heart.

She saw me as I crossed the room, half-standing to raise a hand into the air. I waved back, smiling tentatively. I didn't know why she'd summoned me here, and needed to remain cautious.

"Hi," she said, pressing her hands against the table top as I lowered myself into a chair.

"That looks nice." I indicated the drink before her – a dark-coloured cocktail with lime and sugar around the rim of the glass. "*Mojito*. It's Latin-American. Rum and coke." She took a sip. The smile was still there, but now it was muted.

I hailed a different waitress and ordered a double whisky. I was already half cut and intended to see it through to the end. We sat in an uneasy silence until my drink was brought to the table; then I saluted Polly with my glass and downed half of the generous measure of liquor.

"You look like you needed that." Lights shone above her head and towards the back of the room. They doused her in a hazy glow, painting her hair with a dull lustre. U2 was playing on the sound system, an old song from their early militant days.

"Do I? Need it, I mean. Do I need a drink for what you going to tell me?" I stared her down, refusing to budge. She'd already hurt me enough for two lifetimes, and I didn't intend to spend the rest of this one in thrall to her presence.

"I see you're all business this evening, Simon. I was hoping we could be civilised."

U2 was replaced by The Clash: *London Calling*. Whoever was in charge of the sounds had good taste.

"I'm sorry." I wasn't quite sure if that was true, but I said it anyway, thinking that if I was lucky I might just end up believing it. "I always seem to be on guard whenever we meet." There was so much that I wanted to say, there were so many questions that I needed to ask... but I could voice none of them. Every time I tried, the words got stuck in my throat. It was as if we were facing each other across an empty field littered with buried landmines, and any false step would set off a chain reaction of psychic detonations.

"I've done a lot of thinking since we split. There's been a lot to sort out, to consider." She grasped her glass but didn't raise it to her red lips; she parted them, her dark red tongue slipping out to moisten the area. "Danny is old enough that he can make sense of the hurt we do to each other. He's unhappy. It's affecting him at school. He's started bullying another kid, and when I ask him why he can't seem to put the reason into words."

So our son had inherited our inability to communicate, and was taking it out on those around him. "Shit. That's bad." Still, even now, I could not say what needed saying; could not form the words we both wanted to hear. I didn't even know what they were.

"So I've made a decision – one you won't like." She paused. Took a drink. Expecting me to react. Instead I just sat and waited. "I'm moving back down south, to live with my mum for a while. She has that big house and no one to put in it. Danny and I can live in one half; she can live in the other, like a granny annexe."

I opened my mouth to speak but nothing came out. Realising how stupid I must look, I finished my whisky, and then looked around to summon the waitress to bring me another. She was lounging on the bar, talking to the young man who had set up camp there and washing the fake brass trappings with a ragged cloth.

I kept staring until they noticed me. I could feel Polly's eyes burning into my cheek, but didn't want to turn towards her. The waitress nodded, poured another double, and brought it over. "Sorry," she said. Then she walked back to the young man, swaying her hips like a catwalk model.

"You don't have much to say for yourself."

Finally I turned again to face her, my eyes stinging with tears. "Would anything I said change your mind?"

Her eyes were shiny with moisture, too; they glimmered as she slowly shook her head. "No. I'm afraid my mind's already made up. I have to think of Danny – we have to think about our son." She pressed her lips together, just like she used to when she put on her lipstick before we enjoyed a night out. "It's not like it's another country. Just a couple of hundred miles away. You can come and visit. He can visit you for weekends. You'll probably see more of him than you do now."

We both knew the lie of what she said, but I was too tired, too body-shocked to point it out. If I was honest, even if I had not been so worn out and hollow, I would have said nothing. We never did. We always kept quiet, letting the pain burrow inside like a grub, working its way deep into our bodies where it would be smothered and gradually digested.

3

When I got back to The North Bar it was shortly after 8 p.m. Polly's blows hadn't taken long to fall, and the damage they did was quick, sharp and precise.

I kept drinking whisky and listened to the maudlin tunes on the jukebox. Diane came back just after nine. By that time I was shit-faced, could barely even stand up. She was drunk, too; her gait was unsteady and she bumped into a table, spilling drinks, as she wove her way across the room to where I was sitting.

"You look like I feel," I said, placing a hand on her bare arm.

"I feel like a fuck," she countered, winking at me and settling heavily onto a stool. I began to realise that she was probably the local barroom slut: everyone certainly seemed to know her, the other clientele nodding and smiling and making dirty little quips as she passed by their tables. But I didn't care. Meaningless sex on a night like this was all that I could hope for.

"Let's drink first. The rest can come later." I got up and went to the bar; returned to the table with two fistfuls of liquid damage.

"It looks to me like you're a man on a mission." Her words were slurred, her cheeks were flushed.

"I'd say it's already a case of mission accomplished." I raised my glass.

She belched quietly, and then raised her own. "Cheers."

I recall having a few more drinks in there before moving on to somewhere else. We walked by the canals, down from the train station, and she clawed at my arse with those strong, hard hands.

We kissed clumsily and almost fell into the water. I watched a shopping trolley float by over her shoulder as she licked my neck.

There were other bars – lots of rough rooms with odd graffiti daubed on the inside walls and wooden planks across the broken windows. Someone started a fight in one of these places; I got caught up in the scuffle, pulled into the crowd. When we left there we were laughing, me with a bloody nose, and I remember trying to fuck her up against a rough brick wall with my trousers around my ankles. Her tongue was pleasantly gritty, like that of a cat, and her body trembled as if she feared me...

Then I was alone. I had no idea where Diane had gone, or when she had left me. When I opened my eyes I was sitting in a lightless alley, an overflowing trash bin to my left, ripped plastic bags disgorging their contents onto the wet ground.

It was raining again. I raised my head and opened my mouth, enjoying the cold wetness against my face. The stars looked improbably distant; I strained to pick them out against the rippling black sky.

Leaning against the metal bin, I climbed to my feet. There was a rip in my trouser leg; my left shoe was hanging off my foot and the sock was soaking wet. I dusted myself down, feeling dizzy and still very drunk. The world tilted sharply, and Polly's brutal decision still rang in my ears like the distant pealing of a funeral bell.

I staggered towards the mouth of the alley, planning to orient myself as soon as I could see the street lights. God knew where I was – none of this looked even slightly familiar. The walls of dirty tenements leaned over me, windows smeared dark with the muck of sin and poverty. Again I heard music; everywhere I went , music seemed to find me – just like having a personal soundtrack. Somewhere far off, a car engine roared. A firework went off but when I searched the sky for its trail I found nothing but darkness. Darkness and rain.

Something behind me – a sound, the suggestion of being watched? – made me turn around and stare back along the alley. I looked beyond the bin, ignoring the bags that bulged like soft and monstrous bodies from its gaping maw, and my gaze fell upon a lone figure. It was a woman, and she was watching me.

"Hello," I said, narrowing my eyes, trying to make out her features in the sketch of night. The woman did not move. She stood with her hands by her sides and her legs slightly parted, the toes pointing outward.

"Could you help me? I don't know where I am."

I took a step back into the alley towards her, hoping that she might at least tell me where I was and give me directions back to the main drag.

Within a few steps I began to recognise her face in the shadows. It was Polly, and she was wearing a long dark coat with a turned up collar. Her legs were bare and her fists were clenched. She had let her hair fall out of the hair band, and it lay against her shoulders like strange moss. Her face was slightly elongated, narrow, the cheeks sunken. Her mouth was open; it was a perfect black circle. I could see no teeth. There was little evidence of a tongue.

"Polly? What are you doing here?" I increased my pace as I moved heedlessly along the alley, aware that I was leaving the light far behind. Something wasn't right, but I ignored it. Maybe Polly was in trouble and had been searching for me. The senselessness of this thought didn't even register in my confused mind.

Slowly, she began to move. She raised one of her arms, stiffly, as if it was injured, the range of movement diminished by a debilitating wound. When the arm reached chest level, she twisted her wrist so that the thumb faced upwards. Then, one by one, she opened her fingers to show me what she was holding in her fist.

I tripped on a mound of rubbish, going down into a mass of soggy cardboard boxes, evil-smelling waste and sharp-topped tin cans. My legs slipped on the uneven road surface and I sprawled like an old lady slipping on an icy path. When I looked up, Polly was gone. The air shimmered with the rumour of her recent presence; pressure built up in my ears, threatening to pop.

It was only when I regained my feet that I realised I was weeping. My shoulders shook, my cheeks were wet, and my chest hitched as I sobbed for a reason that somehow eluded me.

4

Next morning I woke in a state of shock, as if roused from uneasy sleep by violent motion. The night before came back to me in crude snippets, snapshots from a gallery of shame: the dodgy bars, the awkward sex, that final nightmare vision in the alleyway and my tears of... what? Regret? Loss? Even now, the reason for my breakdown was out of reach.

I knew I was drinking too much, and that it was becoming a problem, but I was beginning to rely on the buzz to get me through the day. Drink is a subtle lover: it whispers to you of other lands, of distant pain-free places, and offers you shimmering glimpses of how things can be. Then, in the morning, it hits you with a hammer and laughs in your face.

I managed to get out of bed and made it to the bathroom. In the mirror, my face was a ghastly mask: pasty skin, hollow cheeks, and bloated flesh around the eyes. I looked exactly like I felt, and within moments I was bending over the toilet bowl emptying my gut of yesterday's indulgences. There was a burning sensation in my stomach, as if I'd swallowed poison, and after a short while there was nothing left to vomit up but my stomach lining.

I cleaned my teeth but still could not get rid of the bitter, acidic taste in my mouth. The toothbrush kept slipping from my grip because my hands were weak and uncoordinated. Even the bland routines of daily hygiene were becoming chores.

In the kitchen, I drank endless cups of coffee and tried to bring myself around. It didn't work, and I kept thinking about the bottle of Jack Daniels in the cupboard. The bottle, I knew, was over half full. *Just a snifter,* I thought. *A cheeky double to get me back on track.*

I walked over to the cupboard and opened the door. Then I took out the bottle, grabbed a glass from the draining board and poured the drink. I smelled it before I tasted it, and gagged. But that didn't stop me. I closed my eyes, lifted the glass, and downed a small measure of my own damnation.

Later, sitting on the sofa and trying to remember what it was I had to do that day, I became gradually aware of the telephone ringing. I wasn't sure how long it had been ringing, but the tone had probably taken some time to penetrate the fug of my hang-over – which was nowhere near as bad as it should be since I'd headed it off at the pass with the JD.

I loped across the room and picked up the phone. It felt odd in my hand, an alien artefact I may once have dreamed of.

"Hello."

"Daddy. Will you bring me a present?"

It was the Little Man. Suddenly a series of cogs and mecha-nisms clicked into place: today was my time with Danny. Every other Saturday I got to see him; take him to the park, feed the ducks, eat lunch in an awful Fun Pub.

"Hey, Soldier. How's my boy?"

"Fine. When will you be here?"

I blinked away tears. This was wrong; this was shitty. I couldn't believe I'd allowed the drink to get in the way of the only quality time left in my life. "I'll be there in an hour, mate. Daddy got held up, but now he's on his way. That okay?"

"Will you bring me a present?"

"Yeah, Danny. I'll bring you a present. And we can go and feed the ducks in the park."

"Yay! I like ducks." Then he hung up the phone. I imagined Polly standing behind him, knowing all too well why I was late. I checked my watch: 11 a.m. I should have been there thirty min-utes ago. Shit. This was the first time I'd ever let him down, and because of last night's flashpoint meeting, Polly would be only too eager to remind me of my responsibilities.

I took a quick shower and left the flat, hoping that traffic would be light. The route to the M1 Motorway was relatively clear; families in little hatchbacks and delivery trucks steered by mostly overweight middle aged men crossed lazily between lanes. The M1 towards Wakefield had become a road I was fa-miliar with, so my attention wandered as I drove.

I didn't want Polly to move south. My time with Danny was precious and I wanted to keep him as close as I could. If he was living two hundred miles away rather than twenty, I'd see him less and less as the years passed. By the time he hit his teenage years, I'd have become a duty, a bloke up in Leeds he visited briefly twice a year. Whereas if he still lived in the area, we might at least stand a chance of salvaging some kind of father-son relationship.

A tiny car overtook me on my right, the driver gritting his teeth and glaring through the windscreen. I turned and watched him, wondering why he was in such a hurry. Was he late for weekend father duties, too?

The rain had stopped at some point during the night but the roads were still black with moisture. The sky was low and leaden; it undulated with a strange slow rhythm, and I was put in mind of some glacial ocean. The clouds looked like whales, shifting lazily across their domain; a few of them might be sea monsters left over from a time before man had lost his ancient beliefs and superstitions.

I switched on the radio but the mindless bleating of regional deejays failed to inspire me. The last CD I'd played was still in the stereo slot, so I pressed play and waited to hear what it was. There was a slight pause before Thom Yorke's unearthly tones crept in over sonorous guitars. The music suited my mood so I let it play.

A private hire bus was parked on the hard shoulder. The passengers stared desultorily through the smeared windows while the driver bent over the open bonnet. Smoke poured from the engine, forming a little dissipating cloud above the front end of the vehicle. The driver's beefy hand moved through the air like a fat fish as he tried to clear his view of the damage.

A little further on the sky darkened; more rain threatened to pour from its depths. I glanced to my left, at a parking lay-by along the side of the motorway. There was a broken wooden bench, an overflowing litter bin, and stunted trees were gathered round the area in a sulky group. Halfway up one of the trees, arms and legs wrapped around the bare autumn branches, was a man. He sat on a wide bulge in the side of the tree trunk, his head turned towards the road. Beneath the grumbling sky, his face was dark and troubling. His mouth was a large black, glistening circle, forced open to a point well beyond the range of natural motion. I could not see his eyes, yet I felt his gaze upon me. His right hand slipped from its branch, and as he opened his fist something dropped to the ground below the tree.

Who were these people, and why was I seeing them? My first thought was that they were ghosts, wandering the world in search of release. But if that were the case, why had I seen Polly? She was alive and real, not a figment of my stressed imagination. Just what was her connection to these frightening figures, and what had she been holding in her hand?

I strained to see some kind of sense in these visions. Was it just the drink playing tricks on me? I was certainly consuming enough hard liquor to force me to hallucinate; I was already having blank spots and acting out of character, so why not add a dash of delirium to the cocktail?

I looked in the rear-view mirror, the parking place by now far behind. I saw the trees, the bench, the sullen sky... but the man was no longer there, or perhaps the angle was wrong and he was simply out of sight.

By the time I reached Wakefield it was raining again. It always seemed to be raining or about to rain, and any respite was always brief and filled with a doom-laden sense that the rain would return some time soon.

It was impossible to make plans, to sensibly organise anything involving being outdoors, without having a back-up plan to enable you to retreat and take shelter.

I stood on the doorstep of the house where I used to live, the home I used to own. It looked different, altered, even though nothing had changed. The transformation was on a level more fundamental than was immediately obvious: the bricks and mortar had evolved into something I didn't recognise; the windows reflected the light from a world I could no longer enter without permission; the plants and flowers in the garden had grown in soil upon which my feet had never trod.

Polly opened the door and stood back from the threshold, as if daring me to cross. "He's been waiting for you."

I was caught on the doorstep, stuck between two worlds, neither of which I fully understood. "I know. I'm sorry. I lost track of time..."

"You were drunk."

I had no answer; she knew me – even the recent me, the changed me – far too well. Panicked and grasping, I diverted the course of the conversation: "I saw you last night. Late on. Where had you been?"

She looked at me like I was something she'd brought in on the sole of her shoe. Her eyes widened in what for a terrifying moment I suspected might be disgust. "What are you talking about, Simon? I went home right after our pathetic little meeting. If you want to know the truth, I sat up until midnight crying into my fucking coffee."

Words failed me; they slithered around my mouth like worms, unknowable, ungraspable, beyond my control. "I... what I mean is... well, it looked like you. I thought it was you."

"Are you still pissed, Simon? I mean, I fucking refuse to let you near my son if you're still drunk."

I shook my head, took a single tentative step forward, my hands raised in neither defence nor attack, and gaped like a fish: my mouth opened and closed on dead air, decayed promises, and my breath was toxic.

"Get in here," she said. The disgust on her face was now apparent. Was I really so pathetic? Had I sunk so very low in her estimation that whatever affection she had once felt for me was gone, banished to the brittle edges of memory?

I followed Polly through into the living room, noting that the pictures hanging on the walls were ones I'd never seen before. They were not to my taste, nor could I recall Polly ever being drawn to this style of art. Again, it was a demonstration of how little we really knew each other; an example of the way we'd failed utterly to communicate at any level.

Danny was sitting on the floor in front of the television, his eyes locked on the screen. Tom and Jerry chased each other across a fully laden banquet table, using utensils as weapons. My son failed to notice me as I stood in the doorway.

"Daddy's here," said Polly, entering and leaning down to kiss him on the top of the head.

He stood and turned in a single graceful movement, then ran to me, smiling, laughing, with his good little heart full of love and life and energy. "Daddy! Yay! You got me a present?"

"Yes, Little Man. I have a present for you." I caught him as he leapt into my arms, swinging him around and pulling him to my chest. His hair smelled clean and fresh, his skin was silk-soft and slightly chill to the touch.

"What you got, Daddy? I want my present. *Pleeeeeease*."

Laughing, I fished inside my pocket and pulled out the toy I'd bought in the petrol station. It was a stuffed beanie version of Spongebob Squarepants, with suckers on the palms of its hands where you were meant to attach it to the car window. A simple thing, costing no more than a few pounds, but Danny loved it. Spongebob was his favourite. I was a good enough father to at least retain that pointless snippet of information.

"Yay! Spongebob! Yay!" He danced around the room, hugging the silly little toy. Polly smiled at me, but it was a brief gesture and not one that I could afford to read anything into: just a sad, slightly tired smile. I noted the dark smudges beneath her eyes and her unwashed hair. Guilt rose within me; I was responsible for her having another late night, just like the ones she'd gone through when I was out drinking when we were together. Back then, I'd never called to let her know where I was or who I was with.

I would have given anything to take it all back: my eyes, my arms, my legs. My dirty rotten soul.

The rain had turned to drizzle, so we decided to go to the park anyway. I helped Danny into his winter coat and held his hand too tightly as we left the house and walked to the car. Polly stood on the step waving, her face a small pale blob in the dour air. I sat behind the wheel and watched her, wishing that just for a moment the clouds would clear and we might see each other as we really were, naked and unadorned, all armour stripped away. The sky darkened; the clouds massed, huge leviathans grouping together for protection in an unruly sea.

We fed the ducks and Danny played on the wet swings, the soaked slide, the damp roundabout. There were no other kids around, and when the rainfall once again intensified, we went back to the car. His grip on my hand was a reminder of everything I had lost, and was still losing. I didn't want him to ever let go.

Thank God the rain hid my tears; it isn't fitting for a boy to see his father weep.

5

I didn't get home until late, and when I entered the flat my answer phone was flashing to indicate that I had a message. No one ever rang me; I had no friends. Who the hell was calling, and what could they possibly want from me?

I took off my coat, poured a large whisky, and pressed the button to receive the message.

"Simon? Hello, mate, it's Mick. From work. Listen, I heard about what happened with you and that wanker Brendan yesterday. I'm going to a party tonight at my girlfriend's place, and thought you might like to come along. No pressure. Here's the address..."

I listened to the message twice, both annoyed and grateful for Mick's invitation. We'd worked together for five years and this was the first time he'd asked me out anywhere outside of the office. There had been a few lunchtime pints, the occasional after work social event, but never before had he offered me any kind of genuine friendship. Was I now some kind of charity case, the type of man whom colleagues felt sorry for and tried to throw a lifeline?

But Mick was a good guy. His heart was in the right place. I checked the fridge for beer and discovered that I had only one bottle left. The whisky was dwindling, the vodka gone. It was a choice between popping out to the off licence later or going to the party and getting drunk with other people rather than sitting alone.

I decided to attend the party, more out of a vague sense of desperation than anything else: I figured it was less sad to drink with people you didn't know than it was to drink yourself into a lonely stupor.

The place was in an area not far from where I lived but I didn't fancy the walk, so I ordered a taxi and finished off my alcohol supply while I waited for it to arrive. The taxi drove through streets I wasn't that familiar with, past derelict high rises and a burned out church; cars were propped up on bricks, their wheels stripped; gangs of youths hung around on corners outside wire-wreathed shops with dusty window displays. The driver never spoke; he hummed along instead to whatever weird music was playing on his radio.

I got out of the taxi outside a terraced house on a dingy street. A handful of people stood on the dreary lawn smoking cigarettes in the drizzle, a light with a red filter shone bleakly in the small front room, dance music spilled out of the open front door.

I made my way along the path and entered the house, ignored by the smokers. A tall, pale woman sat on the stairs talking quietly into a mobile phone, not even bothering to compete with the music. She looked up at me, smiled. She wore a stainless steel dental brace on her front teeth. I raised a hand and continued along a narrow hallway into what I suspected was the kitchen. Here were cans and bottles on every available surface. A tubby man was bending over to open the fridge. He took out a can of lager, turned, smiled, and walked through another door into the room with the red light.

"Hi." I turned to see the tall woman from the stairs as she entered the room. She was wearing a long, flowing hippy-style dress and no shoes. Her feet were magnificently long, the toes slender and elegant. She had long red hair and light eyes. Her skin was so pale that it was almost white.

"Hi," I said again, grasping a bottle, any bottle, from the table. "I'm a friend of Mick's."

She looked at me with a quizzical expression, tilting her head to one side and pursing her lips. She looked achingly cute, but I knew that was the alcohol speaking to me.

"Mick who?"

I searched my brain for Mick's surname, but it wouldn't come. "Erm... shit, I forget. I work with him, at Gleason's"

She shook her head, the expression now one of mild amusement. The light caught her braces, glinting off the burnished steel wire when she opened her mouth.

"Bishop. Mick Bishop. That's his name." I drank vodka straight from the bottle, grimaced at the taste. When I looked at the bottle in my hand I didn't recognise the brand.

"Thirsty? Here, take this." Her thin hand took a small shot glass from a nearby shelf. She walked over, towering above me, and handed me the glass. She really was the tallest women I had ever met. In that weird moment, when our hands touched, I thought she was beautiful.

"Thanks." I poured the no-name vodka onto the glass, my hands shaking. I drank two shots before I was able to even look her in the eye.

"I don't know anyone called Mick Bishop." She was still standing before me, right up inside my personal space. I didn't want her to move away.

"Oh. Fuck. Have I come to the wrong party?"

"No," she said, smiling, touching my hand again. "There's no such thing as the wrong party."

As was becoming my habit lately, I didn't know what to say, how to respond. So I took another drink. What was going on here? It seemed that suddenly, in the depths of my desperation, I had become irresistible to women. No, not every woman: just a certain type, someone equally as damaged as me. I glanced at this girl's bloodless lips, the ugly braces, the tattoos on her calves, the faint, white and almost unnoticeable – unless you were look-ing for them – scars on her wrists and forearms. "What's your name?"

"Names don't really matter. They aren't important. What matters is how we connect, how we *communicate*." She moved closer, our hips touching through the thin material of her dress. Her hand – so thin, so elegant – came up and she brushed her piano-players' fingers against my stubbled cheek.

"Yeah," I said.. "I suppose so."

The nameless woman rubbed her lower body against me; her sheer height alone felt like a sexual threat. "Do you know the best way to communicate?" Her face seemed suddenly huge, monstrous as it lowered towards me, snatching away my view of the ceiling.

I stepped back, shocked and appalled by my reaction to this attempted seduction, lost in a moment over which I had no con-trol. "I think I should be going now. My friend – he'll be expect-ing me." I ducked under her outstretched arms and made for the door, still carrying the vodka bottle. It was almost full; no way was I going to leave it behind.

At the end of the hallway, clustered around the front door,

was a group of people. They were deep in conversation, animated almost to the point of aggression. Two men stood face to face; their mouths were twisted into snarls. A few women stood at the perimeter of this ensemble, trying to calm things down. I fled up the stairs, looking for the bathroom.

She stood at the top of the stairs, watching me. She had been watching me for some time – perhaps ever since I'd entered the house. The patterned wallpaper was ugly and out of date, the carpet was filthy, dead flowers littered the windowsill behind her, their dried-out leaves spilling onto the floor.

"Diane?"

It was the kind of coincidence that only ever happened in stories or films, and for a brief moment I was taken out of myself and saw my entire existence as the plot of a book, with some obsessive writer tapping away at the keyboard to create every scene that made up the sordid little story of my life. It was a strange moment, surreal in its intensity; I shifted sideways out of myself, turned and looked at the jaded man who stood before a woman at the top of a long, dark flight of stairs, lost in the weird fiction of his life.

"What are you doing here?" She took a step forward, coming out of the shadows, her eyes wide and bright. "I never expected to see you again." She held out one of her broad hands, the fingers splaying open, drawing me in. The snake tattoo wriggled under her chin.

"I don't know. I was supposed to be somewhere else, in another place. It's like a cosmic communication breakdown: everything I'm told has another, entirely different meaning."

"Come here." Her eyes held a sadness that was beyond my ability to fathom; its depths swam with strange things, otherworldly thoughts and images.

I went to her, my arms at my sides, my face thrust forward. She leaned in and kissed me, her lips dry, sticking to my teeth as I opened my mouth to accept her tasteless tongue. We moved towards a closed door at the far end of the landing, our movements driven by a force bigger than us both,

"They tell me no one ever uses this room. It's been locked for years. Somebody once died in there – a previous tenant. It's supposed to be haunted. I got the key from a girl downstairs, a tall, pale girl who talks in riddles. She has metal teeth, like a cage for her words."

Diane opened the door. It swung inwards, pushing back a mass of dusty darkness; a million silent screams were caught up in that web of airborne particles, desperate to be unleashed upon the world. Diane gently pushed me inside, sticking close, her breasts pressed against my back, her arms straying around my waist from behind to fumble at my crotch.

She closed the door, trapping us there, in the dead dust and the heavy air and the atmosphere of neglect.

The bed was dusty, too, a fine layer covering the bed sheets. She pulled back the sheets and slipped between them, pushing her skirt down over her hips. She undressed lying on her back, shrugging of her clothes as if they were a second, unwanted skin. I watched her, entranced, taken in by the smooth curve of a thigh, the musky promise of the damp thatch between her short, wide legs.

I followed her down, still fully clothed. She fumbled with the zip on my jeans, loosening my belt, wrapping her sturdy legs around me and tugging down my pants with her agile feet. I was already hard; I had been hard forever, ready for her since our last barely remembered meeting.

"Don't speak." She whispered directly into my ear. Her breath was warm and wet. The words were maggots crawling, burrowing their way inside my skull. "Say nothing. Just fuck."

At first our rhythm was off and I kept slipping out of her, but she quickly guided me back inside. After several minutes something clicked and we moved together, our bodies singing the same debauched tune. I grasped her hard buttocks, raking the flesh; she held the sides of my head, pulling the hair above my ears so hard that it hurt. Our desperation created something that held a rude beauty, a nasty poetry that only we could hear. The silence in the room thickened; even our breathing was quiet, as if heard from behind a barrier.

It lasted forever and was over in minutes. I rolled off her, strangely elated. Her leg rested against my thigh; one of her hands held onto my dwindling prick, unwilling to let go of the heat radiating from my core.

Several figures stood in the grubby darkness, gathered around the bed and staring down at us. I couldn't be sure if the image was real or just a continuation of the same set of visions I'd been experiencing for days. The figures' outlines were blurred, almost bleeding into the blackness that still filled the room like a thickening fluid.

Each of the figures was locked into a familiar silent scream. Huge black toothless maws that seemed to breathe in the night, or perhaps exhale it like a vapour. They were unmoving, like shop window mannequins. I strained to discern individual features, but it was too dark and my eyes were watering from exertion. Just as I began to think that they were indeed real, the figures were gone. They did not fade, nor did they *pop* out of existence like cartoon phantoms.

They simply became a part of the darkness, as if returning to their natural state.

Diane got up and padded naked across the room. She looked in the mirror that hung on the wall near a closet. I could see no reflection in the glass; the mirror was dark, like a window into another world. She combed her hair with her wide, clumsy fingers, and then patted it down, flattening it where it stuck out in bunches from the sides of her head.

"Diane?"

She did not respond. There was something strange – something awful and almost obscene – about her movements. I could not pin the sensation down, but it felt wrong to observe her in this way, a little like watching someone die.

"Diane."

Slowly, smoothly, as if on casters, she turned to face me. Her hands were held fisted at each side of her face. Her mouth was wide, a perfect black circle. She stood there, nailed to the spot, as I struggled out of bed and pulled up my pants, and fastened my trousers. When I glanced back at the bed, Diane lay sleeping where I'd left her; I looked again at the spot next to the wall-mounted mirror, and the silently screaming effigy had not moved.

I don't know how I found my way downstairs, but the next time I was able to think clearly I was stumbling along an ill-lit street, following the white line in the middle of the road. There was a bottle in my hand. It was almost full. When it was empty, I'd find an all-night store and restock. There was always somewhere open; always someone willing to sell you a bottle of slow suicide.

I drank, demanding that the spirit inside the bottle erase the memory of this night.

6

The news of Polly's death reached me early the following day. Once again I'd pre-empted a hangover by drinking my breakfast. I resisted the urge to try whisky on my cornflakes and opted instead to forget about the cereal and head straight for the bottle. I didn't even bother washing a glass; the feel of the bottleneck against my lips was becoming something of a comfort.

I answered the phone, and before I could even speak Polly's mother launched into an angry tirade:

"Are you happy now, you bastard?" I'd never heard her swear before, and it startled me. "You've done it. You've finally killed her." Choking sobs, a muted cry that she was struggling to control.

"Debra... what is it? What's happened?" My mind churned; it felt like someone had upended a blender in my brain and switched it on at full blast.

"She's dead. Haven't you heard? A hit and run late last night. She was on her way back from trying to see you."

I thought it was a joke, a stupid fucking set-up. Mick getting back at me for not attending his girlfriend's party, or someone I didn't know choosing me as some kind of random victim for a terrible prank.

"Debra..."

"She went to see you at your place. To sort things out, to get things settled before she moved. You weren't in – probably out getting drunk or stoned, or fucking some whore. So she turned around and set off back home." Again, her use of profanity almost floored me. "She was hit by a car when she crossed the road. Still had her car keys and her mobile phone in her hand when they found her, lying in the gutter with her bones broken and her skull smashed!"

I couldn't grasp this, not any of it. Everything was moving too fast; the wheels were falling off whatever crazy fairground ride I'd stepped onto without knowing.

"Debra..."

"Is that all you can say? Is there nothing else? You sad, selfish little prick. I wish I could kill you. I wish I could stab you in that cold, black heart and watch you die!"

The phone went dead.

Polly was dead?

It couldn't be true.

"Fuck you," I screamed. "Why have you done this?" I railed at the imaginary author of my life, the stupid little god of my stupid little tale. Was he smiling, pleased with the scene he had just created? Did my pain please him? Was he, even now, thinking about where it might be published?

Unable to communicate even with myself, I grabbed the whisky bottle and began to drink. I didn't stop until I'd forgotten my own name, until I'd pissed myself and shit myself and murdered myself inside my head a thousand times.

~φ~

It was dark. Night. The front of my shirt was covered in vomit. My trousers were dirty, the knees torn and bloodied. My hands were bloody, the knuckles scraped; my face ached, bruises forming around my eyes. I suspected that my nose was broken.

I had no memory of anything after the phone call from Polly's mother. There was just a huge blank, dead space: a period of rage and insanity from which I'd only just emerged. I was amazed that I was even alive; my body hurt so much that I assumed I'd been in a fight – or several fights.

Nothing mattered. It was all just so much nonsense.

I looked around me, unsure where I was. The landscape was urban, ruin tearing at its edges. Empty buildings loomed over me, their jagged sightless windows not even registering my presence. I looked at my watch, but my wrist was bare. I was not wearing any shoes.

A man sat on a concrete windowsill halfway up a tall derelict building. He hung onto the narrow ledge with his feet, like a bird, yet remained still as a statue. A weird urban gargoyle, he was showing me the by now familiar silent scream. One hand rested against the outside of the window mullion; the other was clenched tightly in his lap.

"What do you want from me?" As expected, there came no reply. He just sat there, that terrible black mouth open, a fleshy tunnel leading down into a night far darker than any I had lived through.

I never saw them anywhere that was busy, just these places – quiet places, lonely places: a motorway embankment late at night, the window of an unpopulated tower block, the far end of an empty alley. These ghosts, these beings, they skulked in all the forgotten corners, the unthought-of crevices, the unloved parts of our environment where dreams never touched and humanity simply passed between the gaps.

I had a notion that they were the ghosts of the living; sad spectres of those unable to communicate their pain, appearing in these lonely and loveless spots to scream silently into the dark, left behind to lament their own unheard grief.

It made a grim sort of sense that people like me needed an outlet for all the things that were never said, all the emotions not vocalised, every single tender moment held inside instead of being offered, like a gift, to the one who needed it most. I imagined my own stoic ghost standing in a darkened room, clinging to the side of a derelict building, or perhaps crouching in some forgotten corner of a closed-down factory floor.

But the realisation had come too late; the damage was already done. I remembered Polly's apparition, how it had appeared to me in that late night alleyway, like a premonition of her death. Is that what they were, ghosts of the future? Images of the dead manifesting even before these people died, like a faulty piece of film briefly jumping forward a scene before returning again to the correct timeline?

In that case, had I effectively been warned of Polly's death before it actually happened? And in my selfish cloud of uncommunicative pain, had I then ignored that warning? I tried to recall my feelings when I'd first seen her in the alley – how I'd felt, what I'd thought. I came up blank; my memory refused to play the game.

Before I could pursue this line of thought any further, she stepped out of a shadowy doorway, moving without moving, simply looming forward in the gloom.

It was Polly, and her mouth was a circular black patch obscuring the bottom half of her face. The flesh around the ugly cavity was puckered and creased, as if twisted out of true. The lips were thin, stretched out of shape, and there were no gums, no teeth... just that unnatural coal-gleaming blackness at the core of the inverted funnel of her mouth.

She stood like a statue, a work of art, and all I could do was go to her.

The doorway at her back, the one she'd appeared from, showed a short, dark hallway with a series of uneven steps at the end which led down to some hidden lower level. A presence that was either vast or composed of several smaller elements receded along the hallway, shifting at speed as it flowed down the canted steps.

As I approached Polly her features remained unclear. The closer I got, the more I appreciated that I was in the presence of an unworldly being. Was she actually some strange angel, a manifestation of God's anger at his children? But no, I didn't believe in God. Heaven was a place in childhood picture books; there was only hell, and that hell was located deep within the human heart.

Yet still I stood before her like a worshipper beholding all that he has ever placed his belief in. Her face was blurred, as if covered by a thin sheet of gauze. That awful eel-like mouth didn't even twitch.

Then, surprisingly, she moved her arm, raising it slowly, the motion almost mechanical. I imagined clockwork cogs and motors working to provide the impetus behind this unnatural automation. She was like an exhibit in a museum, a pristine example of some ancient form of engineering dedicated to mimicking the human form.

The arm stopped moving when it reached waist level. I stared down at her fist, awed by the faint illumination given off by her white skin. The tips of her fingers were smooth and round; she had no fingernails.

The fist slowly opened, fingers arcing upwards like the petals of a mysterious and exotic plant. One by one they opened to reveal her smooth palm, unlined and beautiful, like the skin of a baby's belly. I held my breath as her hand straightened out, becoming flat.

Curled in a loose spiral on her palm, like a sleeping snake, was a clump of meat, torn and ragged at one end. There was blood, but it looked black in the dim light. I reached out and picked up the tongue, holding it up to my face. I glanced at her mouth – peering into the depths of it, able to see right into the silent darkness that dwelled at her core, and had always been there, clotted and compressed: a total absence of communication.

Disgusted, I dropped the tongue, watching it unfurl as it fell though the air and landed at my feet, lost in the rubble and the brick dust and the shredded paper that covered the path. When I looked up again, Polly was diminishing along the dark hallway, already taking the stairs. Her body dropped slowly, floating downward through the musty air rather than physically descending the stone steps.

I followed. What else could I do?

Moving along the hallway, I headed for the top of those stairs. It was quiet in there: the silence was like a sheet, a soft, vast covering spread over the interior. I thought of furniture covered by dust sheets in an empty house, of deep snow drifts settling in a thick blanket over cars and post boxes, and of white sheets draped over the resting dead.

The stairs led down into a series of concrete chambers, passages that led off into other rooms, most of them unoccupied but some containing the suggestion of figures bunched together in small unmoving formations. There were other things moving in the darkness, shifting in packs through the gloom. They could have been animals, but from what little of them that I could see they didn't resemble any species of creature I had ever studied at school.

I followed my unresponsive guide through the darkness. There were no lights down here, but the walls themselves emitted a sleazy luminescence, like a bright fungal decay. It was like being deep underwater: all sound was smothered, my ears rang with the pressure of being down so deep, travelling so far.

Square concrete planters filled with dry, sandy soil were arranged against the walls along the narrow passageways, each one containing a strange grey plant whose leaves resembled human tongues. I saw a hand nailed to a wall beside a bricked-up opening, its fingers pulled so far apart that the skin between was torn. Elsewhere there was a primitive wooden frame festooned with severed heads shorn of their hair – like a bizarre hat rack. Their eyelids were held open with pins; each dead face possessed a cold, endless stare.

These sights didn't disturb or disgust me; they interested me in the same way that a startling art exhibit might draw me into its orbit. This was humanity reduced to gaudy decoration. Whatever landlords oversaw this place, and wherever they were from, they admired the form but failed to recognise the spirit that was held within.

Carefully skinned faces had been stretched over delicate wire frameworks; disembodied feet stood patiently in mismatched pairs outside closed doors; bulky, bloodless torsos were scattered on the floors of dim rooms like abstract throw-cushions.

I felt like I'd wandered into the middle of some grand experiment; this entire place had the controlled atmosphere of a laboratory, where students of some bleak science toiled in darkness to perfect an obscure series of clinical tests.

We came to a frameless doorway. Polly (could I still even call her by that name?) stepped inside, eaten up by the hungry dark. I paused at the threshold, realising that this was the last time I would ever have a choice, any kind of choice, about anything...

I stepped into the room, feeling darkness close over me like the sea.

A group of figures stood in the middle of the room, positioned well away from the clammy walls where other, less recognisable shapes clung like oversized limpets on the sides of great flat rocks. The figures were grouped in a loose circle and blocking my view of whatever lay at their centre.

I walked towards the group, feeling nothing – all my senses were dulled, as if someone had surgically removed my nervous system and sent me back out into the world with no way of experiencing it as a human being. I was a robot, an empty shell. Nothing could touch me.

Beyond the figures was a rectangle of black: a sealed doorway. A broken electric sign hung above the lintel, its cover broken and rubber-insulated wires dangling like exposed veins:

No Exit.

I gritted my teeth, still only capable of feeling a vague echo of emotion, as if I were not really there but watching events unfold through a secret two-way mirror.

Then, slowly, the group parted, sliding away to reveal what they had been clustered around. Something dropped from the ceiling to my left, hanging down in thick syrupy loops to pool in a corner and take on another shape. There was the suggestion of long, thin limbs, crystalline eyes and multiple gaping mouths.

The individual the group had been gathered around was small, dressed in a pair of dark jeans and a warm winter coat. His hair had been neatly combed – I remember that more than anything. It is always the small things, the tiny, barely negligible details, which cause the most pain.

"Danny?" I dropped heavily to my knees on the filthy floor.

He didn't move. His thin arms hung limply at his sides, the hands clenched into tiny fists, the knuckles whitening from the strength of his grip. His mouth formed a perfect letter "O", but it was black as coal, and glistened with the bleak, pearlescent glimmer of fossil fuel.

"Little Man..."

I wept for all the words I'd never spoken, all the opportunities for genuine connection that I'd wasted; I mourned those moments now passed, the ignored days and forgotten nights. Rain on stones; a river running to a forgotten sea.

I cried for us all – for Polly, Danny and me – and I promised myself that I would see my son one last time, and tell him that I loved him before he was taken away for good, and before my own useless mouth formed a circular black hole and my tongue became an offering, a limp token of my inability to say all the things I should have said but never did, never could, and now never would....

"*My son...*"

Kneeling there in that small, cramped room, I thought of all the words that had become ghosts in all the wasted years of my dismal, wasted life.

Then, lowering my heavy head and closing my tired, tired eyes, I finally accepted the fact that I had nothing more to say.

~φ~

My Name is Natasha Putkin

My name is Natasha Putkin. I must remember that. Names are what define us. They tell us who we are and where we are from. Sometimes they even tell us what must be done. I am twenty-one years old and was born in a small farming town in Siberia. All that seems like a lifetime ago – like it happened to another person, someone who looked like me and felt like me but was not me. If I remember my name I can just about hold onto the link between me and that girl. It is dark and warm in here. I never get cold, not like I used to back home. It is always warm here, in this place. Warm. And safe. He came into the room earlier, walking around with big loud, staggering steps and snuffling in the corners, probably looking for something. I think he was drunk. He sat on the bed and started to sing – an old ballad about fishermen lost at sea. The mattress springs whined above me like a broken guitar. The tune went on for a long time. I think I nodded off for a while – the sound of his snoring was horrible, a long drawn-out snorting – and when I regained my senses he was leaving. He did not disturb me, not this time. Perhaps he thinks I have not been punished enough, and he will leave me in here until I have learned my lesson. He is fat and ugly, smelly like an old farm animal. He has a wife. Her name is Hilda. I think she likes me – at least she puts up with my presence in her house, letting me take care of things around the place. And him, of course – she is more than happy to let me take care of him, cleaning up after him and tending to his demands. It means that she does not have to suffer his attentions, his hot, wet mouth and the things he whispers in your ear when he is on top of you, squirming and squealing like a bleeding hog…

I am not sure how long I have been in the box this time. Sometimes he lets me out after a few hours, sometimes I am locked inside for days. The longest time – after I last asked to use the telephone to ring my parents – he left me in here for over a week. I had no food, no water. I was weak and only half conscious when he finally let me out, and when he did Hilda nursed me back to health. When I was back on my feet again the telephone had been taken out. Sometimes, when I am cleaning the house, I stare out of the windows at the aching blue sky and the quivering trees. I am afraid of so much space; miles and miles of unfamiliar streets and homes, all waiting beyond the thin sheet of glass. If I reach out, touch the glass, I can almost feel the chaos out there shivering through my fingertips like the vibrations through a stereo speaker. They have no children, and whenever I ask Hilda if she ever wanted to start a family her eyes go flat and dull, like old pennies at the bottom of a well. She is much older than him and I suspect that she is well past the age of breeding. Her skin is wrinkled, like my mother's, and her small hands shake all the time that she is sober – which is not often. He brings her drink every day, the bottles wrapped in rustling brown paper. I used to live and work on the family farm. We raised pigs for slaughter. I killed my first pig when I was ten years old. I had no brothers, so was expected to work like a boy. At first I did not like the blood, but soon realised that it was essential, a necessary thing so that we might survive.

A memory: White snow; cold air; the squealing of the piglets. I stand in the barn, shivering in the early morning chill. My father says: "I know it is not easy, baba, but it is something that must be done." I watch him as he hangs the two big hogs and draws a thin sharp blade across one of the exposed pink throats. Then it is my turn. I drift away, attaining an inner focus to allow me to kill the second pig. I do not see my hand holding the knife, or the animal's dirty death throes. I am somewhere else: deep inside myself. A place I'd rather be. Pigs are not human. It is easy to watch a pig die.

I am thirsty. My lips are dry, the skin is cracked. I flex my hands at my sides to keep the circulation going, but they feel light and clumsy, as if they do not really belong to me. I stretch my muscles, opening my legs until my knees meet the wood on either side. I raise my arms so that my elbows rest on the floor, and press my fists into the wooden lid. It is so dark that I cannot see. I know there are air holes, but they let in no light. He allows me a cushion for my head, but there are no blankets – the heat builds up at night, and with blankets I might suffocate. He does not want me to die. He only wants me to be sorry for what I did. It was wrong of me to ask if I might go for a walk, just to the end of the street and back, like last time. He will allow it again only when he thinks I deserve it, and as long as I do not ask. I must work hard for my privileges, just like I did back on the farm. If I listen hard I can hear the sound of traffic on the road into town. It is a busy route and the house is almost on top of it. No one has noticed that I am here, even on those occasions when he lets me of the house to stretch my legs in the garden. It is a small garden, yet Hilda keeps it nice. There are roses and other pretty flowers, and a high wall shielding us from the road. I could scale that wall if I wanted - he does not watch me when I am out there, he trusts me to come back inside when he calls. I always come back inside. Out there is too much that I do not know, but in here I know every inch, every shadow. Once I walked right up to the wall, stared at the rough stones and the dark mortar squeezed into the gaps. I imagined myself putting one hand over the other and climbing the wall, then dropping down on the other side. But the traffic sounds were too loud - almost defeating. They invaded my ears and filled my head, and I was gripped by a terror that was both larger than me and yet smaller than my narrow box under the single bed. If I did choose to climb the wall and run into the road to wave down a passing car or truck, I know that he would kill my family. I know this because he has told me, many times. He knows where they live, what they look like, and claims to know a man in my home town who, if called upon, will slit my mother and father's throats like the pigs we slaughtered. I have to believe him when he tells me this. I have no choice. I have been here in this house for seven years, since I was fifteen, when he took me off the street and forced me into the back of his car after paying my parents a lot of money (or so he says). I know no other way of life. The time I had before has been erased, like chalk marks on a stone wall. I do, however, have my doubts about what he tells me. He claims to know many people in many countries who are just like him – but this house is old and falling apart. The furniture is moth-eaten, the windows are dirty. There is no money. He never goes far, not even to work. He is idle and slovenly, preferring to let his wife work while he sits in his chair and scratches his crotch, eating, always eating, like a fat pig. I wish I had the courage to question him, but I have lived under these conditions for so long that any-thing else seems too large and frightening. If I did leave him, where would I go? Who would I run to? According to him, the neighbours would bring me back. He says they all have their own little Natasha's, trapped like me in wooden boxes beneath similar beds in identical gloomy bedrooms.

A memory: The low-ceilinged rooms of my mother and father's house. The smell of old blood in the large kitchen. Pots and pans. My mother's wide forearms. My father's smile – a rare sight, but one that often sustains me. Pork sizzling on the grill, its fatty odour overpowering.

My body tenses whenever I hear footsteps in the hall. Sometimes the door opens and someone takes a few cautious steps inside, then pauses, as if listening for the sound of my breathing. I suspect it is Hilda, checking that I have not suffocated. If I die, she will have to resume her role as his partner, and I know that would be the worst thing in the world as far as she is concerned. With me alive, she is left alone – I keep him distracted so that she can sit and get drunk in another room.

I hear her crying at night. I am not sure why she weeps, but the sound is dreadful, filled with a loss and regret that

I cannot even begin to understand... I think I might have fallen asleep again, just for a moment or two. Or perhaps I retreated inside myself, to the place he cannot touch. When I open my eyes he is out there, on the other side of the box. He has probably lifted the edge of the divan to access the box – there is a door in the side where I roll in and out. I can sense his fingers tracing the pattern of the grain. If I concentrate I can hear him breathing. It is a horrible sound, like ancient, faulty bellows trying to make a draft.

I fear that it might be time to come out.

I hear the clasps open and wait for the side of the box to swing down, letting in the light. I am blinded for a few seconds, and unable to move. My limbs have seized up. My jaw is locked tight.

I feel his chunky hands upon me as he guides me out of the box, clutching at my belly and breasts. I can smell whisky on his breath. The sound of his hoggish moaning and grunting is loud in my ears. The light is too much, I still cannot see beyond its sharp barrier. The wooden flap claws at my back as he drags me out and lifts me onto the bed, pawing at me with his blunt fingers. Then, unexpectedly, he steps away, still grunting, and leaves me on my back on the hard mattress. I wish I could see because I am sure that he is weeping. His footsteps retreat, much lighter than they should be, different from how they usually sound. The door closes but he does not lock it. I stare at the door for a long time, wondering if it will open again. Timber creaks as he leans against the other side of the door. I hear a voice, low and strained, but it does not belong to him. It is a woman's voice, but empty, like a machine, and the noises it makes are nowhere near words. I am frightened and confused. Why has Hilda let me out of the box? This has never happened before – she is not even allowed inside this room. I lie still for a while, waiting for my eyesight to adjust. Slowly, gradually, the light returns my vision. I see the familiar bare room, the splintered boards and grubby curtains. I rub my face with a steady hand, turning so that I am supported on one elbow.

On the unpainted cabinet that stands by the side of the bed, there rests a gun. I stare at the gun, wondering if this is a trick, a test. The sound of traffic outside becomes louder, clearer, and for a moment I am overcome by tastes and smells that I have never experienced before. Tears soak my cheeks but I do not know why I am crying. I swing my legs off the bed, sit facing the door, and pick up the gun. It is heavy. The metal is still warm. It smells of freedom, and that scares me more than anything else I can imagine. Because he had no sons, my father taught me to shoot and hunt at an early age. This gun is nothing like the ancient Russian hunting rifle I am used to, but I think I can work out how to use it. My finger curls under the trigger guard. I am smiling. It feels unnatural. I will need to learn how to smile all over again. There is no sound now beyond the closed door. I stand, holding the gun. Then I open the door, slowly, expecting him to run at me and force me to the floor, laughing. Dusty light spills across the threshold, bathing my feet and the bottom of my shins. I can now hear Hilda crying in another room. The television is on, an American game show. Traffic passes by outside, whispering a strange message in my ear. As I step out into the hall, I catch sight of him through the living room doorframe. All I see is his thick pink arm resting on the side of a chair as he snoozes in front of the game show. The faded blue tattoos. Crumbs. The horrible little black hairs – like the thick, spiny hairs on a pig's back.

It is easy to watch a pig die.

After what feels like forever I take a small step forward, then a bigger one. The floorboards do not make a sound. I feel like I am floating. I have been here for seven years and the promise of freedom is the most terrifying thing I can imagine. What will I do? Where will I go? Who else will ever love me? There are so many things to consider, a buzzing swarm of thoughts threatens to overwhelm me. But I must not forget who I am, where I am from, or what has been done to me. I must never forget.

A memory: My father says: "I know it is not easy, baba, but it is something that must be done."

My name is Natasha Putkin. I must remember that. Names are what define us. They tell us who we are and where we are from. Sometimes they even tell us what must be done.

~φ~

S. G. Browne

S. G. Browne grew up in Northern California and graduated from the University of the Pacific before moving to Hollywood, where he worked for several years doing post-production for the Disney Studios. Eventually, he moved to Santa Cruz to wait tables and write books.

He is the author of *Breathers* and *Fated*, both dark comedies and social satires with a supernatural or fantastic slant. *Breathers*, his debut novel, was a Bram Stoker Award finalist that has also been optioned for film by Fox Searchlight Pictures. His third novel, *Lucky Bastard*, is slated for release in 2012.

He currently lives in San Francisco.

You can visit him online at www.sgbrowne.com.

Dream Girls

I never expected to be lounging in a hammock in my back yard, drinking a cold Corona while my ex-wife power washed the house in a black Spandex mesh underwired teddy with matching thong underwear. Then again, I never expected to have sex with six different women in one day.

Every time I have sex with another woman, I wonder if it's real, if I'm just dreaming the life of the ancient gods of Olympus, attended by my own versions of Athena and Hera and Aphrodite. Then my disbelief explodes in an orgasm as real as the existence of extraterrestrial intelligence and the conspiracy to assassinate John F. Kennedy.

I am forty-five years old and having the best sex of my life.

I finish my beer and reach out to set it down, but before the empty bottle can touch the flagstone, it's plucked out of my hand and replaced with a new, cold Corona with a lime. When I glance up, my ex-wife is walking away with my empty beer bottle, the thong displaying her miraculous ass.

Even with the technology that makes it possible for her to look so good, it's amazing that after eight years of marriage and another seven since the divorce, my ex-wife looks exactly the way I remember her when she was twenty-seven.

I, on the other hand, look every bit like my four and a half decades. According to the averages, I've got another sixty years to go before I vacate my body and it gets carted off to the composting home, which is really more of a factory than a home. But semantics are a big thing when you're trying to make everyone feel more comfortable about death, even when seven in ten people live to see one hundred.

Of course, if I didn't smoke half-a-pack a day and go through a case of beer every week, I'd be looking at a good chance of becoming a centenarian. Fortunately, the third of my vices isn't likely to shorten my life. At least not directly.

Hell, anything in excess can lead to complications, but we're talking about sexual obsession here, not drug addiction. And it's not like I'm breaking any laws.

Still, that doesn't prevent the American Fundamentalists and other religious groups from making a big fuss in Washington. I don't know what they expect the government to do. It's not like the President or Congress plan on installing sex monitors in everyone's bedrooms. Orwell got a number of things right, but telescreens and the Thought Police weren't some of them – not to mention the year. Hell, he missed that by nearly a century.

Sex is another thing Orwell got wrong about the future. In Orwell's *1984*, intercourse was an afterthought at best – a secret, pleasureless act that seemed to have no place in society other than for procreation. But as we approach the cusp of the twenty-second century, sex is in the spotlight, celebrated and commercialized, packaged for no other reason than pleasure. And the pinnacle of that pleasure, the height of hedonism, arrived with the introduction of Dream Girls.

Now I'll be the first to admit that the political and social uproar surrounding Dream Girls isn't without merit. After all, it's not often a consumer product brings up issues of slavery, prostitution, invasion of privacy, and first amendment rights, but I've always been in favor of letting the people choose their poison. Society is bound to collapse sooner or later, whether internally or from an asteroid like the one that brought the dinosaur's party to a premature end, so why stop everyone from having some fun while they're here?

You ask me, people take life too damn seriously. They need to spend less time worrying about what's right and wrong and more time relaxing and drinking a nice, cold beer.

I take several long pulls from my Corona while my ex-wife power washes sun-baked bird shit off the siding above the dining room window, leaving white discolorations. I realize too late I should have grabbed some paint at the hardware store, but I figure I can pick it up tomorrow morning and have Debbie touch up the siding after she finishes re-staining the deck.

If I could afford it I'd get another pair of hands to help her, but I don't earn enough money to become a triad. Unless you take home at least six figures a year, you're best bet to have a threesome is to troll the nearest college campus.

I finish off most of the second Corona and close my eyes, rocking softly in the hammock, lulled by the white noise from the power washer, my thoughts drifting into dream sequences from my college years. When I open my eyes, my ex-wife is gone, the power washer silent. At first I'm annoyed. Then Ashley Allen, the hot little blonde who lived across from me my junior year in college, appears with another Corona, wearing nothing but a smile and looking just as good as she did twenty-four years ago.

She hands me my beer, then climbs into the hammock with me and unzips my shorts without a word. I lean back and the Corona slips out of my hand, the bottle shattering on the flagstone in an explosion of foam.

You ask any warm-blooded, heterosexual male to name one sexual fantasy, and he's apt to reply that he'd like to have sex with two women at the same time – preferably attractive ones with nice bodies and no inhibitions. Maybe throw in a giant Twister mat and a couple of gallons of baby oil. You ask that same warm-blooded male if he'd like to have sex with a different woman every night for the rest of his life with no commitments, no complications, and no consequences, and he's likely to ask where he can sign up.

In spite of society's attempts to alter or influence our behavior, heterosexual men are genetically wired to have sex with as many women as possible. Spread our seed. Ensure the propagation of our DNA. We're like those rhesus monkeys in that experiment where they put a male monkey in a cage with a female monkey and then let them go at it until the male monkey rolls over and starts snoring. Then they take out the female monkey and replace her with another female. She taps the male on the shoulder, he perks up and says "Hey, you're new," and they go at it until he once more grows bored with her company. Then she gets replaced.

It goes on like this for hours, a revolving door of female monkeys.

Switch. Fuck. Repeat.

It's a regular primate porno.

Human men aren't much different. Given the opportunity and a free pass from any unwanted emotional entanglements, we'd have sex with as many women as possible. Marriage is an unnatural hindrance to our intended purpose.

So we cheat.

We watch on-line porn.

We masturbate to fantasies of other women.

Monogamy doesn't stand a chance when it's up against millions of years of genetic code.

But with the rigorous morals of American society chained to its Puritan heritage, we've had to unload buckets of cash and act like gentlemen just to get a piece of ass. Either that or we've had to risk the specter of AIDS in the back room of some dingy hotel with an overused prostitute.

Dream Girls changed all that.

For what men used to have to spend on an engagement ring for a lifetime of commitment to one woman, we can now make a down payment on a lifetime of sex with every woman we ever wanted to sleep with, make love to, hump, fuck, bang, nail, or screw.

No commitments. No complications. No consequences.

The technology is pretty simple – a combination of human and alien DNA with a high speed internal processor that makes the Pentium XXXII seem like the computer equivalent of a snail. The human DNA provides the form, appearance, and feel of a woman, while the internal central processing unit gives the body sentience. The alien DNA is responsible for the rapid growth during the cloning process, allowing the Dream Girl to be manufactured in as little as four weeks. The alien DNA is also what allows the Dream Girl to morph into any woman the man desires her to be.

A porn star. A supermodel. Your ex-wife.

All it takes is a physical or mental image and the Dream Girl's CPU can convert the image into reality. Masturbation and fantasizing have become as outdated as analog. The fantasy is real and attainable, only a thought away.

I look up and watch Ashley, her naked twenty-year-old body so firm and smooth that I can barely maintain my stamina. It doesn't help that she's going at me with the unbridled enthusiasm of a young woman.

Initially, the CPU didn't have a regulator to prevent the Dream Girl from morphing into teenagers or adolescent girls, leading to charges of child pornography, but those problems have been ironed out – though in some states you can still have sex with a seventeen-year-old with her consent, which isn't much of a problem considering you own her.

I haven't had sex with anyone under eighteen yet. And I never had sex with Ashley either during or after college, but she's as hungry and insatiable as I imagined she would be. And with a body less than half my age, I can't imagine anything better than getting fucked in a hammock by a twenty year old blonde. But occasionally during sex, my mind wanders to potential possibilities, so by the time she comes, Ashley has morphed into the nineteen-year-old brunette who works behind the counter at the local Starbucks.

In the six months I've owned my Dream Girl, I've had sex with one-hundred-and-twenty-seven different women. Sometimes they're women I've found in electronic issues of *Playboy*, *Penthouse*, and other soft core porn magazines. Other times they're women I see on the street or at the local pub or in the market squeezing vegetables. My personal favorite is the eighteen-year-old sister of a girl I dated after college.

Like any other technology that transforms society, the Dream Girl has led to numerous legislation and lawsuits ranging from state pornography statutes to civil rights. The ACLU has fought a class-action case, so far unsuccessfully, claiming invasion of privacy on several counts – including unlawful impersonation of an individual and having sex with a clone of a woman without the woman's consent.

Personally, I think the lawsuit is pretty specious. After all, men have been invading women's privacy for centuries with their imaginations – undressing them with their minds, visualizing them naked with their legs spread or on their hands and knees, fucking a fantasy. Dream Girls just takes the fantasy one step further.

In addition to the legal battles, there have been countless philosophical debates. Are Dream Girls human? Do they have rights? Can they vote? Is the technology moral? Is it legalized prostitution? Is it legalized slavery? The list goes on and on.

If you ask me, the answer to the first question is a resounding no. They're not human. They weren't created from a human sperm and egg, and instead of a brain they have a highly advanced computer. They weren't technically born, therefore, they don't have a soul. They're a commercial product, nothing more, and I don't recall a commercial product ever having any rights. As for the last two arguments, hell, if you want to get technical, marriage is legalized prostitution. And I've known my fair share of men and women who've felt trapped by their marriage, enslaved by the responsibilities of being a spouse or a parent.

Not surprisingly, Dream Girls has taken the brunt of the blame for the steady decline in marriages and rapid increase in divorces. A lot of people, mostly conservatives, think society is on the path to corruption and destruction and they want the government to intervene for the sake of the country. But asking the government to outlaw Dream Girls is like asking Henry Frankenstein to kill his monster.

Contrary to what the general public was led to believe for the latter half of the twentieth century and the beginning of this one, Marilyn Monroe was the prototype of what would eventually become the Dream Girl. Norma Jean Mortenson may have been born in Los Angeles, CA, in June of 1926, but the technology that allowed John F. Kennedy to have his alleged affair with Marilyn Monroe was born in a lab in Area 51 in the early 1950's, several years after the Roswell incident.

I won't go into how long it took the feds to develop the technology and how many failures they encountered along the way, but by the time Kennedy took office in 1961, they had a prototype ready to test. I don't think they intended to test it in such a high profile place as the Oval Office, but apparently they didn't have much of a choice. Kennedy managed to learn of the new toy the government had created and wanted to try it out.

For a while, everything went smoothly. Kennedy was able to have his public affair with Marilyn, then bang the clone in the Oval Office. The problem was, the Marilyn clone had too much free will and became a liability. It didn't help that the real Marilyn stumbled upon her doppelganger after JFK's birthday in May of 1962, so both Marilyns had to be terminated. JFK wasn't happy about it and threatened to go public.

The rest, as they say, is history.

Like I said, although Orwell was off the mark more often than not, he got a few things right. Even back in the middle of the twentieth century, Big Brother was alive and well.

Once I'm finished with her, the cute little Starbucks barista climbs out of the hammock and saunters away toward the house, her ass shifting back and forth hypnotically. Sometimes I feel like I've been hypnotized, suggestively guided by the brain between my legs, compelled to act without any freedom of choice. But when you're at the mercy of a legal and glorious addiction, one that provides immense physical pleasure and exceeds any sexual fantasy you've ever imagined, it's kind of hard to find the motivation to quit.

No commitments. No complications. No consequences.

And heterosexual men aren't the only ones who've benefitted from this revolutionary technology that promises to fulfill all of our sexual fantasies. Less than a year after Dream Girls hit the market, a masculine equivalent was launched for women called Dream Boys. While initial response was positive and customers flocked to the stores, Dream Boys never really gained the same popularity as their female counterparts.

The problem lies in the fact that men are much more aroused by visual sexual stimulation, while women get turned on more by verbal cues and loving gestures. There's a reason why there are dozens of pornographic magazines geared for men while there's less than a handful available for women. And why women read so many romance novels.

That's the biggest reason for the relative failure of Dream Boys: women want more of an emotional connection with their lover. That turns them on more than a great ass or a sculpted chest or six-pack abs. And while Dream Boys are good at nodding and listening and providing multiple orgasms, they're about as emotionally engaging as a vibrator.

So for most women, it just became an expensive sex doll. Another toy to use when they were lonely. However, Dream Boys have maintained their popularity with gay men and Catholic priests. After all, whether you're gay, straight, or Catholic, if you're a man and there's a naked body in the vicinity to your liking, chances are you're sporting wood.

Just ask JFK, who was both straight and Catholic.

A few years after the Marilyn fiasco, the government tried again with Jayne Mansfield, but that didn't work out any better, so they scrapped the project and put it on hold until a northern California biotech company called Synergystix bought the technology from the government in the middle of the twenty-first century. Synergystix had to tinker with the technology for nearly a decade before they produced a salable product, but once human cloning got past the initial government hurdles, Dream Girls was good to go.

Understandably, Dream Girls have had their share of problems, not the least of which included men who used their Dream Girls to impersonate an ex-wife or a mother-in-law in order to perpetrate a crime or play an elaborate practical joke. It also wasn't uncommon to see men walking around arm in arm with celebrities or somebody else's wife, which obviously led to some problems.

A few years ago, a guy I worked with met me at a bar with his newly acquired Dream Girl, which had morphed into the twenty-five-year-old wife of another co-worker. I couldn't tell the difference and neither could anyone else. You can imagine what happened when the wife's husband showed up.

The dilemma was solved by packaging the Dream Girl with a base unit that has to be plugged into a power source, limiting the Dream Girl's range – kind of like the old cordless phones. If the Dream Girl travels more than a hundred feet or so from the base unit, she'll return to the bald, breastless creature found in the display container at Brookstone or Sharper Image. Of course, if the power goes out, the same transformation occurs, which could pose a problem if you're having sex at the time. To account for this, the base unit comes with a battery back-up of thirty minutes, which is more than enough time to finish taking care of business. Especially when you consider that the average male achieves orgasm in three to five minutes.

At some point, all of the hype and hysteria and legal and political hand-wringing will come to an end and everyone will just get on with their lives – some of us better than others. I'll be the first to admit that the technology still has a few kinks that need to be worked out, but all in all, I think the future of heterosexual relationships is Dream Girls.

In addition to the obvious benefits of having a partner who not only doesn't mind that you have sex with other women but willingly fulfills those fantasies for you, there are numerous reasons why Dream Girls are superior to human women.

They don't have to be romanced. They don't want a commitment or a two-karat diamond ring. They don't talk about their problems. They don't argue. They don't complain about how much you drink or how much you smoke or how much time you spend with your friends. They don't expect you to stop reading the sports page when they're talking. They don't care if you come first. They don't get pregnant. They don't have menstrual cycles or mood swings. They don't contract venereal diseases or AIDS. They don't age. They don't get sick.

And they don't die.

I discovered this last unexpected benefit when the 169th Miss America was out back cleaning the second story gutters of my home in a French-cut lace bikini. I didn't see what happened and there weren't any neighbors around to witness the accident, but apparently the extension ladder shifted or she somehow lost her balance and fell, impaling herself on a decorative wrought iron fence post in the back yard. By the time I reached her, she'd stopped breathing and had lost a good deal of blood.

Angry and disappointed, thinking only of the extended warranty I'd declined to purchase, I lifted my Dream Girl off the post and laid her on the grass. As I stood grieving over the loss of my most prized possession, the wound below her breasts began to heal, closing up and fading away in less than a few minutes. When Miss America opened her eyes and smiled up at me, stretching out on the lawn like a cat that had just awakened from an afternoon nap, I realized her alien DNA had additional benefits besides the morphing feature.

Upon further inspection, I couldn't detect any sign of the wound or any indication of long-term damage. Had she sustained a serious head injury, I have no doubt that her CPU would have been damaged beyond repair, rendering her technically dead. But barring a blow to her head, I wondered if she could survive other accidents.

I wondered if she had more than nine lives.

A few days later, while I was having sex with an ex-girlfriend who dumped me for a woman, I smothered her with a pillow. She fought against me at first, her arms and legs thrashing, but soon her struggles tapered off and she stopped moving. Five minutes after I removed the pillow, she was in the kitchen making me a grilled cheese sandwich.

Since then, I've killed my Dream Girl thirty-seven times and in nearly as many fashions – she's been beaten, whipped, stabbed, hung, strangled, burned, bled, eviscerated, and even dismembered. The limbs take nearly an hour to grow back but she's always as good as new. My method of choice, however, is using a pillow to suffocate her while we're having sex. It's less messy and more intimate.

When I was ten years old and on the cusp of puberty, I discovered masturbation and thought it was the best thing in the world. I also thought I'd truly discovered it and wondered if anyone else knew about the joys of sexual self-gratification. This is like that, only it goes beyond the intensity of raging hormones. It's more primal, a thirst or hunger I didn't know existed but which I can't seem to satisfy. I spend more time killing my Dream Girl now than having sex with her.

I climb out of the hammock and follow the Starbucks girl into my house, where I find her in the kitchen, bending over into the open refrigerator to grab another Corona. She turns to look at me, her nipples hard, her eyes inviting, but I have other plans.

After she uncaps the Corona and inserts a lime, I ask her to get me a hand saw and a six-foot length of nylon cord. She hands me the bottle with a smile, then walks away, morphing back into my ex-wife on her way to the tool shed.

I've been reading in the papers about an increase in violent crimes against women and I wonder if other Dream Girl owners have discovered the Holy Grail of carnal pleasure. I don't know why they would want to risk killing real women, though. After all, since Dream Girls aren't human, I can kill as many women as I want and not have to worry about getting arrested or having my soul burn in hell. It's the perfect situation.

No commitments. No complications. No consequences.

~φ~

Lower Slaughter

"Oooh, look Frank," Sandy said, pointing out the window of the bus toward the stone cottage nestled at the base of a rolling green hill. "Isn't that charming?"

"Hmmm. Very charming," Frank said, though he would have preferred the view beneath a blue sky rather than the gray clouds that had been threatening rain most of the day.

Why they couldn't have taken their vacation someplace warmer escaped him. Maui would have been nice. Even Mazatlan would have been preferable to the gray, drizzly, cold English weather. Take away the roundabouts and the endless charming stone cottages and they might as well have stayed in Seattle.

"I'd like to live in a house like that," Sandy said, looking back at the cottage like a kid trying to catch one last glimpse of Disneyland. "I'd like to move here when we retire and live in a house like that."

Frank grunted. He had no desire to move to England, to retire in the Cotswolds and spend the rest of his life in some charming little country village with a name like Stow-On-The-Wold or Moreton-In-Marsh or any place with a name that had to be hyphenated. After less than three days touring the Cotswolds, Frank was already catching a case of boredom. Small English country towns were like cheap beer – once you've been through five or six, you can't tell the difference anymore.

As the bus entered the outskirts of Bourton-On-The-Water – the quintessential Cotswold village with stone houses, friendly people, and a duck-filled stream that meandered through the center of town – the clouds finally made good on their threat.

"Oh look, Frank," Sandy said, as if the raindrops were coins of gold. "It's started to rain."

Frank glanced around at the dozen or so other passengers on the bus, most of who appeared to be locals on their way back home, not stupid tourists who couldn't see a late spring rain coming. He wished they could have spent their last day relaxing at the B&B in Cheltenham, but Sandy had wanted to take one more adventure before they left England. She made a habit of running last minute errands, barely catching airplane flights, and generally pushing her luck right up to the last second. Somehow she always managed to beat the clock, but Frank knew, sooner or later, she'd run herself right out of time.

The rain began to run down the windows as the bus pulled into town and stopped across from a combination pharmacy and gift shop. The doors of the bus opened and several people stood up to get off.

Sandy nudged Frank. "Let's get out and walk around."

"In this?" Frank asked.

"Oh come on," Sandy said. "It'll be fun."

Frank had dozens of definitions of what he considered *fun* and this wasn't one of them.

"We didn't bring an umbrella," Frank said.

"We'll buy one."

Frank glanced at his watch. "It's after two already. The ride back is a good forty-five minutes, and we still have to pack and eat dinner."

"We'll eat here," Sandy said. "And we can pack tonight after we get back."

Frank looked into his bag of excuses and found it nearly empty, save for some standard, practical rebuttals that had ceased to work years ago.

"Come on," Sandy said. "I don't want to spend our last few hours of light sitting in our room just because of a little rain."

The remaining passengers on the bus all seemed to be waiting for Frank to respond. Even the bus driver watched from the rearview mirror, one hand resting on the door's control lever.

"All right," he said, standing up and throwing his hands in the air. If he'd had a white flag, he would have waved it.

Sandy grabbed Frank's head in both hands, kissing him on the lips. "Thank you," she said, before walking past him toward the front of the bus.

Frank followed her, pausing when he reached the door. Through a cascade of rain, Sandy stood beneath an awning in front of a store that sold scarves and sweaters and other apparel. Frank wondered if they sold umbrellas and rain slickers, maybe even a leash for his wife.

Frank turned to the driver. "When's the last bus leave for Cheltenham?"

"The last bus departs promptly at 5:23pm," the driver said. "Don't be a minute late or you'll miss her."

Frank checked his watch again. "We'll be early," he said.

"That's good thinking," the driver said as Frank stepped off the bus into the rain. "Time has a habit of slipping away out here. And the nights fall faster than you'd think."

Frank turned to ask the driver what he meant, but the doors closed and the bus pulled away, roaring off down the street before disappearing around a curve.

"Frank! Frank, look!"

Frank turned to find his wife pointing up to the sky, where the gray clouds had parted, revealing a large expanse of blue. The rain had stopped.

Sandy turned to Frank, her smile radiant with the enthusiasm of a twelve-year-old girl. "It's clearing up."

Frank watched the large patch of blue spread out across the sky directly above them, pushing the gray out to the edges of town. One minute the rain was falling in buckets and the next minute, God punched a blue hole in the clouds. The only thing more unpredictable than English weather was his American wife.

"Come on, Mr. Worry Wart," Sandy said, guiding him down the street past the shops. "Let's go exploring."

~φ~

For the rest of the afternoon Sandy towed Frank around the village – patronizing every shop, checking the menus at every café, taking every path and alley past every home and garden until they'd seemingly covered Bourton-On-The-Water three times over. The rain had not returned, and with the sun shining and his wife running out of nooks and crannies to explore, Frank was beginning to think he might finally get a chance to park his butt at a table and enjoy a leisurely pint of ale when Sandy found one last unexplored path.

"Look Frank," she said.

A dirt path leading away from the sidewalk cut through a field of yellow heather. At the head of the path stood a wooden sign:

Lower Slaughter 1

Frank pulled out the *Frommer's* England travel guide and flipped through it, looking for a description of Lower Slaughter, but he couldn't find the name listed among the other Cotswold villages.

"It's not in the book," Frank said.

Sandy walked past the sign and started up the path.

"Where are you going?" Frank asked.

"To Lower Slaughter," she said, stopping and looking back. "It's only a mile. We'll be there in twenty minutes."

Frank closed the travel guide and checked his watch. 3:47. A little over an hour-and-a-half until the last bus left. "I think we ought to stick around," he said. "I don't want to miss the bus."

"We won't miss the bus, Mr. Stick-in-the-Mud," Sandy said, hands on her hips. "This is our last day in England and I don't want to miss a thing. Now come on."

He stood next to the sign, watching in distress as his wife turned and marched down the path, then glanced once more at his watch. Twenty minutes there, twenty minutes back, no more than ten minutes for Sandy to explore whatever existed of Lower Slaughter, which couldn't be much to look at if it wasn't listed in the *Frommer's*. Frank just hoped it had a pub.

After letting out a sigh heavy with reluctance, Frank stuffed the travel guide into his jacket pocket and started down the path after his wife.

The path was narrow, no more than three feet wide, and on either side the heather waved back and forth, the yellow, bell-shaped flowers brushing against Frank's jacket. One of the stems snagged his sleeve, tearing loose from the earth. Frank pulled the stem off and tossed it away, wiping his hand against his pants as nectar secreted from the flowers on to his skin. For several seconds his hand felt numb, then the feeling passed.

Frank stared at his hand, checking for a rash or some sort of reaction, but other than a slight tingling there appeared to be no lasting effects. He glanced out across the field of heather, swaying back and forth in the breeze, and thought about the tentacles of a sea anemone waving in the ocean current, waiting for an unsuspecting fish to wander into its bright, inviting, deadly grasp.

He let out a nervous little laugh, one he didn't care for at all, then shook his head and chided himself for letting his imagination get the better of him. He laughed again, more relaxed this time, and continued along the path, making a point to stay clear of the heather as he hurried to catch up with his wife.

The heather soon gave way to a field of tall grass bordered on one side by a small stream that appeared out of nowhere and curved past the grass before it cut through a grove of birch trees. In late May the birches should have been laden with fresh, green foliage. Instead, they had the stark, ghostly appearance of winter. Even the air seemed to have grown colder. Frank shoved his hands into his pockets and grumbled about the erratic English weather.

"Isn't this beautiful?" Sandy asked.

Haunted is more like it, Frank thought.

As if to confirm this, the late afternoon sun vanished behind a wall of gray clouds, casting the landscape in a cold, colorless prelude to dusk.

Up ahead, on the other side of the stream, Frank noticed several strange plants standing over three feet tall and growing on thick, thorny stalks that looked like medieval weapons. Along each stalk grew a dozen or more dual-lobed leaves, the edges of which were lined with sharp spines, while the insides of the leaves were colored a dark crimson. The plants looked like the Venus Flytrap he'd had as a kid, though Frank had never seen any in the wild and he'd never seen any this size. He used to feed his plant flies, tadpoles, and small pieces of ground beef. The plants near the stream looked big enough to consume a small animal.

"Frank," Sandy cried out ahead of him. "What is that?"

When Frank caught up to her he saw a large animal lying motionless in the weeds near the stream. At first glance it appeared to be a mountain lion, but he'd never heard of mountain lions roaming the English country.

As he stepped closer, Frank noticed that although the animal had a powerful body and sharp claws, it had a head that resembled a possum and a long, leathery tail that looked like it belonged to a rat. Whatever it was, it was dead.

"I don't know what it is," Frank said.

From what he could see, the animal appeared to have been partially devoured, probably by scavengers. Or maybe it had been brought down by a larger animal, though Frank couldn't imagine what kind of predator would feed on an animal as powerful as this.

"Come on," Frank said, steering Sandy away from the carcass. "Let's go."

"Maybe we should head back," Sandy said, glancing once at the dead animal, her childish enthusiasm flagging.

Frank should have agreed with her, told her that was the best idea she'd had all day, and led the way back to drink a pint or two before catching the bus. Instead, he offered his wife encouragement because he knew that's what she wanted.

"Lower Slaughter can't be much further," he said. "Why don't we keep going. Once we get there, if you still feel the same way, we'll turn around."

"Okay," Sandy said.

She remained subdued until they reached Lower Slaughter, which turned out to be only a few hundred yards further up the stream. No sooner had they caught their first glimpse of the town when Sandy's gloom slipped away and she transformed into a kid walking through the gates of Willy Wonka's Chocolate Factory, oohing and aahing, pointing at the cobblestone alleys and the small stone cottages and the ducks swimming through the stream. Lower Slaughter was like a smaller, thrift store version of Bourton-On-The-Water – barely more than a city block from end to end and worn out from years of neglect. Frank didn't see any shops or cafes or anything that resembled a pub. And except for an old man pushing a wooden, single-wheeled cart piled with what appeared to be burlap sacks filled with grain or potatoes, there didn't seem to be anyone else around.

"It's so peaceful," Sandy said. "I could spend hours just enjoying the tranquility."

"Yeah, well, we don't have hours," Frank said, regretting that he hadn't turned back when his wife had suggested it. "The bus leaves at 5:23 and I want to get back..."

Frank stared at his watch. Instead of twenty minutes, it had taken them thirty-seven minutes to get here. Even with a brief stop or two along the way, Frank didn't see how it could have taken them more than half-an-hour to walk one mile.

The old man with the wooden cart turned down an alley, losing his balance and dumping the cart on its side, spilling several of the burlap sacks on to the cobblestones. He uttered no complaints and showed no signs of frustration, but silently righted the cart and lifted the sacks back on board. Frank watched the old man absently, trying to figure out where the time had gone, realizing that if they spent more than fifteen minutes here and it took them another thirty-seven minutes to get back, they'd barely have time to catch the bus. He knew Sandy would fight him to stay longer and that he'd probably have to drag her out of here, and he was preparing to do just that, when one of the burlap sacks that had fallen from the cart twitched, as if something inside was trying to get out.

"Frank, look!"

Frank jumped, his heart pounding as he turned to find Sandy standing near a foot bridge that crossed the stream, pointing to the other side at a two-story stone house with a stairway leading past a garden to the front door.

"Isn't it beautiful?" she said as she walked toward the foot bridge, lost in her own little world.

When Frank looked back toward the alley, the old man with the wooden cart was gone.

What was in those sacks?

He decided he didn't want to know. He just wanted to get his wife and get the hell out of here.

"Come on, Frank," Sandy said, already halfway across the foot bridge.

"Where do you think you're going?" Frank asked.

"I want to see if anyone's home."

"We don't have time," Frank said. "We have to leave."

"Oh don't be such a wet blanket." Sandy reached the other side of the stream and stood in front of the house. "It's our last day in England. Let's have some fun."

"Damn it Sandy! We're going to miss the bus!"

"Oh pooh," she said, waving a hand at him before she turned and headed up the stairs.

Frank yelled after her in exasperation, then marched to the foot bridge and started across. In front of him the house sat cold and silent, the stones old and weathered, the windows dark and lifeless. Large pieces of the flagstone stairway had broken off, creating a treacherous path that cut through a weed-filled garden, then disappeared beneath an arbor that was a twisted nest of dead wisteria. Beyond the arbor the grounds existed in deep pools of shadows, while the oak trees behind the house looked like mangled hands. Above the house, the sky was the color of funeral ash.

To Frank's left, the stream continued past a small, grassy pasture, where three goats stood watching him, as if waiting for something to happen. Frank shivered, reminded of a story he'd heard as a child – one about three billy goats and a troll that lived beneath a bridge. In the story, every time the goats tried to cross the bridge to reach the fresh meadow on the other side, the troll would jump out and cry: *Who's that trip-trapping on my bridge?*

Something splashed loudly in the water below him and Frank let out a shout of alarm, racing to the other side of the bridge and turning around, heart pounding, half-expecting a troll to come crawling out from beneath the bridge's shadow. Instead, he saw two ducks flapping their wings and settling back to the surface of the stream.

Frank took a deep breath and turned toward the house, a chill settling into his spine as he walked past the weeds and shadows and crumbling stones.

"Sandy," he called out from the bottom of the steps. "Sandy, come on. We need to get going. It's almost..."

Behind Frank came a loud splashing, accompanied by frantic quacking that escalated and then suddenly stopped. When Frank turned around, the two ducks were gone. All that remained were a few feathers floating on the rippling water.

Frank backed away up the stairs, watching the stream, looking for the ducks, trying to convince himself they'd just flown off. Then he saw several air bubbles rise to the surface of the water.

Part of the flagstone fell away beneath him and he slipped, falling to one knee and nearly tumbling down the stairs to the edge of the stream. He stared at the water, at the bubbles and the feathers floating away, and felt himself slipping, losing his grip, sliding toward the end of an old, frayed rope. Before the rope unraveled, Frank scrambled to his feet and dashed up the stairs beneath the dead, twisting wisteria, stopping when he reached the shadows of the open front door.

"Sandy." Frank's voice came out in a choked whisper. A faint, gray light emanated from beyond the door. He glanced back toward the stream, then took several steps forward. "Sandy?"

Beyond the front stoop, just inside the open door, Frank spied a small, dark shape attached to what appeared to be a dead snake. Only when he reached the edge of the stoop did he realize that the dead snake was the broken strap of Sandy's blue Italian leather purse.

From somewhere deep inside the house, Frank heard a loud, heavy *thump* followed by soft, high-pitched laughter that turned into a series of hungry, slurping sounds. Something scraped along the floor down the front hallway. A black, shapeless shadow slowly approached, growing larger, spreading across the walls. With it came a stench of decay, like wet garbage that's been sitting for too long.

Frank backed away from the front door, watching the shadow grow larger, impossibly large, too big for whatever threw the shadow to fit through the door. The shadow spilled out on to the stoop. Behind it, a pair of yellow eyes appeared in the gloom. Frank turned and ran, down the crumbling flagstone he went, slipping and falling, scraping his hands and banging his shin.

When he reached the bottom of the steps, he raced along the cobblestone path with shadows stretching toward him from the house, reaching out as if trying to grab him and pull him back.

He slipped and fell, crying out in a choked gasp, then scrambled to his feet and started over the foot bridge. Something splashed in the stream below. Frank heard a grunt, followed by a deep, wet, belching chuckle. A pair of hairy, clawed hands grabbed on to the side of the foot bridge. One of them reached out toward him as a low, guttural voice called out:

"Who's that trip-trapping on my bridge?"

Frank screamed as the claws hooked on to one of his trouser legs and sliced across his calf. For an instant he was being dragged toward the edge of the bridge, then the fabirc tore loose and he was running, screaming his throat raw, fleeing down the deserted street and out of town – the asphalt turning to earth and the stone houses giving way to hunched, haunted willows and tall grass that whispered.

Night fell like a shroud.

Frank's knee cracked against stone and he tumbled through the air, landing with a grunt in a patch of weeds. He scrambled to his feet, then fell back to the ground with a cry and grabbed his knee. Clenching his teeth he rolled on to his hands and stood up, putting the weight on his other leg, and looked around.

The clouds had gone and the moon had risen, casting a pale, colorless light across the landscape, turning everything into ghostly shades of black and white. Ahead of him stood the grove of birch trees, bare and skeletal, packed together like spectral guards, the stream an ebony snake winding through them. Behind him sat the two-foot high stone wall he'd run into, hidden by the tall grass. The wall extended out in a U-shape marking a property boundary, though Frank didn't see any sign of a house or a barn or a stable. No help. No sanctuary.

Frank ran a shaky hand across his face and looked back the way he'd come. He shouldn't have run off and left Sandy like that. He had to go back and find her. But when he thought about the shape coming out of the house and the high-pitched laughter and the hands reaching over the side of the footbridge, the shaking in his hand spread to the rest of him. He couldn't go back. Not alone. There was something in the house. Something under the bridge. Something twitching in those burlap bags. He needed help. Someone back in town could help him. Or maybe someone along the way. He didn't recall seeing any homes on the walk from Bourton-On-The-Water, but there had to be someone who could help him, who could find Sandy. Someone had to find her.

Frank leaned back, grabbing his hair with both hands and sliding along the wall to the ground, his fear and guilt coming out in a sudden burst of tears and sobs. He didn't hear the approaching creature until it jumped over the wall less than five feet away.

Frank pressed himself against the wall, throwing his hands up to protect himself, then lowered them enough to glimpse the creature as it scampered away across the stream and into the grass on the other side. Even in the pale moonlight he recognized the large, muscular body of the animal he and Sandy had discovered earlier. Dead the creature had looked docile, in spite of the claws and the snout lined with teeth. But watching one run in the moonlight with its long, rat-like tail snapping back and forth, Frank thought it looked like Satan's familiar.

Behind him, on the other side of the wall, Frank heard something else approaching. He crouched down, expecting another of the creatures to leap over the wall. Instead, a black, sinewy shape passed overhead in a rush of whispers and icy air. Frank saw its wings flap once before it vanished beyond the stream and into the night. Seconds later an animal shrieked, the screams of a cat or a pig being attacked. Then the cries abruptly cut off.

Frank stood up and hobbled away from the wall, gasping and crying, his knee throbbing as he stumbled along the stream, past the birch trees and the tall, bleached grass, vaguely aware he was whimpering. All around him he heard animals crying out, things scurrying about in the grass, gurgling in the stream. And soft, sucking sounds. More than once he thought he heard the whisper of wings flapping behind him. Then the stream and the trees were gone and Frank found himself staggering along the path through the field of yellow heather. In the moonlight the field seemed to glow, as if the flowers were luminescent, and even without a breath of wind, the heather waved back and forth in the still night air.

More than a dozen stems snagged against Frank's jacket, tearing loose from the earth and sticking to his sleeves. Frank shoved his hands into his pockets until he made it through the field, then unzipped his jacket and shed it like an unwanted skin, leaving it on the ground as he stumbled away from the path into Bourton-On-The-Water.

"Help," he shouted, his voice cracked and dry. "Help! Somebody please help me!"

But as he fled past the stone buildings and into the town square, Frank noticed that the street was made of earth not asphalt. And instead of the stream running through the center of town, an old stone well sat in the middle of the square.

Frank turned around in a circle, staring at the dark buildings that surrounded him, his breath coming out ragged and shrill, tears running down his face as his reason unraveled. Behind him, Frank heard a wet, sloshing sound. He spun around and stared at the well as the noises grew louder, echoing off the dark, silent buildings.

Frank backed away from the well as a tentacle appeared, then another and another, until half a dozen tentacles were crawling out of the well toward him. His knee buckled and he fell to the ground. The tentacles slithered toward him. One of them touched his ankle. Frank cried out and rolled away, struggling to his feet and hobbling to the nearest stone building, shoving open the heavy oak door, then slamming it closed and retreating into a far corner of the room.

He huddled there for several minutes, shaking and sobbing, waiting for the tentacles to push open the door or break through the single, small window that sat high up to the right of the door. But all that came through the window was filtered moonlight, illuminating half of the room in a pale, thin glow. A mixture of stale urine and sweat permeated the air. Except for a pile of rags and old blankets that looked like a makeshift bed, the room appeared empty.

Next to the bed, Frank saw a dead animal twisted up in a white, waxy looking cord, but when he looked closer, he saw the animal was a ragged teddy bear with its eyes torn out. He picked up the bear and tried to disentangle the cord, but it wouldn't come loose and stuck to his hand as though coated with glue. Frank pulled at the cord, trying to free his hand, his eyes following the cord away from the teddy bear, into the shadows, up the wall to the ceiling, where it connected to a series of criss-crossed cords that looked like some kind of netting.

Something stirred in the darkness beyond the room. Frank heard a soft clicking an instant before a figure scrabbled out of the darkness along the ceiling, its spindly legs reaching toward him as it descended from the web.

Frank's screams echoed off the stone walls. Outside, a dark shadow passed over the town square, then flew off into the night.

~φ~

When Frank and Sandy Wheeler missed their flight the following day out of Heathrow and weren't heard from for nearly two weeks, their three adult children filed a missing person's report. Two of the children flew out to England to search for their parents, tracing them from London to York, then finally to a bed and breakfast in Cheltenham. From there they visited all the surrounding towns, including Stow-On-The-Wold, Moreton-In-Marsh, and Bourton-On-The-Water. They never found any trace of their parents. Nor did they find a path that led through a field of yellow heather or a sign directing them to Lower Slaughter, which is actually a charming, quiet village nestled in the heart of England's Cotswolds, just a mile's walk or so from Bourton-On-The-Water.

Year in and year out, busloads of tourists visit the Cotswolds, venturing down paths both wide and narrow, some marked on maps and some not. Other than a few minor accidents ranging from trespassing to twisted ankles, most leave the same way they came in. But occasionally, someone wanders off down an unknown path and discovers too late that time has a habit of slipping away. And in England, where the weather can change unexpectedly and doors swing open into dark places, the nights fall faster than you'd think.

~φ~

The Lord of Words

Grant stared at the white, taunting emptiness of the computer monitor – palms resting on the edge of the keyboard, fingers hovering over the keys, words and sentences arriving stillborn or with a fading pulse.

He shifted his gaze from the screen to the night pressing against the window and the lights glowing in the house across the street. The windows looked like eyes watching him, reminding him that he was no longer anonymous, that with the price of success came even greater expectations.

Grant tapped his fingers against the desk, his gaze shifting back and forth from his monitor to the window. Finally, he stood up and reached over to close the blinds. Across the street, Grant saw a man wearing an overcoat and a hat standing between a pair of birch trees. Then he blinked and the figure dissolved into the shadows. Grant pressed his face closer to the window, holding one hand above his eyes to cut out the glare from the desk lamp, but whatever he thought he'd seen was gone.

Grant closed the blinds, then sat down and stared at his monitor. Frustrated, he turned around in his chair as he leaned back and stared at the wall. A bookshelf sat beneath a movie poster from the original *Invasion of the Body Snatchers*, where the images of Kevin McCarthy and Dana Wynter ran for their lives from more than a dozen faceless figures. Above the poster, six feet of vacant white wall stretched to the top of the vaulted ceiling. Grant stared at the wall, thinking how it looked like the blank screen of his computer monitor, and wondered why he'd never hung anything else on the wall.

"What are you doing?"

Grant turned to find his wife, Debbie, looking at him from just outside the doorway.

He stared at her, his eyes blank. "What?"

"What are you doing?" she asked again, as though she'd caught him picking his nose or visiting an Internet porn site.

"Nothing," he said. "I'm just staring at the wall."

"Well stop it," she said. "Crazy people stare at walls. I don't want anyone to think you're crazy."

She studied him a moment longer, then turned around and walked into the bedroom.

Grant glanced back at the wall before returning to his computer, where he spent the next two hours staring at the vacant screen.

~φ~

The following day, Grant sat at his keyboard, typing out fragments of thoughts he deleted as soon as they appeared. For hours he floundered, trying to recapture the feeling of his first two novels when the words had come in a flood. But now it was as if a hand had reached inside his head and shut off a valve.

Grant stood up and paced about the room, pulling books from his shelves and flipping through the pages, searching for the source of the sentences and paragraphs, the wellspring of words. Failing in his pursuit, he sat back down and stared at the monitor, then spun around in his chair and looked at the *Invasion of the Body Snatchers* poster. Shifting his gaze to the expanse of wall above it, Grant tried to focus, taking deep breaths while he stared at the wall, growing aware of the texture, the patterns in the plaster, the shadows that collected in the corners. The longer he stared, the more relaxed he grew. His heart slowed. His breath grew shallow and soft. His arms and legs felt weightless – buoys floating on a lake beneath a blue summer sky.

Inside Grant something opened, like an iris letting in more light, until he almost sensed something beyond the wall, beyond all that whiteness, an understanding just out of reach. He closed his eyes and felt his mind begin to drift.

A car alarm went off outside.

Startled out of his daze, Grant studied the wall, trying to recapture what he'd felt, but it was just a wall. Just sheetrock and plaster and paint. Grant shook his head and let out a bark of laughter, then turned back to his computer, prepared for another afternoon of frustration. Instead, his fingers found the keyboard and began typing, tentative at first, then with more confidence as thoughts and words came in a steady trickle.

Had he bothered to glance out the window, Grant would have seen a pair of shadowed figures in overcoats standing up the street in the shade of an oak tree.

~φ~

"So how's the book coming?" Debbie asked, picking at the half-eaten lasagna on her plate.

"Good," Grant said, which wasn't exactly a lie. For the first time in weeks, he felt like a writer again.

Debbie washed down a bite of her pasta with some wine and cleared her throat. "Have you given any thought to what we talked about last week?"

"Last week?" Grant said.

"Diapers? Little league? Saving for college?" Debbie said. "Ring a bell?"

Early in their marriage, Grant had made it clear he wanted a writing career before he took on the responsibility of raising a family. Now that he'd tasted some measure of success, he didn't want to sacrifice his writing to change diapers or help with homework or shuttle the kids to soccer practice.

"Do we have to talk about this now?" Grant asked.

"If not now, when?" Debbie asked. "Every time I bring this up, you find some way to avoid it."

"I'm not avoiding anything," Grant said. "I just don't want to rush into anything."

"Rush?" Debbie said, letting out a clipped, humorless laugh. "It's been seven years. Define rush."

Sometimes he really hated the fact that he'd married a teacher.

"I don't have the energy to get into this now," Grant said.

"Fine." Debbie stood up and took her plate into the kitchen. "You go sit in front of your computer and do what you have to do, then come talk to me when you decide you have the energy."

~φ~

Two hours later, Grant sat at his computer, the door to his room shut and the last word he'd written earlier that afternoon sitting marooned on the screen, waiting for a subsequent word or expression or thought to give it balance, to carry him forward into the next paragraph:

vacant

But the words had dried up again.

Damn her, he thought. *God damn her.*

Debbie had never understood his need to write. She read his first drafts and celebrated with him when he finished his book and when he found an agent and when both of his novels were published, but she always seemed to regard it as something he would grow out of once he found a real job. She never validated the hours he spent crafting words into pages, creating something immortal, a piece of his soul removed for public viewing.

More than once Grant wondered if his wife secretly wanted him to fail. With her renewed insistence to raise a family, those thoughts returned.

Grant stared at his monitor, at the last word he'd written more than four hours ago

vacant

and tried to remember where the thought had been leading him. But the only place his thoughts seemed to lead was a dead end.

Frustration as familiar as his own heartbeat pounded in Grant's temples. He pushed away from the desk, his chair rolling back, and spun around until he faced away from the computer, from that marooned word floating in the middle of the screen. He stared at the wall, at the vacant white space above the movie poster, then turned around and looked at his computer.

vacant

Turning back to the wall, Grant stood up and walked over to the movie poster. He lifted the poster off the hook and set it aside before returning to his chair, where he sat and stared at the wall. At first he felt nothing. But within minutes the sensation from earlier that afternoon returned, filling Grant with the sense that he'd opened a portal, stood at the edge of an awareness, an understanding just beyond his grasp.

Outside, a car alarm wailed in the distance.

Grant ignored the distraction and continued to stare at the wall. He could almost hear a low hum of indecipherable words that he might understand if only the words could get through.

Abandoning his chair, Grant knelt on the floor in front of the bookshelf and removed the books, then moved the bookshelf out of the way, leaving no obstruction, only the wall stretching eighteen feet above him. He sat on the floor and stared at the wall, at the nothingness, at the two-hundred-and-sixteen square feet of white, vacant space, listening to the steady hum that penetrated his mind, not knowing what he was hearing but believing it was real. He closed his eyes and opened his mind.

A police siren blared past outside, breaking the connection. Grant opened his eyes and stared at the wall, trying to recapture what he'd experienced, but whatever he'd heard and felt was gone.

Sensing that some important discovery had eluded him, he returned to his chair, certain he would sit impotent at his computer for the rest of the night, unable to concentrate. But when he reached for his keyboard, the words gushed out.

Several hours later, when Grant finally went to sleep, fifteen new pages sat on his desk, the best fifteen pages he'd ever written.

~φ~

Over the next week, Grant spent every possible waking moment at his computer. With growing frequency he would sit in front of the wall and close his eyes, listening to the steady hum, trying to decipher its message. Then he would return to his computer and his fingers would type out words and phrases and ideas he barely recalled conceiving. It was as if he'd found a connection to the Creator of Thoughts, to the Lord of Words.

From the other three walls in his room he removed a framed copy of his first book cover, several photographs of he and Debbie, and a Salvador Dali print. His bookcases and filing cabinet and anything that wouldn't fit in his closet were shoved into the hallway, leaving only his desk, his chair, and his computer, with a single lamp to work by into the early morning hours. That's when he did his best writing, when the world outside his room grew silent and the walls hummed.

"What are you doing to your room?" Debbie asked as if accusing him of hiding something.

"It's too cluttered," Grant said.

"It wasn't too cluttered before."

Grant answered her with a shrug.

The next morning, Grant found his smaller bookcase and floor lamp returned to his room, along with several framed photographs hanging on the walls. He removed the pictures and the other unwanted items, then took them and everything else he'd banished from his room downstairs and into the garage. Upon returning to his room, Grant discovered that his manuscript had been disturbed – several of the pages read and replaced. After a quick breakfast, he drove to the hardware store and bought a keyed entry lock doorknob for his room.

Every day, Grant felt an awareness growing inside him, a comprehension of reality he'd never grasped, a reality he'd never known existed. But each time he sensed he was close to making that final connection, something distracted him. Car alarms went off at all hours. Sirens screamed past in the middle of the night. The phone would ring and when he answered, all Grant heard was a dial tone.

With growing frequency, Grant caught glimpses of figures in overcoats and hats standing in the shadows across the street or on his front lawn, watching him. But when he took a second glance or went outside to investigate, all Grant found were shadows.

In spite of their enigmatic existence, and to an extent because of it, Grant believed the figures were responsible for the alarms and the sirens and the phone calls. He didn't know where they came from, but he decided they were some kind of regulators – cosmic gatekeepers sent to prevent him from finding the key that would unlock the secrets behind the walls.

He didn't tell Debbie any of this. She wouldn't understand, even if she believed him. Besides, she was as much a source of distraction as the regulators. The more he thought about it, the more Grant began to think his wife was one of them.

"How come you put a lock on your door?" she asked one night at dinner.

Grant took a bite of his pork chop and mashed potatoes and stared at his plate. "Why does anyone put a lock on a door?"

He moved his pork chop to one side, and then spread his mashed potatoes out across his plate until they resembled a stucco wall.

"What's going on, Grant?" she said. "Why are you doing this?"

"Doing what?" he said, still staring at his plate.

"This," Debbie said. "Being distant, uncommunicative, blocking me out of what's going on in your life."

"I'm not blocking you out," Grant said. "I'm working."

The stack of sheets that represented his new manuscript had grown from fifteen pages to over one hundred. His supply of words seemed endless.

"God damn it, Grant! Look at me."

Grant looked up from his plate. Behind Debbie, a single floral painting hung on the wall. Grant wondered what would happen if he took down the painting, if the walls down here would talk to him, too.

"Grant?"

"What?" he said, shifting his gaze from the wall to his wife.

"What's wrong with you?"

"There's nothing wrong with *me*," he said, staring directly into Debbie's eyes.

Debbie produced a small, uneven smile that faltered and then vanished altogether. "What's that supposed to mean?"

"You know what it means," Grant said.

"I don't know..."

"You're one of them," Grant said.

Debbie stared at him, her face tense. "One of who? What are you talking about?"

"Why did you marry me?"

"Grant, I don't..."

"Why did you marry me?" he nearly shouted.

"I married you because I love you," Debbie said, her eyes filling with tears. "I married you because I wanted to spend my life with you, to have children, to grow old..."

"We're not having children," Grant said.

Debbie stared at him, her chin trembling, tears spilling down her cheeks. "I don't know who you are anymore."

She picked up her plate and stood up. As she walked past Grant into the kitchen doorway, he reached out and grabbed Debbie by the wrist. Startled, she dropped her plate, splattering pork chop and mashed potatoes and green beans across the kitchen's tile floor.

"I want to know the truth," Grant said.

"Let me go," said Debbie, struggling to get away. Her free hand flailed across the counter inside the kitchen doorway, knocking a dirty, two-cup Pyrex measuring glass to the floor, where it exploded into pieces that scattered across the tile.

"I want to know what you're hiding," Grant said.

"I'm not hiding anything!" she cried, pushing against the doorjamb as she tried to pull away.

Grant tightened his grip. "I want to know who those men are outside."

"I don't know!" Debbie's hand fell across the handle of a steak knife and she grabbed it, her left arm swinging up in a wide arc as she leaned back against her husband's grip. The knife came down fast, but Grant let go an instant before the blade could reach his arm.

Debbie stumbled backwards into the kitchen, her left foot coming down on a glob of mashed potatoes. Her feet slipped out from under her, her arms pin wheeling, the steak knife flying out of her hand as she fell to the floor, her head snapping back and hitting the tile with the sound of an enormous egg. The steak knife clattered harmlessly to the floor as Debbie's legs twitched three times and then stopped.

"Debbie?" Grant said. He stood up and walked into the kitchen, past the fragments of plate and glass, past the pork chop and green beans and mashed potatoes, until he reached his wife.

A small, red bubble of saliva rose from between her slightly parted lips and then burst.

That's when Grant noticed the blood spreading out across the floor from the back of Debbie's head. At first Grant thought she'd split her head open. Then he saw the jagged edges of glass and realized the base of his wife's skull had landed on the broken base of the Pyrex measuring cup.

Grant knelt down next to his wife and held her hand. "Debbie," he said, searching for a pulse, for any signs of life. But she remained motionless, her eyes staring up at the ceiling, her lips parted, no heartbeat or breath.

Grant remained on his knees, eyes closed against the tears and anguish he expected would come as dozens of memories spun through his mind – he and Debbie walking on a beach in Kauai, curled up on a couch together reading, making love on the floor where her body now lay lifeless.

Then the walls started to hum.

In his mind, Grant began to see other images of Debbie, not memories but revelations – Debbie whispering into the phone, skulking out the back door, sneaking into his room and reading his manuscript.

When Grant opened his eyes, he was no longer kneeling on the kitchen tile next to his dead wife but on the carpeted floor of his room surrounded by his vacant, white walls that hummed and pulsed. Grant listened. And he understood.

Turning away from the walls, Grant sat down at his computer and began to write.

~φ~

Night passed and morning dawned. On the kitchen floor, Debbie's body grew cold while Grant sat in his room, listening to the walls, words and concepts streaming into his head. His entire body pulsed with knowledge. He could feel it pumping through his veins, sweating from his pores, releasing from his mind – the words coming out in a torrent.

After a while, Grant became aware of a dull ringing in his ears that grew more insistent, stopping and starting again, until he finally recognized the cry of the telephone. He waited for the answering machine to pick up, but the phone kept ringing. When he finally answered, all Grant heard on the other end of the line was a dial tone.

Grant hung up and went to his window, looking for the men in overcoats and hats standing in the shadows. But the sun had risen high enough in the sky to chase away most of the shadows. Still, Grant knew they were out there, watching him.

When the phone rang again a few minutes later, Grant went through the house and unplugged all the lines. After he disconnected the phone in the kitchen, Grant stepped over Debbie's body into the dining room and stood by the table, his eyes fixed on the floral painting on the opposite wall. To his right, the dining room opened into the living room. To his left, past a two-piece cherry hutch that contained his wife's collection of bone china teacups, a set of French doors led to the back patio.

Grant stared at the painting and the wall surrounding it, then looked into the living room, imagining how the room would look with nothing on the walls and no furniture obstructing his view. He thought about how pristine the walls would be, how clear, how endless.

From deep within the house a faint hum started. Grant cocked his head and listened, a smile stealing across his face as he walked to the French doors and opened them. He removed the painting and carried it outside. The dining table and chairs went next, followed by the hutch, which Grant dragged out on to the flagstone patio with disregard, snapping off one of the legs and breaking all but two of the teacups.

The living room took longer to empty. In addition to the paintings, Grant had to move two wingback chairs, an end table, a wall-length bookcase, and a couch. The couch was too heavy to maneuver on his own, so Grant took off the cushions and cut the couch in half with a skill saw before he dragged it outside.

All around him, the house hummed.

Grant moved to the family room, dragging the furniture and entertainment equipment out the sliding glass doors and removing the artwork from the walls. Debbie's body went last, dragged out through the French doors and tossed in a heap with the rest of the debris.

Upstairs, he cleared out his wife's study, shoving everything he could into the closet before dragging her roll-top desk across the hallway and into the master bedroom. When the desk wouldn't fit through the open window, he smashed out the stationary pane, then dumped the desk over the edge, shouting in triumph when the desk exploded on the patio below.

The bedroom dressers went next, followed by a floor lamp, two nightstands, and finally the bed. By the time Grant finished, the afternoon had nearly run itself out. Soft light filtered in through the windows as Grant stood in the middle of the bedroom, listening to the walls, his eyes closed and his arms outstretched. Energy coursed through him. He could almost hear a lock disengaging to a hidden passage.

Downstairs, the doorbell rang.

Grant ignored it at first, but the doorbell kept ringing, its insistent knell boring into his mind like a drill. When he opened his eyes, the walls stopped humming. Aggravated, Grant ran out of the bedroom and down the stairs. An instant before he reached the door, the bell stopped ringing.

He opened the front door, hoping to catch one of the shadowy men, but the porch stood empty. Grant stepped outside and looked around, expecting to see a figure hiding in the bushes or running away, but the only movement he saw was a fluttering of wings as a gathering of swallows flew off into the approaching twilight.

After one last glance around the front yard, Grant walked back inside and closed the door, staring through the peephole before turning to look into the living room. Fading sunlight drifted through the front window, casting shadows against the barren, silent walls. The longer Grant studied the shadows, the more they looked like the shapes of men wearing overcoats and hats, and he began to wonder if the regulators could somehow get inside his house.

Not wanting to take any chances, Grant locked up the house and drove to the hardware store, where he bought a dozen large sheets of plywood, a box of four-inch nails, two gallons of flat white paint, and a one-hundred-foot roll of barbed wire. By the time he returned home, night had stretched out full and black across the sky.

First, Grant strung the barbed wire across the front porch in an impenetrable web, preventing anyone from reaching either the door or the doorbell. As an afterthought, he disconnected the doorbell chime with a hammer. Once he nailed the front door shut, he turned his attention to the downstairs windows.

After removing the shades and curtains, Grant cut the plywood and nailed it into place, then applied two coats of paint, sealing off the windows and enclosing the entire downstairs. Once he finished, he headed upstairs to complete his fortress.

Outside, car alarms sounded up and down the neighboring streets while sirens screamed in the distance.

As midnight approached, Grant stood at the window in his dead wife's study preparing to install the final piece of plywood. In the wash of light from the lamp across the street, Grant glimpsed several figures dressed in overcoats standing in pools of darkness. He waved to them, then gave them the finger before he nailed the plywood into place. Once the last coat of paint was applied, Grant walked into the bedroom, sat down on the floor, and closed his eyes.

The walls hummed louder now, reverberating, as if a circuit of energy surrounded him, increasing in its intensity, penetrating his soul. In the expanded landscape of his mind, Grant saw a barrier, an enormous stone wall that stretched beyond imaginable heights and endlessly in either direction. Although formidable, the wall had developed a network of cracks and fissures. Through the breaches glowed a light, brighter than anything Grant had ever known, pulsing and pressing against the wall, pouring through the cracks, building up an enormous pressure until the wall could no longer contain it.

The wall collapsed in an explosion of light that flooded into Grant, filling him up, drowning him in perception. It was like a portal had opened to another intelligence. A door to heaven. A nexus with God. He screamed, not in pain or fear but in wonder and glory – his body shaking in orgasm, tears flowing down his cheeks as his scream turned to laughter.

Grant had no memory of returning to his room, but he was suddenly at his desk, revelations pouring out across his computer screen as if he'd tapped directly into a conduit of knowledge. He didn't eat. He didn't sleep. He didn't stop to relieve his bladder but continued to write, his fingers never leaving the keyboard, the words never stopping as the sun rose and fell in oblivion and the stack on his desk grew to more than six-hundred pages.

And yet there was more, pages and pages waiting to be written, epiphanies and truths streaming into him faster than he could think. Grant's fingers attacked the keyboard as the stack of pages climbed past seven hundred, then eight hundred. Time passed without heed. Neither food nor sleep mattered, for the power of the words nourished him.

His senses expanded and his reality shifted. The room distorted – the walls and floor and ceiling curving, reshaping, until the corners and edges vanished and his room became a single continuous wall that encompassed him. The monitor stretched and curved like a windshield, through which existed another universe filled with words and thoughts and concepts that formed planets and stars and galaxies. His desk became the command console of a spaceship, his keyboard the controls, lifting him up and away.

He flew through an endless macrocosm, watching the words that formed, absorbing their energy, listening to what they had to teach, reveling in discovery. Days passed, then months. Months turned into years, years into decades, decades into centuries. Still the words came, infinite and wondrous, lyrical and hypnotic, a symphony of consciousness.

From the distant fringes of that consciousness, foreign sounds emerged, discordant and intrusive. They started out low, barely discernable as anything more than static, then grew louder until the sounds were unmistakable.

An alarm, blaring. Someone pounding against a wall. Voices calling out. Sirens in the distance, growing louder.

Some unseen force grabbed Grant, pulling him away from the words and dragging him out of his new universe, past familiar planets and stars, past the sun, sucking him down through layers of gas and clouds, slamming him through his senses, through the roof of his own house, back into his room.

From downstairs came the sound of splintering wood and shattering glass, followed by footsteps thundering into the house and up the stairs. Shadowy figures surrounded him, over-coats flapping like wings, indistinct faces floating beneath wide-brimmed hats. Hands reached out to him, held him, subdued him, twisted him around and bound his limbs. Something stung him in the arm. Grant turned and saw a gloved hand pull away as a needle retracted into the flesh of an index finger.

His thoughts became muddled. Voices and sounds grew distant, distorted. Phantom shapes drifted past. The room slipped out of focus. As he floated through the doorway, Grant glanced back and saw a man in a trench coat and hat feeding his manuscript into a furnace that had once been his closet. Then the room fell away and darkness descended.

~φ~

Grant sat on the edge of the white, sterile bed, the door to the room closed and the late afternoon sun shining through the window on the wall behind him. He'd lost track of how many days he'd been here, but he knew another week must have passed because Debbie had come to visit.

"Dr. Brooks says you're making great strides," she said from a chair opposite Grant, her hair pulled back in a ponytail. In her lap she worked a ball of blue yarn with a pair of knitting needles. "He says you should be ready to go home in another month."

Grant couldn't recall how he'd come to be a patient here. Fragments of images came to him in his sleep – barbed wire strung across his front porch, Debbie's dead body on the kitchen floor, and other memories too bizarre to be real. The doctors and nurses listened to him and talked with him and helped him to make sense out of his dreams. Still, the events preceding his breakdown remained ambiguous.

"When can I start writing again?" Grant asked.

"You know what Dr. Brooks thinks about that," Debbie said as she continued her knitting. "He said any attempt at writing might trigger another episode, so I think we should take his advice and not rush into anything. The last thing you need right now is another case of writer's block."

Sometimes Grant sensed that prior to his breakdown, he'd been working on something monumental, life changing, a novel of unparalleled discovery. But Debbie assured him he hadn't written a word in weeks.

"I think we should take a vacation," Debbie said. "Go somewhere relaxing like the mountains or the beach, spend some time alone while we still can." She set down her knitting needles and held up a single, blue booty. "What do you think?"

Grant stared at the booty, then dropped his gaze to the curve of Debbie's distended abdomen.

"Whoops," Debbie said, looking at her watch. "I've gotta go." She leaned over to stuff her yarn and needles into her bag. When she did, her ponytail fell to one side, revealing a series of jagged, fading scars along the back of her neck.

She stood up and kissed Grant goodbye. "See you next Thursday, honey."

As Debbie opened the door and stepped out of the room, she nodded to someone. For an instant, Grant saw the shadow of a man wearing an overcoat and a hat moving along the hallway wall, then the shadow became a doctor with a clipboard, making his rounds.

The door closed with a hollow click and the room fell silent. Grant closed his eyes and took in a deep breath, held it, then let it out, repeating the breathing while he envisioned an infinite body of water, blue and serene. The exercise was a form of mediation to help him remember, but lately the water kept turning into a sea of plaster.

Grant opened his eyes and stared at the wall. He didn't want to go home and he didn't want to take a vacation. He liked it here. He felt safe. He'd even made a few friends. But mostly he liked his room, with its single bed and blank, white walls. True, the room had a window, but when the sun went down he could almost imagine the window wasn't there.

During the day Grant often sat and stared at the walls, listening to a faint hum that seemed to emanate from somewhere beyond them. Sometimes he thought he could almost discern a message. But at night, when the sounds of the clinic died down and the other patients went to sleep, the words became clearer.

Grant figured getting paper would probably be easy, but the nurses wouldn't give him anything sharp, so he couldn't ask for a ball point pen or a pencil. If only he could get his hands on a Black Berol marker or a piece of chalk. Maybe even a crayon.

Grant stared at the wall and waited for night to come.

Outside, an alarm wailed in the distance.

~φ~

Dr. Lullaby

People still get confused about my name.

I suppose I shouldn't take it personally. After all, it's not like I've ever done any interviews or tried to set the matter straight. I'm not even the one who came up with the moniker. I think *The New York Post* was the first to print it. That was my first big headline. The one that turned me into a local celebrity. Though *celebrity* isn't really the right word, since no one knows for sure who I am. Who any of us are.

Still, you'd think that after all of the press surrounding the events that have transpired over the past few months, people would understand what it is I do. But from what I hear on the street and on talk radio, a lot of people still think I'm some kind of serenading physician or an academic pedophile.

I'm thinking I need to hire a good publicist.

Before I go any further, I should probably explain a few things. So let me start at the beginning. Or maybe we should start in the middle. Isn't that where stories are supposed to start? In the middle? Not with the hero graduating from college and getting a job working for an advertising agency in Manhattan, then getting downsized and blowing through his severance and savings in less than a year and trying to figure out how he's going to earn a living.

You don't start with all of that expository crap.

The wistful reverie.

The character building.

It's not: Lights. Camera. Backstory.

What you start with is action.

~φ~

I'm walking along Canal Street through Chinatown late at night on my way home to my one-bedroom apartment on the

Lower East Side, just a few blocks from the Tenement Museum and right around the corner from The Doughnut Plant, the best doughnuts in Manhattan.

That's a personal endorsement, not a statement of fact.

Anyway, I'm just turning onto Bowery and walking past the New York Jeweler's Exchange when I hear shouting and I see Vic and Charlie across the street in front of the Kowloon Bay Chinese Market. They're not shouting at me but at a couple of young punks who are beating up a homeless man, shoving him and kicking him and laughing.

I run across the street to help but just as I get there, one of the punks suddenly starts throwing up while the other one drops to the ground and goes into convulsions. When Vic and Charlie go over to see if the homeless guy is all right, a third punk comes running up behind them, shouting, a knife in one hand. Before he can take another step, he goes sprawling to the ground and doesn't get up.

Before one of us has a chance to call 911, we hear the police sirens and scatter.

Wait a minute. Let me back up.

~φ~

Three months earlier, I'm sitting in an examination room on a chair with a disposable thermometer in my mouth and a blood pressure cuff around my upper left arm. On the walls around me are posters of the human body. Of vascular systems. Of reproductive organs. Fluorescent lights wash everything in a yellowish hue. A clock ticks away the morning. Outside the closed door, someone is asking for a breath mint.

I notice that my lips have gone numb.

This has never happened before. Usually I don't feel anything more than drowsy or lightheaded, though that doesn't happen as often as it used to. Occasionally I get cotton mouth or feel like I have food poisoning. More often than not, I'll get a headache. Nothing major. We're not talking migraine and vomiting. That would be serious. What I get is pretty typical, nothing 400 milligrams of Ibuprofin won't fix.

But numbness in my lips? That's definitely a first.

The medical technician sitting across from me removes the thermometer and the cuff, then records my temperature and my blood pressure on a chart attached to a clipboard. When the tech isn't looking, I reach up with one finger and poke at my lower lip. I still can't feel it.

"How are you feeling?" he asks.

"Good," I say, hoping I don't drool on my shirt.

"Any problems with your vision?" he asks, looking down at his clipboard.

I shake my head and say no.

"Cognitive functions?"

No.

"Speech?"

I shake my head, though my lips feel as big as Long Island.

"Cotton mouth?"

No.

"Cramps?"

No.

"Any tingling or numbness in your extremities?"

I shake my head. Since my extremities don't include my lips, I'm not technically lying.

"Nausea?"

"Headaches?"

"Rashes?"

Sometimes just hearing the word *rash* makes me want to itch, but I answer in the negative three more times.

"Are you feeling dizzy or light headed?"

Most of the time, the questions are the same.

Headaches.

Nausea.

Diarrhea.

Frequently they'll throw in night sweats or loss of appetite, with an occasional sinus inflammation and the odd sexual performance question. But I've never been asked about an irregular heartbeat. Or renal failure.

No matter what the question, I tell them the truth. Otherwise, I could get into trouble if they find out I've been lying. But I don't want to let them know about my numb lips because I'm afraid I'll end up on some kind of list. And then I'll really be screwed.

So I'm hoping it's just a temporary reaction.

Temporary reactions are easier to dismiss as inconsequential, even though I'm supposed to report anything out of the ordinary.

Gas.

Swelling.

Hot flashes.

Anything of the smallest significance that isn't normal. That I don't experience on a regular, daily basis. Which is a lot harder than it sounds. You have to be focused. You have to pay attention. You have to write down every physical sensation you experience, everything that you eat and drink and how many times a day you empty your bladder or evacuate your bowels.

It's like taking notes in college, only without mid-terms. And you don't get to go on spring break to Ft. Lauderdale and do beer bongs and watch your roommate have sex with a freshman from Duke.

"No," I tell him. "No dizziness."

The tech takes another five minutes to run through the rest of his questions. By the time he sends me off for my blood and urine tests, my lips have returned to normal.

In another room, a phlebotomist wraps an elastic tourniquet around my arm and sterilizes the soft flesh just inside my left elbow.

I'm not a big fan of needles. Even after more than five years, I still have to look away. I can't stand the sight of my own blood. And I flinch when the needle penetrates my skin. I can't even watch movies where someone sticks a needle or a blade into flesh. I know it's not real, just Hollywood special effects, but I still cringe.

I take a deep breath and stare at the wall as the phlebotomist draws half a dozen blood samples into evacuated tubes. Normally she's supposed to ask a list of questions before drawing samples and record my answers on a form:

Am I on anticoagulation therapy?

Do I have a history of fits?

Do I have any bleeding disorders?

Am I pregnant?

Have I fasted?

Instead, she asks me the questions while taking the samples. Except for the one about being pregnant. And this test didn't require me to fast. I'm not a big fan of fasting. I'm not Bahá'í or Buddhist and I've never spent forty days and nights on a mountain with God, so abstaining from food and drink has never been my strong suit.

After she draws my blood, the phlebotomist hands me a sterile plastic specimen container with my name and date on it and points me to the bathroom.

"Try to catch the urine in mid-stream," she says. "It makes for a cleaner sample."

I nod as if this is something I've never heard before. As if this is my first time.

Collecting a specimen mid-stream doesn't mean inserting the specimen cup into the flow of urine. It takes a talented individual to manage that without pissing all over the side of the cup, not to mention all over your hand and splattering the toilet and floor. No. What you do is, first you wash out the urethra. You do this by releasing a short, initial stream into the toilet. Ideally, you'd use an antiseptic pad to sterilize the opening of the urethra first, but most clinics don't require that degree of cleanliness. After the initial stream, you stop, then resume urination into the container, collecting the sample before the stream ends.

I've heard some guys have a hard time peeing on command into a cup, so they collect a sample at home in a sterile container and bring it in. I've never had a problem providing a sample, so I give them a mid-stream catch, then deposit the specimen container in the cabinet, grab my backpack, and head to the waiting room, where the receptionist gives me a list of dietary requirements and a checklist of side-effects.

"Thank you, Mr. Prescott," she says. "See you next week."

~φ~

I'm a professional guinea pig.

Not exactly something you go to college for or intern at a prestigious law firm to gain experience as or dream of being when you're a kid.

"What do you want to be when you grow up?"

"I want to test drugs that might make me vomit or experience uncontrollable flatulence."

This is why they have high school guidance counselors.

Someone to give us direction. Purpose. Some sense of a future that doesn't involve selling yourself for medical research or starring in bad porn. But sometimes circumstances dictate a future you hadn't planned for, so you do what you have to do.

Most professional guinea pigs volunteer for Phase I pharmaceutical clinical trials, where the safety of a potential drug is tested by giving it to more or less healthy subjects and studying any side effects. Phase II trials involve determining dosing requirements and effectiveness. Phase III trials compare a drug's results with standard treatments.

I'm in the first category. The Phase I trials.

I take generic painkillers, heart medications, anti-depressants. Investigative drugs being developed and tested for market entrance.

Drugs for ADD, insomnia, and urinary tract infections.

Drugs for schizophrenia, impotence, and Parkinson's disease.

Drugs with names like Lorazepam and Naproxen and Adderall.

Unlike test subjects in later-stage clinical trials, who are usually sick and enroll in a study to gain access to a new drug, guinea pigs in early-stage trials can't expect any therapeutic benefit. And every time we volunteer to be tested for some new drug, we're putting ourselves at risk. But sometimes life provides opportunities that you never thought you'd have to take, so you take them in spite of the risks. Plus, it's not like I'm doing this for free.

Nobody's volunteering out of the goodness of their heart.

In a typical month, I make $1500, sometimes as much as $3000, but I've never made less than $1000. Generic testing studies usually take place over two weekends and pay anywhere form $600 to $1000. While I only received $500 for my recent Paleolithic diet study, that only lasted a week and didn't require a washout, which is the thirty-day waiting period required between most studies.

A lot of these drugs I've been tested with, the ones that have already passed the final stage of clinical trials and are now legally available by prescription and advertised on television, come with a host of common side-effects in addition to their advertised health benefits.

Blurred vision.

Diarrhea.

Vomiting.

These are the less serious side effects. The ones that don't require you to call your doctor or make you wonder if it's too late to take out life insurance.

But then there are the more serious side effects, the ones you hear rattled off on a commercial like a contest disclaimer.

May cause fainting.

May cause seizures.

May cause hallucinations.

Only one entry per household.

Must be eighteen or over to be eligible.

Residents of California and Arizona must pay tax.

Then there are the drugs that actually cause the very problem they're supposed to be treating.

Drugs to treat diarrhea that can cause diarrhea.

Drugs for sleep disorders that can cause insomnia.

Drugs to combat depression that can cause suicidal thoughts.

One drug, an anti-inflammatory taken for arthritis, tendinitis, bursitis, gout, and menstrual cramps, suggests that you stop taking the medication and seek immediate medical attention if you experience any of the following:

Slurred speech.

Blistering or peeling of the skin.

Coughing up blood or vomit that looks like coffee grounds.

There's more, including jaundice, bloody stools, numbness, and chills. But if my skin is blistering and I'm having trouble speaking and I'm throwing up something that has the consistency of Starbucks Breakfast Blend, I'm thinking maybe this drug needs to be taken off the shelves.

It makes you wonder how something like this gets approved by the FDA while medical marijuana shops get shut down.

Still, the overall safety of all of these new drugs depends on the willingness of someone to test them. Someone who needs the money. Someone who has a lot of time to spare.

Someone who has no better option.

This isn't something computer engineers do. This isn't something college professors do. This isn't something lawyers or CEO's or members of congress do.

This is something the less advantaged do so the rich can get better drugs.

Of course, you can't always depend on a regular paycheck or a steady monthly income from guinea-pigging, which means you have to find other ways to make ends meet.

~φ~

"Get a job you lazy whore," says a forty something married man in a tie and slacks who throws a dollar into my hat as he walks past.

I thank him and wish him a nice day.

"Shove this up your ass," says a guy in his twenties who works at the Children's Zoo and displays a George Washington around his middle finger before tossing the dollar into my hat.

I give him a nod and a smile.

"You're lousy in bed," says a woman in her early thirties who throws a handful of singles into my hat. She gets a couple of steps away, then turns around, marches back over to me, and hisses, "You're the worst fuck I've ever had!"

I press my hands together in front of me and bow my head.

I'm in Central Park, sitting on a bench near the Naumburg Bandshell. The sign I'm displaying today says:

Will take verbal abuse for money.

When I first started using this sign a couple of years ago, I received the standard insults you'd expect, derogatory comments meant for me and my wasted life. For what I represented. For what I'd become.

A social tumor.

A rash on the ass of civilization.

An oozing pus bag of failure.

More often than not, the insults weren't accompanied by a donation. Sometimes I got spit on, which isn't technically verbal abuse, but when you're a panhandler, you can't expect everyone to be on the same page.

But after a while, after people saw me around Central Park with my sign on a regular basis, they started to feel comfortable with me. They started to understand the freedom I was offering. They started to open up.

People don't always have someone to talk to. Someone they can be honest with. Someone who will listen to all of the things they wish they could say without passing judgment. Plus I'm non-threatening. An outsider. A familiar stranger. Someone they don't have to worry about running into at the office or the local bar or family reunions. Unless they happen to hold their reunion in Central Park.

Now when most people approach me, rather than showering me with personal attacks and derogatory invectives about my existence, they vent their frustrations about anything that's troubling them. The problems that they're unable to deal with. Whatever's on their mind that they can't share with anyone else.

Jobs.

Relationships.

Family.

"I hate you, Mom," says a young woman wearing a Columbia University sweatshirt who tosses a wadded up dollar at me. "You've ruined my life."

I get that a lot.

It doesn't matter if the object of their frustration and anger is male or female, mother or father, husband or wife. I'm an androgynous receptacle of disparagement. An ambiguous catch-all of angst.

I'm kind of like a mendicant therapist.

A panhandling priest.

Absolving the sins of my flock for whatever they care to leave as a contribution. Offering a sliding scale of emotional succor.

Sometimes I use other signs with different sayings, like:

Professional panhandler. How can I help you?

Looking for a little humanity. Have you seen him?

If we were both squirrels, I could show you my nuts.

That one doesn't always work so well. Still, it makes me laugh, and a happy panhandler is a prosperous panhandler. But none of the other signs offer the same sense of purpose as the service I'm providing today.

So I sit and I listen and I smile and I thank them for their words and their donations and their abuse and by the end of my four hours, I've earned eighty-seven dollars and change. Which is a good seven dollars more an hour than I typically earn using any of my other signs. At that rate, doing this full-time, I would earn more than forty-five grand a year.

Tax free.

But if I used the same sign every day, it wouldn't carry the same weight. I'd become just another unimaginative panhandler, preying on the good will of my customers. Which is why I like to mix things up. Plus it makes me appreciate days like this.

As I start to collect my money and my sign, a teenager on a skateboard rides up to me, calls me a dream crushing asshole, then throws a handful of quarters at me.

At least I know I'm making a difference.

I pick up the quarters, which have scattered across the concrete at my feet, and call out a "Thank you" to the kid as he starts to ride away, when my lips go numb again. At the same moment the kid glances back to give me the finger, I let out a yawn. The next thing I know, the kid tumbles to the ground in an unconscious heap, his skateboard rolling away into the grass.

I look around to see if anyone else noticed but no one is paying attention. Or at least if they are, they're ignoring it. Which is typical for New York. Everyone wears blinders unless something directly affects them. So I walk over to the kid to see if he's okay.

He's on his back, out cold, his head turned to one side. His lips are moving but I can't hear what he's saying, so I kneel down next to him.

"Hey," I say, shaking him gently by the shoulder. "Are you okay?"

He moves and I think he's coming around. But instead of opening his eyes and sitting up, he rolls on to his side, puts his hands under his head, and curls up in a fetal position.

~φ~

"Anybody have anything weird happen to them lately?" I ask.

"Weird?" says Charlie. "What kind of weird?"

"Weird," I say. "The kind of weird that makes you wonder if there's something going on that you don't know about."

"I have that all the time," says Randy. "It's called *women*."

A few days later I'm at Caffé Reggio on MacDougal in Greenwich Village with Vic, Charlie, Frank, and Randy – four other guinea pigs who test pharmaceutical drugs. This is our monthly meeting where we share info on clinical trials, including how well a study paid, the competence of the venipuncturist, and the quality of the food. All of the important factors that we take into account before volunteering for a trial. We're kind of like a guinea pig coffee klatch.

"When you say *weird*," says Vic, "are you talking about with you or with other people?"

"Other people," I say. "Though I have been kind of tired lately."

"You been upping your carbohydrate intake?" asks Frank.

Certain carbohydrates with a high glycemic index break down fast and cause a steep rise in blood sugar levels, causing an initial rush that's followed by periods of drowsiness. Foods with a high glycemic index include French fries, instant rice, corn flakes, pretzels, and frozen waffles.

"Not really," I say.

"Not really?" says Frank. "What the hell does that mean? You've either been upping your intake or you haven't. Jesus, don't you keep track of what you're consuming?"

Frank takes being a guinea pig very seriously.

"Have you gained weight?" asks Charlie, looking at Frank.

"What the hell has that got to do with anything?" asks Frank, taking a bite of his cannoli.

"It's just a question," says Charlie. "You don't need to get defensive."

"I'm not getting defensive," says Frank, who, to be honest, looks a little plumper these days. "I just don't understand what my weight has to do with Neal's inability to keep accurate records of his caffeine intake."

"Maybe you should chill out," says Randy, scratching at his head.

"Maybe you should shut the fuck up," says Frank, shoving the last of the cannoli into his mouth.

Everyone seems to be a little more irritable today than usual. But when you spend your existence taking experimental prescription drugs that give you headaches and constipation and insomnia, irritability is just a comment away. Not to mention that we don't get any retirement benefits, disability insurance, worker's compensation, or overtime pay. Plus we're not going to get the benefits of the health care developed by the research we're helping to test, since most of us can't even afford health insurance. So we're only one bad trial away from hospital bills and bankruptcy and homelessness.

"Can we get back to Neal's question about things being weird?" says Vic.

"Yeah," says Charlie, who shivers once like he just got a chill. Which is odd because it's eighty degrees out. "What exactly are we talking about here?"

In addition to feeling tired lately, I tell them about the numbness I've started having in my lips.

"Did you report it?" asks Frank.

I shake my head, which causes Frank to go into lecture mode about personal responsibility. Then I tell them about the kid on the skateboard.

"And he passed out the same moment you yawned?" asks Vic.

"Yeah," I say. "At least it seemed like it."

"It was just a coincidence," says Frank.

"Maybe," I say. "But it was a pretty weird coincidence."

"Anybody else have anything weird happen to them?" asks Charlie.

Frank shakes his head while Randy scratches at his, looking like he has something on his mind. Vic lets out a burp and makes a face.

I look over at Vic who glances back at me and I think he's going to say something, but then Randy starts talking about how the last research facility he stayed at over the weekend could use a good public relations director and the conversation turns to business.

We spend the next fifteen to twenty minutes talking about our recent trials, comparing notes, grading clinics. We give each research unit a grade from A to F, factoring in a number of conditions and variables, such as the friendliness of the staff, how much they pay, the drugs being tested, the side effects, and the length of the trial.

It's nice having a support group of your peers to help navigate the waters of being a professional guinea pig. There aren't any agencies out there to help us. So we pretty much have to look out for ourselves.

"Any of you feel nauseous?" asks Vic, out of nowhere, looking around the table. "Not right now but I mean, in general?"

"No," I say.

Everyone else either answers in the negative or shakes his head.

"I feel nauseous sometimes," says Vic. "A lot lately, actually. But only when I burp."

Which explains the face he made a while back.

"My head itches a lot," says Randy, scratching his head. "It never used to."

Frank, who is sitting next to Randy and eating another cannoli, scoots further away.

Then Vic leans forward so only we can hear him and he says, "I think I'm making other people throw up."

~φ~

I walk through the streets of Lower Manhattan, though Tribeca and Soho and Chinatown, past stores and restaurants and subway stations. Past people who need help.

A homeless man talking to himself out in front of St. Peter's Church.

A bag lady moving her five bags down Lafayette Street one at a time.

A drunk passed out on the sidewalk near the Delancey Station entrance.

I read the news every day and see stories about people getting robbed on the subway or mugged in Central Park. The disadvantaged and the elderly and the homeless. Men and women who are simply going about the business of trying to survive their lives.

I think about my life before, living in an apartment on the Upper East Side and working in an ad agency in an office surrounded by false walls, sharing half-hour lunches and two fifteen-minute breaks with colleagues sitting in their own makeshift offices. A honeycomb of cubicles beneath fluorescent lights. I think about losing my job. I think about all of the pharmaceutical drugs I've tested in order to earn a living and what they've done to me. I think about the kid on the skateboard and Vic's confession.

There comes a moment in every person's life when he realizes the purpose of his existence. Sometimes that moment takes years to arrive, moving like a glacier until it starts to nudge you in the right direction. Other times it arrives like a slap in the face. Or a kick in the nuts. Either one gets your attention. One just hurts more than the other.

This is my moment. This is my time.

~φ~

I'm standing at the edge of Madison Square Park across from the Flatiron Building just after two in the morning, eating jellybeans and keeping alert for any sign of trouble. The homeless who sleep in and around Madison Square Park have been getting attacked lately, assaulted and beaten up. Since the police haven't managed to solve the problem, we thought we'd lend a hand.

Inside the park, Vic and Charlie wander around pretending to be drunk and homeless, while Randy waits across the street by the 23rd Street subway entrance, smoking a cigarette. Randy didn't used to smoke. But he says it helps to calm his nerves.

Frank stands next to me, eating an apple fritter. While Frank has started exercising to try to keep some of the extra weight off, he still wears sweats most of the time and likes to indulge himself with doughnuts and ice cream. Plus he says it helps him to focus.

Frank's been a lot more fun to be around since he accepted his new life.

"Mmm," he says, licking the sugar off his lips, then holding a chunk of apple fritter out to me. "You want a bite?"

"No thanks," I say.

I've already had my fill of pretzels and jelly beans, which are pretty high on the glycemic index, though not as high as sourdough bread or instant rice. But they're easier to carry around and they do a good enough job of upping my glucose levels. I just have to make sure I don't become diabetic. Even if I could afford to take something like Amaryl, the last thing I want is to have to worry about my mouth or face swelling up or my eyes turning yellow.

The funny thing about prescription drugs is that most people will take them without even considering what the long-term effects of those drugs might have on them. At least guinea pigs understand what we're getting into, even if it's not a smart career move.

And taking one drug to cure one problem can lead to more problems that require more drugs, until you're essentially medicating your medications.

In a way, we've become like smart phones, only instead of downloading applications, we're downloading prescriptions.

You've got high blood pressure? There's a pill for that.

You're anxious and stressed out? There's a pill for that.

You can't get an erection? There's a pill for that.

We're gradually becoming more and more dependent on pharmaceutical drugs in order for us to survive. Whether we have problems with sleeping, depression, or gaining weight, there's a prescription answer waiting for us at the drugstore.

It's only a matter of time before evolution makes a leap forward and humans start being born with a dependency on pharmaceutical drugs. Or exhibiting permanent side-effects.

Apparently, some of us have already taken that leap.

Laughter drifts to us from inside the park by the Shake Shack. Loud and boisterous, followed by the sound of a bottle breaking. That's the signal from Vic and Charlie. Frank shoves down the rest of his apple fritter and I pocket my jelly beans. Out by the subway entrance, Randy flicks away his unfinished cigarette and jogs across the street into the park.

When we get to the Shake Shack, two punks are hassling Vic by the closed Pick-Up windows while Charlie backs away from a third punk out behind the hamburger stand. Two more punks are over by the Southern Fountain, terrorizing a homeless woman. Frank peels off from me and heads that way with Randy while I stand point and watch to make sure no one gets blind sided or outnumbered. Or in case someone pulls a gun.

Since Vic's got two to deal with, I keep an eye on him in case he needs any help. But when he burps, the two guys hassling him are suddenly clutching their stomachs and stumbling away, falling to their hands and knees, spraying vomit across the sidewalk.

While the local authorities have issued a statement saying that we are vigilantes acting outside of the law and are not to be encouraged, the local press hasn't helped matters by turning us into heroes, glorifying our exploits, and giving us names.

The New York Post refers to Vic as Captain Vomit.

Vic watches the two punks crawl around, moaning and puking, then he lets out a laugh and walks over to the closest one and kicks him in the ribs.

I think Vic enjoys this more than the rest of us.

Out behind the Shake Shack, Charlie is trying to reason with his would-be assailant. That's Charlie for you. Always trying to resolve conflict without violence. But the punk isn't listening. The next instant, Charlie shivers in the mid-September Manhattan night and the punk drops to the ground, shaking and spasming, looking like an epileptic having an orgasm.

Charlie's been dubbed Convulsion Boy.

None of us ever expected this to become our lives, but it's who we are now. We've become drug reaction crime fighters. Side-effect super heroes. Using our unique abilities to stop criminals by making them vomit and go into convulsions.

Among other things.

Over by the Southern Fountain, Randy lights up another cigarette and takes a deep drag as one of the thugs starts going into contortions, scratching at himself and whimpering, his skin blistered and covered with angry red splotches.

Randy is simply called The Rash.

While Randy isn't particularly fond of his nom de plume,

he's embraced his new identity. We all have. We're the modern prescription for an overmedicated society.

May cause skin rashes.

May cause drowsiness.

May cause rapid weight gain.

The last of the thugs cries out as his waist expands and his arms and thighs grow to twice their thickness. Before he has a chance to run away from Frank, the thug busts through the seams on his clothes and falls down, incapacitated, his frame unable to support the extra weight.

Frank's name is Big Fatty.

We're the new breed of crime fighter. A product of our profession. And we're not the only ones. There are others who have apparently discovered that the constant exposure to the testing of pharmaceutical drugs has given them unusual abilities.

Diarrhea Boy. Erection Man. Professor Phlegm.

While most of them seem to be working for the benefit of others, there are some who have chosen to use their newfound powers for personal gain. Not us. We work for the less fortunate. For those who can't stand up for themselves. People like us. Or at least like we used to be. Before we discovered what we'd become.

Two more punks show up late to the party. When they see their buddies throwing up and convulsing and collapsed in a writhing mass of excessive fat, they turn and run toward the southwest corner and the subway entrance. I take off after them.

In the three months since my encounter with the skateboarder in Central Park, I've learned how to harness my new abilities. Now, I can direct my yawns at a single individual in a crowd with a range of up to fifty feet. I can even hit moving targets while running at full speed.

Just before they reach 23rd Street, I yawn and the two punks collapse and go sliding along the sidewalk, coming to rest next to each other by the park entrance, their eyes closed in a deep, unexpected slumber.

They call me Dr. Lullaby.

~φ~

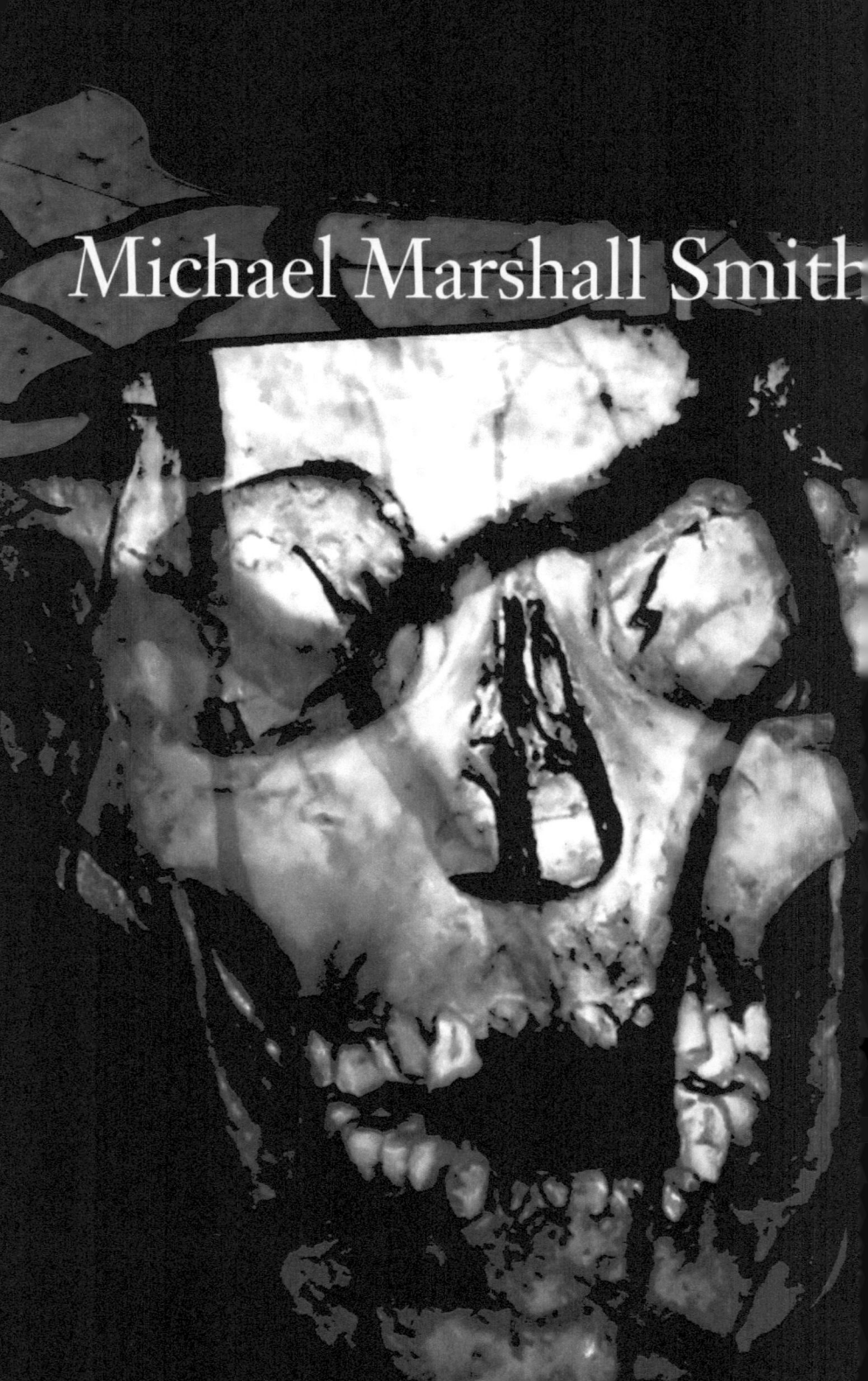

Michael Marshall Smith

Michael Marshall Smith is a novelist and screen-writer. Under this name he has published seventy short stories and three novels – *Only Forward*, *Spares* and *One of Us* – in the process winning the Philip K. Dick Award, International Horror Guild, August Derleth and the Prix Bob Morane in France. He has won the British Fantasy Award for Best Short Fiction four times, more than any other author.

Writing as Michael Marshall, he has also published five internationally-bestselling thrillers, including *The Straw Men*, *The Intruders* and *Bad Things*. *The Intruders* is currently under series development with BBC Television. 2009 also saw the publication of *The Servants*, under the further name M. M. Smith.

He is currently involved in screenwriting projects, including a television pilot set in New York, and an animated horror movie for children. His new Michael Marshall novel *Killer Move* will be published in the US and UK in July 2011.

He lives in North London with his wife, son, and two cats.

Visit his website at: www.michaelmarshallsmith.com

Death Light

I know the moment, the exact second, when I gave up hope. It happened just as afternoon gave itself to twilight, and when it came, it dropped like a stone. It fell on me, and it fell hard, and when it landed, something broke. That's what I think, anyway. Though looking back, it seems it must have started a couple of days before. That's what they say, anyhow, and I cannot find clear memories of that period now so it's hard to disagree. All I can be sure of is the breakage, and that when something breaks, it creates at least two parts.

I'd been in the DGA building on semi-mythical Sunset Boulevard, spectating a half-hour "meeting" in an airy office with an animatronic from the Los Angeles chapter of a well-known mini-major. I'd sat in a disconcertingly large leather chair and sipped a cup of very good coffee, while Jon pimped our creative wares, only making me want to vomit with embarrassment about twice. The studio droid been pleasant and upbeat throughout, assuring us that we were freakishly talented and it would be great for us all to work together, just great, really, incredibly, fabulously... *great* – and he'd be in touch, like, immediately. Seriously. Before we'd left the building, he'd be talking to us again. Before we'd even *arrived today*, wheels would start to turn. This guy was going to bend time itself, in order to us all working together way back before the Big Bang.

Then his pleasant, willowy assistant – her name was something like Hope or Treasure or Magnificence, but after a couple of days of such meetings I'd given up trying to remember them, even though I knew that ten years from now it could be her who ran the studio – had shown Jon and I back out through their epic reception area, smiling pleasantly as she put us in an elevator. Which had also been pleasant, as such things go.

As soon as the elevator doors shut and we were alone, Jon crinkled his eyes and punched me gently on the shoulder, dip-ping from the waist, a triumphant bend in his knees.

"Hey, hey hey!"

I nodded and smiled as best I could, wondering how he could possibly be so dumb as to not realise what had just happened.

The elevator eventually let us out in the vast and silent street-level lobby, and our heels ticked across a shining floor toward glass doors beyond which the real world waited – as real, at least, as it ever got in this part of California. Jon retrieved his rental Le Baron from the underground lot (Budget having been fresh out of Mustangs), clapped me on the back, and nosed out onto Sunset, finding a temporary niche market for low-rent middle-aged producers in the late afternoon traffic, and adding his pair of brake lights to the array.

I watched as his greying coif disappeared, and then, when I was finally alone, let out a long, slow breath.

The guy from the studio wasn't going to be in touch.

Not soon. Not ever.

That much was clear to me, if not to Jon. It wasn't that we'd done anything wrong. It had probably been true before we'd arrived for the meeting, before we'd taken the flight from London three days before. That wasn't the point. It had been one company of many, the person we'd seen merely one executive among thousands plying their vague trade in this bizarre town. I hadn't even bothered to commit the guy's name to memory, knowing that within months he'd have moved up or sideways or down, to be replaced by someone identical. His hair might be a slightly different colour, or he'd be wearing a pant suit and be a woman – but it would effectively be the same guy, with the same combination of excessive confidence and covert vulnerability, bearing an identical trend-crazed decision-paralysis dressed up as cautious acumen. That wasn't the problem. What I'd realised was that there simply wasn't any point going through this charade, in turning up to meetings where everyone maintained a "relationship" without any real possibility of anything whatsoever coming of it. That there was no point believing in sudden and inevitable good fortune, or that a deal was just around the corner if I wanted it enough – that I could use my will to bend reality and make it give me what I'd always wanted.

Reality, it turned out, was a lot more stubborn than it looked. Reality was tough.

Reality could kick my arse.

Or "ass", as they said out here.

I felt like a child, a forlorn kid finally understanding that, however long he searched under the tree, Santa Claus really hadn't brought him a bike this year... And that next year wasn't looking good, either, what with the whole thing having been a made-up story from the get-go. I finally understood that the movie business in general had made a vast, unspoken decision, and probably made it before I was born.

It would get along without me.

I started slowly walking west along Sunset. I could have accepted a lift back to the hotel, but hadn't been able to bear the prospect. I'd told Jon I wanted to soak up the atmosphere – and I had – but now that was exactly what I *didn't* want to do. What had been exciting and energising an hour ago now felt exhausted, grey and sad. It was like seeing the woman you love, after she's told you she's been seeing somebody else for six months. She is still lovely, still all you want, but now looks new and distant, while you feel like somebody old and left behind: looking in, watching her, through glass which is thick and stained.

And those last six months, that time you thought you'd spent together... It turns out she hadn't really been there at all.

Anyone can walk into Hollywood's lobby. So long as you've got a screenplay or two or are allied to a half-assed wannabe producer like Jon, you can walk up to the bar and buy yourself a drink. Watch the players. Dream your little dreams. But there are other rooms, the ones where the real players lurk, waiting to cut the real/reel deals. Suites where the stars lounge, ready to take your work and pay you a little for it, while making themselves ever more rich, and famous, and indispensable. And there are the ballrooms too, icons like Chateau Marmont, which I happened to be passing – along with others which were doubtless far more fashionable these days but which I was insufficiently cool to have been told about. You could walk into any of those places right off the street, but that wasn't the point. Like a vampire, if you want to do real business, you have to be invited in.

Until this afternoon I'd believed that my time would come, that I would be receiving the secret handshake and guided through the right door.

Now suddenly I didn't.

And I felt a fool.

I found myself remembering conversations which had never taken place, things I'd imagined people saying of me, fantasies to warm long sessions at the keyboard:

"This guy's not just one of those writers who turn up in neat jeans and nod and smile, then go home to spend the afternoon drinking bourbon and kicking the cat."

"I hear you, Bob. He understands punctuation and everything. He's the real deal. His apostrophes are fucking legendary."

"Let's get him locked down before someone else snatches him out of our hands. Three picture first look, duplex office on the lot. Make it so, stat."

"We're talking high seven figures?"

"Eight to be safe."

"Plus a house to work in. Or two."

"Hell – just give him Malibu."

Was it bourbon? Or scotch? I had never been entirely clear of the difference. Whatever. Half a large bottle of *something*, at any rate, is what I believed I'd be drinking per afternoon if I lived in LA for very long.

As I passed the site of the old Marlboro Man billboard, I suddenly realised that I'd been so wrapped up in maudlin introspection that I hadn't even had my post-meeting cigarette. I stopped and lit one – a salute in the direction of the vanished icon, amazed that he hadn't yet been replaced with Cranberry Juice Woman, or Low Impact Aerobics Person, Zero Carbohydrate Guy or whatever the hell the locals were telling themselves would make them live forever these days.

At the top of La Cienega I ground to a halt.

I knew what my evening held. An interminable dinner in some restaurant I'd be supposed to be impressed by, with Jon and an American version of Jon boring each other senseless with largely fictitious tales of projects in progress, projects in development, projects in projection: projects which would never –

and *should* never – see the light of day. A reprise of Jon's pitch of my screenplay, with everything but the most facile description of the plot utterly wrong – followed by double decaf espressos and a three-way flurry of unheartfelt declarations of intent to work with each other at some point in a never-to-be-determined future.

I'll get my people to take your people out into the parking lot and kick the living crap out of them.

And validate my parking, shit-head.

For a moment I considered keeping walking, taking Sunset as far as the sunset, all the way to Santa Monica and the sea. It would take what – an hour or two? I could get a beer, sit and look out over the ocean from the palisades. Let the sight of the Pacific wash it all away.

But I turned my head, and looked down the hill.

My hotel waited at the bottom of it. I needed to shower and change, see if there'd been any calls, pump myself up for dinner, just in case. You never know, right? That's the spirit. It could happen, any day, and believing the game is already lost doesn't mean you can stop playing. Not when you've wanted to be a screenwriter since you first heard the word. Not when you've lived and breathed film and television for thirty years.

Not when that desire had become been pretty much all you are.

It was during the first steps down La Cienega, towards the evening and tomorrow's list of pointless meetings which I'd go to anyway, because that's what you do, even when you've realised there's no point, that I felt my heart break.

~φ~

The first I knew about it was when I emerged from the elevator in the lobby of Ma Maison, and noticed a black-and-white sitting outside the main doors to the hotel. I was coughing wildly at the time – far too many cigarettes the night before - and heading for the Concierges' desk, where I was hoping to glom some information on how to get to the Paramount lot with as little grief as possible. I thought nothing about the police car beyond a twinge of voyeuristic curiosity – *wonder who's been caught doing what?* I was halfway across the lobby, about level with the huge flower arrangement, when all hell broke loose.

"Stay the fuck where you are!"

"Get your hands up! Police!"

Startled, I was turning to see who was being screamed at, hoping I wasn't in the line of fire, when something heavy sent me thudding into a marble pedestal.

A sharp pain cracked across my face and shoulders as I collided with it. Then I was engulfed by the combined shattering and rustling of two hundred dollars' worth of flowers, and a huge vase, hitting the floor.

I've been shot, I thought. *Jesus.*

I got a wipe pan of shocked faces as I tried to yank my face up from the floor, and then my head was shoved back down again. I managed to avert my face just in time, and felt my right cheekbone crack with the cold floor. I assumed someone had come up behind me, and was keeping my head down to prevent me from getting in the way of another shot. They say that you don't feel a bullet, not immediately, and I was wondering if I'd been hit, and how badly. I was suffused with vertiginous disbelief, a feeling of being plunged into the kind of situation I'd assumed only happened to characters in films and books.

Though my face and chest hurt, there didn't seem to be blood jetting out of any part of my body. As the initial shouts and screams died down to coos and whispers, I realised the person who'd pushed my head down was sitting on my back, yanking my arms around behind me.

Twisting my eyes forward I could now see the legs of a policeman, standing about two yards in front.

Behind him I saw the day Concierge, an elegant Latino woman. She normally favoured me with an efficient smile, recognising me as someone who would always need advice on how to get somewhere. Now she was staring at me as if I were an unpredictable household pet. So were the other occupants of the lobby. None seemed to be taking cover from anyone any more.

"Try anything," a brutal voice snarled into my ear, from very close range, "And you won't make it to the precinct. Understand? Don't you try a *fucking thing.*"

His breath was hot in my ear. Suddenly I was back on my feet again, and I realised the guy on my back was a policeman, that my hands had been cuffed, and that something *very bad indeed was going on.*

"What's happening?" I asked, shakily. My face hurt all over, and I was scared shitless now.

"Nick Williams?" the cop asked. I stared at him. He stared back, green eyes full of something very cold.

"Yes," I said. "What..."

"You're under arrest."

"For what?" I stammered, and the cop calmly backhanded me across the face. Meanwhile the one behind was yanking me back and forth, checking for weapons – which of course I didn't have.

"I'm going read you your rights," the first cop said, "During which time you're going to *shut the fuck up*, and then you're coming with us."

As he Miranda-ed me I merely blinked, nonplussed, aware of people around the edges of the lobby, staring faces, some of which I recognised from passing glimpses in elevators, the hotel bar, the sun deck. A terrible gout of shame suddenly cut through the confusion and pain, and I was seized with the need to signal to them that I wasn't suddenly different: that I was still the affable young man whom they'd nodded at, and bid good morning; that I wasn't guilty of anything.

But by then the cops were bundling me toward the main doors. The bellhops held them open, refusing to meet my eye. That, more than anything, brought home the reality of what was happening. These were friendly guys – the quality of the staff was one of the reasons I always stayed at Ma Maison. They smiled when they saw you, they recognised you from last time, and they held the door open with a grin when you came back from a meeting, regardless of how pointless it might have been.

But now it was like the police were just carrying a heavy carpet, something soiled, something their eyes skated over. I was swept out of the lobby and into humid warmth outside, then shoved into the back of the police car. The cop who'd cuffed me got in the back beside me, one hand firmly clamped around my arm. The other got in front, hit the siren, and pulled off at high speed.

"Look," I said. I was trying to sound calm. It didn't work. My voice was trembling as much as the rest of me. "What have I done?"

The cop used one hand to swivel me slightly away from him, and punched me very hard in the kidney.

I abruptly lost the will to live, and coughed wordlessly in pain. Then he grabbed my hair and banged my face into the back of the seat in front.

I slumped back, feeling warm liquid, blood, seeping out of my nose. The car was tearing down Beverley Boulevard, the driver keeping his eyes on the road. I took deep breaths, willing myself to become calm.

"Please," I said eventually. "*Please* will you tell me *what it is I'm supposed to have done?*"

The cop next to me laughed. The one in front grunted in counterpoint. I understood they were appreciating the humour of me denying what I had self-evidently done. They seemed very hyped up, excited, as if out on a limb, and I wondered if they were supposed to have made this arrest.

"Please," I said, trying not to snuffle, though enough blood had come out of my nose to start dripping off my chin. "What? *What is going on?*"

"You're under arrest," the cop next to me said, "For the murder of two women and a police officer. Now shut up before I do something you'll regret."

I turned slowly and stared out of the window.

~φ~

The police station was much as you'd expect. I'd only ever seen them on the TV or cinema screen before, and it was kind of like that, only more crowded and noisier and far more scary. Also, in the cop shows people are generally dragged in to universal apathy. There was none of this when I was pulled in front of what I assume was a Desk Sergeant or whatever the American equivalent is.

"Wow," he said. "Now that's what I *call* a likeness."

I was hurriedly finger-printed and then hauled down a corridor and into a room, faces turning to watch me all the way. Some were just intensely curious. The cops amongst them looked actively frightening, however, and I wasn't surprised. From what I'd gathered, cops tend to take a very dim view of people who kill one of their own. I realised I was probably lucky to have made it to the station in one piece. It could only be because I was worth more to the arresting officers as a trophy collar than as a trophy dead person, or so my extensive third-hand knowledge of law and order (from books and the screen) suggested. That should have been comforting, but it wasn't. None of it was in the least bit comforting.

I was locked in the room with a huge cop standing in front of the door. At first I was worried that his job was to beat the shit out of me, but he just stood there, staring at me. My arms were still cuffed, which prevented me from doing the thing foremost in my mind – lighting a cigarette. In all the time since the sudden outbreak of nightmare in the Ma Maison lobby, I'd thought of only three things. Phoning my parents. Phoning my girlfriend. And having a cigarette. I had a pack in my jacket. Probably they were squashed flat, but I didn't care. I wanted one. So much so that I turned to the cop by the door and gathered the courage to speak.

"Look," I said, and that's as far as I got.

"*Shut the fuck up,*" the cop shouted, going from 0 to psycho-furious in no seconds flat.

I shut the fuck up. Probably I couldn't have had one anyway. The only thing on the bare walls of the room was a huge NO SMOKING sign. I'd assumed that cops all around the world smoked, but maybe in LA even they weren't allowed. Maybe in LA they all played racquetball instead.

Ten minutes later two policemen turned up. They were plain clothes, and from the way the cop in the door got out of their way I assumed at least one of them was pretty senior.

The taller of the two, a man in his late forties, with a charcoal grey suit and the most intimidating face I'd ever seen, sat down opposite me. The other, a stocky man wearing a shabbier suit, in a colour I'd have to describe as "tan," went and stood next to the window.

For a moment neither said anything. They simply stared at me. I had another wave of vertigo, as every crime novel I've read, and every thriller I've seen, came home to roost. The guy sitting in front of me, I guessed, was probably the Lieutenant. He had to be. Probably everyone called him "Loot", and he was firm but fair with his officers. The thug by the window, who looked like every maverick detective in every film I'd ever watched, was probably exactly that. Presumably had an ex-wife and a drinking problem and two daughters that he got on with surprisingly well. A 1980s-era James Woods could have played him perfectly, but now I guess you'd settle for a Mark Wahlberg or similar, or maybe take a chance and sign Robert Downey Jr. I suddenly felt eerily sure that the lieutenant – you would have cast Eastwood thirty years ago, or maybe saved some money and gone for Ed Harris, who could still do the job now – was going to offer me a cigarette. They stared at me a little longer, still looking angry. I wondered if this was down to the fact that a couple of beat cops had snapped me off the streets, instead of them.

Then the older one reached into his pocket and pulled out a pack of cigarettes. I thought I hid my happiness, but obviously I was wrong.

"What's funny?" the Detective snapped. "Believe me, asshole, there's *nothing* funny about the place you're in."

The Lieutenant meanwhile lit a cigarette, took a deep drag on it, and then went back to staring at me.

I looked down at the table, and silently rehearsed the available facts. The available fact, singular.

I wasn't guilty.

Whatever these guys had made me for, and however they'd reached that conclusion, I hadn't done it. I had to keep reminding myself of that.

I waited until I was calm enough for a stray thought to enter my head – one concerning the fact I was late for a meeting, and Jon would be getting annoyed – and then I looked back up.

"Would you please tell me," I said, for what felt like the hundredth time, "Why I'm here?"

Tan Suit laughed. The lieutenant kept staring, then got the pack of cigarettes out again, took one from the packet, lit it, and stuck it in my mouth.

I took a deep lug, and looked in the man's eyes to see that they looked very slightly friendlier.

"Thank you," I said. "You would be 'good cop', right?"

Both men's eyes flickered. I was *horrified* at what had just come out of my mouth. I was scared shitless, and my mouth was running off as if I'd suddenly become a minor character in a terrible television cop show.

"I know I'm supposed to have killed two women and a policeman,' I said, trying to raise my game. "One of the arresting officers told me, in between punches. The thing is... I haven't killed anyone."

The lieutenant just kept looking at me.

"I've been in LA four days," I said. "I'm a writer. I go to meetings and then I go back to my hotel where I read and eat room service and generally... uh, do that kind of thing." I was losing the thread of my argument. I was babbling. I couldn't remember what I'd been intending to say, and so I retreated to my core position. "I haven't killed anyone. Why would I *do* that?"

The Detective suddenly reached across, grabbed the cigarette from my mouth and hurled it into the wall. A small shower of sparks drifted down in the air.

"Mal Hopkins was a friend of mine, you *cunt*," he shouted.

The lieutenant held his hand up, and at that moment I really thought I'd lost it. They really were good and bad-copping me. This couldn't be happening. Way too much coffee with breakfast in my room, maybe, or a late burst jet-lag suddenly cutting in, or the weariness of my revelation on Sunset of the afternoon before just suddenly making everything seem like a tired joke.

It had to be something like that. This was too much like a dream, a string of cop clichés hacked together for my own mind for its amusement. Mind games with cigarettes. Nice Mr. Lieutenant, nasty Mr. Tan Suit. The cop who died being a friend of the scary cop. I couldn't have got away with writing this stuff. It was too formulaic to be true. Even Jon would turn his nose up at it.

"I didn't do anything," I said, again.

It was the one thing I was sure of, and I felt as though I might as well keep saying it.

The lieutenant reached into another pocket and pulled out a piece of paper. He unfolded it and held it up, comparing it with my face, then laid it down on the desk. A flick of his wrist turned it round so I could see it. I couldn't say anything for about ten seconds.

"Jesus," I said, eventually. "That's me."

I looked up at the Lieutenant. He had a strange expression on his face. Then I looked back down at the picture. It was a photo-fit, but one subsequently tweaked by an artist to pull out eye-witness detail that a basic composite would have lacked. It showed a man with a goatee beard and a short pony-tail. A long nose, full lips, and bony cheeks. Not gorgeous, by any standards, but it was the best drawing of me I could imagine.

"Where's this *from*?" I asked.

"You don't deny it resembles you?" the lieutenant said.

I shook my head. "No," I said. "I mean, it's a perfect likeness."

The Detective made a dour, triumphal sound in the background, but his boss didn't take his eyes off my face. He picked up the drawing, looked at it, and me, one last time, and then returned it to his pocket.

~φ~

They took me out of the room and down a corridor. At the end was a room in which another five men were standing. Some looked like criminals, others more like plainclothes cops. They were all roughly the same size and build as me, and a couple had goatees. A uniformed policeman roughly wiped the blood off the lower half of my face with a cloth, and then we were filed into another, smaller room, which had glass along one side.

I was in a line-up.

Jesus Christ.

I knew what was happening, and I still couldn't believe it. Someone on the other side of the glass would be looking for a man who looked like the one in the drawing I'd just been shown.

With a numbing sense of panic I realised that they would pick me out. They were bound to. The drawing looked exactly *like* me. How could they not pick me out?

We stood for a while, then a voice from a speaker in the ceiling asked us to turn to the right. We did so. Then, also on instruction, we turned to the left, before returning to facing the front again.

It took about ten minutes, and then we were led out and I was put back in the interrogation room again.

~φ~

Half an hour later, the lieutenant came back. He was alone this time. He sat facing me, got out a pack of cigarettes and lit one for me, watching my face carefully. I took as deep a drag as I could, given that the cigarette was in my mouth and staying there, as my hands were still behind my back. I've never really got the hang of the no-hands school of smoking. The smoke gets in my eyes. I breathed out heavily, shakily.

"Thank you," I said.

"Looks like you needed that," he said, his hands flat on the table, keeping his eyes firmly on me.

"Yes," I said, with smoker's ingrained defensiveness. "I needed that."

"How many do you smoke a day?" he asked.

I suspected I was being softened up for something, but this was the first civil conversation I'd had all day. "About twenty-five, thirty. Forty when I'm a trip like this. Hyped up, jet-lagged, too much coffee, stress, I wind up smoking a lot more."

He nodded, then reached across into my jacket pocket. He pulled out the contents – a duty free lighter and two packs of Marlboro Lights (the official cigarette of the entertainment in-dustry), one of them half-empty. He placed all this in the centre of the table, like an exhibit.

"I assume the witness picked me out?"

"Yep," he said.

When he didn't say anything further, I tried speaking again. "And that wouldn't have had anything to do with me being the only person in the line-up with a bruised face?"

The lieutenant surprised me by smiling. I didn't know whether to smile back, so I didn't. Quite apart from anything else, my face genuinely hurt a lot.

"My name is John Considine," he said. "I'm a Lieutenant in Homicide. I'm telling you that so you know the name of the guy who's on this case. And believe me, I'm *on this case*."

"Okay," I said. I didn't know how else to respond. I was beginning to suspect that something very unpleasant must have happened to the two women and the cop.

"You were picked out of the line-up, right away and without hesitation. But as you've pointed out, your, uh, facial marking could have been a factor. That's untidy. It's one of three reasons you're sitting here and not in the tank with a bunch of guys who might want to curry favour with us by beating the shit out of a cop-killer."

I nodded, not understanding where this was leading, but sensing things weren't getting any worse, at least.

"So... What happens now?"

"What happens now is that you're going to stay here, while I check out the account that you're about to give me of your movements for the last twenty four hours."

I took another lug on the cigarette, indicated that the lit end was beginning to get uncomfortably close to the end of my nose, and he took it.

"I got up around 7a.m. yesterday," I said. "Then I had breakfast with Jon, the producer I'm here with, and we went to a meeting at Bottom Line Productions."

"Time?"

"Nine-thirty," I said. "Then Di Marco Pictures in Santa Monica, at 11:00. We came back to the hotel around 12:30. I had lunch on the sun deck, again with Jon, we had a meeting at Showtime all afternoon, and then a meet-and-greet with Running Time Entertainment, on Sunset."

"What did you do then?"

"Walked back to the hotel, showered, called my girlfriend, in England, and then a dinner meeting with Jon and a guy somewhere in West Hollywood."

"What was the name of the other guy?"

I wracked my brains. I'd been very tired by that stage, jet-lagged, and keeping myself going on a string of Budweisers. It was hard to remember anything about the evening at all. Then, thank God, it came to me.

"Jack Simons," I said. "He's an agent at Douglas Jenson. He supposed to be helping us package some project which is clearly never going to happen."

Considine scribbled some of this on a pad, and then looked up sardonically. "Got to love the power of positive thinking."

"Sadly it's not as convincing as bitter experience."

"What time did you finish eating?"

"Around nine. Jon went off to meet some other contact. I think. I'd had enough schmoozing for one evening, so I took a cab back to the hotel."

"Did you get the driver's name, name of the car firm?"

"No. The cab was green. The driver was stoned. It wasn't a relaxing ride."

Considine wrote some more stuff down. "What then?"

"Back to the hotel. I checked at the concierge's desk because a parcel was supposed to have arrived for me during the day, and hadn't. They still didn't have it. I went up to my room. I ordered coffee on room service."

"Time?"

"I don't know. I guess about ten-thirty. Then I watched a movie."

"On television?"

"No, on the, you know, the in-house service thing. I watched *The Grudge* again, which I think started at eleven. It wasn't any better the second time, but I needed something to stop me crashing too early. Then I went to bed, I guess around twelve-thirty, one o'clock."

Considine stood up. "Don't go anywhere," he said. I guess it was a joke.

Two hours later he was back, with a uniform in tow. The uniform undid the handcuffs and left. I brought my arms slowly round in front, wincing all the way. I took a cigarette from my own packet and lit it.

"Mr Simons has verified that you and Jon Nash had dinner with him," Considine said. "We traced the cab driver, who remembers your 'Hugh Grant' accent and the fact you tipped high. He was still wasted when we talked to him. You're lucky he didn't crash the cab. Room service at Ma Maison has a record of your order for coffee, and the girl who delivered it identified your face from the composite. The hotel media system has a record of a movie being charged to your room, commencing at 11:05."

My insides felt like they'd turned to water.

It *had* to all check out, because it was all true. But by then it was mid-afternoon, and parts of my head were beginning to believe I must have done *something*, or at least that the information I'd given would inexplicably turn out to be untrue. That someone would have lied, to put me in trouble. That... I don't know.

That all this would all keep on happening, for ever.

"What does that mean?" I said.

"That you can't have killed one of the victims, the one we have a witness for. She was killed between 9:30 and 10:30 p.m. last night."

I suddenly felt completely fucked. My arms started shaking, and I went dizzy. It must have been relief I was feeling, but it felt like malaria.

"What were the other two things?" I asked, when I could. "The other reasons you left me in here?"

He turned from the window and looked at me, appraisingly.

"Your reaction on seeing the photo fit. Any normal guilty person, when they see something like that, denies the resemblance. They pick on something small, because there's always *some* inaccuracy. They invent twin brothers, they say space aliens have a mask of their face and they use it when they're down here impregnating Earth women, yes suh, that's how it is. They don't just sit there and go 'Yep, that's me.' Okay, you could have been bluffing. Trying to be clever. But I don't think you were. Your eyes popped out your head when you saw it."

"It's an amazing likeness," I said. "My girlfriend's an artist. She draws me all the time, but she's seldom got as close as that. What was the other reason?"

"I can't tell you," Considine said. "Just there's something else about you which gives cause to reasonable doubt that you are the guy I'm looking for."

"What happens now?" I asked. I felt hot, tired, as if all of my blood had turned sour, or dried out.

"You can go," he said, and opened the door.

~φ~

He got someone to call me a cab, and I picked it up outside the station. The driver wanted to talk, but I didn't. The ride went slowly, far more slowly than the journey to the station had seemed to that morning. My face hurt a lot, and I knew that I'd missed two important meetings. Jon was going to be pissed off.

It was only as the cab was pulling up outside the lobby that it occurred to me how I had left the premises – cuffed and dragged out by two cops. I tried to remember if there was some other way into the hotel, but my head ached and I couldn't come up with one.

I paid the cab off and walked towards the entrance. One of the bellhops reached over and opened the door. He hadn't been there when I'd made my unusual departure earlier, and he gave me a cheery smile as usual.

Inside I turned left and went to the Concierge's Desk. The tall woman was still on duty, and I stood in front of her for a moment, letting her eyes flit over my face, willing her to make something of it. I was finally beginning to become cautiously angry about the events of the morning, and realising that had I been American, I'd be filing suit against the LAPD already, hiring a publicist, and planning my own reality show – WHEN SCREENWRITERS ARE WRONGLY ACCUSED.

I asked if my package had turned up yet. She looked down quickly, as if suddenly aware she'd been staring, and consulted her list. I noticed, pointlessly, and not for the first time, how attractive she was.

"Yes," she said, nodding. "It's already been taken up to your room."

That at least was something to be mildly happy about: Cheap American-priced software for my laptop. I was about to go, when on impulse I turned back to her.

"It wasn't me," I said. "They made a mistake."

"I know, sir," she said, quickly, her face transparently apologetic, as if grateful for the chance. "The police called here to check some information. The man sounded angry when we told him."

I bet myself that the man was Mr. Tan Suit, and nodded. "Okay then."

Up on the eighth floor I walked slowly down the corridor and let myself into 805. The room was frigid, blessed by the hotel's exuberant air-conditioning, and it felt good.

I walked over to the window. I always choose a room on the North side, because they get a good view over the hills. On a clear day, when the smog isn't too heavy, you get a good view the Hollywood sign, which feels symbolically like a good thing. Inspirational, I guess.

The view seemed different today, and didn't make me feel better. The sign just looked like something off a postcard, as if it had no bearing on me at all.

You're a tourist, it said. *That's all.*

As I turned from it, I caught sight of myself in the mirror on the wall. My right cheek looked lumpy and was beginning to discolour, and a couple of other spots looked unusual. It didn't look anywhere as bad as it felt, however, which was galling. I hurt like hell, and I wanted the outside world to know it.

The message light on the phone was flashing. There were four voicemails from Jon, spaced at regular intervals throughout the morning, inquiring as to where the fuck I was, with increasing urgency and irritation. The last message said he's gone to the eXpow meeting by himself, and wouldn't be back until mid-evening, and WTF???, and on and on.

I thought about calling Anne, then remembered the time difference and realised she'd be asleep. Suddenly I felt very alone, a Brit scribbler in a city which evidently didn't like me a whole lot.

With an air of vague defiance I walked to the window, lit a cigarette and smoked it in the city's general direction.

~φ~

At five o'clock I was sitting in the room's armchair, dressed in a post-shower bathrobe and staring out at the sheen over the hills. I was drinking a bottle of cranberry juice from the minibar. A half-finished jug of coffee sat on the table, surrounded by the chaos of my loose change (I never seem to be able to tame it when I'm in America – it just grows and grows). I'd felt a curious gratitude when the room service had arrived, and fought the urge to ludicrously overtip the waiter. These guys had alibied me. Even though I was innocent, that felt like a big favour. By now I'd calmed down enough to be tremblingly furious with the two cops who'd arrested me. There was a red welt across my chest, from my collision the pedestal in the lobby. My cheekbone had started to come up in earnest now, one eye was blackening, and all in all I looked like crap.

I'd been *unarmed*.

Christ, never mind that – I was *innocent*.

Considine's spiel at the end was most likely an attempt to stop me pressing charges. It had been unnecessary, of course. My policy in foreign countries is to keep my head down, get on with my work, and not antagonise the natives. It's my policy when at home, too. I was inexpressibly glad that the whole situation had gone away, but I was angry that I'd needed someone else's efforts to clear me, that I hadn't just exuded innocence. It was irrational, but I felt both used and stupid, and was rehearsing after-the-event strategies, things I should have said, ways I should have been.

Pointless. I remembered that at least I had my software. I find new bits of software genuinely exciting – not least because it's written in a language I don't understand *at all*, and so there's no chance of some fucker wheedling me into rewriting it to a stupid deadline, and for not enough money. Normally I left the stuff shrink-wrapped until I got home, but today I felt I could do with something to get my mind off current events. I was going to have to deal with Jon later, which would be trying. At the moment I felt as if any lip from him could result in a fight, which would not a good idea for my career, or anything else. Punching out a producer in the bar of Ma Maison – even a no-hoper like Jon – would be a bad move on any number of grounds. Though the Writers' Union might put up a statue to me.

So I poured myself another coffee, swore mildly at the fact that they'd brought cream, rather than the milk I'd explicitly asked for, and looked around the room for the package. A first trawl didn't bring anything to light, so I stood up and poked around for it.

It didn't take long to establish it wasn't there. My jaw clenched. I reached out for the phone. Then I stopped, turned abruptly and walked over to my suitcase. Rather than bawl someone out down the phone, which would do me no good, I'd go down to the desk, gently enquire as to where the *fucking Christing Hell* my software was, and then sit in the bar reading a book and drinking Budweisers. Many, many Budweisers. Not only would that be preferable to staying in a room which was beginning to develop a smog of its own, but it might mean I was in a more receptive mood when Jon returned to the hotel.

I dressed, left a message on his voice mail, and went downstairs. The tall woman was about to go off duty when I got down to the desk, a man shaped like a small hairy fridge poised to take her place. He turned toward me as I approached, ready and able to assist, but the woman – whose badge I noticed, for the first time, declared that she was called Alicia (staff don't have surnames at this hotel) – saw me coming, and seemed to impress upon the man that she would like to deal with me. At least that's what I thought happened, but it could have been wishful thinking. At that moment I was prepared to leap at the idea that someone wanted to be nice to me. More likely she'd flagged me as a "problematic and demanding" guest.

I smiled, to show I wasn't going to bite, and told her my package wasn't in my room. Instead of rolling her eyes and generally implying that Sir was a bit of a retard, she reached for her ledger.

She ran her finger down the day's deliveries, then held it politely out to show me that a package for N. Williams had been received, and ticked as delivered to the room. I bore this patiently.

"Right," I said, "That's as may be. But it's not in my room, unless the guy hid it somewhere."

"He would have put it on the bedside table."

I was aware of this, having had stuff delivered to the room on previous trips, and nodded with a resigned smile. "It's not there." I repeated.

She turned to her terminal. Her long, slim fingers pattered over the keys for a few moments, and then she smiled brightly.

"Ahh!" she said contentedly. "There are two of you."

I stared at her. The woman saw my confusion, and angled the monitor towards me. On the screen, in little green points of light, I saw my own name. And under it, in the lists of guests, there it was again – Mr. Williams.

"The boy has delivered your package to the wrong Mr. Williams."

She seemed pleased at having solved the mystery, but I wished she'd phrased it that way in the first place. Being in a hotel with another person of the same surname was a possibility I'd considered before, having once ordered an "adult" CD-ROM. After making the order I'd spent twenty-four hours plagued with the complete and utter Fear, fully expecting the porn to be delivered to someone else, opened, and then brought irately back down to reception. I pictured the staff mounting the disc on a plinth, pointing spotlights at it, and standing around with their arms folded waiting for me: none of them knowing or caring it had been my girlfriend's idea to buy the bloody thing in the first place.

Thank God this time it was only Photoshop plug-ins.

"Good," I said. "So..."

"I'll call Mr. Williams," Alicia said, and pattered the keyboard again. She frowned. "He is called Nick too," she said. "That's a coincidence. He's in Room 805."

"That's *my* room," I said.

"Oh. Then this must be your information I'm looking at. I'll check the other one."

A few more seconds of typing, and then she frowned at the monitor, her fingers still.

"There must be some mistake," she said.

She swivelled the monitor toward me again. Two guest record windows were open side by side on the screen.

Both were for a Mr. Williams, first name Nick. And both were registered to room 805.

"Someone must have entered your information twice," she suggested, eventually.

"Wouldn't the system notice that both were allocated the same room?" My throat felt dry. I needed a beer quite soon. And another cigarette. Always another of those.

"Not necessarily," Alicia said, blushing slightly. "The two Mr. Williams could be... good *friends*."

"Okay, I hear what you're saying, but there *is* no other Mr. Williams," I said. "Take it from me. So... where's my package?"

"I'll look into it right now," Alicia said, suddenly business-like. I don't know whether it was because she found the problem genuinely absorbing, or if she was nettled about not being able to clock off. "Perhaps you could sit in the bar, and I'll come to you when I've found out what the problem is?"

I thanked her, and trouped over towards the bar area on the terrace, where a semi-talented pianist was playing jazz standards, thankfully fairly quietly. I found a nook as far away from him as possible. After a moment a waitress came over, and set a bowl of nuts and a napkin down on the table in front of me.

"Hello, Mr. Williams," she said. "What will you be having this evening?"

I didn't recognise her. I was a little surprised at being addressed by name, and immediately paranoid, wondering if news of this morning's events had spread through the staff. More probably she'd just served me on some previous evening, when I was already a little too beer-relaxed to notice faces and remember them.

I ordered a Bud and she strode off, leaving me to my book. I lit a cigarette and tried to settle down to it. After no more than a few seconds I heard a tutting sound, and looked up. A young American couple were sitting at the next table, and both were frowning shrewishly at me.

"Excuse me?" I said.

"Would you mind not smoking?" the man said, loudly.

"Yes I would," I said. "We are outside, and the requisite distance from an open doorway. There are ashtrays on the tables. I am a smoker, and I am smoking. If you don't like it, you're welcome to sit somewhere else. Have a nice day."

They gawped at me like a pair of affronted owls. I stared back, not in the mood to back down. I'd about had it for one day, and especially had it on the subject of smoking. LA is fucking insane on the subject. You can't even smoke where you like on the street, but have to traipse a sufficient distance down the road and lurk with other social misfits, losers and criminals. If you're a smoker in LA you feel like you're always being watched, as if some dread force is after you, one which has taken protection of the body to the level of psychosis. LA's going to be the first city where you can't smoke *at all*, I'm sure, and yet half the time you can't even see the celebrated sign for all the car fumes, and you're swimming neck-high in smog that's thicker than water and sparkles and fizzes in the dark.

"You realise you're killing me," the woman said.

"All part of the service," I replied, in my fruitiest English accent, and her boyfriend stood up. He was tall and had the wholesome, corn-fed look that virile non-smoker Americans like to affect. He'd doubtless been a line-backer or running front or some such thing in college, and looked capable of making me unhappy.

So much for not antagonising the natives.

Luckily, at that moment half the staff in the hotel arrived at my table. The waitress turned up with my beer, and Alicia also materialised with a bellhop in tow. I turned to deal with them, half-aware of the young couple as they huffily gathered their stuff together and headed for the interior of the bar, where no one was smoking, juggling knives or in any other way imperilling other people's health and safety.

Alicia was polite and friendly, which just made me feel even more of a fuckwit. The bellhop with her was the very one who had delivered my package to room 805, early that afternoon. He remembered it clearly, including the small change spread over my table, and the large stack of pulp detective novels I was currently trawling through in a search for plots I could steal.

A little spark of anger went off in my head, like a bubble of foul gas in a stream, and then I just sighed. I thanked the bell-boy, who about-turned and walked off. Alicia lingered a moment longer, apologising for the problems I was having, and then went away, hopefully to a better evening than the one I was having.

Maybe the package really was in my room, and I'd been too weirded-out to look for it properly. Maybe not, and someone had stolen it, in which case I could deal with that in the morning, if at all. The software hadn't been very expensive. Probably I should just order it again and chalk it and the whole day down to experience.

I lit another cigarette, tried to blow the first mouthful of smoke toward the room where the young couple were sitting glowering at me, and settled down to drinking heavily.

~φ~

Jon showed up at ten, by which time I was six Budweisers down and feeling significantly more mellow. I still ached, but the chair was comfortable and the young Americans had disappeared, presumably to have a colonic irrigation. I was coming to realise that tomorrow would be another day, one on which I wouldn't have been rousted by over-zealous police and could reorder the software which was beginning to assume Holy Grail status in my mind. Or else I could cab over to an Apple Centre, and buy it there, which might be simpler. Or just download it, for Christ's sake.

Jon's tirade stopped in the middle of his first sentence, when he saw the bruises on my face. I gave him an abridged account of events. He talked forgivable bollocks about suing the police, filled me in on the meetings I'd missed, and reminded me what we had lined up for tomorrow. When he showed signs of wanting me to go through my day in more detail, I finished my beer, made my excuses and left.

In the elevator I discovered that all the beer I'd drunk had had an effect I somehow hadn't envisaged. It had made me quite drunk. I stood with my head against the cool side of the elevator, listening to soft pings and distant thrumming. At one point the elevator stopped at a floor and I straightened up unsteadily, but no one got on. The doors closed again, and we continued up towards the sky.

I found my room comparatively easily. It felt warmer than I was expecting, and I peered at the air conditioning control to find it had been switched off. I didn't understand this. I keep the A/C up very high. I like it that way. Sometimes the housemaid turned it off or down when she came in to turn the sheets, but tonight I'd successfully repelled her before I went downstairs.

I flicked the switch back up, and turned to face the room, which was dark, lit only by the bedside and table lamps. It was then that I saw a cardboard box sitting on the table by the window. The box was brown, covered in stickers, and had the unmistakable air of being full of software. From somewhere in the bowels of the hotel's delivery system, my package had been burped up.

Instantly forgetting the air-conditioning conundrum, I stumbled across the room towards it.

The top of the box was already open.

Inside was a mass of those polystyrene things which are used to pad packages and fuck up the environment. I stared at it, feeling more violated than at any time since, well, since that morning. Probably it was just someone who had received the package in error – maybe the other Mr. Williams, who at that stage I'd forgotten had never actually existed – and opened it accidentally. Either way, someone had opened my fucking package.

I took a handful of packing material out of the box, and then another. During the second handful I felt something. A box, much smaller than I would have expected software to be packaged in. I picked the larger box up and tipped the contents onto the bed.

Ten packets of Marlboro Lights fell out.

Nothing else.

I sat down on the bed. It felt as if the whole day had condensed down to this point. I should have felt angry, perplexed. But I didn't.

This wasn't an accident.

The fact that whoever had done this had got my brand of cigarettes right proved it, and it simply didn't feel like a joke. It felt macabre.

Who could have done it? Not Jon. It was entirely out of character. If not him, then who? Alicia downstairs knew about my never-ending quest, as did the bellhop she'd brought to my table in the bar. Maybe the bellhop had seen an empty pack of cigarettes in the trash – but why would this seem like a good thing to do?

It wasn't a joke. It was antagonistic. More than that. It felt like a threat.

The couple in the bar had looked daggers at me for an hour before flouncing out, but suspecting them of this was running straight into the realms of abject paranoia.

Apart from that, I couldn't think of anyone except...

The Lieutenant. The man who'd searched through my pockets and found two packs of Marlboro Light. Who'd asked me about my smoking. Who'd thought he'd had good reason to accuse me of crimes which were evidently heinous.

He could have done this. Or maybe not him, but someone else from the department. Maybe Mr. Tan Suit.

It wasn't over, after all. They were still after me.

I stalked across to the minibar, wrenched it open, and grabbed another beer. By the time I'd wrestled the cap off and taken the first mouthful, I knew what I was going to do. In a strange way, I felt *glad* it wasn't over. I'd been snatched out of my life that morning, thrown into some second, parallel reality. Then, through no skill or goodness of my own, I'd been belched out again, thrown clear of the machine. I'd received no sense of closure, still felt a victim of forces which I didn't understand and couldn't control.

If it wasn't over, fine. But I wasn't going to just sit there and let it happen to me.

I grabbed the phone. The hotel operator put me through to the L.A.P.D. general switchboard, and five minutes of careful enunciation got me through to somewhere specific, where a phone rang and rang. Eventually someone picked it up and grunted.

I asked for Lieutenant Considine, and heard the sound of the handset being dropped on a desk. A couple of minutes later someone picked it up again.

"Considine," a voice said, sounding tired.

"It's Nick Williams," I said, my heart thumping. "I've just had a package delivered to my hotel room. It should have had software in it, but instead it's got ten packets of Marlboro Light. Does this mean anything to you? Is this supposed to be some kind of joke?"

There was a long pause. When Considine spoke again he sounded different. "Where are you?"

"In my room," I said. "At Ma Maison."

"Stay there," he said, and the line went dead.

It was as I was putting the phone down that I thought I heard the quiet sound of my hotel room door, shutting, as someone left.

~φ~

"No of course we didn't send it," Considine snapped, after looking through the box, and a telephone conversation with the hotel's security manager. "Like everyone else, you've seen far too many movies."

"So who did it?"

"I don't know."

"Bullshit," I said. Bear in mind I'd drunk my own volume in Budweiser by then, and had a weird day. "You didn't come racing over here just because someone solved my cigarette needs for the next week."

"I can't tell you any more."

"Your guys made me look an idiot, like a *criminal*, in front of the guests and staff of this hotel. Not to mention making my face look like this. Added to which, someone *broke into my hotel room*. This is a warning."

Considine didn't deny that, which worried me.

"So?" I said, insistently.

He looked at me. "The third reason you got an extra chance today," he said, "Is that you smoke."

"I don't..." I said, but he talked over me.

"Understand that I'm telling you this because you got a hard time this morning, and because I'm concerned about this box, and what it means. What I'm going to tell you is confidential. The third murder happened last night. A waitress called Janie Peltz was stabbed in her apartment – not so far from this hotel – at around 10.00 pm. Her room-mate came home at midnight to find Janie's body on the kitchen floor, naked and messed up. The face and torso were covered in burn marks, made with the lighted tip of a cigarette. These weren't little burns. They were deep enough to stick the tip of your little finger in."

I looked at the end of my cigarette, suddenly less keen on smoking it. Considine noticed.

"Right," he said. "But there's more. The torso was ripped open in two places, either side of the sternum. The killer had broken through the ribcage with an unknown implement, revealing the lungs. Into each he had stuffed a pack of Merits, the cigarettes smoked by Ms. Peltz."

"Christ," I said, stubbing my cigarette out in the ashtray. It was horrific, but it was also absurd. I got a sudden glimpse of what it must be to be the kind of person who would do such a thing. Psychotic, yet with a kernel of triviality and ludicrousness and retarded literalism at the core, undermining the majesty of madness and turning it into a dark and stupid circus.

The writer in me was callous enough to wish I had a pen and paper, to note that down.

"As the room-mate was staring at this, she heard a noise and the murderer emerged from the bathroom. It was dark, but she got a good look because he came right up to her, stared in her eyes, and guess what?"

"I don't know."

"He asked her if she smoked. She said no. He punched her in the face, hard enough to knock her out, and left."

"And the M.O. was the same in the other two murders?" I asked.

He raised an eyebrow. "'M.O.'?"

I indicated the stack of crime novels on my other table.

"Yeah," he said. "It was. Except nobody saw him on those occasions."

"Even for LA, that seems excessive."

"What's that supposed to mean?" Considine said, looking at me closely. I hoped I hadn't made a blunder.

"Well, I mean, I come from England. We know smoking's bad for you, but we're more relaxed about it. We banned it indoors, but otherwise, you want to kill yourself, go ahead. Just don't blow it directly up my nose. In this town people are *militant*. It's like I'm assaulting someone if I have a smoke in the same zip code as them. I feel like a pariah the whole time."

"We're a dying breed," Considine said.

One part of my mind was working over what he had told me. The other was sitting a little way off, watching, marvelling at what was happening. I wasn't another cop. I was a script-writer, and an unknown, un-produced and probably useless one at that. Yet here I was, in an LA hotel room, shooting the breeze with homicide brass. I got another flash of the feeling I'd had in the station. *Someone's scripting this.*

"What do I do?" I asked.

He shrugged. "Nobody saw anyone enter or leave your room. They'll be long gone now. How much longer are you in town?"

"Two days," I said.

"Watch your back, is my advice. If you see anything you don't like," he added, handing me a card, "Call me."

He stood up and picked up the cardboard box and the cigarettes strewn over the bed. He noticed my own ample stock of cigarettes, leaning over against the wall in their duty free carton.

"Maybe you should consider cutting down," he said.

"Never," I said. "That would be giving in."

~φ~

Ten minutes after he'd gone, I left my room, peered both ways down the corridor, and headed to the lift. I'd spent the intervening time standing by the window, looking at the lights which stretched into the hills, looking up at the Hollywood sign. I couldn't seem to settle. I felt like... I didn't know what. Like someone was out to get me, and who I was didn't matter any more.

I certainly hadn't felt like going to bed. Considine's conversation with hotel security had been perfunctory: for all I knew, the guy could still be in the building, and I didn't fancy lying in bed and waiting for the sound of someone trying the door.

I decided to go and see if the bar was still in operation. It was after midnight, and I didn't know how things operated in American hotels, but I felt I needed to be doing something. On the one hand I felt as if I'd been up for three days, but I also felt very awake. Albeit drunk.

The elevator doors opened onto a lobby which was cool and a little darker than usual. Reception was still open, and there was twenty four hour room service, I knew, so most likely there was always something going on down here. But otherwise it looked like things were shut for the night. I turned left and walked into the lounge. No one was sitting at any of the tables, and the waitresses' cubby hole up against the wall was deserted. I decided to make sure, and walked through the archway to the bar. Now that I was down here, I didn't want to go back upstairs. Even a cup of coffee would do.

The bar was dead, however, glasses neatly stacked along the side. The tall and morose barman was nowhere to be seen. I turned forlornly and walked out onto the terrace, pointlessly, reconciling myself to coffee in my room. Then I noticed the chair where I'd been sitting earlier in the evening, and something caught my eye.

A book, lying on the table. And a pack of cigarettes.

I walked over, puzzled. The table sat in its own little area of lamplight, and looked inviting, but it seemed odd someone should remain there when they couldn't get any refreshment. Then I caught sight of the title of the book and the brand of the cigarettes.

The book was *House-Hunting Blues*, a half-decent detective novel by a guy called Egerton Royle. It was one of the books I had in the stack in my room.

The cigarettes were Marlboro Lights.

For a moment I confusedly assumed I must have left them when I left the bar earlier, and felt embarrassed. Then I remembered carrying my book and cigarettes up in the elevator, and that I was reading a different book.

At that moment I was startled by a door opening. It was the door to the kitchens, and the waitress I'd seen earlier came sailing out of it.

"Hello, Mr. Williams," she said cheerfully, her voice soft in the gloom of the lounge. "Still here?"

"Yes," I said, confused. "Well, I'm back, anyway."

She hovered, obviously waiting to see if I wanted anything. "I know the bar's closed," I said, on autopilot, "But can I get another Budweiser down here?"

"But you just paid your *tab*," she said, feigning comic irritation. It was nicely done. Half the waitresses in Ma Maison are actresses or singers. The rest are probably directors.

"That was hours ago," I said.

She pouted, as if I was making a joke.

"Okay," she said. "Sit down and I'll be right out." She turned, but then stopped and looked back at me. "Are you okay, Sir?"

"Yes," I said distantly, "I'm fine."

She went, and I dismissed her from my mind. I *wasn't* okay. I'd noticed the cellophane was still on the bottom half of the pack of Marlboro on the table. Not every smoker leaves it there. But I do.

More disturbingly, there was a coffee stain on the cover of the book, and I moved closer to look at it. It was in the right place – or the *wrong* place. It was exactly where a friend of mine had drunkenly placed a coffee mug, around the time I'd first read *House Hunting Blues*, about a year ago. I'd been annoyed – I like to keep my books in pristine condition – and remembered the position exactly.

I sat in the chair where I'd sat earlier, facing the table. The cigarettes were where I always put them, in easy reach. The book was laid as if I had just popped away to the gents, or set it down to use my phone.

"Here you are," the waitress said, placing a frosted glass of Budweiser in front of me.

I settled the tab and she marched off, on the way to deliver some food to somebody. Somebody who was sitting happily in their room in this nice hotel.

I couldn't have been sitting here in the last hour, of course. I'd been up in my room with Considine. But slowly I began to read other things into the way the waitress had greeted me. *Still here*, she'd said, as if I hadn't left an hour or two earlier. Maybe she *had* thought I'd been joking about paying my tab hours ago. Maybe she thought I'd just done it only moments before.

Maybe someone had. Someone who had been sitting in this chair, reading my book, smoking my brand of cigarettes.

And when I'd sat down here at the beginning of the evening, she'd greeted me by name – though I didn't remember her. Maybe I *had* never seen her before, as I'd believed. Maybe she'd seen... someone else. Someone with the same name, and who signed the tab with the same room number. Someone who looked a lot like me, but wasn't?

There was no ashtray on the table, which was weird. All the others had one. I suppose the waitress could have cleared it away, but some of the others I could see still had butts in them. It was almost as if whoever had been sitting in the chair had deliberately moved an ashtray away, despite having cigarettes with him.

As if he wanted to make a point of not smoking.

These thoughts took a short time to run through my head. Someone who looked like me had stolen one of my books, and sat here. He'd drunk beer, but hadn't smoked any cigarettes.

Someone who looked like me, but didn't smoke.

Someone who looked exactly like me.

I couldn't call Considine again. Or... could I? I should, surely. This kind of thing was his job. I took a nervous sip of beer. Whoever this guy was, he was spiralling closer. He was trying to send a message. About what, I wasn't sure. I suddenly knew what he was trying to do, however. He was starting to intermingle his life with mine, to the point where some of the blame for the terrible things he'd done would start to seep toward me.

The real blame wouldn't be mine, of course, but if he began to be seen where I should be seen, then he was making me a part of it. Our lives would become seamless, we would become the same person, and I would be guilty too. Who was he? How did he look so much like me? And what was he trying to do to us?

There was a soft sound to one side of me, and I looked up wildly. Expecting... what? A mirror image of myself. A murderer.

But it wasn't. I took me a moment to realise who I *was* seeing, because she wasn't dressed in the hotel's black uniform, but in jeans and a blouse.

It was Alicia, and in her right hand she was holding a lit cigarette.

"Hello Nick," she said.

"Christ," I said, my heart thumping. "Don't you ever get to go home?" She smiled, and I was reminded of the waitress again. *Oh you fooler,* her face seemed to say.

And since when had she called me by my first name?

"We should go up now," Alicia said, softly. "It wouldn't be good for me to be seen with you. I'll go first, you follow. Okay?"

I just stared at her, baffled, and she walked towards the elevators. When the doors opened she turned, and flashed a small, demure smile before going in.

I waited for about five minutes, feeling more and more afraid. What was going on? What had he said to her? What had he got me into?

I am stupid.

I am so very stupid.

When I realised, I stood up and ran to the elevators. I banged the button with my fist until the doors opened, and then I leapt in and slapped the button for the eighth floor. The carriage seemed to take forever to climb. When the doors finally opened I tore out of the elevator and down the corridor, fumbling the key from my pocket as I ran. I slipped taking a corner and almost fell, but then fetched breathlessly up outside the door. Alicia was nowhere to be seen, but this *had* to have been where she meant. She had to have been coming up here.

She had arranged something with *him*, thinking it was me...

I jammed the key into the door and turned. Nothing happened. I tried again.

It was locked from the inside.

Then I heard a sound from the room, a muffled scream, and I knew for sure that he was in there, and that my life was never going to be the same again.

~φ~

I'm in a town in Maine at the moment, somewhere very small, in the woods. It was as far as I could go without leaving the country. I cannot get out of the USA. I left the hotel with my wallet and the clothes I stood up in, but even if I had my passport, I'm sure I'd get stopped if I tried to fly. Everything else is gone. Yesterday I called my parents and girlfriend and said goodbye.

Whatever happens, I'll never see England again.

I ran. There was nothing else I could do. I saw the first newspaper reports the following day, and then followed it on the web. Deep cigarette burns at regular intervals over the torso, except where it had been cut open in order for packs of Marlboro Light to be inserted. A ridiculous piece of symbolism, like someone parodying every psycho movie of the last twenty years. This time the murderer had also hacked off the victim's arms and legs. These had been arranged in a pattern on the floor. The detectives didn't know what the pattern was supposed to represent, and I don't think they'll ever work it out. It's nothing but the traced inner workings of a smog which fizzes and sparks in the dark, the shape of cigarette smoke as it bends in the wind.

One of the hands was missing. The right hand.

Her smoking hand.

The next day there were more details. The box was mentioned, the box which my software was supposed to have been delivered in. The only fingerprints found on it matched the prints all over Alicia's watch, which had been torn off and inserted in her throat. The murderer had never done that before, and could only have done so to make absolutely sure I was nailed – because these prints matched those taken from a suspect questioned on the day of the murder, an English writer now the subject of a country-wide APB. The paper I was reading was up in arms about the fact that this man had been released from custody, to kill again. There were calls for Considine to lose his job. When I read the story, sitting on a train going across Virginia, I wanted to call him up, and tell him it wasn't his fault. I didn't, of course.

Then yesterday there was a photo, a blow-up of the man believed to be the murderer, captured on video as he left the hotel in the early hours. It was grainy, but it was plenty clear enough.

It was me.

But it wasn't. I was halfway to the airport by then. At least... I think I was. It's unclear in my mind. I can't remember what really happened over the last few days, and what I made up, what I fictionalised. Yesterday evening, as I sat rocking back and forth on my motel bed, I had a sudden recollection of paying a stoned cab driver to tell a lie, if anyone asked – to put me somewhere that I'd not actually been, to give me a window of opportunity. Did that actually happen, or is my mind just trying to adjust the plot for it to make sense, to back-fill reality to that it flows from A to B?

I'm not sure. But it wasn't me. I didn't kill any of them. Not really. Something happened, and someone arrived to lay waste to my life, as a punishment, and a revenge. For what I was doing to him, I guess. To us.

I don't know how much longer I'm going to be able to last out. I'm running out of cash, fast, and I can't use my credit cards. It's possible I could get a manual job somewhere, washing dishes or something, but it would be a risk. My face is all over everything, and the Internet is no friend to someone who's trying to hide.

At the very least I have to lie very low for a while, until the initial heat is off. My only real hope is that he will kill again in Los Angeles, and divert attention away from the rest of the country. I believe he would most like to kill there, because it is that place which gave him birth. I don't think that he will kill again in that place, however. He... can't, because I'm not there. Maybe he's always been here, or nearby, loathing what I do to our body, though the smoking, and wanting some form of redress. He couldn't have done it without help, however. He couldn't have done it without LA's love. He wasn't insane enough.

Every day I wake up, expecting something to have happened in the town nearby, expecting to hear the sound of sirens. Every morning I check the bag I bought to carry the few things I've acquired, to see if Alicia's hand has appeared in there, to tell me that he is closing in, to remind me he always will be near. He is clever, but he went too far, fucked us up too completely. I can never go back now, and I have nothing left to lose.

He does, though.

He can lose the thing he has been protecting all along – our body, and our precious life. I think he knows what I'm going to do, but I'm going to make him wait.

As I sit here writing, I have four packets of Marlboro Lights in front of me, and I'm going to finish them today. Tomorrow I will do the same. And again the next day, and again. For as long as it takes. Until I get cancer.

Until the fucker dies.

~φ~

The Stuff That Goes On In Their Heads

I first heard the name on Monday night, when I was putting him to bed. Kathy was out for an early dinner and catch-up with a friend, and so it had been the Ethan-and-Daddy Show from late afternoon. The recurring plot of this regular series boils down to me preparing one of the pasta dishes which have gained my son's tacit approval (and getting him to focus on eating it before it turns into a congealed mass), the two of us then watching his allotted one-per-day ration of *Ben 10: Alien Force*. After its conclusion I coax him up to the bathroom, and into the bath – usually against sustained and imaginative resistance – followed by the even more protracted process of getting him to *leave* the bath once more, Ethan having in the interim realized that the nice, warm tub is the best place in the world to be, and one he is not prepared to leave at any cost. Then there's the putting-on-of-pajamas and the brushing-of-the-teeth and various other tasks which sound (and should be) simple and quick but always seem to end up taking *forever* – little tranches of time which add up to really *quite a lot of time* when taken together, time that I'll never get back. We had Ethan relatively late in life (he's six, making me exactly forty years his senior) but what the older parent may lack in energy and vim is hopefully tempered by what they bring in terms of perspective, and so I understand well enough that it won't be so very long before my presence in the bathroom (or anywhere else) will not be enjoyed or even tolerated by a child who'll grow up faster than seems possible. Two more lots of six years, and he'll be leaving home. I get that. I try, therefore, to take all these little tribulations in good spirit, and to enjoy their fleeting presence in my life. But still, at the end of a long day, you do kind of wish they'd just brush their bloody teeth, by themselves, without all the stalling and prevarication.

For *the love of god.*

Eventually we got clear of the bathroom and processed in state to Ethan's bedroom – him leading the way, regal in pint-sized dressing gown, chattering about this and that. He resisted getting into bed for a while, but without any real purpose, and in a pro forma manner, as if he knew this part was merely part of a ritual, and he was doing it for my sake more than for himself. Eventually he yawned massively and headed toward the bed. He was tired. He always is on Mondays and Wednesdays, because of after-school club. The trick with tired children is to resist in a passive, judo-style fashion, putting up no specific barriers for them to kick against, instead letting them use their own strength against themselves. This, at least, I have learned.

When he was finally tucked up under the covers I asked him how his day had been. I'd meant to do it earlier, but forgot, which meant the enquiry was doomed to failure. Ethan appears to blank the working day within minutes of leaving the school gates, as if what happens within has no more reality than a dream, and melts like ice under the fierce sun of The Outside World. Or perhaps the opposite is true, and there's a fundamental reality about the universe of the school that is impossible to convey to we shades who live in the unconvincing hinterland outside.

Either way, he appeared as usual to have zero recollection of what had occurred between nine a.m. and four p.m. that day. When pushed for a definitive account, however, he issued a brief statement saying that it had been "fine."

"And how was after-school club?"

Many of the kids who go to The Reynolds School have parents who both work. This means the school runs a slick and profitable range of activities to tide tots over from the end of actual school to the point where their stressed-out handlers can pick them up. Ethan's after-school diversion on Mondays is swimming. This is a bit pointless, I can't help thinking. Partly because Monday happens also to be when his class does swimming anyway – and so all his piscine endeavors are concentrated on the same day; and mainly because said classes seem to boil down to the children spending most of the half hour shivering on the edge of the pool, waiting for their brief turn to splash about. Ethan's already pretty confident in the water – courtesy of a vacation in Florida last year – but untutored in terms of strokes, beyond a hectic doggy-paddle that is full of sound and fury but conveys little in the way of forward motion. We hoped the after-school club would help refine this. So far, he seems to be going backwards.

"Terrible," Ethan said.

"Terrible?" This is strong for him. He usually confines pronouncements of quality to "fine" or "okay", occasionally peaking in a devil-may-care "good". I suspect the deployment of "great" would require the school suddenly deciding to hand out free chocolate. I'd never heard "terrible" before, either. "Why?"

"Arthur Milford was mean to me again."

I snorted. "Arthur *Milford*? What the hell kind of name is that?"

Ethan turned his head in bed to look at me. "What?"

"How *old* is this kid?"

"Six," Ethan said, with gentle care, as if I was crazy. "He's *six*. Like me."

"Sorry, yes," I said. I tend to talk to my son as if he's a miniature adult for much of the time – too much of it, perhaps – but there was no way of explaining to him that the name "Arthur Milford", while theoretically acceptable, seemed more appropriate to a music hall comedian of the 1930s than a six-year-old in 2011. "What do you mean, he was mean to you again?"

"He's always mean to me."

"Really? In what way?"

"Telling me I'm stupid."

"You're not stupid," I said, crossly. "*He's* stupid, if he goes around calling people names. Just ignore him."

"I can't ignore him." Ethan's voice was quiet. "He's always doing it. He pushes me in the corridor, too. Today he said he was going to throw me out of a window."

"*What?* He actually *said* that?"

Ethan looked up at me solemnly. After a moment he looked away. "He didn't actually say it. But he meant it."

"I see," I said, suddenly unsure how much of the entire account was true. "Well, look. If he says mean things to you, just ignore him. Mean boys say mean things. That's just the way it is. But if he pushes you, tell a teacher about it. Immediately."

"I do. They don't do anything about it."

"Well, if it happens again, then tell them again. And tell me, too, okay?"

"Okay, daddy."

And then, as so often in such conversations, the matter was dismissed as if it had never been of import – instead, something I'd been rather tediously insisting on discussing – and my son asked me a series of apparently random questions about the world, which I did my best to answer, and I read him a story and filled up his water cup and read more story, and eventually he went to sleep.

~φ~

We tend to alternate in picking Ethan up (as with most parenting duties), and so Tuesday was Kathy's turn. I had a deadline to chase and so – bar him dashing into my study to say hello when they got back – I barely saw Ethan before I kissed him on the head and said goodnight as Kathy led him up toward bath and bedtime.

Fifty minutes later, by which time I'd made a start on cooking, my wife appeared in the kitchen with the cautiously relieved demeanor of someone who believes they've wrangled an unpredictable child into bed.

"Is he down?"

"I'm not enumerating any domesticated, egg-producing fowl," she said, reaching into the fridge for the open bottle of wine, "But he might be. God willing."

She poured herself a glass and took a long sip before turning to me. "God I'm tired."

"Me too," I said, without a lot of sympathy.

"I know. I'm just saying. By the way – has Ethan mentioned some kid called Arthur to you?"

"Arthur Milford?"

"So he has?"

"Once. Last night. Why – did he come up again?"

"Mmm. And it's not the first time, either."

"Really?"

"Ethan mentioned him last week, and I think the week before, too. They're in after-school swimming together."

"I know. Last night he said this Arthur kid had been mean to him. In fact, he said he'd been mean 'again'."

"Mean in what way?"

"Pushed him in the corridor. Called him stupid." I thought about mentioning the threat to throw Ethan through a window, but decided not to. I didn't think Kathy needed to hear that part, especially as the telling had subsequently made it unclear whether that had taken place in what Ethan called "real life."

"Pushed him *in the corridor*? That means it's not just happening during swimming class."

"I guess. If it's happening at all."

"You don't believe him?"

"No, no, I do. But you know what he's like, Kath. He's all about the baddies and the goodies. It just sounds to me a bit like this Arthur Milford kid is in the script as Ethan's dread Nemesis. And that maybe not all of his exploits are directly related to events in what we'd think of as reality."

"Doesn't mean there isn't a real problem there."

"I know," I said, a little irritated that Kathy seemed to be claiming ownership of the issue, or implying that I wasn't taking it seriously enough. "I told him to talk to the teachers if this kid is mean to him again. And to tell me about it, too."

"Okay."

"But ultimately, that's just the way children are. Boys especially. They give each other grief. They shove. Little girls form cliques and get bitchy and tell other girls they're not their friends. Boys call each other names and thump each other. It has been thus since we lived in caves. It will be so until the sun explodes."

"I know. It's just... Ethan's such a cute kid. He can be a total pain, of course, but he's... so sweet, really, underneath. He doesn't know about all the crap in life yet. I want to protect him from it. I don't want him being hit, just because that's what happens. I don't want him being hurt in any way. I just want... everything to be nice."

"I know," I said, relenting. "Me too."

I rubbed her shoulder on the way over to supervise the closing stages of cooking, and privately raised my State of Awareness of the Arthur Milford situation to DefCon 4 to DefCon 3. Despite what everyone seems to think, the readiness-for-conflict index increases in severity from five to one, with *one* being the highest level (the highest level ever officially recorded is DefCon 2, which obtained for a while during the Cuban Missile Crisis. I knew all this from some half-hearted research for an article I was drafting on Homeland Security).

Be all which as it may, and despite my pompous such-is-life declaration, Kathy was right. I didn't want anyone hassling my kid. Much more of it, and words would need to be spoken.

~φ~

I picked Ethan up the next day, and remembered to ask him about his day as soon as we got into the car. Ethan proved surprisingly well-informed on his own doings, and filled me in on a variety of Montessori-structured activities he'd undertaken (neither Kathy nor I truly understand what Montessori is about, but we believe/hope that it's generally agreed to be A Good Thing, like lower CO_2 levels and being kind to dogs). There was no mention of Arthur Milford. I thought about asking a direct question, but decided that if Ethan hadn't deemed him worth mentioning, there was probably nothing to say.

Ethan went to bed easily that night, in the unpredictable way he sometimes did. We had a laugh during bath-time, he brushed his own teeth without being asked, and then – after quite a short reading – he drifted off to sleep before I was even ready for it. I sat there for five minutes afterwards, enjoying the peace of quietly being in the same space as someone you love very much. There's usually a hidden edge to the observation that nothing's as beautiful as a sleeping child (the point being it's all too often nicer than them being awake), but the fact is... there really isn't. To watch your son, asleep in his comfortable bed, with a tummy full of food that you made him, and a head full of story, arm gripping a furry polar bear you can bought him on a whim but to which he'd taken as if they'd been separated at birth... that's why we're born. That's why everything else is worth it.

Yet sometimes I get so angry with him that I don't know what to do with myself. And he knows it. He must do.

About six hours later I woke slowly in my own bed, dimly aware I could hear a noise that shouldn't exist in a house in the middle of the night. By the time I'd opened my eyes, it was quiet. But as I started to relax back into oblivion, I heard it again.

A quiet sob.

I hauled myself quickly upright, staggered out of bed. Kathy lay dead to the world, which was unusual. She generally sleeps on far more of a hair trigger than me. She evidently was really tired, and I blearily regretted my snipe before dinner the evening before.

I went into the hallway to stand outside Ethan's room and listen. Nothing for a minute, but then I heard the sound again. I opened the door.

Before I even got to the side of his bed, I could tell how hot he was. Children beam their heat out in the night, like little suns. I squatted down and put my hand on his head.

"Ethan," I said. "It's okay. It's just a dream."

He sobbed once more, very quietly.

"*Ethan*, it's okay."

He opened his eyes suddenly. He looked scared. Scared of me.

"It's daddy," I said, disconcerted. "Just daddy, okay?"

His eyes seemed to swim into focus. "Daddy?"

"Yes. It's okay. Everything's okay."

Ethan's eyes swiveled. "Is he still here?"

"Who?"

"Arthur Milford."

The back of my neck tickled. "No. Of course not."

"He was *here*. He came up the stairs and stood outside my room saying things. Then he came in. He stood by my bed and said he was going to..."

"No, he didn't," I said, firmly.

"He *did*."

"Ethan, it was just a dream. No one's in the house apart from you and me and mummy. Nobody can get in. The doors are locked. The alarm system's on."

"Are you *sure*?"

"I'm sure," I said. "I did it myself. I promise you. It's just the three of us, and everything's okay."

Ethan's eyelids were already starting to drift downward. "Okay."

He was asleep five minutes later. I went back to bed, and lay there for an hour before I could get under again. Once I've been woken, I find it hard to get back to sleep.

The next morning I was irritable, and snapped pretty badly at Ethan when he made a laboriously annoying job of putting on his school shoes. I shouldn't have, but I was tired, and for fuck's sake – he should be able to put on his own shoes.

But as I watched him and Kathy walk down the path toward the car, the wailing over and a new détente being hammered out between them, I realized that at some point after coming back to my bed in the night, I'd raised the Arthur Milford Awareness Level to DEFCON 2.

~φ~

On Thursday evening Kathy has yoga, and so The Ethan Going To Bed Show featured daddy in a co-starring role (or supporting actor, more likely, my name below the title and in a notably smaller typeface) for the second night in a row. Bedtime did not, of course follow the same course as the night before. That's not how the shorties roll. Like some snappy young box-er on the way up, they'll pull you in, fake like they're running out of steam, and then unleash a brutal combination that will leave you glancing desperately back at your corner, as you take a standing eight count. I'm getting better at rolling with the punches, shifting the conflict to safer ground and letting the passion defuse, but that night I went back at Ethan like some broken-down old scrapper who knew this was his last chance in the ring, and wanted to go out with a bare knuckles slugfest.

He wouldn't eat his pasta, instead deliberately distributing it over the floor – meanwhile looking me steadily in the eye. He wouldn't come upstairs. He wouldn't get into the bath, and then wouldn't get out, and broke a soap dish. I had to brush his teeth for him, and did it none too gently. He wouldn't get into his pajamas because they "always itched" – the very same pair that he'd cheerfully gone to sleep in the previous night. He wouldn't get into bed, instead breaking out of the room and stomping downstairs, wailing dismally for Kathy, though he knew damned well she was out.

By the time I'd recaptured him, harsh words had been spoken on both sides. I had been designated an "idiot" and a "doofus," and been informed that I was no longer loved. I had likened his behavior to that of a significantly younger child, and had threatened to inform the world at large of this maturity shortfall: his friends, grandparents and Father Christmas had all been invoked as potential recipients of the information. I'd said he was being childish and stupid, and had even called him the very worst word I (or you) know, though thankfully I'd managed to throttle my voice down into inaudibility at the last moment. So he hadn't caught the word. The anger had sure as hell made it though, though. The anger, and probably the pitiful level of powerlessness, too.

I did however finally manage to get him into bed.

He lay there, silently. I sat equally silently in the chair, both of us breathing hard, wild-eyed with silent fury and sour adrenaline.

"Arthur Milford was mean to me today, too," Ethan muttered, suddenly.

I was still pretty close to the edge, and the "too" at the end of his pronouncement nearly pushed me over it into somewhere dark and bad.

I took a breath, and bit my tongue. "Mean in what way?" I managed, eventually.

"In the upstairs corridor. On the third floor."

"Okay – so now I know where the alleged event occurred. But *how* was he mean? *In what actual way?*"

"Why are you being so *mean* to me tonight?"

"I'm... Just tell me, okay? What did he *do*?"

"He pushed me again. *Really* hard. Into the wall. And then... against the window."

"Really?"

"*Yes.*"

"Did you tell a teacher? Like I told you?"

"No."

"*Why?* That's what you've got to do. You *have* to tell a teacher."

"He said... he said that if anyone told a teacher about what he was doing, he'd throw me out of the window for sure."

"*Really?* He actually said it this time?"

"*Yes.*"

"But you've just told *me* about it – so why not a teacher?"

"Arthur said telling you didn't matter. *You* can't do anything. Only the teachers can."

"I see. How interesting."

I decided then and there that I'd had quite enough of Arthur sodding Milford. I'd like to think this was solely because of the evident discomfort he was causing Ethan, during both waking and sleeping hours, but I know some of it was due to pathetic outrage at hearing myself thus dismissed. As a parent, you often encounter moments when you feel impotent, and may often be genuinely unable to affect events. I had to take crap from my own child, evidently: that didn't hold true for someone else's. It was time for Arthur, and his parents, if necessary, to learn that the world did *not* stop at the school gates.

As Ethan and I moved on to talking about other things, gradually opening doors to each other once more, and calming down, I silently determined that the Arthur Milford situation had finally reached DefCon 1.

~φ~

I got to the school a little after two o'clock. My appointment would mean that I'd have time to kill in the area afterwards, before picking Ethan up, but it was the only time the headmistress/owner would deign to see me. It's a small school, privately-owned, and to be fair, I imagine Ms. Reynolds is pretty busy. I was shown to a little office, part of the recent extension on the ground floor, and given a cup of coffee. I sat sipping it, looking up through the glass roof at the side of the building. Two further stories, grey brick, with long bands of windows.

Schools, even small and bijou ones like this, all feel the same. They take you back. I knew that when Ms Reyholds arrived I'd stand up slightly too quickly, and be excessively deferential, though she was ten years younger than me and effectively ran a service industry, in which the customer should always be right. None of that matters. School is where you learn the primal things, the big spells, the place where you become versed in the eternal hierarchies and are appraised of our species' hopes and fears. Being back in one as an adult is like returning in waking hours to some epic battleground in the dreamscape – even if, like me, you had a pretty decent time during your formative years.

It was quiet as I waited, all the little animals corralled into classrooms for the time being, having information and cultural norms stuffed into their wild and chaotic heads.

Eventually the door opened, and the trim figure of Ms. Reynolds entered. "Sorry I'm late."

I stood. "No problem."

She smiled briefly, and perched at an angle on the chair on the other side of the desk. I tried hard not to take against her posture, and the way it signaled a confident belief that this was going to be a short conversation. I sat back down, square-on to the table.

"So. How can I help?"

"I wanted a quick word. About Ethan."

"I'm sure it's temporary," she said, briskly. "I honestly don't think it's anything to worry about."

"What is?" I asked, thrown. "Worry about what?"

"Ah," she said, smoothly covering a moment of confusion. "I talked with your wife about this, yesterday, at the end of school. I assumed she'd mentioned it to you."

"Mentioned what?"

"Ethan's schoolwork. It's taken a dip recently, that's all. Nothing major. It happens with most of them, the boys. From time to time. But we're aware of it, and we're working with Ethan to lift things back up. I can appreciate your concern, but I really..."

"That's not why I'm here."

"Oh. So..."

"I *am* concerned if there's an issue with his work," I said. I was also a little ticked that Kathy hadn't mentioned it to me when she got back from yoga the night before. "But I wanted to talk about the bullying."

"*Bullying?*"

"For the last week, maybe two, Ethan's been talking about being bullied."

Ms. Reynolds swiveled to sit square in her chair. It was clear I'd got her full attention now. "If that's the case, it's a very serious matter," she said.

"It's the case."

She frowned. "One of the teachers did notice a mark on his arm this morning. Very minor. It looked as though someone had gripped his arm. Is that what you're referring to?"

Her eyes were on me. There was probably no way she could know that the mark, which I'd noticed myself when helping Ethan to get dressed that morning, was the result of me shoving him into bed the night before. Not so very hard, but children's skins are sensitive.

And my own father raised me to tell the truth.

"No," I said. "That was me."

"You?"

"There was a disagreement over getting into bed last night. I ended up guided him into it."

She nodded, a minimalist raise of the chin. "So then what *are* you referring to?"

"One of the other boys has been picking on him. Muttering things in after-school swimming class, calling him stupid. Shoving him in the corridors."

"Ethan told you this?"

"Yes. And this boy's even threatened to throw Ethan out of a window."

"Throw him out *of a window?*" Ms Reynolds now looked stricken. "When? When did this happen?"

"Last Monday. And again yesterday." I'd forgotten, for the moment, that this threat hadn't actually been made on Monday

– only implied, or intuited (or fabricated) by Ethan. It didn't matter. Yesterday, it *had* been said. "I'm not happy about this. At all."

"Well of course not," the headmistress said, putting her hands out flat on the table in front of her. "And who does Ethan say is doing all this?"

"Arthur Milford," I said, feeling heavy satisfaction as I handed up the name. Not just at finally stepping up to the plate on behalf of my son, but also through disproving what Arthur had told him – that it was only teachers that could do anything about a situation.

Learn this, you little shit: stuff that happens in the outside world counts, too.

"Arthur Milford?"

"Yes."

"It can't be," she said.

"I'm sure he behaves perfectly when teachers are around."

"No, that's not what I mean. I mean... we don't have an Arthur Milford at this school. Are you *sure* that's the name?"

"Absolutely sure. I've heard it every day this week, including in the middle of Wednesday night, when Ethan had a nightmare about this boy coming into his room and threatening him. Kathy's heard the name too."

The teacher looked baffled. "We did have an Arthur Ely in the school, a few years ago, who was quite big, and boisterous, but he left well before Ethan joined us. And there was a Patrick Milford, I think... Yes. He was here even before Arthur. But again, he's moved on. There's no Milfords here now. No Arthurs either."

"That's the name Ethan used."

"I'm afraid... he may just have made it up. Or one of the other children did."

"What – and the fact there have been kids here with very similar names is just a coincidence?"

"No. Making something up doesn't mean it isn't real. I know this is hard to hear, but... Their parents, everything out there in the world... They're important, of course, you're important. But still not as real to the children as what happens in here."

I nodded, remembering the thoughts I'd had while sitting in the chair waiting, and how it had been when I was a child. "Facts, too," she went on. "Children can get them muddled up. Or half-hear things. Or add two and two and make twenty eleven and a half. Perhaps Ethan got shoved, by accident. Or he and another boy really aren't getting on – or perhaps he's having arguments with a someone who *is* his friend, and so Ethan doesn't want to use his real name. Children remember the names of those who have gone before. Perhaps they use them, too, sometimes. Like mythological figures. I spend all my working hours in this place, but it doesn't mean I understand everything that goes on."

"So you don't think anyone's actually bullying Ethan?"

"I really doubt it – and not just because we do a lot to make sure this kind of thing doesn't happen. None of the other boys or girls have said anything. None of the teachers, either. But trust me, I'll look into it. The moment you've gone. And if there's anything – anything at all – to be concerned about, I'll call you right away. I promise."

"Thank you," I said. I didn't know what to feel. A little foolish, certainly.

She stood up, and reached out her hand. I did the same, and we shook.

"I hope I haven't wasted your time."

"No time spent talking about a child is wasted," she said, and I felt a little less silly. "But do you mind if I offer you a piece of advice?"

"Go ahead," I said, assuming it would be some way of helping Ethan move past this, or of helping him to get his school-work back on track.

"Do be careful about... the ways in which you have physical contact with your son."

I froze, indignation and guilt melting together. The room seemed suddenly larger, and very cold. "What do you mean?"

She looked steadily at me. Her eyes were clear, and kind, and for a moment she didn't looked like a teacher, or Ethan's headmistress, just a woman who meant well and cared about her charges a great deal.

"I know what it's like," she said. "What *they* can be like. I don't have a child of my own, not yet, but I spend a *lot* of time with them. Which is why, every day after I leave here, I go to the gym and get it out of my system for an hour. I kickbox. I'm not very good, but boy do I give those punch bags a thump. And then I go home and have a gin and tonic that would make most people's eyes water. That information is not for general consumption, okay?"

"Okay," I said, smiling.

"Loving children can be hard work. But it's what we do. I know you love Ethan, very much. I'm just saying... be careful. Because of the assumptions others might make, if they see a mark on him. And also because of how *you* feel, about yourself, and about how he'll feel too. Boys need strong fathers. Men who are strong, and kind... and not full of anger and guilt."

I nodded, knowing she was right.

"There's evidently *something* going on in Ethan's universe, and it's good that I know about it. You did the right thing coming in to tell me about it."

"I hope so," I said, anxious now to lighten the mood. "Ethan said last night that's it was okay to tell me about it, but teachers couldn't know. Otherwise, Arthur would, you know."

Ms. Reynolds smiled, and rolled her eyes, as she started to lead me toward the door. "The stuff that goes on in their heads," she said, with just the right amount of irony, and affection.

I realized that I'd started to like Ms. Reynolds, and respect her, and that perhaps I'd start to take a more active role in Ethan's schooling, and that would be good.

She walked with me out of the doors and to the waiting area outside. I had an hour to kill, and had decided to go find a coffee somewhere. To think through what had been said, to find a way of accessing a calm which must still exist somewhere inside me. To lighten up. To remember how to be strong, and kind.

"You did the right thing," she said, once more.

As we shook hands again, there was the sound of glass breaking, somewhere high above. We looked up and saw the third floor, and the broken window there.

Saw the small, boy-shaped figure that came out of it, and started to fall.

~φ~

REMtemps

got into it the same way as most people, I guess. By accident. I was staying the night in Jacksonville, much as anything because I basically didn't have anywhere else to be. I arrived in town late and tired, pissed at winding up there yet again. It seemed like whenever I couldn't find a road to take me anyplace new, I wound up back in that city, like a yo-yo bouncing back to the hand that had thrown it away in the first place.

I was planning on getting out of state early the next day, and after my ride set me down I headed for the blocks round the bus station, where everything is cheaper. Last time I'd worked had been over a week ago, at a bar down near St Augustine. They didn't like the way I talked to the customers. I hadn't cared for their attitude towards pay and working conditions. It had been a short and unproductive relationship.

I walked through the neon and cars, crawling curb, until I found a place in my exalted price range. It went under the inspiring and evocative name of "Pete's Rooms," and the guy behind the desk was wearing one of the worst shirts I've ever seen. I didn't ask him if he was Pete, but it seemed a fair assumption. The shirt looked like a painting of a road accident done by someone who had no talent, but an awful lot of paint to use up. A sign above the desk said the rate was twenty dollars a night, with superbroad web access in every room.

Very reasonable. Extremely so, in fact – yet the shirt, unappealing though it was, looked like it had been made on purpose. Maybe I should have thought about that, but it was late and I couldn't be bothered.

The room was on the fourth floor and small. It wasn't as horrible as it could have been, but the air smelt like it had been there since before I was born. I pulled something to drink from my bag, and dragged the room's one tatty chair over to the window. Outside was a fire escape the rats were probably afraid of using, and below that just yellow lights and noise.

I leant out into humid night and watched people walking up and down the street, all looking for action of some kind. You see them in every city, mangy dogs trying to find the trail their instincts tell them must start around here someplace. I wished them well, but not with much hope or enthusiasm on their behalf. I've tried most types of action, and they don't get you very far. Stealing physical possessions isn't as easy as it sounds, and they're always disappointingly heavy and difficult to sell. Drugs are either too dangerous or too organized, or both. Ripping credit card numbers or running hacker scams can make money, but not much, and not for long. The Feds have the cash and reach to ensure that the net runners they hire are better than or at least equal to those on the street, so sooner rather than later someone's going to drop you in it. It's my opinion you're probably actually better off looking for regular work, but I've just never been very good at keeping it.

I stared out the window until the bottle was done, wondering where I was going next. It felt like everything had ground to a halt, as if I needed something pretty major to get my life started up again. It's felt that way before, but not quite so bleakly. I was thirty-five, with no money, no family, and all the prospects of a sand castle. It was the kind of situation that could get you down, if you studied on it too long.

So I lay on the bed and went to asleep.

~φ~

I woke up early the next morning, feeling strange. Tired. Spacey. Hollow-stomached, and as if someone had put little warm balls of crumpled paper inside my eyes.

My watch said it was seven o'clock, which didn't make sense. Only time I see seven is when I've been awake straight through the night. Waking voluntarily at that time is unheard of.

Then I realised an alarm was going off, and turned my head slowly and carefully to see the console in the bedside table was flashing.

"Message," it said.

I screwed my eyes up tight and looked at it again. It still said I had a message. I rolled over to reach the keyboard and hit the RECEIVE button.

The screen went blank for a moment, and then fed up some text. "You could have earned $367.77 last night," it read. "If you're interested in learning more, come by 135 Highwater today. Quote reference PR43."

I sat up, reached for a cigarette, squinting at the message. I'd never seen one like it before, and I've slept in a lot of different rooms, in hotels and motels and even less salubrious by-the-night accommodations all over the country. The amount mentioned was very specific, and it didn't take me long to remember that my room number was 43. Chances were the "PR" stood for "Pete's Rooms." Rather than just saying "Earn $$$ fast," it seemed to be targeted directly at me.

Intriguing.

$367.77 is a lot of nights' bar work. I changed my shirt and left the hotel.

~φ~

By the time I was nearing the address I was already losing interest. It was likely a scam of some kind, just better-pitched than usual, and I'd done my time in the minor crime mines and I was still waiting for my Gold Card invitation. My head felt fuzzy and worn, as if I'd spent all night doing math in my sleep. A big part of me just wanted to score a carb and protein-intensive breakfast somewhere and then go sit on a bus, watch the sun hazing across window panels until I was somewhere else.

But I didn't. I have a kind of shambling momentum and sticky focus, once I'm started. I followed the streets on the map, surprised to find myself getting closer to the business district. The kind of people who spam consoles in cheap hotels generally work out of virtual holes in the wall, non-places lodged in foreign corners of the net. Highwater was very much a real place, a long road with a lot of big, butch-looking office buildings preening on either side, and when I found 135 I stood on the pavement for a moment, finishing the cigarette they wouldn't let me have inside.

135 was a mountain of black plate glass with a revolving door at the bottom. Unlike many of the other buildings I'd passed, it didn't have videowall panels displaying with tiresome thoroughness the business and success of the people who toiled within. It just sat there, not giving anything away. The lobby, when I went inside, was similarly uncommunicative, and likewise decked out all in black. It was like they'd acquired a job lot of the colour from somewhere and were eager to use it up.

I walked across the marble floor to a desk at the far end, my heels tapping in the cool silence. A woman sat there in a pool of yellow light, looking at me with a raised eyebrow.

"Can I help you?" she asked, her tone making it clear she thought it was very unlikely.

"I don't know. I was told to come here and quote a reference."

Her face didn't light up, but she did reach to tap a button on her keyboard and turn her eyes toward the screen. "And that is?"

"PR43."

She scrolled down through some list for a while. "Okay," she said, eventually. "Here's how it is. Your potential earnings for last night were $367.77, which is quite impressive."

"Thank you. I think."

"You have two options. The first is I give you $171.39, and you go away with no further obligation. The second is that you take the elevator on the right and go up to the 34th floor, where Mr. Rabutni will meet with you presently."

"And you arrive at the $171.39 how, exactly?"

"Your potential earnings less a twenty five dollar handling fee, divided by two and rounded up to the nearest cent."

"How come I only get half the money?"

"Because you're not on contract. You go up and meet Mr. Rabutni, maybe that will change."

"And in that case I get the full $367?"

She raised an eyebrow again. "You're kind of smart, aren't you?"

The elevator was very pleasant. Tinted mirrors, quiet, leisurely upward progress. It spoke of money, and lots of it. Not much happened during the journey.

When the doors opened I found myself faced with a corridor done out in – you guessed it – black. Maybe the architect had been blind or something, hired on some positive discrimination deal. A large chrome sign on the wall said "REMtemps." I walked the way the sign pointed and fetched up at another reception desk. The girl there told me in turn to take a seat. I walked a couple paces from the desk, but didn't sit down. I hate sitting in receptions. I read somewhere it puts you in a subordinate position right off the bat, and I figure I'm starting from a low enough point that there's sense in making it worse. (I'm great at the pre-hiring tactics, you see – it's just a shame it goes to pieces soon afterwards).

"Mr. Stone, good morning."

I turned to see a man in a sober suit standing behind me, hand held out.

I stared at it for a moment, then shook it. "Mr. Rabutni, I assume. How'd you know my name?"

The man smiled. He looked just like anybody else, simply more polished: as if he was a release-standard human instead of the beta versions you normally see lumbering around. His handshake was firm and dry.

"We ran a check on you. We need to know who we're dealing with before we hire them."

"How? I paid cash at the hotel."

Rabutni just smiled again. I guessed it didn't matter how they'd done it. They evidently had their methods.

I was shown into a small room off the main corridor. Mr. Rabutni sat behind a desk, and I lounged back in the other available chair.

"So what's the deal?" I asked, trying to sound relaxed, and perhaps even insouciant. I'm not absolutely sure what the latter is, but I gather it's something that could be good to be in this kind of situation. There was something about the guy opposite which put me on edge, however. He was charming, suave and obviously very rich. But behind the ever-present smile it was also crystal clear that he wasn't someone to fuck with. Plus there was the matter of how he'd been able to run a make on me without any credit card information. Maybe there'd been a video camera hidden in the elevator, and they'd used a frame-grab of my face. That implied he was wiring to some very good information systems.

I don't like people like that. They give people like me The Fear. We don't want to be known about. We don't want to be pulled into the big picture. We just want to be left alone to scratch out our little lives in peace.

"Dreams," he said.

"What about them?"

He leant forward and turned the console on the desk to face me. "See if there's anything you recognize," he said, and pressed a switch.

The console chittered and whirred for a moment, and flashed up "PR43 @ 18/5/2025." The screen bled to black, and then faded up again to show a corridor.

The camera – if that's what it was – walked forward along it a little way. Drab green walls trailed off into the distance. On the left hand side was another corridor. The point of view turned – and showed that it was exactly the same. Going a little quicker now, it tramped that way for a while, before making another turn into yet another identical corridor. There didn't seem to be any shortage of corridors, or of new turnings to make. The floor went on for ever. The walls were featureless, and looked like they were made out of metal. Occasional chips in the paint relieved the monotonous olive, but other than that it just went on and on and on.

I looked up after five minutes, to see Rabutni watching me.

"Ring any bells?" he said.

I shook my head. Rabutni made a note, and then typed something rapidly on the console's keyboard.

"The imagery wasn't distinctive," he said. "I don't think the owner was very imaginative. And you lose a lot, naturally, just getting the visual without any of the emotional content. Try this one instead."

The image on the screen changed, and showed a pair of hands holding a piece of water. I know "piece of water" doesn't make much sense, but that's what it looked like. The hands were nervously fondling the liquid, and a quiet male voice was relayed from the console's speaker.

"Oh, I don't know," it said, doubtfully. "About five? Six and a half, maybe?"

The hands put the water down on a shelf, and picked up another bit. This water was a little smaller.

The voice paused for a moment, then spoke more confidently. "Definitely a two. Two and a third at most."

The hands placed this second piece down on top of the first. The two bits of water didn't meld, but stayed separate. One hand moved out of sight and there was a different sound then, a soft metallic scraping.

That's when I got my first twitch of recall.

Rabutni noticed. "Getting warmer?"

"Maybe," I said, leaning to get a closer look at the console.

The point of view had swiveled slightly, to show a battered filing cabinet. One of the drawers was open, and the hands were carefully picking up pieces of water – which I now saw were arrayed all around, in piles of differing sizes – and putting them one by one into drop files. Every now and then the voice would swear to itself, take out one of the pieces of water and return it to a pile – not necessarily the one it had originally come from.

The hands started moving more and more quickly, putting water in, taking water out, and all the time there was this low background noise of the voice reciting different numbers. I stared at the screen, gradually losing awareness of the office around me, and becoming absorbed. I forgot that Rabutni was even there, and it was largely to myself that I eventually spoke.

"Each of the pieces of water has a different value. Somewhere between one and twenty seven. Each drawer in the filing cabinet has to be filled with the same value of water, but no one told him how to work out how much each piece is worth, or what the total for the drawer has to be."

The screen went blank, and I turned my head to see Rabutni grinning at me.

"You remember," he said.

"That was the one just before I woke up. What the fuck's going on?" I reached unthinkingly into my pocket and pulled out a cigarette.

Instead of shouting at me, Rabutni simply opened a drawer and pulled out an ashtray. "We took a liberty last night," he said. "The proprietor of the hotel has an arrangement with us. We subsidize the cost of his rooms and web access, and provide the consoles."

"Why?"

"We always need new people. This is the best way of finding them. I'd like to offer you a job as a REMtemp."

"You're going to have to unpack that for me."

He did.

He unpacked at some length, in fact. This is the gist.

Five years previously, as I knew, someone had found a way of taking dreams out of people's heads in real time. The government wasn't keen on the idea, and it's still not strictly legal, but a covert industry was born overnight. A device placed near the head of a sufficiently well-off client could keep an eye out for dreams of particular types (alerted by distinctive spikes in alpha and theta waves), and – when they came – divert them out of the dreamer's unconscious mind and into an erasing device.

At first the main trade was in nightmares, naturally. After a while this changed, however, for two reasons. Nightmares usually don't happen very often, and clients balked at buying systems which would only help them out once every two or three months. They would only pay piece rate on a dream-by-dream basis, and the people who'd patented the technology wanted more return on their investment. Also, nightmares are generally handing you useful information. They're giving you news. If you're scared crapless about something, there's a good reason for it – and you'd be better off paying it some mind, rather than just ignoring it all the time.

So instead of nightmares, the market shifted to anxiety dreams. Kind of like nightmares, but not usually as frightening, these are the dreams you get when you're stressed, or tired, or fretting about something. Often they consist of minute and complex tasks which the dreamer has to endlessly go through, often with really understanding what they're doing, and thus constantly having to start again. Then just when you're starting to get a grip on what's going on, you get flipped into something else entirely, and the whole cycle starts again. These kind of dreams usually either cut in just after you've gone to sleep – in which case they'll fuck up your whole night – or in the couple of hours before waking. In either case you get up feeling tired and worn out, in no state to start a working day when it feels like you've already just been through one.

Anxiety dreams are far more frequent than nightmares, and tend to affect precisely the kind of middle and high management executives who were the primary market for dream disposal. The guys who owned the technology changed their pitch, reprinted their brochures, and started making some serious money.

But there was a problem.

It turned out that you couldn't just erase dreams after all. That wasn't the way it worked. Over the course of eighteen months the company started getting more and more complaints, and in the end they worked out what was going on. When you erased a dream, all you destroyed was the imagery, the visuals which had played over the dreamer's inner eye. The substance of the dream, an intangible quality which seemed impossible to isolate, remained. The more dreams a client had removed, the more of this substance was left behind: invisible, indestructible, but carrying some kind of weight. It hung around in the room where the dream had been erased, and after a hundred or so deletions the room would become uninhabitable. It was like walking into a thunderstorm of subconscious impulses – absolutely silent, but impossible to bear. After a few weeks the dreams seemed to coalesce even further, making the air so thick that it became difficult to even enter the room at all.

Unfortunately, the kind of client who could afford dream therapy was exactly the type who was turned on by litigation. After the company had paid a few huge out-of-court settlements on bedrooms which were now impassable, they turned their minds to finding a way out of the problem.

At first they tried diverting the dreams into storage data banks, instead of erasing them. This didn't work either. Some of the dream still seeped out of the hard disks, regardless of how air-tight the casing. Also, dreams take up a phenomenal amount of storage space, and the math on setting up huge server farms to handle the traffic just wasn't stacking up.

Then finally it clicked.

The problem seemed to be that the dreams weren't being used up, and so they game something else a try.

A client's receiving machine was connected to a transmitter placed near the bed of a volunteer, and two anxiety dreams were successfully diverted from the mind of one to the other. The client woke up nicely rested, ready for another hard day in the money mines. The volunteer had a shitty night of dull dreams he couldn't quite remember, but was paid for his troubles. No residue was left in the room. The dream was gone. Problem solved, and the cash started flowing again.

"And that's what you did to me last night?" I asked.

"Yes," Rabutni said. "And I think you'll be glad we did. People have varying ability to use up other people's dreams. Most can handle two a night, three at the most. They get up feeling ragged, drag themselves through the day. Usually they only work every other night – but they still make eight, nine hundred dollars a week. You, on the other hand, appear to be different."

"How's that?"

"You took four dreams last night without breaking sweat. The two you've seen, and another two – one of which was so dull I can't bear to even watch just the visuals. You could probably have taken a couple more."

"Nice to find something I'm good at."

"That's what we're all looking for, Mr. Stone. I don't know why you can do this when other people can't, but it's rare. If you sign up with us, you could make a lot of money."

"How much money?"

"We pay according to dream duration, with bonuses for unusually complex or tedious ones. Last night you pulled down over three hundred dollars' worth – and that doesn't factor in a bonus for the dullest. In an average week, depending how often you worked, you could be earning somewhere between three and five thousand dollars. While you sleep."

I coughed.

He closed the pitch. "And we pay cash. Our business is still in a slightly unstable state with regard to legality, and we find it more convenient to disguise its true nature to some of the authorities. Paying cash is good for us. And, I assume, for you."

I looked at him, biting the inside of my lower lip. Three to five thousand dollars is an *awful* lot of bar work.

"It's up to you," he said, shrugging and smiling that smile.

It wasn't a hard decision.

~φ~

I signed a non-disclosure contract, and that's the way I spent the next two years. I was given a carefully anonymous-looking receiver, and had the process explained to me. Basically the deal was that I could go anywhere in the continental United States, so long as I kept the machine within six feet of my head while I slept. I didn't have to go to bed at any particular time, because the dreams booked to me were spooled into memory. When the device sensed I was in REM sleep, it fed the backlog into my head. The next morning I'd wake up and check the screen on the device to see how much I'd earned. When I slept somewhere with a console, I could connect it up to the device and my nightwork would appear on the screen like a list of email messages: how long the dreams were, when they started and finished, whether they qualified for bonus payment or were just hack work.

And at the bottom of the list, the good news.

A figure in dollars.

Rabutni had been right about my capacity, and I found I could take six or seven dreams a night without much difficulty. Some days I'd be really groggy and find it difficult to concentrate on anything more complex than smoking, but when that happened I'd just take the following night off. After six months I was recalled to REMtemps' offices and asked if I'd like to volunteer for a higher proportion of bonus dreams. I said "Hell, yes," and my earnings took another jump upwards. I set up accounts with a number of different banks, hired a street coder to write me a daemon which would keep the cash constantly on the move between them, so it was more difficult to trace, and concentrated on having fun during my waking hours.

It was a good life. I traveled all over, this time as a person with cash instead of some loser looking for a cheap bed and an easy score. After a while it came to seem natural to wear expensive clothes, to head for the uptown hotels, to wonder which Gold Card to charge things to. I got used to the less material things that money also gets you, like politeness, and respect, and a better class of bed companion.

Every now and then the IRS or some other ratfinks would close in on one particular account, but I was making enough by then that I'd just cut the money loose and set up another stash somewhere else.

There were occasional downsides. The exhaustion which came after a night full of bonuses, or following a day chain-snorting cocaine to iron out the bumps. Being forever on the move, and never having a relationship which lasted longer than a few days. There were periods when I'd go a little wobbly psychologically, and I came to realise that was because I'd spent so many nights having other people's dreams that I hadn't had time for any of my own. When that happened I'd clock off for a week or so, let my mind catch up. Those periods were like holidays, a chance to catch up with what my own subconscious had been up to, and I came to kind of look forward to them.

But the problems were few and far between, and for the most part I was having exactly the kind of life I'd always dreamed of and never really believed I'd have.

I'd found some action which was safe, which I was good at, and which paid big time money.

That should have been enough.

~φ~

One morning I got a call from Rabutni. I was crashed out in a king-sized bed on the top floor of a hotel in New Orleans, the debris of a hard evening's pleasure spread all around me. I couldn't remember the name of the woman beside me, but she was a whiz at answering the phone. By the time I'd realized it was ringing, she already had it up out of its cradle and by her ear.

When she passed it over to me I sat up, head foggy and full of half-remembered tasks and confusions. I suppressed the urge to look at the dream receiver to see how much I'd earned. From the way I felt, I knew it was going to be considerable.

"Mr. Stone," said that voice, and I instantly became more awake. I'd only been phoned by him once before, the time they pulled me in for promotion. "Who was that who answered the phone?"

"I don't know," I said. "I mean, why? What difference?"

"I assume she's someone you've met very 'recently'?"

"You could say that."

I glanced across the room to where the woman was standing. Candy, I think her name may have been. She seemed nice, and I was wondering whether she might be interested in hooking up with me for a while. At that moment she was making coffee. With no clothes on. I was hoping Rabutni would cut to the chase.

"When we're done, get rid of her. Immediately."

"*What?*"

"You met her last night, right? And she's in *your* hotel room. But she answered the phone after a single ring."

"So?"

"She may be working for someone."

I watched as she stirred just the right amount of sugar into my coffee. "Don't talk crap."

Candy winked at me and slipped into the john.

"Get rid of her," Rabutni repeated, "And then come to the office. I have a proposal for you."

The line went dead.

I got out of bed and put the device in my suitcase. The readout said I'd earned over fifteen hundred dollars during the night, a new personal best. Then I got dressed, and when Candy came back out, spruced and fresh and ready to play, I said I had to go out for a while. She took it badly, and then well, and then badly again. She tried a lot of things to get me to stay. When it was clear that wasn't working, she said she'd hang out in the room and wait for me. For however long it took.

Call me someone with low self-esteem, but women don't usually behave that way after a single night in my company. It wasn't proof, but it was enough to make me gather my things and walk out the door, leaving her shouting at my back. In the elevator I did what I'd been told to do in such circumstances, and pressed a button on the side of the dream receiver.

There was a soft "crump" sound from within and the read-out panel went black. The unit was now dead, logic board fused into inexplicability. If the cops or anyone else pulled me over, there was no way of telling what the machine had ever been capable of. No way of proving it in a court of law, anyhow.

On the plane to Jacksonville it occurred to me to wonder why – if Candy had been some kind of government agent – she hadn't simply done whatever she needed to do while I was sleeping. If there was one thing a REMtemp was guaranteed to do most nights, it was catch some zeds. Maybe she'd needed to talk to me, get names or something.

I couldn't work out what had been going on – if anything – and it didn't make much difference. I had to go back to the office anyway, to pick up a replacement receiver. I caught some breakfast before heading for REMtemps, slumped over a table in an upmarket diner. I wondered how many bonus dreams I must have had to earn fifteen hundred bucks, but couldn't get my mind to function well enough to figure it out. It had to be a lot. Usually the fog faded to a soft confusion after a couple hours, but this morning it felt like I'd never slept in my whole life. I didn't want to meet with Rabutni until I felt together enough to cope.

A gallon of coffee and half a pack of cigarettes wired me to the point where I was ready to face him, and I left the diner and staggered into the big black building. The smile I got from the REMtemps receptionist remained patronizing rather than respectful, but that's receptionists for you. I guess they'd probably look down their noses at the President if he happened by.

This time we didn't meet in a side office, but in Rabutni's own den. It was no bigger than your average football pitch, but luckily we sat at the same end so we didn't have to shout.

I told him I'd done what he told me, and he smiled. I added that I'd fritzed the machine, also as per instructions, and that I'd need another one. He smiled again. Then he pitched it to me.

He said he was pleased – very pleased – with the work I'd been doing. Yowsa, was he satisfied. He did everything short of offering me a cigar. Though I hadn't known it, he said, a number of the company's most important clients now asked for me, apparently because I dreamed their dreams better than anyone else. Some REMtemps left little vestiges behind, evidently, elements very personal to the original dreamer which, they couldn't assimilate. I got the whole lot, every little shadow and whisper and scrap. Hence the bonuses.

Hence also the fact that he wanted to offer me a chance at a different – and more lucrative – line of work.

Memories.

As soon as he said the word I started shaking my head. Dreams were one thing. Though not exactly legal, they weren't a big deal. Kind of like smoking dope: every now and the cops target someone to make up a quota or in the hope it'll be a gateway to something more juicy, but most of the time they turned a blind eye. Probably ten percent of the Upper House was using REMtemps' services anyway. And smoking dope, for all I knew.

Memories were different. Though it had been known for a couple of years that they could be externalized in the same way as dreams, doing so was absolutely and completely illegal. Divesting people of their memories was very bad news for the authorities. For a start, it meant that polygraphs – admissible as evidence for ten years – didn't work. If a suspect genuinely had no memory of committing a crime, fooling the polygraph was a breeze. In a way, it wasn't even deception. As far as the guy was concerned, the incident had just never happened.

Plus this:

People are their memories. Pure and simple.

What's happened to you is what you are. If you start taking bits of that away, you become a different person. If you remove the childhood incidents – however dire or quotidian, terrible or trivial – where someone learnt right from wrong, you end up with a guy who's kind of difficult to deal with. He doesn't have second thoughts about anything any more. He just doesn't care. Such people don't understand why they shouldn't steal, or rape, or murder – and that makes them better at it. In the event they do get caught, another memory dump just before the polygraph will blank that line of evidence straight away. This is not good for the courts. It's not good for society in general, as a matter of fact.

A test case eighteen months before had settled the issue. A freelance proxy dreamer who'd agreed to carry a criminal's memory of a certain incident, thus derailing what would otherwise likely have been a successful prosecution, was sentenced to two life terms in prison – exactly half what the real culprit would have received, had he been convicted.

In other words, memories weren't a trade you wanted to get involved in. I said as much to Rabutni.

He heard me out, and when I'd ground to a halt, he let a silence settle. When it had gone on long enough that it seemed like what I'd said had been to another person on some other day, he began.

"Yes," he said. "Memory temping is illegal – and rightly so. If it was legal the criminal justice system would fall apart, and none of us want that."

"Good," I said. "That's settled then. Where do I pick up my new receiver?"

"However," Rabutni continued, as if I'd said nothing at all, "The kind of memories I'm referring to do not relate to criminal activities. I'm talking about little things, and only temporary transferals."

"If they're that trivial, let the clients deal with them," I suggested. "And if they're only getting rid of the memory temporarily, tell them to take a valium instead. Or go out and get steaming drunk."

"And miss out on a chance for us to make more money?" Rabutni asked, eyes ironically wide. "I'm not just talking about the company either, Mr. Stone. This new service is going to pay its employees *very* well."

"The answer's still no."

He kept looking at me, hands folded over one another on the desk in front of him. "*Exceedingly* well."

"Nope, and no thank you. Also, no."

"Ten thousand dollars a memory," he said.

I stopped speaking before my mouth had even framed the next word.

He kept talking. "And the memory can be a single instant,

an individual fact. When the client base is built up you could earn a quarter million dollars every two months. All for holding memory fragments for no more than a week."

He let that sink in for a while, and I thought about it. About pulling in seven figures a year. Wealth has a way of operating on a sliding scale. When you've bought all the things you can at your current level, you start noticing the things you still can't have. And you start wanting those too. Or looked at another way: a couple more years' work, and I'd never have to lift a synapse again. I could retire, fuck off down to Mexico and just do what the hell I liked for the rest of my days.

"No," I said. I knew where I was, and I was doing okay. Dreams were do-able. They faded. Though I'd never tried one, I suspected that memories didn't – even if they were only supposed to be temporary.

"I think you'll find the answer's 'yes'," Rabutni said, "When you ask me again where you pick up your new receiver."

My mind was still dulled from the night's work, and I didn't get what he was driving at. "Where *do* I pick it up?"

"Unless you accept my offer, you don't," he said. "You take memory work, or you're fired."

"You're a fucker, aren't you," I said.

His smile didn't waver, and I realized it wasn't a smile and never had been. "I have heard that opinion expressed, yes."

I looked out the window, more to keep him waiting than any other reason. I wondered about Candy, whether she'd been paid by Rabutni. He would have known that I'd just woken when he called, and that I'd be unable to judge properly after a night full of heavy bonus dreams. Maybe he'd even set it up that way. Didn't make much difference in the end. He had me by the balls, and he knew it. Without dreamwork I was back on the streets, an environment in which I'd never thrived. I had money squirreled away, sure, but not enough. Too much of it had been pissed away.

With the memory work I could buy my own bar, if it came to it.

"Okay," I said.

~φ~

In many ways, the work was pretty much the same. I could still go anywhere, do anything – though I took a lot more trouble to cover my tracks. I ditched my old credit cards, got some new ones under fake ids, and started shifting money out of the country. I was a lot more cautious about who I woke up next to. I worked maybe one, two nights on dreams, just to keep my hand in. Then a couple of times a week I'd get a call and be told to be somewhere secluded, with my new machine, at a particular time.

A tickle in the back of the mind, a momentary blackout, and then someone else's memory was mine. I kept it for an hour, a couple of days, a week at the most, and then a similar session would take it away again.

Most of the memories were straightforward. Once a week a woman would lose the fact she was married, so she'd feel less guilty about spending the afternoon with her lover. An executive would forget what his mother taught him about right and wrong, so as to make screwing over a colleague a little easier. Another woman would pass me a memory of being touched up by her father when she was a kid, to make a Christmas spent with her folks more bearable.

Others were stranger.

Fragments, like a cat walking along a wall, jumping safely to the ground, and then turning a corner and disappearing. A girl's face, laughing. The sound of a stream gurgling past an open window in a bedroom at night. I never got any context, just those little pieces of remembrance, and had no way of working out why someone might pay ten thousand for a vacation from them.

It didn't matter. After the allotted time the client got them back, and they were gone from my head. I could remember what it was that I briefly had a memory of, but there was no confusion. I could tell, once it had gone, what was my experience and what had been someone else's.

It was kind of weird to spend an afternoon, once a week, convinced I could remember getting married to someone called David. But most of the memories were already used to being shunted to the side, and didn't really fuck me up. I could generally hem them in with enough self-awareness to cope with the truths they purported to tell. I don't know if there were any side effects. Maybe a few. I found myself getting tired more easily, and misbehaving less, but that could have been down to a number of factors. I was nearing forty, and had been on the road all my life. Maybe the time was coming when I needed to buy somewhere and settle down. But doing that would mean giving up the memory work, because a still target would be easy for the police to find. I knew what I did was harmless, but they'd be prone to see it another way. I didn't know if I was ready to stop earning yet, and I didn't know whether Rabutni would let me.

So I carried on, caretaking moments of other people's lives, and wishing that once in a while someone would lend me a *good* memory. I toyed with a little heroin every now and then, just to dull the noise of other people's bad times in my head, but only ever used stuff of good quality and in very small quantities. I got occasional headaches. But for the most part it was okay, and if I needed a reason, I just watched the money flowing into my account. This went on for nearly a year.

Until about a month ago, in fact.

~φ~

The guy's name was Chet Williams, and he was a regular client. Four or five times since I'd been doing memory work I'd held a particular one of his for a couple of days. The memory was of his mother, many years ago, when he was very small. He'd been standing in the back yard of the house where he grew up, a yard which faded into a small patch of forest. The day was hot and it was late afternoon, and little Chet had come out of the forest knowing it was going to be supper time soon.

Then suddenly there'd been a shadow over him, and he'd looked up to see his mom standing there, saying his name slowly and softly. She was a tall woman, thin, with a lot of reddish brown hair. In the memory Chet had looked slowly up until he'd found his mother's face. What he needed a break from every now and then was the expression he saw there. A look of fury, hate and disgust – mixed in with a little glee.

The memory always ended abruptly at that moment, and I don't know what the look meant, or what had happened afterwards. I'd always been kind of glad I didn't. Mr. Williams' memory was one of the ones I could understand someone wanting to get away from once in a while.

I came back from lounging round a hotel pool one morning to find I had an email message from an address I didn't recognize. Before I even read it I ran a check on the source. The domain code didn't set any alarm bells ringing with my software, but even so I got the console to hardcopy it without technically opening it.

The mail was from Mr. Williams.

We'd never been in contact before – all transactions were brokered through REMtemps on a double-blind principle – and the only reason I even knew his first name was because it was contained in the memory itself. The message said he wanted to meet with me. He had something he wanted me to carry, and he would make it worth my while.

I stared at the piece of paper for a few moments, then set fire to it and let it burn out in an ashtray. I spent the rest of the day round the pool, and the evening in a bar playing pool and talking shit with the locals.

When I got back I had another message. I went through the same procedure and found it was from Mr. Williams again. It sounded a little more desperate and listed a phone number. It also mentioned a figure.

One hundred thousand dollars.

I watched a movie on the in-house system for a while, but you know how it is. The back brain makes a decision instantly, and no matter how long you put it off, you know what you're going to do.

At about midnight I left the hotel room and went back to the bar. There was a phone box round the back, out of sight, and I called the number from the message.

A nervous-sounding man answered the phone. He took a while to settle down, and had me describe in detail the memory he usually left with me, to make sure I was who I said I was. Then he started sounding more confident, and told me what he wanted.

He had another memory, one which wasn't usually a problem. In fact, it was one of his favorites. Ten years ago he'd gone on vacation with a woman he'd just met, to some place on the beach he'd known for years. They stayed there for a while, hanging out, eating seafood, having a good time. Then he'd come back.

"That's it?" I asked.

"That's it," he said. "But now it's got a little more complicated."

He'd recently met another woman. He liked her a lot. In fact, he was thinking of getting married to her. But before he asked the question, they were going to go away together, just to make sure. He wanted to go to the same town he'd taken the other woman all that time ago.

I still didn't see the problem, and said so. He said they had to go to this exact same place, because it was his favorite in all the world. His special place. But he didn't want to go back there remembering what it had been like with the other woman, the one from a decade before. He thought it wouldn't be fair on the new one, that it might make him see things differently, maybe screw things up. He really loved this new person, didn't want to take the risk of soiling what could be a make or break vacation.

Okay, I said. I could understand what he was saying: many clients had far weirder reasons for wanting to forget something for a spell. In a way I sort of respected his attitude, and wished I had a woman who made me feel that serious. But why couldn't he go through the normal channels?

Because he wanted me specifically, he said. I was the only person he'd used who could soak up every little bit of memory, blank it utterly, like it had never happened. He'd tried using other REMtemps on little things, as an experiment, and they always left something – however tiny – behind.

I still didn't see why we were doing the cloak and dagger stuff. All he had to do was specify me when he booked the storage.

Then he told me.

He was going to be away for ten days.

Rabutni wouldn't accept a booking for more than a week, I knew that. I suspected he was paying off someone in government somewhere. If they heard he was extending the time limit, all bets would be off. Also, the memory Mr. Williams wanted to leave wasn't a fragment. It was for the whole period, from the moment he and the other woman had got on the plane, to when the vacation was over. A whole week.

No one had ever tried to hold anything remotely that long before.

I thought I was going to say no, but instead I found myself telling him the money wasn't enough. I would have to go on leave from REMtemps for a week and a half. If I wanted to I could earn a hundred in that time anyway, without risking pissing Rabutni off.

"Two hundred," he said.

I thought for a moment.

"Two-fifty," he said.

"This means a lot to you, doesn't it?" I asked.

"It means everything."

~φ~

Three days later I sat in a chair in my hotel room in the mid-afternoon and waited for the transmission. Williams had found some hacker with a lashed-up transmitter, who'd somehow been able to acquire the code of my receiver. I made a mental note to find some way of hinting to Rabutni, when this job was done, that the receivers weren't as impregnable as he thought. If he wasn't careful then the black market was going to start cutting into his business. Worse than that, memory temps could find themselves stuffed with of all kinds of shit they weren't expecting, or being paid for. The money for this job was already in my hands, however, and on its way to three different accounts.

We spoke on the phone and arranged a time for him to take the memory back. It was a different number to the one he'd originally given me: presumably the home of the freelance. Then I closed my eyes and got myself ready to receive.

It came moments afterwards. A pulse of noise and smell that filled my mind like the worst headache you've ever had, magnified a million-fold.

I grunted, unable even to shout, and pitched forward onto the carpet, hands and legs going into spasm. I seemed to go deaf and partly blind for a time, but that was the least of my problems.

I thought I was going to die.

After a few minutes the shaking lessened – enough that I could crawl to the bedside table and light a cigarette. I hauled myself up onto the bed and lay face down, waiting for the pain to go away.

It started to, eventually. Half an hour later I was sitting up and drinking scotch, which helped. My sight was clearing and I could once more hear the sound of people horsing around by the pool below my window. I still felt like shit, but had started to believe I was going to be alright.

I simply hadn't considered the difference between getting a quick, single fragment of someone's life, and taking over week's worth of experience in one hit. The brain is designed to accept life piece-meal, moment by moment – not to get a week full of sounds, sights, feelings and tactile impressions condensed into a single bullet of remembrance. If I hadn't already spent years exercising my mind then I'd probably have been slumped in a corner, drooling and staring into nothingness.

As it was, my head was still humming and thudding, trying to wade through what it had received, to sort it into chronology and pattern and sensory types. I could feel countless threads of sensory information squirming over each other, like worms, trying to find some kind of order, some mental box to call home. Sunburn on my shoulder; salt on my lips from a Margarita; someone else's tongue in my mouth; a flash of sunlight on a car window; the sound of water rolling up sand; coolness; a shout. A thousand sentences all at once, some of them leaving my head, others coming in. My brain was lurching under the weight, miss-firing like a heart on the verge of arrest.

I reached unsteadily for the phone. Large amounts of room service was what was on my mind, but first I had to call Williams and let him know the transmission had gone okay. I'm professional about these things.

I dialed the number and waited as it rang, holding the cold glass of my drink up against my forehead and panting slightly. There was no answer.

I tapped the pips and redialed. This time I gave it thirty rings before putting the phone back again. I knew he wasn't going away for two days, so it was no big deal. Probably he was out, making arrangements – or maybe he'd gone home.

By then it was forty minutes since the hit.

I munched slowly through a burger delivered by an offensively self-confident bellboy, keeping half an eye on what was going on in my head. It felt like a hard drive desperately running optimization software, without enough slack to swap all the data around. I seemed to be having real trouble ordering the mass of impressions which I'd been given. Parts from the start of Williams' golden vacation were lodging into place, but other sections were still missing, making the recollection hazy and fragmented and impossible to rationalize.

When I was done with the food I called Williams' number again. I let it ring for a long time and was about to put it down when someone answered.

"Mr. Williams," I said.

"Hello," said a voice I didn't recognize. "Who is this?" There was a weird sound in the background.

"It's Mr. Stone," I answered, slightly taken aback. "Is Mr. Williams there?"

"How the fuck do you expect me to know?" snarled the voice, and the connection was severed.

Sudden very bad feeling.

I tried the number again, immediately. No answer.

Then I called the operator. She told me there was no fault on the line but wouldn't give me the address.

I called the guy who'd set up my bank account daemons. He said he could check some sources and would call me back. I stumbled around the room for ten minutes, gobbling weapons-grade painkillers. The optimization process in my head felt like it was crashing out now, as if it was beginning to unravel out of control, unable to find places to put back the things it had moved: as if the juggler in there was starting to drop a few balls, and beginning to panic.

The phone call came. My hacker friend told me the number was that of a courtesy phone in the first class departure lounge of Miami airport.

I called the other number I had for Williams. The line was dead. I stared at the handset.

Then I blacked out.

~φ~

It had been very hot that week, and humid, each rare breeze as welcome as the brush of cool, slim fingers across the back of your neck. It was clear he had been happy, and excited, but I was still surprised at how much he remembered. Conversations, her laugh, the smell of the sea through the window she insisted on keeping open in the car despite the fact the air-conditioning was on. The sound of her thighs moving across the hot car seat. Some old song playing on the car radio, and hands tapping against the steering wheel in ragged time.

That's the bit I return to, when I can. The very beginning.

When I regained consciousness after the blackout, the first couple of hours of the memory were more or less in order. The woman was in her mid-twenties, very slim, with long black hair. From the moment the plane landed, and all the way through the drive to the hotel, you could feel the joy coming off her in waves. When the car turned into the drive of motel she squealed, as if she'd never seen the sea before. You knew that everything she ever experienced would be like that, time after time: a constant surprise, a discovering. Her name was Rebecca.

She was... she was nice.

The rest of the memory unraveled into the white noise of all the data my mind was still trying to process.

I spent ten minutes in the bathroom washing off the blood which had tipped out of my nose as I lay passed out on the hotel room floor. Then I checked out and drove to Miami, where I bullied and lied flight registers out of the airlines. Williams wasn't listed on any of them.

I traced the first number Williams gave me, flew to Gainesville and kicked the door down.

The house was empty, unfurnished – the cupboards and wardrobe bare. The phone sat in the middle of the floor. It was obvious no one had lived there in a while, because there was no food anywhere and no sheets on the bed so you couldn't lie down and rest your head.

Three days had passed by then, and the first half of Williams' memory was in order in my mind. Even through the haze of a headache that no amount of Tylenol would budge, I came to look forward to remembering more about what they'd done. I envied Williams the time he'd had with Rebecca. I could understand how she'd be difficult to forget.

Another week went by. I'm not sure where I was during that time. I wrote some of it down in a book but I didn't put enough letters in some of the words, and then I forgot where I'd put the book. Williams didn't come back. After two weeks I went to Rabutni.

I had to. I'd tried going back to work, because I knew I couldn't keep stalling him forever: but a run of the mill memory job had left me unconscious for twelve hours. When I woke I'd forgotten a whole slew of new words. They're still gone. I don't know whether they got overwritten, or if part of my brain simply blew out. Probably the latter, because one of my hands shakes a lot of the time now.

Rabutni let me trace back through the records to find who'd fed me the memories of a young boy confronted by his mother in a back yard. Williams didn't seem to be his real name, and no, he didn't live where he said he did. Rabutni was actually pretty kind. After this, he let me throw up in the office toilet, too.

But then he fired me.

~φ~

Most days I drive around, up and down, trying to find the town where they went ten years ago. Twice I've thought I've found it. I know it's somewhere on the Gulf Coast of Florida, but that's an awfully long stretch of sand, with lots of people and places and motels and towns. It could take me all year at this rate. It could take forever and a day. The headaches get worse and worse and worse, and I keep losing things. Ways of using words, to say things like "Look, there is a boat" or something. The ability to think about anything for more than moments at a tie. I mean, "time". It comes and goes like that water you find at the edge of land. Some days it's a little better, but in general it's getting much worse. I'm just too full, I suppose, over-loaded, or perhaps something happened when the bullet hit my brain.

Oh, and the hacker man I'd hired to hide my money hid it *very* well, it turns out. He hid it from me too. He thieved it from me. I know because one day when I could think pretty well I went online and found that there were no accounts there under any of my names, none at all, not even little ones. And thus, no money either.

I'm back right where I started, but even further behind. So far back, it's as if I'd never even been born.

~φ~

I think Rebecca would have liked me, though.

I'm not trying to find the town they stayed because I think Williams or whatever his name really is will be there. I'm going for other reasons, and looking for something different. Why I want to find it I don't really know, because it's too late. For her, for me. I just don't seem to be capable of doing anything else.

Maybe somewhere in the world is Mr. Williams and his new lady wife friend, and they're having fun and playing in the sand somewhere by big water. I hope so, even though he has been very bad to me, and not just to me. Of course it's a maybe that the memory he gave to me wasn't even his in the first place, but some other one did the same to him as he did to me. And maybe back and then back again until they'll never find who went on their holidays with Rebecca. Maybe that is what is. I don't know, but I don't think so. I think it is Mr. Williams who did it. And of course finally in the end I realized there was no new woman, and never had been. He just had this history, this guilt he'd done in his life, and he wanted rid of it. He gave it to me.

Permanently.

Very slowly the rest of it moves into position. At the end of the memory everything is dark and loud and angry, and what takes place happens round a corner and out of sight, in the night time. He was drunk, and things got out of hand.

Her face was so scared.

And then it is all mashed up.

There's blood everywhere and he buried her where people would never see her again. But if anyone can, it is me. I am him, now – the part that did that thing, at least. I was there. Maybe I can find her and say sorry for what I did. She loved me, even if it wasn't really me.

And now I love her. I'll find her. I must.

Rebecca is all that's left of me.

~φ~

DAVE 2.0b2

A man.

Customer Reviews for current version:

@MELTYFACE:
Woot! A new version of Dave! Going to install now!! LOL!!!

@CAPTAINSMOO:
Glad to see an upgrade at last, but I don't really like the new icon or interface changes. Dave seems to have put on weight, and has more lines around the eyes.

@woodenbrane:
Dave sucks! There are lot's beter people around than him. Rip off!

@LUKILUKI:
I like some of the new habits, and actually think the few grey hairs are an improvement. I would have liked to see a little more wiseness (I have submitted a NUMBER of requests for this via the forums), but overall, a decent upgrade.

@NUTTYBOY:
THIS IS BLOODY RUBBISH. IT DOESNT WORK AT ALL AND CRASHES EVERYTHING. THE DEVELOPER IS AN ARSHOLE FUCK TROLL.

@developer:
Hey - I'm Dave's developer. Thanks for the comments... It would help a LOT if everyone would submit proper bug reports (with log files), though, instead of just saying Dave doesn't work.

For example: "Has tendency to get dogmatic after four beers [16/10/2009]". Cheers!

@MACMAN:
I like Dave, and will continue to support his development, although like some other long-term users I have been disappointed by his tendency in recent updates to lack the verve and optimism of previous versions.
> **REPLY from DEVELOPER:** The optimism plug-in proved hard to maintain due to underlying features in Dave's Reality, and has been dropped. I'm working on implementing some new Defeated Resignation options for the next beta.

@Dave'sWife:
Not the upgrade I was hoping for after all this time. The audio monitoring and response functions still don't work as advertised. It's like he doesn't understand a word I say.
> **REPLY from DEVELOPER:** Increased Empathy is on the request list, and I'm working on it. For the time being, please use workarounds like not talking to him when he's tired.

@CoMaTiZe:
This should be FREE! Check out the open source John 0.4.6 instead. Can't stand up or speak or breathe dependably, but its FREE!!!

@fughole:
I tried to use Dave to do my accounts and it got everything wrong. I want my hard-earned cash back.
> **REPLY from DEVELOPER:** Dave has never understood accounts, and never will.

@YRFACEACHES:
LYNDSEY LOHAN FUX NUDE WITH AN OKAPI!!! CLICK HERE!!!!!!

@Dave'sWife:
Dreadful evening. Just dreadful [log attached]

REPLY from DEVELOPER: Yes, I'm aware there are some compatibility issues with Dave 2.0 and YourFriends 3.1. Please try to use them at different times while I work on a patch.

@LowestCommonDenominator:
Does exactly what it says on the tin!!!

@noIDRroid:
Does this upgrade have Telepathy powers?
REPLY from DEVELOPER: No.

@HAPPLYSLAPPLY:
I have absolutely nothing better to do with my time, and so have just read every comment ever made about this software. I don't specifically have anything to add. Christ I'm bored.

@Seriouslytho:
I just tried to run the exercise mode in Dave 2.0b2 and it crashed out after 20 minutes. FIX THIS, YOU BASTARD.
REPLY from DEVELOPER: Try using the "Walk" setting rather than "Run".

@Dave'sWife:
I'm sorry but this just isn't good enough. I've been a long-term supporter of Dave, and have paid the upgrade fee every time, but I'm just not sure I see evidence of meaningful development. Dave 2.0b2 is prey to increasing feature-itis (ability to make basic dinners for the children, occasionally remembering to pick his trousers off the bedroom floor, retention of trivia gleaned from the History Channel) but the basic flaws (lack of flair, decreasing libido, being generally annoying) remain - and are getting worse, if anything. Unless these are fixed in the next beta I'm tempted to try Co-Worker 1.0.
REPLY from DEVELOPER: Please be patient - and see the changelog on the website for under-the-hood improvements that should bear fruit soon. Also, be aware that Co-Worker 1.0 has a virus.

@WESTLOVE555:
Seems to sigh a lot more than he used to. Is this deliberate?

@twazzyPam:
Wat??? Dave is a man? It shuld say so heer. I pade good money for this and wanted a Lady. Money back!!!
    REPLY from DEVELOPER: It *does* say so here, you muppet.

@fughole:
I have consulted with someone I met on FaceBook, who says he is a great lawyer, and he says Dave is not fit for purpose, specifically he can't do my accounts for me like I want. Therefore I am suing you. To avoid this send me all your money now.
    REPLY from DEVELOPER: I don't *have* any money. Dave 2.0 is shareware, relying upon the honestly and decency of users. You do the math.

@PeterSmith:
I've been using Dave since the early days back at college, and generally found him a good fit for my workflow and socialising goals. Well, times have changed, and after test-driving Bob 1.4 for a couple of evenings, I think I'm going to switch. I will keep Dave on my hard drive and XmasCardList, but won't ever use him again.

@CLIVEFISHER: Me to!!

@Dave'sWife:
Okay, fair enough, Co-Worker 1.0 wasn't the solution (though I've had worse snogs). But I'm not getting any younger, am I, and I'm tired of living with a man with no drive, who never seems truly happy, and who never, ever touches me any more. I'm downloading a trial version of Friend of a Friend right now.

@Dave'sWife:
Aha. Now THAT'S what I'm talking about, right there. Oh yeah.

@braindeadplankton: Earn $300 from home!! Click HERE!!!!!!!

@developer:
It is with great regret that I am ceasing development on Dave. I'm simply not gaining enough satisfaction to justify the amounts of time required, and to be honest I think there are problems in the underlying code which will never be resolved. I'd like to thank everyone for their input. Dave should continue to function for some time, but will eventually succumb to an ever-increasing sense of pointlessness and doubt, before eventually crashing forever. No flowers, please.

~φ~

About the Editors

Bill Breedlove is the editor of the anthologies *Candy in the Dumpster, Waiting for October, Like a Chinese Tattoo, Mighty Unclean* and *When the Night Comes Down.* A collection of his short fiction will be published in 2011 by Bad Moon Books. In addition to his monthly column for *The Black Glove*, Bill's work has also appeared in publications such as *Chicago Tribune, In-Sider, The Fortune News, Restaurants & Institutions, Bluefood.cc, Encyclopedia of Actuarial Science* and *Playboy Online*.  His stories can also be found in the books *Tales of Forbidden Passion, Strange Creatures, Tails from the Pet Shop, Book of Dead Things, Cthulhu and the Coeds* and *Blood and Donuts*. He lives in Chicago with his wife, dog and pigeon. His website is www.curiousstories.com.

John Everson is the Bram Stoker Award-winning author of the novels *Covenant, Sacrifice, The 13th, Siren* and the forthcoming *The Pumpkin Man*, all from Leisure Books. His short fiction has been collected in the books *Creeptych, Deadly Nightlusts, Needles & Sins, Vigilantes of Love* and *Cage of Bones & Other Deadly Obsessions*. Over the past 20 years, his short stories have appeared in more than 75 magazines and anthologies  and many have also been translated into Polish and French. He has served as editor of the anthologies *Sins of the Sirens, In Delirium II*, and co-editor of *Spooks!* He lives in Naperville, IL with his wife, son and petulant cockatoo and cockatiel. For information on his fiction, art and music, visit www.johneverson.com.